The Gift

Nicola Pearson

with Timothy O'Rourke, DVM

This book is a work of fiction.
No part of the contents relate to any real person or persons, living or dead.

Acknowledgments

I can't start these acknowledgments without first thanking Dr. Timothy O'Rourke for asking me to write this book. Without his request I don't think I would ever have come up with the idea to write about a small-animal veterinary practice, and I would have lost the chance to learn so much. This has been an incredible journey for me, and I really am indebted to Tim for asking me to take it. And then I am very grateful to Carolyn Hatch for all the details she gave me about veterinary work. She answered my questions and gave me inspiration with some of the stories she shared from her history as a veterinary technician. Thanks also to Dr. Jennifer Johnson, who has a gift for explaining veterinary medicine in a way that is clear and comprehensible to a layperson like me, and to the rest of the staff at Animal Care Clinic in Mount Vernon, Washington, especially Destiny for being a first reader. Thanks also to Kirsten for the amazing job she did copyediting this novel, to Eve Hanninen for her help with the early pages and to my long-standing editor, Jerry Ziegler, for his invaluable feedback with the story. As always, thanks to my husband, Stephen, for letting me describe the things I saw when shadowing Tim and for reading the manuscript so many times. Finally, thanks to every dog in my life who has loved me so unreservedly: you inspired this story.

.

Cover Art:

Graphic design by Jon-Paul Verfaillie

Interior Art:

Drawings by Elizabeth Powell

for Reed and Annie, my greatest gifts,
and all the pets who have graced our lives
~ NP ~

Spike

He knew she was sick. He'd tried every which way to let her know, too, but she wasn't having any of it. He didn't know what to do. He'd spent a lot of time reflecting on how to get her help, and one sunny morning, when he was standing on the front porch, smelling the arrival of spring in the air with the wind chimes jangling softly above his head, it came to him. He needed to get her to the man in whose hands he felt whole. The hands that he'd sensed, right from the beginning, would heal him no matter what. But how could he do that?

He thought some more, watching beads of icy moisture on the barren branches of the magnolia tree tremble in the early morning sunshine. He knew the man with the hands was somewhere close to the river. He remembered that. And he knew that the van that came once a month to clean the carpets was from somewhere close to the river. So what he needed to do was watch for the van and get a ride in it.

If the van could get him to the river, he was sure he could find the man with the hands. And if he could find the man with the hands, he could get her help for her illness.

So that was what he'd do, he decided as two beads of moisture dropped from the tree onto the scraggly grass. He'd watch for the van.

Part One

Chapter 1

Leo was in the middle of a really, really good dream when he felt a whisper-soft kiss on his ear. He started to roll toward it but the sound of his cell phone dragged him into semiconsciousness. He slapped his left hand around on his bedside table, realizing this must be why she'd woken him, and turned away from her nuzzling when his fingers located the phone.

"Mm huh?" he grunted into the sleek rectangle. He knew it was his vet tech, Mackenzie Manning—or Mac, as most people called her—because of the ringtone. He made himself look at the clock on his bedside table: four thirty a.m. *Something must be up.*

"I hate to wake you," she said, her voice warm, resonant. She didn't wake him very often—almost never, in fact—but Dr. Leo Friel was always glad that the one voice he would allow to disturb his sleep for the sake of the clinic was Mac's.

He rolled onto his back again, tugging some of his hair up at the front of his scalp to increase blood flow to his brain. "What is it?"

"Heather Coy called and said her cat's having trouble peeing."

Trouble urinating could be a stone in the cat's urethra, which would back up waste products into the kidneys. Usually clients called saying their cat was constipated when they saw it straining over the litter box, not realizing it was really struggling to pee, but Heather had nearly lost her cat to urinary crystals once before. So she knew what that straining meant. And she knew it was the one thing that would drag Leo out of bed in the early hours. "All right. I'm on my way."

The ear kissing became more pronounced as he hung up and slipped his phone back on the bedside table. Leo turned to face Venus, his five-month-old golden retriever. She pushed her wet puppy nose under his chin and started licking the tip.

"Stop!" he chuckled. "I need to go to work." But Venus just scooted closer, belly flat on the bed, back legs splayed, tail wagging softly from side to side. She moved up to kissing his nose. Leo caressed her with his left hand, then levitated to a sit. He couldn't lay here and snuggle with his puppy. He needed to get to the clinic.

He rubbed his eye sockets with the heels of his hands and then looked at the rest of the bed. It was empty. He felt a pang in the pit of his stomach. He caressed the soft golden fur on Venus's back, feeling her loose puppy skin move with the motion. He leaned forward and cupped her muzzle with both his hands, putting his nose close to hers, and whispered, "How come I can make this relationship work, but I can't do the same with the human ones?"

Behind him he heard a thump thump thump on the floor, and he twisted his head around to see Harley, his older Heinz 57 mongrel with hips too stiff to get up onto the bed anymore. The big black dog with paintball patches of gold and white had propped his chin on the edge of the bed, hoping to be included. "Yes, I love you, too," Leo reassured him with a quick scratch behind one ear.

He swung his legs over Harley, put his feet on the floor, and stood up out of bed. "You stay here, okay?" he ordered both dogs.

He padded into the bathroom, took a leak, and then splashed cold water onto his face one, two, three times. He'd heard Jerry

Seinfeld describe doing this as a wake-up trick—"like reveille," said his interviewer—and decided if it was good enough for Seinfeld, it was good enough for Friel. He towel dried his face and looked in the mirror above the sink, his eyes bleary. He needed to shave, but he'd do that at the clinic, after he'd assessed the cat. With a stone in the urethra, there was no time to waste.

Leo set the towel down on the side of the sink and stretched both hands up into the air. He looped his thumbs together, biceps tensing, and arced slowly right, then left, to warm up his back. At fifty-eight he knew the one part of him he needed to keep supple was his spine. He came to center again, turned away from the sink, and folded forward at the hips, pulling his muscular torso in tight to his legs. In that snug forward bend he counted to twenty while another part of his mind flashed a reminder that he was supposed to be somewhere today. It disappeared before he could catch where. He let the thought go as he unfurled back to a stand. *Okay*, he told himself. *Let's do this.*

*****

The last thing Mac needed was to be woken early by an emergency for the clinic. She'd been at the opening night cast party for the summer Shakespeare production of *Hamlet* till almost one in the morning, so she knew it would be a struggle to get up at her usual time of five thirty. But four twenty? Really? *This had better be an emergency*, she thought as she snatched up the phone, hoping not to wake her husband, Chad. And, of course, it was. On the one morning she could have used an extra five minutes in bed.

But Heather Coy has been a client at the clinic for a dozen years and Mac knew Dr. F thought the world of her, even though she was kind of wacky. Well, more than kind of. "Certifiable" was probably closer to the mark, but nobody ever said anything about it to her. All the staff at the clinic just listened and nodded when Heather told them about the marriage ceremony she'd had with her cat, Buster, and how they got a letter from the President—President John F. Kennedy, mind you, who Mac was pretty sure died before Heather was even born—giving his blessing to their union. Dr. F would look at her, with those big baby blues that worked so well on the female clientele, and ask, "So when did you first notice Buster was limping?" Mac wondered how he kept a straight face at times; but then she knew how laser focused he could get when he was examining a pet, so she imagined he spent a lot of time thinking she could deal with any extraneous jibber jabber. And Mac spent a lot of time telling herself she was glad she was an actress in her spare time.

After Heather called, Mac willed herself to get out of bed. Today was a big day for Dr. F, but she knew there was no way he was going to pass on helping Buster. Plus it should go pretty quickly, she thought, if they could get it done before the clinic opened at seven. She hit his cell-phone number as she stumbled around her little house in the mountains, wondering what she was going to wear. She had a brand-new pair of scrubs with Olaf the Snowman from *Frozen* at the clinic, but she needed something to pull on to get down there.

Dr. F picked up on the third ring as Mac nudged her Jack Russell terrier, Puck, off a pile of clothes her friend Janie had given her for costumes. Janie was curvy, just like Mac, although Mac had a little more in the boob department. Still, she figured there ought to be something in the pile that she could wear.

She told Leo what was going on and, of course, he said he'd be right there. As Mac hung up she found a pair of black spandex leggings in the pile. Perfect! Then she found a baggy gray T-shirt with the words, "It's just a flesh wound," from *Monty Python and the Holy Grail* on the front of it. She chuckled. That was her kind of shirt.

She tugged on the leggings while Puck ran circles around her, and then called Heather Coy back and told her to head on over to the clinic. She hung up, tossed her phone into her purse, pulled the T-shirt over her head, scooped up Puck, and walked him into the bedroom, so he could go back to sleep with Chad.

"You need me to drive you down?" Chad mumbled from his cocoon in the blankets.

"Nah, it's Saturday," whispered Mac, pushing her fists into the bed to lean over and kiss him. "You go back to sleep."

She pulled the bedroom door closed behind her and made a beeline for the bathroom to put on her eyeliner. Mac didn't care what her clothes looked like under her scrubs, but dammit, she was an actress as well as a vet tech. She had to have her makeup on! She applied a quick stroke of kohl black on both lids, to highlight what Chad referred to as the liquid amber of her eyes, then put on a few dabs of foundation and some powder. She looked in the mirror; that would do.

It was just after four thirty by the time she was in her Honda Element, starting the thirty-minute drive west on the North Cascades Highway. The road meandered left and right, alongside the beauty of the great Skagit River, which came down from Canada and through the town of Mount Vernon, where the animal clinic was located, before heading out to the Puget Sound. Chad usually drove, so Mac could nap in the car, but she was glad she'd told him to stay in bed this morning, because she caught that special hour—"The hour before the heavenly-harnessed team / Begins his golden progress in the east"—and saw dawn to sunrise in a watercolor progression of pale pearl to opalescent gold.

She pulled past the "Riverside Animal Clinic" sign at exactly five a.m. and wound around the back to park next to Dr. F's Jeep Cherokee. The clinic sat about twenty feet above the Skagit River, and Mac took a moment to watch the morning sunlight dancing, like so many fairy lights, on the tips of the tiny whitecaps in the teal-green water. When she slid out of her car, she was smiling.

She hustled around to the side door to let herself in and saw that someone had dumped a used black T-shirt with bands of yellow across it, like the utility workers wore, on the ground there. It reeked of urine. She tsked. *Why couldn't they have carried it over to the dumpster rather than leaving it by the door?* She leaned forward to snatch it up, then thought twice about it. Maybe she should put on gloves before touching such a thing.

She swung open the door, stepped inside, and scooted down the short hallway housing the autoclave, microwave, and toaster oven. She continued on through the treatment room, heading for X-ray, to dump her purse. It was quiet when she hurried through treatment, but it didn't take long for the "hey-I'm-here-can-you-see-me?" addition to her day to start. Bark, pause, bark, pause, bark: low, deep, rhythmic.

Mac hung her purse on one of the hooks at the far end of the X-ray table and turned on the light in the adjacent break room. She guessed that the low, steady bark was coming from Ginger, the spaniel-hound mix in the large dog ward. From his kennel he could see through the window in the door and undoubtedly caught Mac shooting past into X-ray.

She slipped into her scrubs as a louder, more insistent WOOWOOWOOWOOWOO joined in with Ginger. That was probably the black Lab cruciate ligament surgery in the kennel farthest from the door. He was due to go home today. He set off the steady, high-pitched whine of the two Great Dane pups next door to him.

Mac sped back out into treatment hearing WOOwhineWOOwhineBarkWOOwhine. She booted up the viewing computer for the digital X-rays, moved down the counter and opened the door to the oxygen closet, which set off the yap yap yap yap yap meow meeOOOWW in the small animal ward next door. She turned on the oxygen tanks just as some critter in the large dog ward added a periodic howl to the dose of dissonance for the day. Mac always wished she could think of it as free jazz, but that would suggest there was music in all the mewing and baying and yapping and howling, when really it was just noise.

She snapped on a pair of latex gloves to go deal with the T-shirt outside. It wasn't going to get any less stinky sitting out in the July sun. She put her head down and started for the door.

Dr. F appeared at the end of the short hallway leading to his office. "You want to go get Buster?" he asked, even though there was very little question in his tone.

Mac rocked awkwardly on her feet, caught between the wants and musts of her job. "Er, sure," she said, knowing Dr. F's impatience when on a mission to help an animal. She'd have to go dump the T-shirt later. She pulled off the gloves, stuffed them in the pocket of her scrubs, and headed out the double doors to fetch Buster.

*****

Five minutes later Mac and Dr. F were both staring at the X-ray of Buster's abdomen. "Do *you* see anything?" the doc asked, leaning forward slightly as if he wasn't close enough.

"I don't. No." Mac was on one side of him, directly in front of the large animal ward, cradling the sleek gray Russian Blue in her arms. Buster tensed as Ginger began to bound up against the door to his kennel, bark-pause-barking. Mac leaned toward the computer screen to remove Buster from Ginger's line of sight.

They peered some more, squinting to see signs of the white circles that would indicate crystals in the urine. Dr. F made a deep hmm of intrigue in his throat. "His bladder wasn't full when I palpated his abdomen," he said, more to himself than to Mac. "And I checked his colon to make sure he wasn't just constipated. It felt normal . . ."

"You want me to get a urine sample?"

Dr. F didn't reply. Mac waited, knowing he was running every scenario through his mind and thinking about his options. After a few seconds he smacked his lips decisively and threw his shoulders back. Mac knew that meant "game on." Now it would be full-speed ahead to cure Buster.

"No. Let's run an ultrasound," Dr. F declared. "Then, if we can't see anything from that, we'll catheterize him, fill his bladder full of radiopaque dye, then re-X-ray him."

"You want me to air fill and X-ray it first?"

The vet's eyes narrowed as he chewed on this for a moment. Mac knew he was worrying over the cost of the extra tests for Heather Coy. "Let me see if I can't get some more information out of the client first," he said. "And then, of course, we'll have to see if you *can* catheterize him."

Mac nodded. If she couldn't, it would be a sure sign of a blocked urethra.

Dr. F lifted his right hand and signaled the list of procedures: thumb, finger, finger. "So client questions, ultrasound, catheter." Buster craned forward and sniffed the doc's raised fingers, then rubbed against them, looking for love. Dr. F smiled and tickled the top of Buster's head before starting toward the double doors out of treatment. "And if all that fails to tell us what we need, then yes, air, dye, air."

Mac scooted Buster back into his pet carrier on the floor of treatment, so she could go dispose of the stinky T-shirt while the ultrasound machine warmed up. Buster growled argumentatively, and Mac scratched him behind the ear to appease him. She felt a small, fresh wound.

"Have you been fighting?" she asked. She tipped his head down and parted his fur to take a closer at the wound. It needed cleaning, but it didn't seem to be bothering him. He nudged his head up and around under her fingers, like he wanted her to pet him some more, then stepped toward her. Mac laughed. "Yeah, think again, little man," she said and closed the door to the pet carrier on him. "You're in there till I'm ready for you." He huffed his nose up in the air, emitted a tiny mewl, then lowered himself, front legs folded underneath his chest, and promptly closed his eyes.

Mac buzzed back into X-ray and plugged in the ultrasound machine. If she was really quick, maybe she'd even have time to fix her hair in the bathroom before they took a second look at Buster. She dashed through treatment, tugging the latex gloves back on, and stepped back out into the gathering daylight. She bent forward and grabbed a corner of the T-shirt, but when she pulled, it didn't lift up off the ground. Mac felt a warning prickle on the back of her neck. She crouched down, holding the back of her left hand against her nose to mitigate the smell. The T-shirt was oversized brushed cotton and looked like it had been kicked around in the dirt. She unfolded the fabric with the fingers of her right hand. *"What the . . . ?"* she uttered.

Without a second thought, she scooped the whole works up and ran toward X-ray.

*****

Leo peered through the peephole to exam room 1 to see if that's where Heather Coy was waiting for news of Buster. He spied her narrow shape and spiky hair, even though she was facing away from him, her fingers clutched tightly around her upper arms like she was trying to hold in her fears with the fiercest of hugs. He hoped she was calm enough that she could give him the information he needed to help Buster. Leo decided to take the cat's chart in with him to prompt her and headed back into treatment to fetch it. But as he walked through the double doors he saw Mac speed by holding something out in front of her. He instantly switched gears.

He grabbed his stethoscope off its hook and hurried after her into X-ray, recoiling at the acrid aroma filling the small space. He assumed it was coming from the big black T-shirt with the yellow stripes on it that she'd laid on the X-ray table. As Leo came around to stand beside her, Mac threw open the T-shirt to reveal an unconscious and badly wounded dog. Leo could see immediately that the dog's left rear leg was broken and his right hip was protruding at an angle that made him think it was dislocated. He watched Mac carefully ease the lower half of the lifeless canine into the air to pull the shirt out from under it. He checked as Mac freed the rest of the T-shirt from under the pup's shoulders and head. It was a male.

Leo unclipped the raggedy blue collar around the dog's neck. It had a rusty ring on it that wasn't fully closed. Maybe it had held a nametag at one point, but not anymore. There was a scrap of fiber tied around it in one place that might have been the edge of a bandana.

"Any indication who he belongs to?" asked Mac.

Leo shook his head no. He gave her the collar, and she took it with the T-shirt to the garbage out in treatment. Leo flipped over the dog's lip to see his teeth and check the color of his gums. There wasn't much tartar on the teeth, so this was a young dog. Maybe a year old. He put the bell of the stethoscope on the dog's chest and listened. It sounded like there was fluid in the lung cavity. And his heartbeat was faint.

Leo pulled the stethoscope from his ears and hooked it around his neck. He felt the dog's abdomen. It was squishy. He leaned forward and tapped on it, listening for the gurgle of moving liquid. He heard it, a sure sign of internal bleeding. He ran his hand over the dog's right hip and felt the end of the femur detached from its socket. He noted the pronounced separation of the dog's ribcage from his belly as he parted the matted and dirt-encrusted fur; fleas ran every which way. Poor thing, thought Leo. Not only had he suffered an extreme trauma, but also it looked like he'd been a victim of neglect.

Mac bustled back into the room with a handheld plastic box and moved it over the top of the dog's spine. "Let's see if you've got a chip in you," she said. The machine didn't beep, and no number flashed on the tiny screen. "Nope," she said and slipped it in the pocket of her scrubs.

Leo was still staring at the pup, chewing over his predicament. He could feel Mac's eyes on him and avoided looking at her because he knew they would be filled with pleading. Pleading for him to save this dog, the one thing Leo was sure he couldn't do.

"Hit by a car would be my guess," he said, staring down at the dog.

"Yeah, that's what I thought."

"Although the state of his coat and his emaciation make me think he wasn't living a great life to start with."

"Somebody loved him enough to leave him here," Mac shot back.

Leo's stomach tightened. He'd hoped Mac could be realistic. This poor dog had no owner to claim responsibility for him if Leo *did* fix him up. No owner, not much of a pulse, and a slew of ailments that would require immediate surgery.

"He looks like a basenji," was all he said.

"Uh-huh. Except his tail isn't curled."

"That could be because he's unconscious."

"He looks kinda big for a purebred basenji," Mac remarked, her fingers tickling the fur between the dog's pointed ears. "Even as skinny as he is."

"And his coat's thicker," Leo concurred.

"But I love the rusty red," she said. Leo felt her eyes on him again. "Don't you think that's a great color?"

Leo nodded. "I bet the top of him looks like a shiny copper pot when he's all cleaned up."

There was a moment of silence as they both stood side by side, staring at the dog, neither of them wanting to bring up the inevitable. Mac eventually did the deed.

"Are we going to clean him up?" she asked.

Leo looked at her, his forehead tipped down, his eyebrows up. It was a cautionary look. "He's got a pneumothorax, a bad break in that left leg, his right hip's dislocated, and he's bleeding internally." He shook his head no. "I can't help him."

Mac's spirit visibly collapsed. "I put down three dogs yesterday afternoon. I can't do one first thing today."

Leo's tone softened but his resolve was fixed. "What about Buster?" he said. "I can't make him wait even as long as it would take me to do a quick fix on this dog. And this dog needs a lot more than a quick fix."

"Did you talk to Heather Coy yet?"

Leo shook his head no.

"I could put this one on oxygen and get some initial X-rays while you do that. You know how quick I can be."

"His gums are pale blue," Leo insisted. "And it's not like he's got an owner waiting on him—unless . . . was there a note in the T-shirt?"

Mac looked down at her hands. She shook her head no. Leo could tell she was close to tears, and he empathized. One of the hardest things the staff had to do at the clinic was put animals down. It drained them of all their reserves of joy, like letting air out of a balloon. He touched her shoulder and said, as gently as he could, "I don't think this dog's going to regain consciousness."

She looked up at him, her eyes wet, and Leo did the only thing he knew to do: he moved forward with his decision. He slipped his hands under the limp body of the dog and lifted him just enough to get a rough weight for the Fatal-Plus. "Not much more than eighteen pounds, I'd guess, so get three ccs of the blue stuff." He lowered the dog and made eye contact with Mac once more. "It's time," he said.

She walked heavily out of X-ray, muttering loudly enough that Leo could hear it, "Sometimes I *hate* my job!"

*****

While Leo waited for Mac to return with the pentobarbital sodium, the ultrasound machine blinked the name of the manufacturer across the screen to indicate it was ready for use. He didn't notice. He was bent over the dying pup, his left hand cupped under the dog's head while his right caressed his ear and face. "It won't be long now," he whispered. The other side to the pain of having to euthanize animals was the knowledge that they wouldn't have to suffer any longer.

Leo ran his right forefinger under the dog's chin, stroking the tip of his fur back and forth, back and forth. Even as unwashed and bedraggled as this dog was, his fur was incredibly soft. Like a dandelion head gone to seed. Leo knew the dog was completely out of it, but he held him nonetheless, not wanting the pup to feel alone in the little time he had left before he received the injection of Fatal-Plus.

"I'm sorry, buddy," he whispered to the basenji, feeling something familiar in the pup. He wondered how hard his year of life had been and whether he was glad to be letting go. He also wondered why somebody had brought him this far and yet not stayed to see if he could be saved. Money, probably, Leo thought. He was a vet with a reputation for not letting the finances get in the way of helping an animal, but maybe that reputation hadn't reached as far as the owner of this pet.

Leo smacked his lips together and looked up at the wall in front of him, his eyes settling on the chart of the X-ray guidelines. He felt the shallow, rhythmic breathing of the dog vibrate through him, like a background beat, as his mind wandered from never letting money get in the way of treatment, to the reputation he had with his clients, to that jarring conversation in the mall.

It had been about eighteen months ago, and it still stung when Leo thought about it. He had been out with his wife, Sheena, on one of their rare shopping trips together, when they ran into a client—a heavyset banker with a cheerful disposition—who was fond of pugs. He'd been doing business with Leo for more than a decade.

The banker looked tickled, running into Leo like that. "I don't think I've ever seen you outside the clinic." Then he joked, "It must be Christmas."

Which it was. Well, almost. It was about a week before Christmas.

"No, I'm glad to see you do take breaks," the banker went on more seriously. "Although don't get me wrong, I appreciate the long hours you put in at the clinic. Very much. In fact, if it weren't for that, I might never have met you." The client turned to Sheena and explained. "My wife and I woke up one morning to find our pug, Napoleon, struggling to breathe, and the only small-animal clinic we could find open at seven in the morning was your husband's. Of course, that was back fifteen years ago, before there were emergency clinics for small animals, but still. He was there when we needed him. And he's been there every time we've needed him ever since." The banker smiled across at Leo and patted Sheena on the shoulder as he started to move away. "You're married to a really great guy," he said with such sincerity that Leo felt humbled.

"Yeah, he obviously doesn't know you at *all*," scoffed Sheena as she and Leo continued on their way. Leo was so gobsmacked that he stopped right there, in the middle of the mall, and let her march away from him.

He was still gobsmacked that she could have said such a thing. *Why?* he wanted to know. Was *that* how little she thought of him?

Of course, he never asked. He never said a word, in fact. He just regrouped from the roller coaster he'd been on and hurried after her. Which may have been a mistake, now that he thought about it, because not saying anything to Sheena about how much this comment hurt had given her permission to unleash all the spite she'd been saving up against him. Which had sounded the death knell on their marriage.

He still didn't get where all that spite had come from. He'd tried to give Sheena everything she wanted, and they had two great kids together, so why had she fallen out of love with him? He knew he'd been too young in his first marriage, but his second one—he'd really thought his second marriage would stand the test of time. Yet it hadn't.

Leo could see Mac relocking the controlled-substances safe in treatment. He felt a sudden deep and pervasive sadness. Was it him? Did he just not deserve to be loved for some reason?

Something rasped gently against his right thumb. Leo looked down. The basenji was mustering everything he had to lick Leo's hand. This little dog that Leo thought was virtually dead, that he *knew* was completely unconscious, seemed to have dragged himself awake to make a gesture of reassurance. For Leo, not for himself. And as Leo stared down at the pup, not believing what had just transpired, the dog turned a pair of soft brown eyes on him with such a look of love in them that Leo felt himself choke up.

"Thank you," he voiced, tenderly rubbing his finger on the side of the dog's face. "I needed that."

The canine let his head fall back down into Leo's left hand and closed his eyes.

Mac slouched back into the room, holding the needle with the three ccs of Fatal-Plus.

"Get the oxygen," Leo instructed with a nod of his chin toward treatment. "Let's see if we can't save this little guy."

Chapter 2

The change of direction was quick and focused to handle the sudden ramping up of their workload. That didn't faze Mac. It often happened like that at the clinic. This morning she had to be super streamlined though, since Dr. F wasn't even supposed to be here and now she'd added to his workload by asking him to save this stray. She was surprised he'd made such a sudden turn around but she didn't get the impression he wanted to explain why. She forced herself not to ask as she handed him the blue stuff to take back to the safe. After all, that had been the way of things with him lately. He seemed to be—how would she put it?—not distracted, that wasn't it—more like unmoored. Like he was drifting when he wasn't tethered to surgery. Not in his work with the animals but definitely in his communications with her.

She let him go past her then turned around and followed him out of X-ray. The lack of bounce in his stride told her something was bothering him. She pushed into surgery and grabbed the mobile oxygen machine, her right foot propped against the door to keep it open. Maybe what he had on for today was making him anxious because of his separation from Sheena and the looming "D" word. She remembered how much it weighed on her to be in the same room as her ex before their divorce, and she didn't have to weigh it against the needs of an animal clinic. She glanced across at him relocking the safe as she wheeled the oxygen out of surgery. "Uneasy lies the head that wears the crown," she thought.

But despite his worries today was a *good* day for Dr. F she reminded herself. "Are we giving this stray a name?" she called out hoping to take him out of himself.

"Let me think on it," he called back. He smiled across at her as he picked up a chart from his workstation.

She smiled back. That was more like it. She wheeled the oxygen into X-ray and lined it up under the hose coming down from the ceiling. She screwed the two hoses together then lifted the mask off the stand and slipped it over the pup's nose. She watched, waiting for the inflatable rubber bag to fill, but the basenji's breathing was too shallow. She squeezed up on the bag, like she was crimping wet hair, and watched the pup's chest lift, then fall. She squeezed twice more, then sped out of X-ray, scooped Buster out of his carrier in his sleeping curl and raced him back into X-ray.

She set the cat down on the table and immediately squeezed the basenji's oxygen bag again. Buster began to unravel at the other end of the table, sniffing the air in a way that suggested he couldn't believe what he was smelling. His nose led him to turn his head left, and when he spotted the dog, he bared his teeth and gahh-hissed at the pup.

"Oh shush," Mac told the cat. "He's much worse off than you."

Buster stood, turned around, and settled back down facing away from the dog, his front legs folded under him, his tail wrapped around the side of his torso. Mac chuckled at his haughty delicacy. She ran her left hand down his back and around his tail, nudging his belly with the back of her hand as she did so. She repeated the motion and Buster relaxed, falling onto his side and lifting his front paws, so his belly was exposed. Perfect for Mac's ultrasound needs.

With her right hand still squeezing the dog's oxygen bag, she picked up the ultrasound probe and rolled it over Buster's abdomen, aiming for his bladder. There was always a delay before the image registered on the screen, and Mac glanced around at the stray as she waited. His little chest was lifting and falling, lifting and falling. She ran her mind through what she needed to do: X-ray his leg, his hip, and maybe his belly if Dr. F thought he was bleeding internally.

She turned back to the ultrasound screen and saw that the image had cleared. She leaned forward, hunting for the tiny, white, sand-like particles that would suggest crystals in the cat's urine. One of the things she enjoyed doing was shaking the probe over them to make the bladder look like a snow globe. She wasn't going to get to do that today, she realized, because she didn't see any crystals in there. Maybe Dr. F would spot them. She glanced out the open doorway, looking for her boss. She thought she'd heard him come back into treatment, but she couldn't see him. Buster's front paws bumped playfully against Mac's left hand—*pet me, pet me*—but she couldn't because she needed her right hand to keep the basenji breathing. She smiled at Buster, hoping he wouldn't get bored before the doc arrived. "Dr. Friel, are you there?" she called out.

Dr. F stepped in front of the lift table, opposite the door to X-ray, but he didn't acknowledge Mac. He was standing in profile to her, his left hand pushed into his mop of brown hair with its growing patina of gray. The hand in the hair was usually a sign that Dr. F was trying to close out the daily dose of dissonance while he talked on his cell phone. Making sure not to lose hold of either the oxygen bag or the probe on Buster's belly, Mac leaned over the X-ray table to peer around the doorway and see the clock on the wall next to the viewing station: five thirty-five. *Who would the doc be talking to so early in the morning?* she wondered.

Buster took Mac's proximity as permission to play with her long dark hair, and he snagged a length between his claws as she lifted her head back up. "Ow," she complained, letting go of the oxygen bag for a second to free her locks from the cat's clutches. "You sure don't seem to be suffering for someone who's got a stone blocking his urethra," she commented.

She was back to squeezing the oxygen bag when she heard Dr. F's quick, light, athletic tread behind her. She turned to look at him and could tell by the crease in his forehead that he'd not heard good news. "What?" she asked.

"Noah Rengen—you know who I mean?"

"Sure. With the chocolate Lab."

"Mocha. Yes."

Now Mac's brow creased, too, because if she was thinking of the right dog, and she was sure she was, then Mocha was close to delivering puppies. "What's going on?"

"That was Noah's dad on the phone. He said Mocha's at sixty-four days of gestation and has been straining for hours, but now it looks like she's given up."

"Uterine inertia?"

"That's what I'm thinking."

"Are they bringing her in?"

"Uh-huh." Dr. F edged between the wall and the ultrasound machine to put himself where he could see the screen. "We'll have to do a C-section."

"Oh." Mac was surprised. He bent over the ultrasound, so his face was closer to the screen and, without thinking about it, Mac positioned the probe over Buster's bladder again. "Do you have time for a C-section this morning?" she asked.

"Can you move it to the kidneys?" Dr. F answered, an indication that he was already too intent on the ultrasound to have heard her question. A small nag at the back of Mac's mind said she hoped he hadn't forgotten what today was, but then she thought, *No. No way.*

*****

"They're not showing up," Leo declared a few moments later, as he straightened himself to a stand.

"No. I couldn't see them either. Maybe they're radiolucent."

"You've got the kind that hides from the X-ray," Leo teased the cat.

Mac went to switch off the ultrasound, but Leo stopped her.

"Here, run the probe over the basenji's belly," he said. "Let's see if we can't get a heads-up on what's bleeding in there."

"Okay." Mac was still pumping the oxygen bag with her right hand and needed to wheel the machine closer to the stray to use the probe on him.

Leo caught her dilemma without her having to voice it; they were used to working without words, maybe because they spent so much time assessing animals. He edged back, so Mac could step right unencumbered, and wheeled the ultrasound machine over to the ailing dog for her. Mac ran the probe over the dog's belly, which was skinny but definitely liquidy.

"There!" Leo pounced, pointing at the screen. "His spleen's enlarged. That's probably why he came in unconscious."

Mac nodded. "Lethargy," she murmured. "Between that and not getting enough oxygen . . ."

"And shock."

Leo stood upright again and took the probe from Mac. He laid it on the keyboard, wheeled the ultrasound machine back into the corner, and unplugged it.

"What do you want to do?" she asked him.

"You still have to do his X-rays, right?" replied Leo, walking back toward the basenji.

"Yes."

"Okay, then let's deal with the pneumothorax, so you can take the X-rays. After that we'll prioritize what comes next." He searched through the fur on the dog's chest for the puncture wound. "Here it is," he said, exposing a bloody opening on the left side. He thought for a moment; he still had to take care of Buster, but it shouldn't take too long to sew up this wound. "Okay," he said, having made a determination. "I'll put Buster back in his carrier and get us some needle packs."

He ruffled Buster's belly again. "We're going to have to put some dye in your bladder," he told the cat, "to make those urinary crystals come out of hiding." Buster lifted his back paws and batted Leo's hand. "They certainly don't seem to be affecting his mood."

"I noticed that, too."

Leo scooped the cat up in his arms and walked with a spring in his step toward the door, his mood back to optimistic and energized.

"Can you bring me a clipper?" Mac requested.

Leo nodded. And then disappeared on the other side of the lift table.

*****

The treatment room at Riverside Animal Clinic was large enough to allow uninterrupted movement in all directions, just the way Leo wanted it. During regular clinic hours, the double doors leading to reception and the exam rooms popped open again and again as staff came in to check the board for the list of surgeries, to ask Leo and Mac questions, or to bring back animals, and that never seemed to get in the way of what was already going on inside treatment. Leo wanted this, got it, and was proud of it. He could still hear the conversation he'd had with the architect twenty years previous, in which he'd said he didn't mind what the general footprint of the clinic looked like, but the treatment room was the heart, and as such, he wanted unconstricted flow and a pulse that made the animals feel safe.

To the right of the double doors was a computer station and telephone, a short hallway leading to Leo's office, then a deep rectangular alcove housing a refrigerator, microscope, sink, and another computer. Mac could often be found in that alcove when she wasn't busy with animals; it was a small, out-of-the-way space where she could update her controlled-substance log or look for openings in Leo's schedule on the computer. The whiteboard, with the daily list of animals being held in the wards and procedures they needed, was on the back wall, next to the oxygen closet, and the surgery itself, the one room where Leo and Mac could work almost undisturbed, was left of the double doors, next to X-ray. Everything else in treatment took place in the four main workstations directly opposite the double doors.

The architect had designed the room with two multishelved rectangular posts four and a half feet apart in the center of the room. On the front and back of both posts were stainless-steel workstations. The whole setup looked like the letter *H* without the line across the center and allowed for plenty of back-and-forth and to-and-fro without staff bumping into each other. The workstations closest to surgery comprised a wet sink, for procedures on cats and dental work, and a lift table on the back of the post, so Leo could examine larger dogs without having to crawl around on the floor in an exam room. The lift table was the only workstation perpendicular to the posts, so there would be room for a huddle of people around the animal without blocking access to X-ray or the large animal ward. Leo was always impressed with how well this worked.

The workstation in front of the computer table to the right of the double doors, was covered in manila file folders containing charts needing to be updated. The workstation behind it, closest to where the staff came in through the side door, was usually covered in barista drinks, sweet snacks, and sometimes bags of veggies. "This is not a kitchen!" Leo would gripe when the table got too cluttered, and the staff would indulge him by moving their stuff, leaving it clear until the next time Leo set his own to-go cup on that table. Then they'd cover it in drinks again.

Four computers and three sinks meant nobody ever had to wait to access a patient file or rinse their hands. That feature alone kept the space humming. Over the years they'd used this room, the flow had become so streamlined Leo found himself following it, like a groove in the highway, even when there was no one else around. At five foot ten, trim and athletic, he had a swift gait at the best of times, but in treatment, he dodged and weaved with the agility of a light-heavyweight champion, boxing to beat whatever was threatening the animal in his care.

Once Buster was safely back in his pet carrier, Leo swung between the workstations, around the wet sink, and into surgery. He crossed to the upper cabinets on the sidewall, opened one, and picked out a sterile suture pack for the inside chest cavity of the basenji. He chose another for Mac to suture the outside.

He grabbed a pair of rat-tooth forceps and needle drivers from the counter, turned around, and lifted the clippers off the stainless-steel surgery table. He was on his way out of surgery when he remembered antibiotics. They'd need a flush and IV antibiotics for the stray. He picked up a bag of lactated Ringer's solution for the cefazolin and headed out. He added a squirt bottle of surgical soap, some cotton balls, and gauze pads from the wet sink to his full hands, then turned into X-ray and dropped everything down onto the table next to the stray.

"Thanks," said Mac.

She'd already hooked the dog up to the gas to avoid his waking during the procedure, so Leo rolled the IV stand closer to her. He darted back out to get an antibiotic flush, and even though it didn't take him but a moment, Mac had the IV tube connected to the dog's vein—one handed!—by the time he came back. Leo loved working with Mac.

Without discussing it, they switched places, so he could squeeze the oxygen bag while Mac prepared the wound site. While she shaved, Leo stared at the X-ray guidelines on the wall again, feeling the edges of his stomach begin to gnaw with hunger. He wished he'd drunk more of the coffee he'd bought on the way to the clinic, too. Mac finished and they switched places again.

Leo bent over the wound and, in his practiced, muscle-memory way, lifted the tissue with the forceps, pierced it with the curved needle, and fed the needle through to the opposing tissue. He repeated the motion, pulling the thread through until just half an inch remained exposed. His fingers crossed and recrossed, moved apart and back together, looping and pulling the sutures like skaters on an ice rink until the exposed end was captured and a tidy stitch had been formed. He snipped the ends and moved on to the next stitch.

It took four to close the wound, and when Leo tied off the last, he gave the nod to Mac to stop squeezing the oxygen bag. She did, and they both watched to see if the basenji could breathe by himself now. They held very still, hoping, and exhaled in unison when they saw the dog's chest suddenly lift.

"Okay, you suture the skin, take the X-rays, and I'll get the dye for Buster."

"You want a stomach X-ray, too, or just the leg and the hip?"

Leo flipped the basenji's lip again and pushed on his gum. It pinked up just enough to reassure him they had time.

"Let's wait on X-raying his stomach. Hopefully his color will keep improving now that he's breathing again."

He turned and was out the door when Mac called out, "The dye's in the refrigerator."

Leo stopped midstride. He'd been on his way to the drawer next to the wet sink, where the dye was supposed to live, and wanted to know who among the staff had thought to put it in the fridge, of all places! He bit down on his tongue, holding that particular gripe back. No point sweating the small stuff. As long as the animals were well taken care of, that was his inner mantra.

"Where in the refrigerator?" he asked.

"Third shelf down. Toward the back."

Leo nodded, made an arc around the wet sink, and headed for the fridge.

*****

It didn't take Mac more than a couple of minutes to suture the skin closed over the basenji's chest wound. As she pulled and looped the thread between her fingers in that rhythmic, repetitive way she found so relaxing, she could hear Dr. F grumbling at the refrigerator. She knew it wouldn't be long before she found out why.

"Which shelf did you say again?" he called out, tension in his tone.

"The third one down. Behind the antibiotics."

Mac snipped the final suture and this time heard Dr. F vocalize, "How many times do I have to tell people not to put food in this refrigerator!"

Mac walked out of X-ray and put the scissors on the wet sink, then dropped the needles in the sharps bin, snapped off her gloves, and dropped them in the trash. "Those aren't yours?" she asked, keeping her tone neutral.

"I don't eat this kind of stuff," Dr. F complained and pulled two eight-ounce plastic tubs of some kind of salad out of the fridge and tossed them on the catchall table where everyone deposited their drinks. And snacks.

Mac crossed to the table and picked up one of the plastic tubs. She took the lid off and wrinkled her nose in displeasure. "Maybe not this kind," she joked. "'It looks ill, it eats drily; marry 'tis a withered pear.'"

"What's that from?" grumbled Dr. F.

"*All's Well*. The countess. Of course, she was talking about virginity . . ."

She walked both offending food containers to the garbage at the end of the hallway to the side door. When she came back into treatment, Dr. F straightened himself up, frustrated. "There isn't any dye in here," he complained.

"Is one of these coffees for me?" Mac asked, pointing at the two red paper cups with white lids on the table in front of her.

"Yes. The taller one."

"Thanks." She picked up the twelve-ounce drink and took a sip of the black Americano with one sugar in it. Dr. F knew how his vet tech took her morning caffeine, and she was very glad he did. "Did you look behind the antibiotics?" she asked before setting the coffee down and crossing into X-ray. She knew it wouldn't be long before Dr. F found the dye, and then he'd want her over at the wet sink to inject it into Buster, so she really needed to get on the X-rays.

She depressed the lever under the table with her foot, and the window with the settings buttons for the X-ray machine popped out. She moved the column over the basenji's left leg, checked the chart on the wall, and entered fifteen pounds for his weight, since she was X-raying an extremity. She chose the appropriate time for that weight and hit "Start." She waited through the pause and moved over to the acquisitions computer hanging on the wall in the corner to her right as soon as she heard the buzz of completion. She looked at the X-ray on the screen. It looked good. She named the file and sent it over to the viewing station.

When she went to X-ray the right hip she saw Dr. F taking a swig of his coffee. He held up a box of Omnipaque dye for her to see. He'd found it. He pointed to his left, meaning he'd meet her at the wet sink. Mac nodded.

She X-rayed the basenji's right hip, looked at it on the computer, sent it over to the viewing station, and checked the dog's blood oxygen on the monitor. It was a little low, so she turned up the oxygen and switched gears to work on Buster.

*****

Leo put the dye on the blue rubberized mat that covered the steel bars over the wet sink, turned to fetch Buster out of his carrier, and passed Mac on her way to the safe to get the injectable. They passed each other in a lazy figure eight. Leo scooped Buster up out of his carrier, Mac grabbed the dose of anesthetic, and they each swung back in one fluid move, like a well-rehearsed barn dance, to end up on opposite sides of the wet sink.

Leo lifted a pair of latex gloves out of the box on the shelf to his right, and when he turned back around, Mac was tossing away a wet cotton ball. "Did you already give him the injectable?" he asked her.

"Not yet, no. I just cleaned up the little wound behind his right ear."

Leo parted the hair at the base of the ear and examined the wound. "That's fresh," he said as Buster stretched his mouth into a wide-open yawn, then snapped his head vigorously to return his coif to normal.

"Uh-huh. I was thinking last night."

"Hmm." Leo stared down at the beautiful smoke-gray cat, wondering how long—exactly—he'd been straining over his litter box. Heather Coy hadn't given him a definitive answer when he'd asked her that question, but if Buster had been out much of the night, she wouldn't have seen him constantly wanting to urinate. Although he didn't seem to want to urinate now. Leo looked up to see Mac, now gloved, too, waiting patiently with the small dose of ketamine.

"What are you thinking?" she asked.

"I hope it's not a tumor," Leo replied. He really didn't want to give Heather that kind of news.

He stood patiently, caressing Buster's head, while Mac injected the cat with something to make him sleepy. Or sleepier. She finished, and Leo felt Buster's head become heavy in his hand. He waited again, for Mac to intubate the cat, then he laid Buster's head down on the rubber mat. He lifted Buster's hind legs cranially, so Mac could catheterize him, and tuned out what remained of the daily dissonance as he watched her work. He thought about how far she'd come from that young woman just off a painful divorce, applying for the position of receptionist in the clinic. How even though she'd hidden in the shadows, he'd glimpsed her intelligence, like a firefly in the woods, and encouraged her to follow it to the vet-tech exam. She had passed, of course, with a near-perfect score, and had been his right hand ever since.

"That slipped in okay," he said, nodding at the catheter.

"Uh-huh. I didn't feel any blockage."

Mac attached a syringe to the end of the catheter and drained Buster's bladder of urine. She unhooked it, then attached a syringe full of air and emptied that back into Buster's bladder. She lifted the cat and carried him into X-ray while Leo loaded the Omnipaque dye into a syringe. She was back before he finished tossing the box in the recycle bin.

"How's the basenji doing?" he asked.

"His breathing's stronger," Mac remarked as she emptied the air out of Buster's bladder.

"You sent his X-rays over?" asked Leo, filling Buster's bladder with dye.

"I did, yes."

"All right. I'll try to look at them in between X-rays of this one."

Mac nodded, scooped Buster up again, and headed back to X-ray.

Leo bounced over to the viewing station on the back wall and studied the previous X-ray of Buster, with his bladder full of air. Still no visible crystals. "What name did you put on the X-rays for the basenji?" he asked Mac as she walked toward him with Buster in her arms.

"Stray."

Leo looked for that under "Today" in the files and double-clicked on it. The first X-ray was of the dog's left leg, and the bone was broken clean through. He trotted back to the wet sink and immediately held Buster's legs cranially again, so Mac could empty the bladder of dye. "We'll need to put a pin through both parts of that bone on the stray and then wire it in place. It's a clean break, but it might take us a while."

"D'you want to save that for tomorrow? I can come in if you like."

Leo bobbed his head on his shoulders. He didn't want to give up his Sunday off if he didn't have to. "Let's see how today goes first," he said.

"But . . ."

Leo took off again, now that Mac had put more air in Buster's bladder, so he could look at the X-ray with the dye. He heard her swish past on his left, heading back into X-ray with Buster, as he scanned the film for anomalies in the bladder. Still nothing. He switched to the basenji's film and looked at the dog's right hip. It was dislocated but not broken as far as he could tell. They could probably fix that next.

"I sent it over," Mac called out.

Leo flipped back to Buster's bladder. He scoured every inch of the film for signs of the telltale crystals.

"Anything?" said Mac from behind him, making him jump he was so focused.

"Nope," said Leo. He was stumped. He held his chin between his thumb and forefinger, pondering the timeline of Buster's emergency. It didn't make sense.

"Did Heather say when she first saw him straining to pee?" asked Mac, who had moved away to take out Buster's catheter. Leo wandered over to the wet sink and stood opposite her. She'd articulated what was nagging at him.

He shook his head no, unconsciously stroking Buster's belly as an antidote to the things that were worrying him. The cat slept on, oblivious to all the fuss being made over him. "She was acting kind of squirrely, and I put it down to her being scared. Now I'm beginning to wonder." He inhaled air through his nose, tipping his head up as he did so, and turned over the pieces of the puzzle in his mind. He knew Heather Coy had escaped an abusive marriage, and he suspected she had some form of PTSD as a result. He also knew that what kept her balanced, even if it did sometimes make her *sound* unbalanced, was her relationship with Buster. Would this make her overprotective toward the cat? Sure. But had she ever brought him in without something being wrong? No. So what was he missing in Buster's diagnosis?

Mac finished putting the gas away, peeled off her gloves and tossed them in the garbage under the wet sink, then slipped her hands under Buster to lift him up. "Do you want us to go in and talk to her together?" she asked.

Leo nodded. "We need to do something if we're to figure this out. She might say more with you in the room."

"Okay, I'll put Buster in the small animal ward to sleep off the gas. Shall I move the basenji to a ward, too?"

The vet shook his head no, his mind still finishing with Buster, his stomach aching even more noticeably from hunger now. He blinked across at Mac, her arms full of the large gray cat. "Not yet. I want to look at his color again before we go in to see Heather, and set that left hip back in place, too." He caught a look of disparagement in Mac's eyes and thought it was because he was delaying treatment for the cat. He tipped his forehead down at her. "I really don't think Buster's emergent."

"O-kay," she answered, like she didn't disagree. Then she turned her head and looked up at the clock on the wall behind her. "But how far out did Noah's dad say they were with Mocha?"

Leo glanced up at the clock, too. "Forty-five minutes," he said. Then he did a double take at the clock; it was after six already! His stomach tightened again as adrenaline pumped through his system. "We'd better get moving," he said.

Chapter 3

Leo moved ahead of Mac and opened the door to the small animal ward.

"I need time to make at least one large surgical pack," she informed him as she stepped forward.

"Before the C-section?"

Mac nodded. "We only have one sterile pack in the surgical closet, and we'll use that for the C-section. I should make at least one and get it in the autoclave for sterilizing before the clinic opens; otherwise we could get caught without."

"I can help," offered Leo.

Mac marched past without making eye contact, and Leo knew she'd given him her answer. Mac could be very particular about the way the surgical packs were put together. He watched her lay Buster on the soft towel inside the shoulder-high kennel as the three other cats and two Chihuahuas vied for her attention by getting louder. She closed the door on Buster, made kissing sounds at the animals to his left, then reached into the kennel to the right and petted Gus, a mature cat with a recurring stomach disorder.

"Is he doing okay?" Leo asked as she checked the cat's IV.

He saw Gus lean into Mac's hand, obviously enjoying the human contact. Mac's face softened into a small smile and Leo knew that the cat had filled her full of good love.

"He is," she answered. She closed the door to the kennel and looked up at him. "Okay," she said, "let's do this."

*****

They moved back into X-ray in tandem, and Dr. F leaned against the table, ready to do a closed reduction on the basenji's femur.

"Maybe turn up the gas a little?" he said to Mac. She leaned over and increased it to three, making a mental note to turn it back down in a while. She watched the dog's breathing as Dr. F manipulated the head of the femoral bone back into the socket. They both heard the click when it made it.

"Okay, two X-rays, if you would. VD and lateral," said Dr. F as he buzzed out of X-ray over to the viewing station.

Mac turned the gas back down on the pup. She started with the lateral since the dog was already on its side, and then she gently eased him onto his back for the ventrodorsal. She sent both X-rays over. "You want me to put it in an Ehmer sling?" she called out, because a luxated femur like the one he'd just set indicated the ligament was destroyed, so the hip might not stay in place if it wasn't bandaged correctly.

"Yes," replied Dr. F. "But can you do that a little later?"

"Sure."

She saw him snap away from the viewing station, indicating the hip looked good and he was ready to go see Heather. Mac waylaid him with a finger in the air. She needed a shot of coffee. She crossed treatment, picked up her cup, and took a long, hot swig. A jolt ran through her. She picked up Dr. F's cup and passed it to him, not really expecting him to take it, but he did. And slowed down enough to drink. Mac knew they'd both been running on fumes as they put the needs of the two animals in their care ahead of their own. It felt good to pause.

Somebody had left a box of chocolate-chip granola bars sitting on the catchall workstation, and she pulled one out. She looked at Dr. F with her eyebrows raised: *Want one?* He pushed his lips up and swayed his head on his shoulders this way and that, then said, "Sure." Normally neither of them ate that kind of stuff, but Mac hadn't had any breakfast and she was pretty sure the doc hadn't either. "It's granola, right?" she said to him as he took the snack out of her hand. "That could be breakfast."

They stood and munched, the woobarkwoobark with intermittent yapmeows going on around them, and glugged the last of their coffees. Dr. F took the wrapper and cup from Mac to throw in the trash, and they both turned at the sound of his cell phone ringing on his desk in his office. "You want to get that?" Mac asked.

"Do we have time?"

She shrugged. "I'd like to fix my hair and brush my teeth."

"Good," he said, waving a finger in the air. "I'll see you at the door."

*****

They walked into exam room 1 together, and as soon as Mac saw Heather's face, she noticed the puffiness around her eyes. She'd been crying. She hid it well, though, thought Mac, with that tough set to her jaw, short, spiky hair, and army surplus gear. But with Heather, the clues were always in the eyes. Today the hazel orbs were like pinballs in their sockets, knocking this way and that like she was high on meth. But Mac knew Heather Coy didn't do drugs; she just had a past that kept her wired. She wanted to slip her arm around the anxious client, but when Heather was ramped up on fear, Mac knew she could be shy about being touched. So she waited, propping her back against the counter next to the door.

Dr. F stepped ahead of Mac and to the left, setting Buster's file down on the waist-high examination table that came out of the sidewall. Heather was sitting in one of the chairs on the other side of the table, opposite Mac, next to an open door with a view out to reception. Dr. F leaned on the table at an angle, forearms down, hands clasped together, so he could make direct eye contact with Heather.

"The good news is," he said to Heather, "we haven't found stones or crystals in Buster's urine, and he doesn't seem to be in any distress."

Heather's eyes dropped to her hands. She was holding a tattered tissue, and Mac watched her pluck at the edges frantically. Dr. F paused, obviously waiting for Heather to look at him again. When she didn't he slid his forearms forward on the table, and the slight movement drew her back to him. Mac saw Heather's eyes switch this way and that, then meet Dr. F's as he asked, "Can you tell me how long you saw Buster straining over the litter box? Because he may just have passed the stone."

Now Heather's eyes pinged over to Mac, a definite look of panic in them. She stared down at her tissue again, twitching her lips forward and back, forward and back. Mac guessed she was trying to find the best way to answer Dr. F's question.

"The thing is," said Heather finally, flinging her head up to make eye contact with Dr. F. She looked hostile, angry. "He was out all night *cheating* on me. And I warned him, I *warned* him, if he did that one more time, I'd have him neutered." She sniffed belligerently and looked out through the open door. "So that's why I brought him in. I want you to cut them off."

Dr. F shifted his eyes toward Mac, and she saw a storm on the horizon of those big blue pools. She flashed her own back at him, beacons of warning—*don't go there!*—and the storm receded. He had to know it wasn't Mac's fault that Heather had lied to get him out of bed so early in the morning.

Dr. F sighed and stood upright again. "The thing is," he started to say.

Heather spun back his way and cut him off, speeding up her explanation, which made her sound even more crazy. "He didn't come home till almost four a.m.! I lay awake worrying myself half to death, and then he walked in looking proud as punch, like he'd nailed every pussy in the neighborhood! I said, 'I didn't let you put a ring on my finger so you could go all tomcat on me!' but he just climbed up on to the bed and purred like he hadn't done anything wrong." She dropped her head again and sniffed two, three times.

Dr. F glanced at Mac. She made a tiny shrug to let him know that she had no clue what to say.

Heather went on without looking at either of them, a sob rising through her words. "I put up with it last time it happened because . . . well, he's a cat and I know he has needs." She swiped at her eyes with the back of her hand, the tissue being virtually useless at this point. "Needs I can't take care of. But I can't deal with the *stress* of worrying about him all night. So I thought if I brought him to you . . ." She paused. Dr. F didn't say anything. Heather lifted her head to look at him once more, her eyes wet with tears. "I'm sorry I made you come out in the middle of the night."

"It's okay," he said, walking around the examination table with his arms out, ready to give her a hug. She stepped up into the hug and let him console her. "Another emergency was waiting for us when we got here, so it's just as well I came in early. Are you going to be okay?" he asked as he let go of her and stepped back. He tipped his head down, drawing her eyes back up to his again.

She nodded yes.

"Good. Buster's still out from the anesthetic, and we need to help this other emergency plus get ready for a third one we have coming in. We might be able to get Buster back to you before we start on that, or you can head on home and come back later to pick him up."

"I'd rather wait," said Heather, pulling on the tissue again.

"Okay, that's fine." Dr. F walked around the examining table and picked up Buster's chart. "You can stay in here for now, but once the clinic opens, you might have to move out to reception. Pema—you know, who works the front desk?" Heather nodded without looking up. "She should be getting here pretty soon. She'll put some coffee on for you."

"Can I close this door?" Heather asked, like it was no big deal. But the wisp of poignancy behind her bravado made Mac know it was.

"Of course," said Dr. F.

As Mac made her way out with him she heard Heather close the other door and assumed it was to give herself a private space to cry. She slid open a drawer in the counter that she'd been propped against and pulled out a box of tissues. "Those are for you," she whispered to Heather. Then closed the door behind her.

Dr. F was standing inside treatment, waiting for Mac. "I was going to tell her that Buster's already *been* neutered," he said, his face creased in confusion.

"In the state she's in," joked Mac, "that would be like you telling her she can't be married to her cat."

*****

Leo caught the humor in Mac's retort, but his mind was already running through the order of what he needed to do next to help the two animals in his care, and whether he could get it done before Steve arrived with Mocha. He could hear his cell phone ringing on his desk again and wondered if that was his daughter calling back. He hadn't got to his phone in time to answer her earlier, and she hadn't left a message. Maybe this time she would. He glanced at the clock on the wall: it was six twenty-five already. "Let's jump on the splenectomy," he said.

Mac looked up at the clock, too. "Isn't that kind of a risk?"

"It shouldn't take us more than thirty minutes, and the Rengens are still at least twenty minutes out. Plus, by the time they get here, the rest of the staff will have arrived, and we'll have help."

"Yes, but what about the surgical packs? If I use the one we have for the basenji, I won't have one for the C-section."

"How long will it take you to put one together?"

Mac shrugged. "Five minutes?"

"Okay, you do that and get it in the autoclave, and I'll prep the basenji for surgery."

Mac shook her head no. "That won't work. It's the first use of the autoclave for the day, so the surgical tray will take forty-five minutes to sterilize and another forty-five minutes to dry."

Leo thought about this for a second. "Okay, then we'll use the packaged instruments from the drawers in surgery for the spleen. You have a sterile gown for me?"

She nodded again and he nodded back, the all's well sign.

Leo heard his cell phone ring yet again and was glad it wasn't in his pocket. He'd have to put it on vibrate, he thought. His mind flashed back to that reminder that had skimmed through his brain first thing this morning, the one that he hadn't been able to identify. Maybe that was what the phone calls were about. But before he could take that thought further, he had the stray in his arms and was nudging the door to surgery open with his foot.

*****

Mac walked over to the cabinets by the wet sink and lifted out two large surgical trays, figuring if she could throw instruments into one in five minutes, she could throw them into two. The only thing that sometimes slowed her down was tying the cloth around them.

She dropped in the usual—two pairs of scissors, three different hemostat forceps, needle driver, clamps—covered them with gauze squares and paper towels, and then began her overly exacting way of tying the green drape cloth around the tray. She had learned how to prepare trays when she worked as an assistant in a clinic on an army base way up in Alaska, where her first husband was stationed. The army veterinarians made the assistants play football with the trays after they tied them—no tape—and they had to go back and do them again if the cloth fell apart when tossed. The army's motto was that the tools had to *stay* sterile after they came out of the autoclave, and it was a lesson Mac had never forgotten. Sometimes she tied and retied the cloths until she got them *just* right, and nothing bugged her more than finding a tray in the sterile closet that didn't meet football standards. That was one thing she could get a little OCD about.

She tugged on the second green cloth just as the doc's face appeared at the door to surgery; he was ready for her. Fortunately the cloth stayed tied but she still needed to put the surgical packs in the autoclave, which meant she'd have to make him wait.

Then Waylon breezed in and she knew she'd been saved. The tall, skinny vet assistant with his tight, chestnut curls and patchy beard had only been working for the clinic for a couple of months but his willingness to pick up the slack had earned him big points with Mac. In fact the only thing that bothered her about him was that sometimes his reactions to the work were kind of immature; but he was only twenty-seven and the closer she got to forty-five, the younger twenty-seven seemed.

She bobbed her chin at him, and Waylon gave her the *whaddaya need?* bob back. She pointed at the surgical tray, then at the short hallway where the autoclave lived. Waylon strode toward her without hesitation. She glanced up at the board and saw there were two feline spays and a cherry eye scheduled for that morning. "And will you prep me three small trays?" she asked. "There's only one spare in the closet."

"If you promise not to give me the stink eye when I do it

wrong," he said.

"Yeah. No. Can't promise that," Mac quipped.

He dropped his head and shoulders and went all Eeyore on her. "O-kay," he said. "I'll do them anyway."

She chuckled and stored a small mental note to herself to talk to him about auditioning for the next Shakespeare production. Then she grabbed a mask and headed in to help Dr. F.

*****

As Mac shot into surgery, Leo shot out and went directly to the sink to scrub up. As he doused his hands with chlorhexidine soap and began to lather, he heard his cell phone ringing in the distance. He glanced up at the clock above the double doors: it was six thirty-five. Whoever was bugging him would have to wait until he got the basenji's bleed under control. He rinsed his hands and forearms, shook them over the sink, and headed back to surgery, holding them up in the air in front of him.

He pushed the door open with his butt and swung into the one island of calm in the clinic. Leo liked surgery, not just because he got to fix things in here but also because it was a place where he could close out the daily dissonance, put the constant barrage of questions on hold, not have to explain himself, and focus. Not that he and Mac didn't get interrupted in there; they did. The door opened frequently with need-to-know-right-now questions, but the fact that he couldn't stop in the middle of a surgery put him on the outside of the huddle, running unimpeded toward the goal line, and he liked that. Mac did, too. Surgery was restful compared to everything else they had to do at the clinic.

Mac already had a gaggle of instruments laid out on the counter by the wall, and when Leo walked in, she reached up to the sterile closet and pulled out a gown and a drape pack. She untied the gown, shook it, and held it open for him to walk into, then ripped the tape off the drapes.

She gave the one with the rectangular opening in the center of it to Leo, and he laid it across the basenji, so the dog was covered everywhere except over his abdomen. "His breathing's good," he remarked.

"Uh-huh," agreed Mac. She flung a smaller sterile drape over the mobile surgical tray and quickly dropped a scalpel from its blue plastic wrapper down onto it. Just in time for Leo to spin around and pick it up, and, as he made his first incision through the skin over the basenji's belly, Mac ripped open seal after seal on sterile surgical instruments, dropping them all on the tray ready for him to use. She added a stack of gauze squares, and quickly threw a towel at Leo's feet as the first blood gushed out of the belly down to the floor.

"Perfect timing," he remarked, mopping the incision with three squares of gauze. Once he could see clearly, he slipped his right hand in and felt it land immediately on the tubular-shaped spleen. He looped his fingers around it and eased the purple-brown organ out of the dog's body. More blood ran out across the green drape, then dribbled down onto the towel.

"There's the tear," he said to Mac, pointing at the bloody opening in the spleen with his scalpel. He looked down at the towel by his feet. "I wouldn't have thought it was big enough for this amount of blood," he muttered. "Maybe there's a hole in the diaphragm."

He slipped the fingers of his right hand into the dog and felt around the diaphragm to see if there was an opening. He felt nothing. Not even a bulge in the diaphragm to suggest it had been squeezed like a balloon until the air popped out somewhere else in the form of a hernia.

He dropped his chin to his collarbone to ease the tension in the back of his neck. He heard his stomach growl. He ignored the hunger pains and focused on the task in front of him. Dissecting and tying off the multiple blood vessels going in and out of the spleen was a lengthy, involved process. Fortunately because Leo had trained to do this thirty years ago, when keeping an animal under anesthetic was way more risky than it was today, he tended to work quickly. Quickly and efficiently.

The minutes sped by once he started dissecting, the rhythmic clicking of the hand on the clock reminding him of raindrops dripping from trees in the forest. His mind drifted back to Heather, and how ramped up on fear she'd been. *Was it fear over his reaction when he found out there was nothing wrong with Buster?* he wondered. *Or fear of losing Buster because he'd been out for much of the night. She had to know that Buster was neutered so then—*

Mac interrupted his thoughts as she passed him a wad of gauze to mop the blood.

"Thanks." He stopped work for a second and looked at her. "D'you have any idea what was going on with Heather?"

"No," she said. "Although I was just thinking about that, too."

Leo bent forward and continued dissecting.

"I have this whole scenario in my head where she's sleeping and Buster comes in through the cat door and the noise wakes her up and triggers her PTSD. She reaches for Buster to protect her—because she has no clue he's gone out rabble-rousing—and when she finds out he's not on the bed beside her, she gets even more panicked. So she grabs her phone and calls the only person she knows is fool enough to answer at that hour. Me. Then she has to come up with some kind of reason for her call."

Leo glanced up at her. "You think?"

Mac shrugged. "I'm an actress, remember? So I'm always looking for motivation." She paused, then added, "She could just be crazy."

Leo chuckled. He'd come to the gastrosplenic ligament and reached for the Allis tissue forceps on the tray. He noticed Mac was looking past him, her eyes crinkled above her mask. He also noticed that the dogs had suddenly got louder out in the ward. JJ had arrived.

"Do you want to let her know about the incoming C-section?" he asked.

Mac nodded and nudged her head to the right; an encouragement for JJ to come in.

Leo went back to dissecting as the door to surgery opened behind him. The daily dissonance clashed like cymbals into the quiet of the room. All the animals wanted JJ's attention. JJ was the go-to assistant for *a-n-y-thing* that needed doing at the clinic: feeding the animals in the wards, washing their beds, holding argumentative pets so they could get shots or stitches out, monitoring the gas and oxygen during surgery. JJ had Mac's back while Mac had Leo's, and she did everything required, often before being asked and with a work ethic that made Mac happy. And when Mac was happy, Leo's day went much smoother. He still hadn't figured out how the dogs in the ward saw JJ. She was a petite Korean American, barely five feet tall, without an ounce of spare flesh on her, but the minute she sailed into treatment, they started with their "HEY HI YOU'RE HERE CAN YOU SEE ME I'M HUNGRY" barks.

"What d'you need?" came her voice from behind Leo.

"Can you bring in a warming bed? We've got an emergency C-section coming in."

"Is that who's shaking the front doors?"

Leo listened but he couldn't hear anything over the racket from the dogs. "Are they shaking?" he asked.

"I thought that's what I heard when I came around from my car in the parking lot," said JJ.

"And Pema's not here yet?"

"Not that I've seen," JJ answered. "But I've only just got here. And it's still only quarter of seven."

"I thought it would take Steve longer to get here," murmured Leo dissecting cleanly through the last blood vessel. He tied it off and lifted the spleen up into the air. He looked at Mac; she gave him a sarcastic eyebrow raise, which he ignored. He dropped the spleen in a saline bowl and glanced over his shoulder at JJ. She was standing in the barely open door, holding a mask to her face. "Okay, you do what you need to do, and I'll go take care of the Rengens—that's who's here for the C-section—when I've sutured this one," he told her.

"Noah Rengen?" said JJ. They all knew about the little boy's attachment to his dog.

"Yep," chimed Leo and Mac.

"Okay, I'll try to be quick," said JJ and was gone before the door could swing closed.

"When is she not quick?" Mac remarked.

Leo laughed. Then set to work suturing the basenji.

*****

Five minutes later, Leo stepped out of surgery and rolled his shoulders like he'd just taken off a heavy backpack. His eyes were bleary, his body felt like it was moving in slow motion, and there was sweat trickling down from his forehead around his eyes. He was drained. But he wouldn't trade this feeling for any other.

He loved surgery. To see a dog come into the clinic with his head down, his breathing labored, and a hind leg that obviously couldn't take any weight, then see the same dog—six months after he'd fixed him up—skitter around the clinic like a puppy again, well, that just made him feel like a rock star. Of course it wasn't nearly that glamorous. He was more like a mechanic than a rock star. Although mechanicss could take all the parts out of an engine and leave them on the shop floor while they talked on the telephone, and he didn't dare do that with an animal. So why, then, did his wife always think he could?

The debate over whose job was more important could still claw at the back of Leo's throat. He had never looked for a pedestal to stand on for what he did. In fact, when he thought about people's professions, he found himself admiring snowplow drivers and power-company employees who went out in the middle of the night, in conditions that most people wouldn't brave, and put things back to right again. No, all Leo needed to be sure of the value of his work was this gelatinized feeling he got after helping an animal. Like he'd given it his all.

He trudged around the wet sink, past someone tying a cloth around a small surgical tray, willing himself not to let his mind roll towards the negative. Not today, when he'd tried to do something good for an animal. An animal he might *really* get to meet now. The thought made him smile just as he heard a voice say, "Morning, Dr. F."

It didn't occur to Leo that this salutation might require a reply until he was outside the door to his bathroom. He looked back and threw out, "Morning," then saw Waylon smile at him from over by the wet sink. *Waylon was here already?* queried Leo.

He stepped into the bathroom and turned the faucet in the sink full on. He bent forward, filled his hands, and threw the water over his face once, twice, three times. He filled his hands again and sloshed the water up into his hair. He did that again and then stood upright, letting the cold drips run down his face and neck and onto his scrubs. He shuddered like a wet dog and felt his whole being come alive again.

He glanced in the mirror, saw the sweat stains that had come through to his scrub shirt, and tugged it off with his T-shirt in one swift move. He sloshed some water under his pits, patted them dry, and filled them with deodorant. He pulled on a clean white T-shirt, followed by a fresh dark-blue scrub top, and combed his wet hair away from his face with his fingers. He glanced in the mirror one more time, then swung a clean, beige towel under his arm. Time to go see how he could help Mocha.

Spike

He'd gotten himself turned around, and he didn't know where exactly. Most likely where he'd had to go away from the river to get around that building with all the motorbikes outside it. He certainly didn't want to get caught in the middle of those.

His mistake had been getting out of the van too soon. He'd ducked out once they got to the river, because he was sure he could make it from there, but he hadn't figured on all these buildings blocking his way.

And now it was raining. A cold, bone-chilling rain that felt like it might be carrying some late snow with it. He hunkered down for a while at a coffee shop, but then he started to get scared that she'd be worried about him. In fact, the more he delayed, the more he thought he could hear her sighs. He *knew* she was worried about him. Moving forward was the only option even though it was getting dark.

He stood on the street corner outside the coffee shop, turning his head slowly in all directions, trying to get a sense of where he was. If he went downhill, he felt pretty sure he'd run into the river again, but all the roads looked flat from where he was standing.

He decided to look for a place to stay for the night, then get a fresh start in the morning when he wasn't so tired. And cold. The rain was like an ice sheet coming down from the sky. His coat was saturated. He walked back under the sagging awning over the entrance to the coffee shop and shook it off. Then he started down the street toward the neon lights he could see in the distance, hoping to find a place to sleep.

Chapter 4

When Leo came around the corner into reception, carrying the towel and his stethoscope, he blinked at the sudden suffusion of sunlight. *When had it become morning?* he wondered. He tipped his head up, enjoying the feel of the sun on his face as he unlocked the front doors for the tall, wiry man smiling at him from the other side. Leo knew that Steve wasn't smiling because he was happy, but because it was a default position for his particular temperament. Steve was one of Leo's more genial clients, knowledgeable, articulate, and very willing to do whatever it took to help his pets, especially Mocha, because she belonged to his six-year-old son, Noah. Leo pulled the door open and the already hot July day whooshed toward him like heat from a furnace.

"I'm so sorry we had to make you open up, Dr. Friel," said Steve, his right shoulder tipped down and forward in his regular posture of self-effacement.

"It's totally fine," said Leo. He flapped his hand to dismiss any feelings of guilt Steve might have. "Where is she?"

"In the van, with Noah," said Steve, pointing at the green

Chrysler Town & Country just a few feet away in the parking lot.

Leo stepped outside, wishing he were dressed in shorts and a T-shirt like Steve, and hustled around the small area of grass and shrubs in front of the clinic, Steve keeping pace beside him. "How long has she been in labor?" he asked.

"Most of the night."

"And you say it's not advancing?"

"Not that I can tell. Although I'm not experienced in this at all."

Leo nodded. Mocha had been bred to be a service dog, and originally she belonged to one of Steve's neighbors. But the puppy had noticed the quiet little boy who didn't want to talk to anyone in the house next door, and wriggled her way under the shared fence to play with Noah. And then she did it again. And again and again and again. It wasn't long before everyone saw the positive effect that Mocha was having on Noah. Steve had approached his neighbor about keeping the dog. She'd agreed, but only on the condition that Steve would let Mocha have one litter of puppies to replace her in the service-dog world. Mocha was now two years old and this was that litter.

They got to the van and walked around to the passenger side, where the sliding door was wide open. Mocha was spread out on the floor, her head toward the door. Noah was sitting beside her, his legs dangling outside the vehicle, his hand resting gently on her shoulder. He didn't look at his dad or the vet.

Leo crouched down and placed the beige towel on the floor of the van beside Mocha. He lifted her lip and pressed his forefinger into her gum. It paled, then pinked up again as soon as he relieved the pressure; her capillary reflex was good. He listened to her heart through his stethoscope, concerned that her calcium had passed directly into her milk, leaving her with insufficient calcium for muscular contractions. Her heartbeat was strong and steady, so no calcium deficit that he could tell. He pulled the stethoscope off and gently stroked the top of Mocha's head. He was about to stand up when Noah leapt to his feet and clutched him around the neck. The six-year-old put his lips close to Leo's ear and whispered, "Please don't let her die."

Leo's heart skipped a beat. Noah's mother had died giving birth to his baby brother, and Noah, who was only three at the time, had stopped talking. His large and small motor skills stopped improving, his social skills with anyone outside his direct family disappeared altogether, and even inside his family, he became withdrawn. No one knew what to do. Until last year, when Mocha came along. She was only eight months old when she squeezed her way under the fence and nudged Noah out of his solitude and into playing. And Steve told Leo that the more the puppy brought Noah out of himself, the more Noah seemed to teach her the things she needed to know to be a good dog.

Leo had no doubt. Every day he saw what animals could do for their humans and vice versa. With one arm around Noah and the other caressing Mocha's head, Leo could feel their bond filtering through him, like morning sunlight through the trees, and it fed that part of him that lived to be a vet. He thought about how Mac had asked him, "Do you have time for a C-section this morning?" and something flashed through his mind. The same something that had flashed through first thing this morning, when he was in his bathroom at home. He still couldn't make out what it was though, so he pushed it aside, smacked his lips together and whispered back to Noah, "I'm on it."

*****

Mac finished stitching the basenji and whisked away the green drapes all at the same time.

"You want a blanket?" JJ asked, taking the drapes from her and unclipping the clamps.

"He's not very heavy," Mac replied, discarding the needle in the sharps bin. She pulled off her latex gloves and began unhooking the dog from the gas and oxygen. "But we have to watch that broken leg. Will you stay with him?"

"Till he's awake?" JJ dropped the clamps in the tray to be sterilized, picked the bloody towel up off the floor, and headed for the door. "Sure."

As she left, Mac pulled the endotracheal tube out of the basenji's throat and started to free him from all the cords that connected him to the monitor. She worked quickly, knowing she had to get the room ready for the potential C-section. She imagined how pressured Dr. F must be feeling. This was supposed to be one of his days off yet here he was, putting in the extra time to help clients because he knew how much their furry friends meant to them. *The clinic needed a second, full-time vet, that was the problem*, she thought. Well, no. The real problem was that Dr. F's daughter, Carly, had backed out of becoming that second vet. And after she'd done such a stellar internship with them. Everyone at the clinic had come to appreciate how Carly took on the things her dad didn't prefer doing, leaving him free to focus on surgery. And then she'd gone and fallen in love, and suddenly being a vet didn't matter to her so much as helping her husband-to-be open a climbing gym.

Mac made a clicking sound of resignation in the side of her cheek as she looked down at the sleeping basenji. "If thou remember'st not the slightest folly that ever love did make thee run into / Thou hast not loved," she whispered to him. "That's from *As You Like It*." She ran her hand gently over his bedraggled fur. "Are you a Shakespeare kind of dog? Or are you more of a modernist?" She paused, plucking some of the dirt out of his fur. She imagined the red would sharpen to a lovely rose gold when it was clean. She watched the dog's breathing; it was good and steady. "I'm looking forward to meeting you," she told him.

The door opened behind her and JJ came back in with a blanket. "Do we have an owner for this dog?" she asked.

"Uh-uh, no."

"So you talked Dr. F into fixing him up?"

Mac lifted the basenji and JJ spread the blanket on the operating table underneath him. "Not really. I tried but he was adamant there was nothing we could do for him." She laid the pup down on the blanket. "He sent me to get the blue stuff but then, when I got back with it, he'd changed his mind." She noticed the blanket felt warm against her hands. "Did you get this out of the dryer?"

"Yep."

"Honestly, I don't know what came over him," Mac continued, scooping the basenji up with the blanket. "He just suddenly wanted to save this one."

JJ reached her right hand forward and ran her fingers over the fur on the sleeping dog's chin. "Was it you, little man? Did you win his heart?" She bent closer to the dog and whispered, " Or was it just the doc being capricious."

Mac laughed. "That's a good word. I was thinking distracted because of the divorce—"

"Are they getting divorced?"

"He hasn't said." Mac leaned in closer to JJ. "But I've seen some appointments with his lawyer on his calendar."

JJ pulled the sides of her mouth down.

"Yeah, that's what I thought. I figured that's why he's been so out of it recently. But I like capricious better. Is that one of your words of the day?"

"Yep. Got it two days ago." JJ moved to the door and held it wide open. "I was hoping to find a place to use it," she added as Mac moved through with the basenji across her forearms.

Mac stopped immediately outside the door to let Dr. F and Steve Rengen go through into X-ray. They were carrying Mocha on a towel between them and she knew their load was heavier than hers. Plus JJ had to get around her to open the door to the ward.

"Who's that?" came a voice to her right.

She looked down and saw Noah Rengen standing by the lift table, pointing up at the dog in her arms. "This is a stray we found this morning. He'd been hit by a car."

"Is he going to be okay?"

"I think so, yes," said Mac. "Dr. Friel fixed him up, and now he's going to rest."

"Will Mocha be in the bed next to him after she has her puppies?" he asked.

Mac bobbed her head, yes. "We can make that happen," she said.

"Good. Then they'll be company for each other."

Mac smiled at him and moved on, past JJ, into the large animal ward. Some of the dogs lunged against their kennel doors, but Mac paid them no mind as she scooted down the narrow space in front of the kennels and found an open one. She laid the basenji down on his blanket and left him with JJ.

Dr. F and Steve already had Mocha up on the X-ray table. "Do we know how much she weighs?" Mac asked as she slid into the room behind them.

"I'll check her chart," said Dr. F

"Thanks."

Mac paused after Dr. F and Steve left. She looked at the beautiful chocolate Lab, lying on her side, panting hard, her stomach distended. "How're you doing?" she whispered, running her hand under the dog's muzzle. Mocha showed no response, and Mac knew she was tired from the unproductive labor. Probably scared, too.

She stretched the dog's back legs out away from her belly and her front legs forward a little so she could get a full extension of her stomach. "We just need to see if the puppies are folded," she told Mocha. "Or breech," This time, the dog opened a soulful eye in her direction. Mac stroked her head between her eyes. "It'll be all right," she assured the dog.

She bent forward to slip her lead apron over her head, and when she stood up again she noticed Noah watching her through the open doorway. The little boy looked very, very serious, and Mac felt uncomfortable under his steady gaze. She was used to audiences for her acting, but when it came to real life—or, in this case, real life and death—she didn't like being watched so much. Especially when the audience had such a haunted look in his eyes.

"Dr. F," she called softly, knowing she was interrupting his explanation of a C-section to Steve. He appeared immediately in the doorway, his hand out for Noah to take.

The little boy let himself be led away with his dad, and Mac heard Dr. F saying, "Can you feed the turtle in reception for me?" as they all disappeared out of sight.

She breathed a sigh of relief and turned back to Mocha. "Okay, m'dear," she said, opening the aperture on the light so it covered the dog's belly. "Let's take a look at your puppies."

*****

"Is it over?" Dr. F called out, heading directly to the viewing station as he came back into treatment.

"Uh-huh," Mac called back.

Waylon looked across at her, from where he was writing something on the board for today's surgery schedule. She beckoned him toward her, and he snapped the lid back on the red marker, let it hang down beside the board, then strolled around Dr. F and into X-ray.

"We taking her into surgery?" he asked.

"I'm not sure yet. I'm waiting on Dr. F to tell me what the X-ray looks like."

"I can't find it," he called out.

Waylon snickered.

Mac gave him a warning look. "You wait with Mocha," she

instructed, then sashayed out of X-ray and came up behind Dr. F to look at the computer.

"Oh, here it is," said Dr. F, finding the file as soon as Mac appeared beside him. He clicked on Steve's name, and Mocha's uterus blinked up onto the screen.

Mac leaned forward at the same time as Dr. F. The phone rang next to her elbow. Without thinking, she answered it.

"Yes, I'm calling to find out how Cleo's doing and if I can pick her up this morning?" said a female voice at the other end.

"I'm sorry. Who?" Mac asked as Dr. F pointed at the folded fetus in the entrance to the birth canal. Mac nodded; she'd seen it too.

"My Rottweiler, Cleo," said the caller. "I'm s'posed to be able to pick her up today, but I was told to call first."

Mac glanced to her right, at the board, even though she knew there wasn't a Cleo in the wards. "What was she in for?" she asked.

"She had to have her right leg amputated."

Mac paused. They hadn't done an amputation yesterday. Or any day in the last month, for that matter. "Are you sure you have the right number?" she asked.

The caller repeated the number she had dialed and, naturally, it was the one for Riverside Animal Clinic. Mac tried a different tack. "And what's the name of the clinic where Cleo had the surgery?"

This seemed to confuse the caller. "Well, I'm not . . . ," she started without finishing. Then asked, "Are you in a vet's office?"

"This is Riverside Animal Clinic, yes."

"What's it called again?"

"Riverside Animal Clinic."

"Oh no, that's not right," said the voice on the other end. "Cleo's at a place with River *Road* in the name. What was it again?" Mac heard a scratching sound, like the caller was shuffling paper close to the receiver. "Oh, that's it. River Road Animal Hospital."

"Is that in Skagit County?".

"No, no. King County."

"Oh, no wonder," said Mac, smiling into the phone. "I thought I didn't recognize the name. We're in Skagit County, so it's not one I know."

"You can't tell me how Cleo's doing?" insisted the woman, and there was such urgency in her tone Mac almost wanted to help. But, of course, she couldn't.

"Mmm, no," she said. "You'll have to call River Road Animal Hospital for that information."

"Can you give me that number?"

This had already taken longer than Mac wanted, and from her cursory count, Mocha had at least nine puppies that needed delivering. "I'm afraid we don't open for another five minutes, so our computers aren't up yet."

"All right, I'll find it somewhere else," said the caller with an edge to her voice. The line went dead.

"Looks like nine to me," Dr. F declared, pushing back from the viewing station now that he had Mac's attention again. She nodded.

They broke apart without discussing it, Dr. F headed for the key to the controlled-substances safe that held the anesthetic and Mac back to X-ray.

"What was her weight?" she called out.

"Seventy-nine pounds. I'll get a half dose of ketamine, and we'll get those puppies out of her."

*****

Leo hustled into reception to update Steve on what he'd seen in Mocha's X-ray. Father and son were sitting next to each other, their heads bowed close together in whispered conversation. Beyond them Leo could see the Skagit River bouncing sunlight like a prism as it raced downstream. He really liked that view when the sun was out. He stopped at the end of the long, angled counter that defined reception, and smiled a greeting at Pema. Like so many of his staff, Pema turned her hand to whatever was needed around the clinic, although she usually worked reception. She was young, maybe in her late twenties, with long, dark hair and caramel-colored skin, and just last week she'd informed Leo she would be leaving her job at the clinic after the New Year to go adventuring with her husband. He was disappointed; Pema had been with him nine years. Of course he was lucky that so many of his staff gave him loyal service for so many years, but that just made it harder to see them go.

"Hi, Dr. F," she said, walking toward him, holding a handful of charts. "Do you know what time Dr. Murphy is coming in today?"

Leo had forgotten he'd asked Mac to schedule a relief vet for today. "I don't know. Maybe ten o'clock? Maybe earlier. I know we have two spays to do . . ."

"Okay. I was just wondering if I could schedule her for any appointments, because the parking lot is filling up."

Pema pointed out the windows behind Leo, and he spun around to see three cars that he hadn't seen earlier. And he couldn't see the whole parking lot from where he was standing, so there were probably more. "Well, you can always schedule them with me," he said. Pema's mouth dropped open, and her eyebrows came together in a look of confusion. Leo wondered why. But then he also wondered why he'd scheduled a relief vet to come and do two spays when he could undoubtedly have done them himself.

Before he could answer that question—or even ask it of Pema—he heard a chair scrape against the floor and turned to see Steve standing up. Leo waved for him to sit down again and walked the last few steps across reception to be in front of both Rengens. He crouched close to the floor, so they could look into his face from their seats. "We took an X-ray," he said, "and saw that one of the puppies is folded, so its head is tucked in toward its tummy and it's trying to come out shoulders first." Leo illustrated his explanation by putting his hands on his own shoulders and lowering his head slightly. When he looked back up, Noah's brown eyes were staring intently at him. "A puppy can't come out shoulders first," Leo went on, "and since the puppy that's folded is at the head of the line to be born, it's blocking the way for all the other puppies. So we're going to go in surgically and take the puppies out by Cesarean section."

Noah shifted forward on his seat a little. "Do you know how many puppies are inside Mocha?" he asked.

"Nine, we think," Leo replied.

Noah looked up at his dad, and for the first time since they'd arrived, Leo saw excitement in his face. *"Nine,"* he repeated, long and slow, like somebody had just told him he was getting ice cream for dinner. His dad smiled down at him. Noah turned back to Leo. "Do you have a picture?" he asked.

"The X-ray," the vet confirmed. "Do you want to come see?"

"Oh yes, please." Noah nodded and jumped down from his seat.

Leo led both of them back across reception as first one phone line, then another, started ringing. The day had begun, he thought. He heard Pema singsong into the telephone, "Riverside Animal Clinic. Would you hold, please?" twice.

Leo heard his own phone ringing again in his office as he pushed open the double door with his back and held it open for the Rengens to pass through. Who knew he'd be in such demand this morning?

He walked them over to the viewing station and brought up the image of Mocha's uterus again. "Here they are," he said and ran his finger across the row of fetuses. He caught sight of Waylon coming out of surgery, which meant Mac was in there prepping Mocha. "Can you help Noah count the puppies," he asked, "so I can go scrub up?"

Waylon nodded yes, but before Leo could turn around and head for the sink, JJ appeared in the door to the large animal ward and mouthed, "He's awake."

Leo changed gears like he was on automatic. He felt a buzz of excitement even though it didn't make any sense. Animals had a way of sneaking into his heart, but this one must have pumped it full of love. JJ stepped back to let him through. Leo turned into the ward and saw the bedraggled pup look up at him; then his tail flickered before it began to wag in earnest. "You remember me, huh?" said the vet, crouching down in the open door to the kennel. On both sides of them dogs barked and whined—METOOMETOOMETOO—but Leo barely noticed them, captivated as he was by the look in the basenji's eyes. The dog so wanted to please Leo that even though he was still groggy from surgery, he rolled his spine inward and padded his front legs back toward his body, to get up on all fours. "No, no, little guy," said Leo. "Don't try to stand up with that leg."

The vet crab walked farther into the kennel and encouraged the dog to lie back down by gently stroking the length of his body. The basenji let himself be guided by the vet's touch, and once down, offered a front and back leg up in the air to expose his belly. Leo ran his fingertips lightly over the shaved belly as his trained eye took in the position of the rear leg.

"That hip's obviously not bothering him," came Mac's voice.

Leo looked around to see her leaning in the doorway. "No, that's what I was thinking," he replied, shifting farther right to allow Mac space enough to come in and pet the dog. "You're feeling much better, aren't you?" he said to the pup.

The stray wound his head around and licked Leo on his wrist, his tail thumping the floor.

"I'd say so," chuckled Mac.

"But there's still no curl to your tail, so we'll have to figure out what's in you besides basenji," said Leo.

The dog flicked his head around to Mac, as if wondering whether he could talk her into petting him, too. She responded by bobbing down alongside Leo and cupping the dog's face in her hand. "You're a bright-eyed little thing," she said, running her thumbs back and forth on both sides of his muzzle. He closed his eyes and leaned into the caress.

"I'd like you to splint that back leg," said Leo, rising to a stand. The basenji perked his head up again, as if not wanting to lose sight of Leo.

Mac rose also. She pulled a splint and a roll of self-adherent bandage from the pocket of her scrubs. She'd been ready.

"Hot orange?" questioned Leo, pointing at the bandage.

"Summer colors."

Leo rolled his eyes. "I'm glad you order these things."

"You want me to give him a sedative, too?"

"Maybe not yet. Splint him and give him something easy to eat . . ."

"Chicken and rice," Mac said over to JJ, who nodded and slipped away from the entrance to the ward to get it.

"And I'll check back on him in an hour."

Mac's brow crumpled in confusion the same way Pema's had earlier.

"What?" he said, as he made for the door.

"Will you be here in an hour?" she called after him.

Leo kept moving across treatment, shaking his head that she would even ask that question. "Why wouldn't I be?" he called back, then disappeared down the hallway to his office before he could hear her answer.

*****

Mac didn't bother answering. She knew the doc wouldn't hear her with the door open on the presently deafening daily dissonance. Plus he probably wasn't listening anyway. Maybe wasn't even remembering. She stroked the basenji, who was still watching the door as if expecting Leo to come back, and confided, "'But men are men; the best sometimes forget.'"

"*Othello?*" asked JJ, returning with a can of special dog food.

"You got it," said Mac. "Hold him for me, would you?"

But JJ didn't need to be asked. She had already deposited the tinned dog food on a counter outside the kennel and bobbed down to cradle the basenji's head, and Mac knew it was because she'd seen the splints and bandage on the floor next to him.

Mac worked in silence, JJ kneeling beside her. She put a pad around the obvious break in the dog's hind leg, splints on either side of it, then wrapped everything with the sticky bandage. The dog didn't wiggle.

"He's pretty accommodating for a basenji," JJ remarked as stood back up with Mac.

"He's a sweetheart."

Mac watched the basenji as she made her way out of the ward, in case he tried to stand up, but he just plopped his head down on his two front paws and looked past her at the door again. "I think Dr. F's got a new best friend," she whispered to JJ.

She put the remainder of the hot orange bandage roll next to the wet sink, pulled a clean paper mask out of the box and looped it over her ears. JJ followed suit. They pushed into surgery where Waylon was waiting with the sleeping Mocha.

"She good?" Mac asked, hoping the pre-anesthetic had taken so she could intubate Mocha.

"Yep. She's good," he answered.

They traded places while JJ started prepping the fluids on the oxygen machine. Mac opened Mocha's mouth to maneuver the endo-tube into place "We're going to need some bedding laundered for the kennels," she told Waylon before he left. "And give the stray in kennel four half the tin of dog food on the counter, please," she added, before he was out of earshot.

She tubed Mocha, taped it in place, and glanced around for her clippers. JJ handed them to her.. "Thanks," said Mac. Their roles were so rehearsed in surgery, they performed them almost seamlessly. Mac loved this about working with JJ.

She shaved part of Mocha's leg while JJ hooked the dog up to the monitor.

"The basenji looks like he's gonna be real pretty," said JJ as they worked.

"Yeah, when we can get him cleaned up," agreed Mac.

"When's Dr. F going to pin his leg? Because I could bathe him right after."

"Tomorrow, I guess," Mac answered. She pierced Mocha's skin with a needle then connected her to the IV. "If he lives that long."

"Who? The basenji? Or Dr. F?"

"The doc, of course. I think he's completely forgotten what today is."

"Uh-oh."

"Exactly."

JJ snorted with laughter, then moved the box with the heat pad in it to the end of the operating table, ready for the puppies. "Well, I'm guessing he's gonna find out," she declared.

*****

Leo stared down at his cell phone buzzing across his desk like an irate bee. Sheena again. This was what, the fourth or fifth time this morning? He sighed, long and loud, and reached his hand out toward the phone. Before it got there, however, it drifted left and picked up his Seahawks surgical cap instead. *How did that happen?* he wondered. He pulled the cap down over his hair and began stuffing the stray ends in underneath it. Was that deliberate on his part? Or was it more like muscle memory, to protect himself from being unsettled before surgery, something he'd vowed would no longer be acceptable now that they were separated.

The ringing stopped and Leo snatched up his phone and put it on silent. He slid it back down on his desk where it started vibrating almost immediately with another call from Sheena. He was about to relent and answer the damn thing when Pema poked her head around the door and saved him.

"Dr. F, I have a client on the line who says she thinks the Amoxicillin she got for her cat has gone bad . . ."

"Why does she think that?" he asked, moving toward her, then around her to head back out to treatment.

Pema followed him. "She said it's black instead of pink."

Treatment was empty and Leo was headed to the sink to scrub up when his body overrode him again and took him toward the kennels. "Yes, that doesn't sound right," he told Pema, He walked into the large dog ward and made straight for the basenji, adding "It goes that way if it's not refrigerated."

The basenji woke at the sound of Leo's voice. A calm came over Leo as he crouched down and ran his hand gently down the length of the pup's body. The dog's eyes were bright, his breathing steady, and Leo flipped his lip to check the color of his gums again. "You're looking pretty good," he told the dog.

"He ate the food I gave him," said Waylon from behind Leo. The vet looked around and saw Waylon, his arms around a pile of towels and blankets.

"How much did you give him?'

"Half the tin."

Leo nodded and rose to a stand again. "Okay, well, just keep an eye on him, if you would."

"Sure thing," said Waylon. He continued down the row of kennels.

The basenji watched Leo.

"The client said she had the Amoxicillin in the refrigerator," Pema continued, having stepped into the ward behind Leo. "It was just black when she opened it today."

"Who's the client?" he asked.

"Dana Erdahl."

Leo nodded. One of their more challenging clients. The basenji whined and looked down at his broken leg. "Yeah, I'm sorry about the hot orange," said Leo. "We'll get you a better color once I patch up your leg." He glanced around at Pema. "All right. Tell her she can have another bottle if she wants to come pick it up." Leo crouched down close to the basenji again. "And you," he said, looking into the dog's warm brown eyes. "You need a name. I was thinking Lono, for the Hawaiian god of peace and prosperity. What d'you think of that?"

The stray scrabbled forward on his belly and tucked his head into Leo's hands, which were resting, folded, between his bent knees. Leo chuckled and rubbed the dog's ears with both hands. "Yeah? You like that?" He touched his nose to the end of the basenji's, then let him go. "You'll be much more pleasant to pet when you don't smell so bad." He rose and bounced back toward the door feeling rejuvenated. "Change the name on his kennel door, would you, Waylon? To Lono."

"Leo and Lono," mused Pema, stepping back to let Leo go past her. She smiled. "I like that."

Leo strode over to the sink, turned the faucet full on, then bent forward. He hadn't really thought of the dog being his, but the way Pema conjoined the names made it seem so. He let the water run over his hands and forearms; maybe she was right. "Thanks," he said.

"So should I charge Ms. Erdahl for the new prescription?" asked Pema. She walked behind Leo and propped herself against the other end of the counter where he was scrubbing up. She crossed one foot over the other.

Leo shook his head. "No. How many days left in the prescription?"

Pema opened the chart she was holding and read. "Three."

Behind Leo JJ came out of surgery and grabbed a short stack of small, clean towels off the pile by the door.

Waylon stepped out of the large animal ward, the bundle of

dirty bedding and towels now up to his chin. "Do I wash these on a warm cycle?" he asked JJ.

"Yep. And replace the towels with some from this stack."

Pema called across to JJ, like she didn't want to miss her chance. "Mr. Yu's coming for Ginger in about fifteen minutes and asked that we squeeze his anal gland."

"Waylon can do that," Leo put in, shaking his arms over the sink.

Waylon stopped mid step, tipped his head back, and opened his mouth wide in a silent grimace—*GAHHHH!* Pema scrunched her lips together like she was trying not to laugh, and JJ disappeared back into surgery, grinning behind her mask.

Oblivious to the staff's clowning, Leo turned off the faucet with his right elbow and told Pema, "Set out a one-ounce bottle of Amoxicillin for Dana Erdahl's cat. That should be enough to finish out the prescription."

"Okay, thanks. And your daughter called," she said, looking down at the note she was holding against the chart.

"Carly?"

"Uh-huh."

Leo frowned; Carly called his cell *and* the clinic? "All right. I'll call her back after the C-section."

"And the man who owns the two Chihuahuas getting spayed today," Pema went on quickly, standing upright as Leo walked away from her, his wet hands and forearms up in the air. "He wants to know if he can pick them up at noon?"

Leo cracked the door to surgery open with his right hip. "Not if they're getting spayed, he can't."

Then he stepped inside his special realm, and let the door swing closed on the outside distractions.

*****

Mac and JJ were both giggling like schoolgirls when Dr. F walked into surgery. "What?" he asked.

"Just that you detailed Waylon to squeeze Ginger's anal gland," Mac informed him.

Dr. F dried his hands on a sterile towel and walked into the gown Mac was holding open for him. "He's got to learn sometime."

"As long as I'm not standing next to him when he's still figuring it out," joked Mac.

She tied Dr. F's gown in the back, then flapped open a sterile drape, and for a few moments they worked with calculated precision, like costumers laying out fabric, to cover all but Mocha's distended abdomen. Dr. F finished by rolling his shoulders back and looking up above him. "Adjust the light, please," he said.

Mac tipped the light over the surgery table, so it illuminated the spot where he would be working. Dr. F reached around and picked up a scalpel. The room settled as he sliced through the skin down by the lower horn of the uterus. Mac mopped the blood around the incision with gauze, one eye on Mocha's breathing. JJ watched the monitor, holding a suction hose for when the puppies came out. She had put the clean towels next to Mac for the puppies to land on before they moved to the box with the heat pad in it, and placed a sterile towel against Mocha's belly to absorb the fluid from the uterus.

Dr. F repositioned his scalpel and started to cut again. The silence in the room intensified, as if all three humans were holding their breath while the vet cautiously sliced down through Mocha's subcutaneous fat, hoping not to break too many blood vessels.

The door opened a fraction. Mac looked up to see Pema's head in the opening. She was holding a mask up to her mouth.

"Dr. F?" said Pema.

"Yes?"

"The Chihuahuas' owner said he's from Canada and he's only down for the day, so he needs to pick up the puppies this morning."

"That's fine, he can do that. But that means we won't spay them today." The doc's eyes lifted to look at Mac. "This scalpel's dull."

Mac mopped away the blood around the incision again, then reached behind her for a second sterile scalpel blade. She handed it across to him.

"He wants to know why they weren't spayed yesterday, when he brought them in?" Pema asked as Dr. F reached into Mocha and gently lifted out her uterus. He laid it up against the sterile towel and quickly replaced the blade in this scalpel.

"What time did he bring them in?"

"It was after three," Mac replied.

"That's why, then," Dr. F said back to Pema. "That's not enough time to prep an animal for surgery and have us be able to monitor it *after* the surgery before we close for the day. I'm sure you told him to have the dogs at the clinic by nine." He made a neat cut down into Mocha's uterus. Fluid gushed out onto the sterile towel. He reached in and slipped out the first amniotic sac.

"I did, yes." She paused while Dr. F broke the sac, cut the umbilical cord, and gently dropped the puppy on the towels next to Mac. JJ leaned forward and suctioned the mucous out of the puppy's nose and mouth as Mac rubbed back and forth on its body to get it breathing.

"The client says he can't come back Monday to pick the puppies up."

"Then he can take them home today," explained Dr. F as he reached into the uterus for the second sac. "And make an appointment to bring them back for spaying at some other time when he can leave them overnight after the procedure."

"Okay," said Pema. "And Leslie van den Endt, whose dog had a cruciate ligament surgery, said there's a bulge on the outside of the wound area and she wants you to look at it."

"That's fine. Schedule it for about an hour from now," murmured Dr. F. He brought his left hand over to meet the slippery fetal sac before lifting it onto the sterile towel.

There was a moment of silence. Pema looked at Mac. "But . . . ?"

Mac gave a tight shake of her head: *Not now!* She didn't know what Dr. F was thinking either, when he was supposed to have been out of the clinic before it opened for business, but she knew better than to get into it when he was rupturing a fetal sac. Once the puppy came out of that protective environment, they had only a certain amount of time to get it breathing; the doc wouldn't welcome his attention being pulled elsewhere.

"Okay, thanks," said Pema and slipped her head back out of the door.

The first puppy mewed to life. "We like that sound," Dr. F said as he dropped the second pup onto the towels.

Mac handed the first puppy off to JJ, so she could put in the warm box until it could be reunited with its mother, then started rubbing the second one to life.

Suddenly there was a loud SLAM, THWACK THWACK somewhere close by.

"What was that?" questioned Dr. F, looking across the table at Mac.

Mac had a pretty good idea what it was, but she didn't want to be the one to say. Fortunately she didn't have to. Because just as Dr. F went to reach for the third sac, the door to surgery burst open and there, on the threshold, stood Carly. In her wedding dress. Holding a mask over her mouth.

"What the hell, Dad?" she yelled.

Mac saw the doc's eyes bug wide open. *Now he gets it,* she thought.

Everyone at the clinic knew that Carly was a feisty one. She was short, pert, and extremely athletic, like her dad, but *unlike* her dad, she had a mouth on her that she wasn't afraid to use. "You were supposed to be at my house over an hour ago," she yelled on, "and

I've been calling and calling your cell phone!!"

The calm had left the room as soon as Carly slammed open the door, and now her anger hung heavy in the air like smoke in a low-pressure zone. Mac looked from Carly to Dr. F. She couldn't begin to imagine what he might find to say to make this better. Carly's brown eyes pierced the room, staring directly at him, like she was daring him to try to justify his lateness. Mac imagined him apologizing, she imagined him explaining what he was up to, she even imagined him telling his daughter to close the door, but what he actually said was priceless. With his blue eyes as wide as they got, shiny with love, he said just three words. "You. Look. *Beautiful!*"

The smoke instantly dissipated, as if the doc had thrown fairy dust into the air and magicked the mad right out of his daughter. Carly's dark eyes arced up toward the ceiling and around, then came back to meet her father's, and Mac could see the crinkles around the edges of them. Carly was smiling behind her mask.

Mac's hands had been doing a steady back-and-forth on the tiny, hairless puppy while this was all going on, and she suddenly felt its chest heave. She looked down just in time to see it mew its entry into the world. She passed it over to JJ as Carly pushed the door open all the way and stepped into the room, scooping the long train of her dress in behind her. "You think?" she ventured.

"I do. I *do!*" Dr. F announced with such enthusiasm that Carly's eyes crinkled again.

Mac looked at her. She was gorgeous in her dress of satin that sparkled slightly when she moved, like snow under the moonlight. It cinched around her waist, accenting her figure, then fell in long, loose folds down to the ground. Her brown hair shone in artful curls around the nape of her neck, and she wore a crowning lei of tightly woven white pikake flowers. Mac guessed Carly's sister, Clarissa, must have brought that over fresh from Hawaii.

But as much as Dr. F's kind words quashed his daughter's anger, Mac got the impression they hadn't stopped her from wondering why he wasn't ready for her wedding. She could see the young woman turning the question over in her mind as she watched her dad slip his hand back into Mocha's uterus.

"I thought you'd at least be in your suit by now, Dad," she said, her voice gentler but still insistent. "It's going to take us an hour and a half to drive up to the lodge for the wedding. We should have been on the road by now."

Mac switched her focus back to Dr. F and wondered if, in addition to keeping the delivery going, he wasn't also trying to avoid explaining himself.

"I hope you didn't forget," Carly insisted.

Dr. F flinched, knocking his scalpel down to the floor. *"Forget?"* he argued. Mac turned around to get him another scalpel and heard him murmur, "I think this is the one that's folded."

Everyone in surgery was silent as he felt around the amniotic sac, working to disengage it from Mocha's uterus. Mac saw him close his eyes, trading sight for touch, and she knew he was breathing into his fingertips so they could relax past the slipperiness and gently encourage the sac to give. Which it did in one sudden, jellied gush that the doc dexterously scooped out onto the towel next to Mocha's belly.

"Of course I didn't forget," he went on, the breath he'd been holding tumbling out around his words.

Mac handed him the new scalpel staring at his mask to see if his nose had grown.

Carly pressed the point. "Then how come you're not dressed?"

"I have my suit ready," Dr. F assured her, slicing through the membrane and freeing the puppy. He dropped it on the towels next to Mac and whispered, "D'you think I can send Waylon to my house to fetch it?"

"You *did* forget!" Carly accused.

"Okay, okay, so maybe I forgot a little," Dr. F admitted, clamping the umbilical cord. "But I got called out for a blocked urethra very early this morning . . ."

"That's why Heather Coy's pacing reception, looking like she's high on speed?" asked Carly.

"Yep," Mac confirmed.

Dr. F went on with his explanation as he snipped the cord. "And then the Rengens' dog needed this C-section—"

"That's *Noah's* dog?" interrupted Carly her tone so completely different, so hushed and respectful, that everyone looked across at her.

That's when Mac saw something that was worth the early wake up call and all the emotional shifts the morning had brought so far. She saw Carly glide toward her dad, transfixed, her eyes wide, fascinated as they took in the newborn pup. And she saw Dr. F watching his daughter equally transfixed because he was seeing her experience that special moment: the moment when her heart sparked against her vocation, like a match on the side of a box, to light the flame that would guide the rest of her life.

JJ held out a pair of latex gloves. Carly clipped her mask over her ears, took the gloves, pulled them on, and spread her hands out to her dad like an offering. He looked into her eyes, and Mac glimpsed the father-daughter tenderness between them; then he dropped the pup into Carly's hands and went back to work.

Carly cradled the puppy against her stomach as JJ suctioned, rubbing it gently to nudge it into life. Peace descended on the surgery again, and Mac felt her shoulders relax in relief. Then her eyes widened as she saw the dark-red stain spreading over Carly's midriff. Dr. F dropped the fourth puppy onto the towels and must have caught the look in Mac's eyes because he spun around to see what she was seeing.

"Oh honey," he exclaimed. "Your dress!"

But Carly was obviously lost in the bliss of helping animals for she just sighed, massaging the puppy's lungs between her fingers and her belly, and murmured, "That's okay."

"But what will you wear to your wedding?"

"Is there a spare pair of scrubs around?" she asked, looking at both Mac and JJ.

"I think so," said Mac.

"Yes," seconded JJ.

The puppy sprang to life under Carly's steady ministrations, and Mac saw her look down and shiver with glee at having helped. "Then that's what I'll wear," she declared, handing the pup off to JJ. She wheeled around to face her dad, both eyes gleaming. "May as well let my honey know before the fact that he's getting himself hitched to a vet!"

Part Two

Spike

The good news was the weather had cleared up. After what seemed like endless dreary days, the sun had finally come out and led him back to the river. No, that wasn't right. It was the *tulips* that had led him back to the river. He'd seen their dark yellow blossoms against the light blue of the sky when he was trudging along a road just east of the fields. It was such a rush to catch that glimpse of bright after seeing nothing but gray for so long that he couldn't help himself; he had to go check it out. That was a lucky break, because as soon as he got to the tulips, he found the river close by, and suddenly he was back on track.

The bad news was that there was way more private property along the river than he'd thought there would be, and he was leery of crossing it in case someone came after him. People could be very territorial. So he kept taking the long route around. Which set him back even more from getting to the man with the hands, and now he was running out of options for places to stay. He hadn't brought anything with him, not thinking he'd be gone this long, and the last place had given him a definite no. He'd find somewhere else, he was sure: a place where maybe he could convince them to let him help out in exchange for a bed for the night. He was a great helper when given the chance. It was the convincing that was difficult. He had a hard time connecting with some people.

Which was likely to become a greater problem in the short term because his spirit was flagging. He hadn't had a decent meal in a while, and he was pretty sure he smelled bad. Not the best combination when trying to convince a stranger to give him a chance.

But he had to try. All he needed was one more lucky break, and he'd be there.

Chapter 5

Leo flew across the last quarter mile of the trail on Dreamer, his heart pumping as he held on with his knees, head low to avoid hitting the branches on either side of them. The hooves of his American paint horse pounded across the duff, her body leaning left and right with the narrow trail, and he could feel her joy. This was what she needed, what they both needed. She stretched out the last few hundred feet, seeing the openness of his sprawling pasture ahead of them, and he sat up when they got to it, pulling back on the reins to slow her to a canter. Leo was breathing hard, his lungs full of the fresh oxygen of the forest that surrounded his aerie high up on the hill overlooking the Skagit Valley. Not that his ten acres were really a nest; more like a high mountain farm where the only things growing were the animals.

He slowed Dreamer even further, and she purred into the air, shaking her head with the pleasure of it all. He leaned forward and patted the side of her neck. "Thanks, baby," he whispered and she purred again. Yesterday had been a hard day for him. It wasn't always easy juggling being a boss with answering to the client, and it frustrated him when the staff made it clear they thought he'd dropped the ball. But taking care of the client was what had *made* his business in the first place, and what kept making it all these years on.

Of course his staff couldn't have known that yesterday was the wrong day to give him a hard time about anything. Not after the prickly phone conversation he'd had with his lawyer, John Elbert, about the divorce.

"You're going to have to give up one of them," John had informed him with an appropriate amount of regret in his voice. "Either your house or your business. So my advice is you decide which one before someone—the mediator or the judge—does it for you." He'd paused, presumably to let Leo digest this, then added, "If you come at this from a conciliatory angle, you're liable to emerge with fewer parts missing."

Leo wasn't sure he wanted to be conciliatory. Heck, he wasn't sure he wanted the divorce. But he wasn't getting any choice in that, so then why did he have to choose what part of his life to give up?

He mopped sweat from his forehead on the arm of his T-shirt, then tipped his head back and let his face cool in the fine, soft early-fall rain. And that wasn't even the worst of yesterday, he thought. The worst was when he'd had to put down Sweetness. He'd cared for that little white cat for over a decade, and in more ways than just being her vet. She was such a gentle creature, and Leo had always wondered if she'd lived up to her name or if she'd been named for that sweetness she epitomized. Her owners were kind people, but Sweetness was an outdoor cat and it was apparent they'd stopped paying attention to her health. They'd brought her in regularly for her shots over the years, but when Leo touched her yesterday, clumps of fur fell off in his fingers. And she was emaciated. Kidney disease, he told them. Sweetness looked up at him, her eyes clouded with ill health, her breathing labored, and he could feel her saying, "Please, stop the pain. Please." So he did.

He dropped his face again and tugged gently on the reins,

wanting to think about something other than the way Sweetness, like so many cats, had purred as the dose of Fatal-Plus flowed through the bloodstream to take her into her final sleep. He walked Dreamer to the high point of his pasture, where he could look down over the river. Feathery clouds partially obscured his view of the Skagit, but he could still see stretches of that enticing teal green, like antique jade, that marked the water at this time of year. Glacial flour, that was what caused that color: from the river rubbing up against the mountains and eroding tiny rock particles, then carrying them, suspended in its water, down to the Puget Sound. Not only was the color entrancing, but Leo liked the notion that one day, not in his lifetime, but one day, these mountains would be where the Puget Sound was now. Nature's moving tapestry.

A dull ache replaced the burn in his chest at the thought that this view would soon no longer be his. That's what he was going to tell John today when he saw him; that he'd give up his home. He couldn't give up his clinic, not with all the people dependent on him for a living. Not to mention the clients, and their pets. His eyes skimmed across the clouds like a skipping rock over water until they took him to a place high up in the Cascades where it was just him and his horse in a vast, untainted wilderness. Sometimes he wished he could just ride to that place, leave all the trappings of civilization behind him. Not that he really felt he'd fallen into traps, he thought as he pulled Dreamer around and walked her back across the pasture toward the house. She stopped midway to chew on some grass, and Leo gazed at the A-frame log house that he'd called home for twenty-some years. It was modest in size, open plan throughout the downstairs, with spacious windows in the kitchen and dining area looking out to the meadow on the backside of his property. He thought back to lying out on the upper deck with Sheena, bewitched by the shooting stars in the night sky; to bringing his baby daughters home from the hospital and the dogs crowding the front door to meet them; to laughing with Sheena as they watched the girls slide across the wood floor in their socks, pretending to ice skate. The ache in his chest spread. How they'd got from there to competing over whose job was most important he didn't know.

His gaze dropped and he saw Harley watching him from the long covered front porch amid an array of colorful gourds from the garden. The old dog's hips didn't allow him to join them on the morning ride anymore and the cataracts in his eyes surely stopped him from being able to see Leo clearly right now, and yet the vet knew he was being looked at with so much love. How could he move Harley from the only place he'd ever known as home?

Before his thoughts could continue to spiral down, he heard a sound behind him and looked around just in time to see Lono and Venus barreling out of the end of the trail. *Right on cue*, he thought.

"What took you so long?" he called out and Lono dodged in front of Venus then circled her nimbly, as if to imply she was too slow.

"Yeah, right," Leo laughed, "blame it on her."

He marveled at the newest member of his family, not just because the pup was intelligent and incredibly agile, but because he always seemed to know when Leo needed him. As if he were somehow tuned into Leo's internal monologue. Although nothing surprised Leo when it came to dogs' perception. If he had his way there would be a dog in every classroom, that's how sure he was of their ability to intuit what people needed most.

He watched Venus struggling to keep pace with Lono and applauded her mentally. She was pushing hard, the flesh on her torso rolling awkwardly on her too-short legs, and Leo could picture the strands of calcium in her bones stretching like taffy as a result of the workout.

He switched his focus to Lono. Unlike Venus, who kept her muzzle down, intent, concentrated, Lono always ran with his head up, his legs prancing easily like a show horse's. Leo narrowed his eyes and watched the pup's left rear leg bend, stretch, and land without hesitation, a sure sign that his femur had gone back to doing what it was supposed to do.

The break had been clean through, a definite advantage for surgery, but it had taken a good forty-five minutes to pin the two parts back together. "I'm going to need to wire it," Leo had said to Mac once he'd exposed both ends of the break. He could hold the two parts of the femur end to end with a pin, but he couldn't stop torsion if he didn't wire the break closed.

Mac slid open the drawer behind her. "What size drill bit?" she asked.

"Two millimeter, please."

Her hand shifted through the blue sterile bags. She pulled one out, tore open the seal, and dropped the sterile drill bit on the mobile surgical tray. "How was the wedding?" she asked.

Leo tightened the bit in the casement of the drill. "Exactly how I expected it to be with Carly as the bride." He leaned down and drilled at an angle into one end of the break, like pushing a needle through fabric. When it popped through to the other side, he took his finger off the trigger and looked at Mac. "Emotional, beautiful, well attended. And then the reception was a raucous blast. I haven't danced so much in a long time." He cleaned the tiny curls of bone matter off the drill bit with his gloved fingers. He flipped the drill around so it was facing toward him, shifting his weight to be parallel to it, and drilled through the other end of the break.

"Did she get married in those scrubs we found her?"

"No," said Leo, having forgotten about the scrubs. "She wore her mother's wedding dress." He set the drill down and sifted through the instruments on the tray for a length of surgical wire. "Sheena had someone bring it to the lodge as soon as she found out what had happened to Carly's dress. She didn't even get upset about it," he went on, having found what he wanted and started to push the wire through the lower hole. "She was just gracious and practical and very thoughtful . . ." He looped the outer end of the wire to secure it. "And her dress fit Carly perfectly. Made me feel," —he punched the center of his chest with his fist— "you know, like it hurt."

"I bet."

Leo pushed the pin up through the top end of the femur then spent some minutes gently stretching the muscles that had tightened around the femur when it broke so he could slip the pin down into the lower end. It was like trying to stretch a lid that was too small over the mouth of a bottle without breaking either of them but eventually the muscles gave, enabling Leo to push the pin down into the bottom section of the femur and connect the parts of the bone.

Now for the exacting work, he thought. For the bone to heal properly, the two parts had to go back together exactly as they were before they broke apart. Leo crouched, to be at eye level with the broken parts. He twisted them first one way, then another, trying to find where they slotted back together. It was like a two-piece jigsaw puzzle with hundreds of possible solutions but only one that was right.

Mac crouched also, to guide him from the other side of the table.

"Does that look right?" he asked.

"No. I have a tiny shard this side that doesn't have an opening."

"Okay."

Leo rotated the bone ends a few millimeters more.

"Maybe keep one still," said Mac, lifting her left hand as if to stop his right without touching him.

"Okay," he agreed. "But only because you gave up your Sunday morning to come help me."

"Yeah, don't think you're getting off that cheap. Next month I might be after you to give me an extra day or two off to take Chad to Disneyland for our 10th anniversary."

"I'll have forgotten by then," said Leo, sparring with her.

"But I won't."

Leo smiled. Mac was an excellent sparring partner. "Did I get it now?" he asked, looking back down at the femur.

"Ummmm—" She was peering hard at the connection on her side, tilting her head to see it from a different angle. "No," she said.

Leo examined his side. He thought it looked right. Then he saw where a jagged point didn't have a matching groove. He slowly rotated the upper end this time. "No, I was thinking I'd pay you back for your help this morning by recommending to my niece that she go see your Ophelia."

"Well good luck with that," said Mac. "'Cause I'm playing Gertrude."

"Hamlet's mom?"

"Yep. Hold on a sec," she said, putting her hand out again for him to stop.

"It's not right this side," he informed her.

"Oh. Carry on then."

Leo blinked, feeling some sweat trickle down onto his eyelash. Mac must have noticed because she lifted herself a little higher, reached across the table and mopped his brow.

"No, I told you," she said returning to their banter. "I'm too old to play the ingénues now."

"You're a lot younger than me."

"That's not saying much."

"Watch it."

Mac chuckled. "Honestly though, I don't mind being older. I get to play roles with 'some relish of the saltiness of time.'"

"Talking of roles," said Leo, keeping his hands still while he lifted his head to recalibrate. "How did the relief vet work out yesterday?"

"Dr. Murphy? She never showed up—"

"What?"

"—but she sent a substitute. A friend of hers who just graduated vet school—Dr. Weastenhaver. Ella. And she was great. Whipped out the two feline spays and the cherry eye like she did them every day. And was very easy to work with. She wanted to tidy up an ear crop, too, but the client specifically requested you do it."

Leo examined the bone ends. He still couldn't make them mesh. "Did it fail?"

"What? The ear crop?"

"Uh-huh."

"Kind of. Mostly because the client didn't want to drive back here from Oregon to get the dressing changed, so he did it himself. Plus he took the stitches out by himself. He assured me he splinted the ears after he took the stitches out, but one of the ears flops. At the top."

"So what's he want me to do?"

"Maybe cut a little more off both ears."

Leo didn't say anything. He wasn't a fan of doing ear crops in the first place, but he knew that clients would just crop the dog's ears themselves if they couldn't get professional help, and that could be very dangerous for the animal. And now if the dog's ears didn't look the way the client wanted them, the client would find another way to try to correct them. He didn't want that happening either. "I'll have to look at the ears," he said. He worked in silence for a few moments, willing the pieces of bone to find their way back together. When he could see it wasn't working, he inhaled deeply and tried to relax. "Can we get this Dr. Ella again?" he mumbled.

Mac shook her head no. "That's the thing. She's got a job over in Spokane that she starts next week. *And* Dr. Murphy asked that we not give up on her. Said something just came up that she couldn't get out of but it wouldn't happen again."

"Hmmm." Leo wasn't sure about that. He felt the bone ends suddenly connect the way he thought they should connect and dropped whatever it was they'd been talking about. "I've got it, right?"

Mac checked his handiwork. "Yes," she answered.

And just like that it was done. He'd wired the bone, and now, twelve weeks on, anyone looking at Lono would never guess he had a six-inch piece of metal in his leg. Or that he'd been a near-death, bedraggled little stray at that time, too.

The dogs raced the last few feet toward him and finished with Lono running a lap around Dreamer while Venus plopped down on the grass under the big horse's nose, panting. The American paint horse snorted a gentle greeting, and Venus rolled onto her back, her feet up in the air.

Leo shivered, the sweat beginning to cool under his cotton T-shirt. He clicked in the side of his mouth; Dreamer moved forward, and Venus jumped up and ran for the porch to join Harley. Lono stayed firmly at Leo's side as he walked Dreamer back to the big, beautiful barn he'd had built to give Sheena a place to make the sauces and pickles, chutneys and jams she sold commercially. The gambrel-roofed barn had a wide central bay for vehicles and farm equipment, with horse stalls to one side and the commercial kitchen on the other. Leo felt his jaw tighten in acrimony; maybe the kitchen would actually get used if Sheena ended up with the property.

He followed Lono around the side of the barn toward Dreamer's stall and let his mind flip to what he might do with the one precious hour he had remaining before he had to head down to his appointment. He'd brush Dreamer, shower, and get some coffee, then maybe he'd walk Harley around the garden. Maybe even pull a couple of the tomato plants now that their season was at an end. If it didn't rain too much, of course, he told himself. He glanced up and saw the dense, dark clouds coming his way and almost laughed. Who was he kidding?

He walked Dreamer in under the sheet-metal roof and heard his cell phone ringing in the pocket of his jean jacket hanging on the outside of her stall. It was the clinic. Did he want to talk to work in the sliver of time he had left to himself this morning? As he climbed down off Dreamer he wondered if he wanted to talk to them *at all* today, given how unappreciated they'd made him feel yesterday?

Lono appeared in front of him and gently dropped a ball at his feet. "I take it that's a no," he said to the pup. And a red tail with a white tip swished through the air in glee.

*****

Mac looked at the clock again. Waylon was standing by the fridge, JJ over by the wet sink, all of them wondering what to do. It was almost nine a.m. already; Dr. Murphy was an hour late. The first two appointments of the morning were out in reception, and three pets had been dropped off for surgeries. One of them was already making a terrible racket. It sounded like the wail of an emergency vehicle overlaid with the desperate howling of an animal in distress. It was making Mac want to run and hide. "What is *that*?" she asked.

"That's the beagle," Waylon responded. "I put her in the Lost Boys ward because her owner warned me she was loud."

"He was right about that," said Mac rubbing her temple with her fingertips. This did not bode well for the day. "Close the door to the large animal ward, would you?" she asked Waylon. "That might keep some of her noise out."

"Sure thing," he replied and moved to do as requested.

Mac stared at the board again.

"I can get the vaccines ready for the shepherd," JJ offered.

"What's he here for?"

"DA2PP and *Bordetella*."

"Okay, sure."

"And do you want me to shave the IV site on the beagle?" asked Waylon.

"If that'll get her to shut up for two seconds then I'm in favor of it," said Mac, even though she wasn't convinced this was a good use of Waylon's time. Fortunately closing the door had muffled the beagle's complaining. "What else do we have for appointments?"

she asked, marching over to the computer in the corner to the right of the double door. She touched the mouse to bring up the appointments' schedule. "We've got three health certificates," she said, pointing at the screen. She looked over her shoulder at Waylon. "You could start the paperwork for those."

"Okay," he said. He was holding some charts against his belly. "None of those are here yet, right?"

"No, but two are due in fifteen minutes."

"We're going to have some angry clients if we don't start clearing reception," warned JJ, as if Mac didn't already know that.

She pushed up off the desk. "I'll try Dr. F again."

Before she could pick up the phone, Pema put her head in through the door and announced, "She just called. She said she's maybe ten minutes out." Then she winced and her tone became embarrassed. "And Dana Erdahl's in with her dog, Snickers."

"I thought we weren't seeing Dana Erdahl anymore," complained JJ.

Mac threw her hands up; she didn't know what the heck was going on. "Dr. F told me he was going to send her a letter . . ."

Pema squirmed. "She said Snickers needs a C-section."

"Oh great!" complained Mac. "And us without a vet."

"I'm here," said a female voice coming in the side door, by the autoclave. "I was closer than I thought. Sorry, my GPS sent me down the wrong highway." A forty-something, petite brunette in blue scrubs blew into treatment, an aging shorthaired pointer at her side, and the abnormally quiet room burst into life. Her shoulder-length hair was dark, almost black, with silvery tendrils here and there, accenting the inky blue of her eyes perfectly. But it was the way she carried herself that was compelling. Mac stared, openmouthed. Here was her Cleopatra. She was about to play that role at the community theatre and had been looking for someone to model herself after as the Egyptian queen. Someone who wasn't exactly beautiful but who knew she had allure and could project it to draw people toward her. Like a siren. She glanced at Waylon; he was staring, too.

"I was heading to Bothell instead of this way," explained Dr. Murphy, dumping her tote bag on the floor under the surgery board. "Is it okay if I leave this here?" she asked as an afterthought.

"Sure," said Mac, "although JJ could take it into the office if you like."

"Where's that?" asked Dr. Murphy.

"Through here," answered the vet tech, pointing at the hallway to her right.

"That's okay," the relief vet said with a dismissive flap of her hand. "It's fine where it is for right now. I'm Kelly Murphy," she said, holding both hands up in the air like she was guilty. "And this is my dog, Kent. It's okay if he's here, right?"

They all turned to look at the shorthaired pointer, who was sniffing a small sofa dog bed under the viewing station. As soon as their eyes were on him, the dog drew back his head and sneezed profusely, a big gob of snot shooting out of his nose onto the side of the dog bed. JJ snatched up a paper towel and bustled over to clean it up.

"Sorry about that," said Dr. Murphy, cringing slightly. "He's got some kind of sinus thing going on, and I've been resisting putting him on Prednisone."

The shorthaired pointer sneezed twice more, both times shedding white gunk, before he climbed into the dog bed and turned circles, sniffing with his newly cleansed nostrils.

Waylon's eyes widened.

"What?" asked Dr. Murphy, her wavy, dark hair bouncing as her head spun side to side, looking at all their faces. "Does that bed belong to someone important?"

"Dr. Friel's dog, Lono," Mac informed her.

"Oh, he won't mind Kent sharing for the day," said Dr. Murphy with yet another dismissive flap of her hand. "Where is Dr. Friel anyway?" she asked, noticing the surgery board and backing up to read it.

"Well it's his day off," Mac explained, "but he also has an appointment with his divorce lawyer."

"Oh, that's right. Now I remember. He said something about that in the message he left." She lifted a pair of cheater glasses that she had hanging on a string of plastic beads around her neck and held them in front of her eyes to read the board. "I don't envy him," she muttered. "That's how I lost my practice. Divorce. My ex didn't want it—and trust me," she said, dropping the glasses and turning to face them all again, one hand out to suggest she wanted to be clear on this, "he wouldn't have got it if he had wanted it—but while I was busy defending my share of the assets from our thirteen-year union, my veterinary partner made off with my client list. And left me some real doozy bills." She smiled tightly. "So I had to declare bankruptcy." She slapped her hands together, then pointed back at the board. "Moving right on," she said, "am I the only vet doing these procedures today? Or is Carly here, too?"

Mac liked that she'd done her homework and knew Carly was part of the team now. "Carly's still only part time," she explained, "so she can help her husband set up his climbing gym." She spread her arms at her sides with a flourish. "So it's just you and us for the day."

"Okay," said Dr. Murphy. She took the charts out of Waylon's hands like it was something she did all the time. He did not resist. She flipped the top one open and lifted her glasses to read.

Mac smiled. This woman was going to fit in just fine.

Dr. Murphy dropped her glasses and motioned for Waylon to precede her. "Take me to the anal gland that needs squeezing."

*****

The rain was pelting against the big windows in the conference room at the law office, long gray strands of misery hitting rhythmically against the wide panes. Leo was standing close enough to touch the glass, although he had his hands in the pockets of his cream-colored chinos, but the sound in the otherwise silent room was lulling him into a kind of blurry-eyed staring as his mind drifted this way and that.

He thought first of Lono sitting out on the front seat of his Jeep, probably curled up in a tight ball on the sweatshirt Leo had dropped there. He wanted to leave the little stray at home with Venus, in the spacious kennel he'd built in the barn alongside the horse stalls, but he could never get the little minx to stay there.

He'd walked him out to the kennel with Venus the morning after he'd taken him home for the first time and turned his back for one moment, to put food in their bowls, only to turn back around and find Lono gone! Then he'd spent an anxious forty minutes calling, waiting, and looking for the basenji in between brushing and feeding Dreamer, settling Venus, running back into the house to check on Harley and grabbing his gear for work. He finally gave up, deciding the pup would have to fend for himself. He'd been a stray when he'd come into Leo's life; maybe he'd go back to being a stray now that he wasn't confined to the clinic. Seconds later Leo opened the door to his Jeep and found Lono sitting on the passenger side, waiting for him.

He'd scratched his head, looking around his feet at the concrete floor in the central bay of the barn, wondering how the dog had managed to hop up through the open window into the vehicle when he was still groggy from surgery and had a cumbersome pale-blue cast on his left rear leg. He hadn't been able to figure it out. But rather than waste more time getting him back in the kennel, Leo had acquiesced to the dog's wish to go with him to work. And he'd been acquiescing ever since.

His eyes shifted from the dark, rain-shadowed street below the law office out to the bright lights of the sprawling buy-everything-in-one-place store that had been recently built on the agricultural flats, close to the Skagit River. Leo could still remember when this window had an almost uninterrupted view of Mount Baker, way off in the distance. Now he suspected the flat-topped mountain could still be seen when it wasn't socked in by rain clouds, but only as an afterthought to all the development in the foreground.

His mind moved back to his garden and all that he might have gotten done today if he hadn't had to come down to see his lawyer. And if it hadn't been raining, of course. For sure he would have started the process of putting the garden to sleep for the winter before the first frosts forced his hand.

He heard a quiet footfall behind him and turned to see John coming into the room holding two yellow legal pads and two pens. John Elbert was young, younger than Leo by about ten or fifteen years, and physically unremarkable. Not a power presence or a head turner; just an ordinary, amiable guy with thinning blondish hair and a lean countenance. But Leo knew that John's ability to fade into the background physically belied his inordinate tenacity. He was like a miniature pinscher with big, soft round eyes that wouldn't let go once he had his teeth in something. Or someone.

He tried to read the lawyer's face for signs of the news he was about to share, but John looked relaxed as he dropped the legal pads onto the conference table and placed a pen beside each one. Leo felt his spirits lift; maybe this wouldn't be as bad as he feared.

John pulled out one of the rolling office chairs from under the table and moved in front of it. "Maybe you should sit to hear this," he said.

And Leo's spirits fell, like the rainwater, into a puddle of gloom at his feet.

*****

It was when Mac went out to check on something for one of the clients needing a health certificate that Dana Erdahl accosted her. "Are you going to do this C-section on Snickers or not?" she snapped across reception, not bothering to get up and walk toward Mac to make the conversation at least semiprivate.

Mac didn't take the bait. She held her index finger up to Dana and said, "Just one second," then turned, with a smile, to the slender, dark-haired lady holding two border collies on leashes. "Ms. Hedlund?"

The woman smiled back. "Yes."

"You're taking Keevah to Ireland, is that right?"

"Yes. They're holding the sheepdog trials there this year, unusually, and my husband is one of the judges. So he wants to take Keevah with him and have him compete."

"Okay, well, I've got a call in to the state vet to see if they know of anything special that Ireland requires on the health certificate, so that might take a few minutes more."

"That's fine. I don't mind waiting."

Dana Erdahl harrumphed loudly.

"But you also need a health certificate for Jazzy to go to Colorado?" asked Mac, looking down at the USDA form in her hand.

"Yes. She's going to Colorado with me while my husband goes to Ireland with Keevah." Ms. Hedlund laughed. "I don't know who's getting the better deal, to be honest, although I'd love to go to Ireland, of course."

"Yeah, me, too," agreed Mac, edging over toward Dana. "If you don't mind, I'm just going to check on this dog, and then you can follow me back to exam 3 . . ."

"No, that's fine."

"I hope Dr. Friel's going to get to Snickers soon," Dana said as soon as Mac knelt in front of Snickers. "Because I don't know how much longer she can wait."

"How long has she been pushing?" the vet tech asked, noticing immediately how emaciated Snickers looked. She didn't like the sound of her breathing, so she put on the stethoscope she'd carried out and listened to her chest.

"Since this morning," said Dana, although she sounded like she was talking through a closed car window as Mac listened to the crackle in Snickers's breathing. She wished she were in a car, with Dana on the outside. A car that she could speed away in, because she was dreading telling Dana that Dr. F wasn't in today. She'd called him twice to see if he could come in to do the C-section on Snickers and hadn't been able to reach him, so now Waylon was calling Carly to see if she could come in and do it. Because if she couldn't, Mac wasn't sure they could get through everything they had on the board today.

She pulled off the stethoscope and wrapped it around her neck, leaning back to rest her butt on her feet. "I'm pretty sure the doctor's going to want an X-ray to see if there's a puppy in the birth canal, but let me check."

"Another X-ray? That just sounds like a delaying tactic to me!" Dana snapped.

"I'm sorry that you're having to wait. We're really busy today," said Mac, rising to her feet again.

"I know she needs a C-section," Dana went on, ignoring Mac's apology. "You forget I was a vet tech for twenty years."

"'Of thee, thy record never can be missed,'" Mac disputed, sotto voce, as she started across reception, motioning for Ms. Hedlund to follow her.

"What was that?"

Mac turned back to face Dana, a smile fixed on her face. "I said Dr. Murphy will be right out to talk to you."

"Dr. Murphy? Who's Dr. Murphy?" Dana called out after her as Mac disappeared into exam 3. "And where is Dr. Friel?"

*****

Leo was staring at John, wondering if the lawyer had made a mistake. "Why would she want the clinic?" he asked, stunned. "I won't be able to make a living if she takes the clinic. That doesn't make sense. Won't I have to pay her some kind of maintenance?"

"We're getting to that," said John, pulling his chair in closer to the conference table. "She doesn't *just* want the clinic," he went on in a tone that suggested he had a much bigger bomb to drop.

Leo rolled his chair back from the table and propped his right foot on his left knee, trying to relax. "What else does she want?' he said and heard the edge in his voice slice through the hushed room.

"She wants you to run it for the next five years while she gets her degree in veterinary medicine—"

"What?!" spluttered Leo, shooting forward in his seat again.

"—and she'll forgo any maintenance from you the court would award her in the divorce in exchange for half the revenue you generate—"

"*Half* my revenue?"

"—and leave you the other half while you're still working and the house on the hill when you give over the clinic to her entirely."

Leo felt like his head was going to explode. Sheena? A veterinarian? While he lived, what, *where*? "So wait, who gets to live in the house for the next five years?"

"She does."

"So she gets the house *and* the business?!"

John held one hand up in the air. "She doesn't want the house. She just wants to keep it as collateral, in case you run the clinic into the ground."

"How does she think I'm going to *stop* that from happening if she gets half my revenue?" argued Leo. He clenched and unclenched his jaw in anger. What John had just told him stood before him like a battalion of armed fighters on a ridge, and his mind was rolling out ideas for a counterattack. "I'd have no reason to keep the business solvent," he said, a bitter taste in his mouth from just saying the words. "Not if she's going to turn me into her veterinary bitch. No business, no payments to her!" he decreed, slicing his right hand through the air definitively. "Simple as that."

"Except it's not," countered John. He tapped his pen repetitively on the yellow legal pad in front of him, like it was a nervous habit. "She wants a minimum of $5,000 a month, and if she doesn't get it from the clinic's revenue, you'll just have to pay it some other way."

Leo's mouth dropped open. His whole life was being held ransom. "I can't make my payroll and give her half my revenue. I just can't."

John sighed. "I understand. And I told her lawyer that when I called her yesterday."

"But?"

"There was some suggestion that you either work harder or raise your rates."

Leo shoved his chair back, levitating to a stand. He strode away from John, needing someplace devoid of a human being to put this welter of emotion he was experiencing. He stopped at the end of the conference table, wishing he could explode out of the windows and disappear. He felt his phone vibrate in the top pocket of his dress shirt and pulled it out reflexively. It was the clinic again. "Look," he said, turning back to face John, "I need to call the clinic and I need to let my dog out of the car."

John lifted the edge of the court documents from Sheena's lawyer with his thumb and forefinger like they were fragile. Or maybe contaminated. "Unfortunately we're just starting here. We need to put our heads together and draft a reasonable counterproposal."

That's what Leo had been afraid of, and he was in no shape to be reasonable right now. "I'm going to take a break to do what I need to do, and then we can take whatever time it takes . . ."

"O-kay," conceded John, sitting back in his chair and twirling his pen with the fingers of both hands. "Except I blocked out the rest of the morning for you, and I have to be in court this afternoon." He canted his head, studying Leo, and the vet got the impression that he was picturing how he could both let him break out and save face at the same time. John sat forward again and let go of his pen. "Why don't you take a break with your dog," he said, gathering up the papers and tapping them into a tidy pile on the tabletop. "And I'll hunt us up some lunch. Do you think you can be back here by one?"

"Yes," said Leo, more loudly than he'd intended. Then he bolted for the door.

*****

"Can I have you come look at this Labradoodle in reception?" Mac asked Dr. Murphy, holding up the chart that belonged to Snickers. "She's in labor, and her owner thinks she needs a C-section."

JJ was clipping the toenails on a wailing vizsla, whose owner was standing by, looking embarrassed, and Waylon was talking on the phone over by the surgery board, blocking the sound of the wailing out with one hand over his free ear. He hung up and punched the air, victorious.

"Carly's on her way in," he shouted across to Mac.

"Great. We need her," said Dr. Murphy. "Especially if we have to squeeze in a C-section before you close. Which is at two today, right?"

Mac nodded. "Yes. Thursdays we close at two." At least she hoped they'd get to close by two because she wanted the extra time to prepare for dress rehearsal of *Antony and Cleopatra*. Especially now that she knew how she wanted to look

"Good. I promised my twins I'd go to their soccer practice this afternoon," said Dr. Murphy, "because they have their first game on Saturday." She rolled her dark blue eyes up as if considering what she'd just said. "Is Saturday the thirtieth?"

"September 30th, yes," Mac confirmed.

"Okay good. So I *have* to make their practice to give them some pointers today."

"Do you play soccer?" Waylon asked, smiling across at Dr. Murphy.

"Used to," she replied. "In fact, it helped pay for my undergrad degree. Until I hurt my shoulder slamming into another player when I was doing a header into the goal." She rubbed her left shoulder with her right hand as she said it.

"Did you get the goal," he asked.

"I did. And a shoulder injury that hasn't been right since. So now I just help my girls play," she said, gracing Waylon with a wide, warm smile.

Mac pushed open the door to treatment, and held it open for Dr. Murphy.

The relief vet sailed through then stopped in the hallway, before they rounded the corner to reception. "Why does this owner think a C-section is required?" she asked.

"Because the labor's not progressing," Mac answered. She dropped her voice and added, "But the owner's bred her every time she's come into heat these last two years."

Dr. Murphy hmmed under her breath. "Maybe her uterus is too tired to do this anymore," she muttered. "Can you prep the beagle with the mammary gland tumor after you show me this woman in reception?"

"Oh I'd be glad to," admitted Mac. "A little gas is just what that beagle needs."

"Is that the one that sounds like a fire siren?"

"Yep," said Mac as they went around the corner. "Makes me wish the Lost Boys was sound proofed." Ahead of them she glimpsed Pema opening the front door to one of their clients: an older English woman called Vera, whose accent Mac liked imitating when she needed to sound British on stage. Vera was struggling to collapse her umbrella under shelter of the roof while trying to maintain her hold on two big, bulky pit bulls. Mac glanced around reception. Harry Rea was here with his Shih Tzu, it looked like the demon cat, Earl Grey, was in a cat carrier on the floor although Mac couldn't see his owner anywhere, and then there was a young woman with a cocker spaniel that she didn't recognize and Ms. Hedlund with her two border collies. Plus Snickers. *This should be interesting,* she thought to herself.

"Thank you very much," Vera said to Pema, her voice rich and frothy like a cup of hot chocolate. The dogs bulldozed in ahead of her, panting and choking against their collars, the claws tapping loudly against the tile floor. They both shook in the middle of the room, spraying rainwater in every direction. The Shih Tzu yipped his assertion of alpha status from his seat on his owner's lap and the cocker spaniel barked repetitively. The pit bulls jumped around to face both dogs, their shortened tails wiggling, and rumbled their authority from deep in their chests.

"Can I take Snickers into a room?" Dana wailed as Pema hustled past her to get back behind the counter and sign in the new arrivals. "I don't want her to get caught in the middle of a fight."

"My dogs aren't aggressive with other dogs," Vera reassured Dana, although her tone suggested she was clearly offended by the idea.

"I don't think we have any exam rooms available right now," Pema told Dana.

"Actually you can bring her into exam 1," Dr. Murphy called out from the mouth of the hallway, circling her right arm in the air to encourage Dana to come forward. "I'm sorry I had to make you wait," she rushed on. "We're a little behind with appointments, as you might have seen, and with Dr. Friel out today, I'm running to catch up. I'm Dr. Murphy, by the way, and Carly's on her way in. She's familiar with your dog, I know." Her face softened and her manner became solicitous as Dana made her way toward her, her very pregnant bitch still struggling to get herself up on all four paws. "Will Snickers be okay to walk as far as exam 1?" she asked.

"Oh yes, she's fine," said Dana as Snickers lumbered after her.

Mac was impressed with Dr. Murphy's pampering ability. Not only did she have sex appeal, but she had a great way with the clients. Dr. F would be impressed. And maybe a little smitten, too. Mac sighed to herself; maybe that was one headache they didn't need at the clinic.

Dana gave Pema a snarky smirk on her way by, and Mac watched Pema's face flush red with embarrassment.

"We took the vizsla in exam 1 back to treatment," Mac told her once Dana and Dr. Murphy had gone into the room. "That's the only reason it's empty now."

"Although she needn't have worried," Vera added. "My dogs never fight with other dogs. They're little bastards with each other," she admitted, making a funny face, "but never with other dogs."

Mac remembered the antagonism between the pit bulls from their previous visit to the clinic. She chuckled as she walked back to treatment; at more than one hundred pounds apiece, she thought, the last thing she'd call these pit bull brothers was little.

*****

Leo stopped, realizing he'd walked a lot farther along the trail by the river than he'd intended. If he wasn't careful, he'd end up at his own clinic—while it still *was* his own clinic, he huffed to himself—and on his day off, no less! Mind you, he thought, peering through the rain in the direction of the clinic, that might save him from going back to the lawyer's office and trying to find a reasonable solution to an unreasonable situation. He felt his jaw tighten again. Yeah, no, he said to himself, there was no way he was going to stop by the clinic when he felt like a porcupine with quills erect, liable to jab anyone who got too close.

He spun in a circle, not knowing where to put himself, and looked down at Lono, who was looking up at him, his eyes bright with love. That's when he noticed how hard it was raining. Lono's coat was slicked down flat against his skin. He felt a rush of tenderness for the little dog. "How do you do it, huh?" he asked, bending down to run his hand over the one place the dog was still dry: under his muzzle. "How do you put up with me without complaining?"

The phone vibrated in Leo's pocket again, and he slapped his hand against it. He had to call the clinic back. But not here, he said to himself, noticing suddenly how cold the rainwater felt against his skin. *Lono must be freezing,* he thought. The day hadn't started out that cold, but it had certainly crept toward the kind of dank dreariness that could chill a person to the core. And he hadn't noticed because anger was fueling his inner heat.

"Okay," he said to Lono, pushing himself upright again and peering down the road toward the center of town. "Let's go back to the picnic shelter."

He walked faster now, almost jogging, hoping that he could find a way to dry his dog down before he had to go back into John's office. He shouldn't have gone so far, he realized, but fury had propelled him forward. Fury over Sheena's constant complaints about how much he charged for his veterinary work. "I *know* my rates are lower than other vets," he'd told her so many times. "But I'd rather do four surgeries a morning to make what I need to cover my expenses than stand around waiting for someone to be able to afford one." She *knew* how much it meant to him not to have to put down pet after pet after pet because their owners couldn't afford medical treatment for them, and she knew that he'd fired a bookkeeper once because they clashed over rates, and yet still she harped on him about it.

But Leo had stood firm; he didn't want to raise his rates. He loved working. So now she was going to try an end run around him using the divorce? Well, he wouldn't go for it. He didn't care what John said; he'd rather close his business down and live on the beach in Hawaii than gouge his clients. And Sheena could go pound sand for her $5,000 a month.

He got in under cover of the picnic shelter, his breath steaming the air in front of his face, and pulled his phone out of his pocket. Between the rain on the roof over the picnic table and the steady stream of traffic slapping through water on the roadway alongside the trail, Leo realized it was going to be hard to hear. He turned away from the road and walked around the picnic table to put himself closer to the river, crouching forward as he touched the clinic's number, as if his body would somehow create a quiet zone. Lono did a head-to-toe body shake beside Leo as he put the phone to his ear, but the vet could see he was shivering under his bedraggled fur. He wished he had a towel to mop some of the moisture off the little guy. He encouraged Lono toward him by rustling the fingers of his free hand in the air and put one leg on either side of the dog when he sat, hoping to warm him with his body heat.

Someone picked up the phone at the clinic, and Leo's head shot up as his ear filled with the angry sounds of barking and yipping and growling and panting.

"Riverside Animal Clinic," he heard Pema say into the receiver. "How can I help you?"

"What's going on?" he queried, forgetting even to tell her who it was he was so surprised by the ruckus on the other end of the line.

"Oh hi, Dr. F," Pema answered, cheery as ever. The growling sounds got louder, openmouthed, and angry, but Pema just seemed to smile into the receiver as she said, "It's nothing."

"Are you sure?" he asked, hearing a kind of slamming sound.

"Oop," she said, like she was trying to avoid something. "Everything's fine," she assured him. "Did you want to talk to Mac?"

"If she's available."

"She in surgery right now with Dr. Murphy . . ."

Her voice faded out as if she'd turned her head away from the phone, and Leo heard tumbling sounds on top of the growling and panting and barking, as if something was being thrown to the floor.

"Okay, well, I only called because someone's been trying to . . ." He heard a huge crash, huge enough that it made him jump and Lono startle. "What in the world is . . . ?"

"CanIcallyouback?" blurted Pema and hung up before he could answer.

Leo stared down at the phone in his hand. What in the heck had just happened? Did Pema hang up on him? Pema never hung up on him! And what was that terrible crash he'd heard? It sounded like the clinic was under attack. But she would have told him. Wouldn't she? He hit redial and waited while it rang once, twice, three times. He hung up. Why would he bother her if she was trying to deal with something? He heard the sound of the crash in his mind again. What if it was something he really didn't want to deal with right now? Couldn't deal with? He looked out at the river, his eyes resting on the somber iron gray of its surface in the rain. Maybe that's why Pema had hung up on him. She didn't want him to have to deal with it on his day off. He slipped the phone back into his pocket and let his hands hang down at his sides. He didn't know what was going on at the clinic, but the thought that Pema might be trying to spare him from it touched him to the core of his being in the way the rain had not. It made him feel guilty for not having answered the calls from the clinic earlier, when he was still at home. His staff might bug him at times but he did appreciate their loyalty. And their willingness to handle whatever was thrown at them, by him as well as by the clients. He looked out at the river again and was struck by how it no longer looked gray. It looked silver. As if thinking about his staff's sterling support had made his viewpoint more shiny.

And Sheena wanted to take that away from him?

A little wet nose kissed the tips of his fingers on one hand, dislocating Leo from thoughts. He looked down at his bedraggled dog. "You think I should go back and fight?" he asked.

Lono kissed his fingers again.

"Yep," the vet agreed, feeling the ire rise in him again. "Me, too." He scratched the underside of Lono's chin as he looked out at the river again. Never piss off an Irishman, that was what his grandmother used to say.

And Leo was now seriously pissed off.

Spike

It had been so hard. He tried not to think of how she must be worried, even though he was getting her thoughts like vibrations in his soul. She would be so happy when he sorted this all out. That was what kept him moving along: the look on her face when she found out what he'd been up to.

Today had been very hot. He'd gotten more and more thirsty as he walked, but his stomach had also been bugging him. He'd eaten some egg this morning, and it hadn't tasted right. Maybe it had given him gut rot. Now he was just tired, and more than a little discouraged.

He stopped at another coffee shop. It was closed, as late as it was, but he doubted anyone would mind if he sat out front. He nodded off for a moment. Maybe for a long moment because things got pretty quiet around him. Then someone honked out on the road in front of him and startled him awake.

Reluctantly he got up and peered down the street, wondering how much farther. That's when he saw something. Something familiar. Could it be . . . ? Did he dare hope? His eyes were watery with fatigue, and there was only a half moon in the sky, so he was having trouble trusting what he thought he was seeing, but he didn't let that stop him.

He walked forward, feeling the hairs on the back of his neck prickle with excitement. The more he walked, the more sure he became. And before he knew it, he felt himself jogging, then running, then running harder, no longer weary or hungry or anxious but excited to *be* there. He'd found it! He'd actually found it!

He bounded out across the road and heard a monstrous, ear-splitting squeal followed by . . .

Blackness.

Chapter 6

Mac was there when the fight started, except it didn't look like a fight. It looked more like male posturing between two headstrong brothers.

She had been securing the beagle spread eagle on the operating table when JJ came in through the door holding up some papers. "Dr. Murphy's signed off on the health certificates for the border collies," she said.

"Okay. Can you watch this one so I can go give them to Ms. Hedlund?"

"Sure," said JJ, switching places with Mac and giving her the health certificates.

"Is Dr. Murphy scrubbing up?" Mac asked.

JJ shook her head no. "She had to run out to her car for something. But she said she was going to scrub up next."

"And where's Waylon?"

"Taking a blanket into Snickers in exam 1."

Mac stopped, her hand on the door ready to push it open. "Why?"

"Because Dana wants to wait till Carly can take care of Snickers and Carly is in exam 2 with the cocker spaniel."

"But why didn't Waylon take Snickers to the ward?"

JJ rolled her eyes and shook her head like she didn't get it either. "You'd have to ask Dr. Murphy."

Mac tsked then hurried out of surgery, across treatment through the double doors and out into the hallway. She could hear some low growls coming from reception but nothing that sounded too unusual. Before she rounded the corner she heard Vera say, "Pink-y!" like she was warning him. Then, "Perky, if you don't behave—"

Once she turned the corner she could see the pit bulls facing each other in the center of reception. Their muscles were taut, their hackles were up and their claws were making skittering sounds on the floor as they moved first one way then the other in the game of assertion. Harry Rea's Shih Tzu was straining in his arms, looking like he wanted to get in on the action, and Earl Grey had been tucked in his carrier under the seat now occupied by his owner.

Mac switched her focus to Ms. Hedlund, who was watching her approach from over by the doors, obviously eager to leave. "I'm sorry this took so long," she said holding out the health certificates as she moved past Vera, who was trying to disentangle the mess her dogs had made of their leashes.

"That's okay. I can see you're busy," said Ms. Hedlund, pulling the door open as soon as she had the paperwork in her hand.

The pit bulls added snapping and snarling to their feud and Mac raised her voice to call out after her, "Have a great trip."

She swung around and saw Pinky and Perky in a very involved interlock over by the turtle tank. She was hoping they wouldn't knock into it when they *did* knock into it, sloshing water down onto the floor. "You're acting like a pair of football hooligans," Vera yelled at them, flinging down their leashes. "And I've had enough. If you can't behave I'm going to *make* you behave!" With that she snatched up her purse and started scrabbling through it in search of something.

Hopefully a cattle prod, Mac thought to herself as she walked past Pema, whose eyes were pleading with her to intervene. Mac knew Pema was prone to embarrassment, especially when things weren't going smoothly, and she had considered trying to break up the canine scrum but she really needed to get back to surgery. Plus she was pretty sure Vera had this.

She sailed down the short hallway hearing the phone ring and what sounded like one of the dogs smacking into a chair. Or maybe it was Vera smacking a chair into a dog, she chuckled to herself. Then she heard Pema's cheery voice sing out, "Oh hi, Dr. F," and Mac assumed they were back to business as usual.

*****

"You're sure about this now?"

"I am, yes," Leo told John. They were eating roast beef sandwiches that the lawyer had brought up from the sandwich shop on the bottom floor of his building, and Leo's appetite was increasing with his decisiveness. He didn't want to go through this divorce, but it felt good to have come to the conclusion that he was willing to fight for what he wanted out of it. "She can have the house and land on the hill, and if she wants to train to be a vet, I guess I'll help her financially. I probably won't have a choice in that," he added ruefully as he lifted his sandwich up toward his mouth. "But I'm not giving up my clinic." He bit down ravenously on the roast beef and Havarti.

Leo chewed his mouthful and pulled a tiny piece of roast beef off the side of his sandwich. He held it out for Lono, who was curled beside him on the floor of the conference room. When Leo got back to John's office, the lawyer had gaped at his chinos.

"You look like you got pretty damp out there," he'd joked as he motioned for the vet to sit at the conference table again, in front of one of the waxed paper lunch boxes that he'd placed where the legal pads had been.

"It was raining pretty hard, and I walked my dog a lot farther than I planned," Leo explained.

"Did you put him back in your vehicle?"

"Uh-huh."

"Didn't he get wet, too?"

"Very."

"Then why don't you bring him in? He'll dry off better in here, won't he, than in your vehicle? Plus this is going to take a while."

"I thought we were just having lunch," said Leo.

"We are. But then you need to fill out some paperwork for me," explained John, lifting a multipage document off the pile next to his lunch box.

"I can fill that out at home," Leo countered.

"Mmm," hummed John. "Maybe not. Some of the questions are pretty intrusive, so you might avoid it if you took it home. At least, that's what I'd do. I'd rather you filled it out here after I leave for court, so I'll have it to work with." He fixed Leo with a knowing look. "Might take you a while, though, so go. Get your pup."

"You're sure?"

"Absolutely. You won't like me much if he ends up catching a cold."

It was the first time Leo had really thought of John in any other light than his legal advisor. "Are you a dog person?" he asked.

"I am," confessed the lawyer. "Well, I always have been, but my wife was allergic to dogs, so I couldn't have one as an adult. Until recently."

"What changed?"

"My wife. She left me," said John with a shrug of his eyebrows. "So I went out and got myself a puppy."

"What kind did you get?"

"A Portuguese water dog. Like Obama."

There was a glint in John's eye as he said this, and Leo wondered if this revelation was some kind of challenge to declare his political leaning. He'd decided not to confuse things, talking politics. Instead he'd made for the door, saying, "You should bring your pup to see me when he needs his first checkup."

"I've already made an appointment."

And now Lono was curled up on Leo's denim jacket.

"I don't mind if he lies on the carpet," John had reassured him when Leo laid his jacket on the floor for Lono.

"Yes, but he feels safe this way. He knows that's where he's s'posed to be." And Leo didn't say it but he also felt safe knowing Lono was curled up on his jacket next to him.

"I don't mind fighting for you to keep the clinic," said John, wiping the sides of his mouth with a paper napkin. "And I think it's a valid thing to do. But it will take longer than just agreeing to what Sheena wants."

"I'm not in a hurry," said Leo.

"No. But you might resent the time away from work this is going to require."

Leo thought about that as he swallowed what was in his mouth. He picked up his bottle of water, looking at the windows again. It wasn't nearly as dark now that the rain had let up. He took a swig of his water to cleanse his palate and realized that John was right; he couldn't be in two places at the same time. And if he was here, drafting counterproposals to Sheena's demands, he wouldn't be at the clinic, helping people's pets. "I think my daughter will be able to cover for me most of the time," he told John. He leaned back in his chair and smiled. "And to be honest, in our daily routine, there's pretty much nothing that my vet tech can't handle."

*****

Dr. Murphy had just finished cutting around the tumor when a massive crash pierced the peace and rattled the surgical instruments in their tray.

"What was *that*?" she said.

"I have no idea," replied Mac, although she did have an idea but she wasn't going to acknowledge it until someone came and confirmed it. Then she heard what sounded like a hurricane bursting into treatment, snatching up tools and trays and equipment in its path and flinging them all across the room.

Dr. Murphy had the tumor pinched in forceps and was about to drop it on the surgical tray but she stopped and questioned Mac with a look.

"Yeah, I think it might be a dog fight," stated Mac without enthusiasm.

The door to surgery sprang open and JJ whipped in then stood with her back against it like she was hiding.

"Is it the pit bulls?" asked Mac.

"Uh-huh. And I think I may have screwed up," said JJ.

"How?"

"When they pitched through the doors to treatment, I grabbed the nearest thing to squirt at them—you know, to cool their jets—and didn't realize till I'd done it that it was chlorhexidine."

"That's just soap," said Dr. Murphy. "It's not going to hurt them." She stopped opening the suture kit in her hand and looked across at JJ. "You didn't get any in their eyes, did you?"

JJ shook her head no. "I don't think so. They were wound up so tight together that I couldn't even see their faces. And they managed to kick the sharps bin up into the air just as I squirted, so most of the chlorhexidine ended up on the floor."

A loud thud on the door behind her bounced JJ forward. She quickly backed up and spread her feet apart to rest against the doorjambs, maintaining her hold on the mask over her mouth.

"Who's out there with them?" asked Mac.

"No one. Carly's still in exam 2. I was hoping you'd come deal with them."

Mac was the clinic's best offense against aggressive dogs. She was good at giving them the eye: the eye that said she was in charge, not them. "Can JJ take over in here?" she asked Dr. Murphy.

"Of course."

Mac squared her shoulders and headed for the door, ready to take on the pugilists.

"What are they here for?" she heard Dr. Murphy ask JJ.

"Suture removal postneutering."

"Oh, I'm guessing they've long since taken care of that," joked the vet.

Mac peeked through the window to see if the dogs were still on the other side of the door. They weren't so she slammed the door open to make a strong entrance. The brothers' brawl was now happening over by the catchall workstation, a trail of blood and slime and used gauze pads left in their wake from the leashes dragging on the floor behind them. The dogs' only response to Mac's entrance was to bang into the leg of the workstation, adding spilled coffee and sodas and water to the war zone they were making of treatment.

First things first, thought Mac. She marched over to the phone by the viewing station and punched the button for reception. Pema picked up immediately. "Where's Vera?" she demanded.

"She's here but she says she can't help." Pema's voice became muffled, as if she'd cupped the mouthpiece with her hand so she couldn't be overheard. "She says she had them neutered to stop them from being so aggressive, and she doesn't know what more she can do."

"I could suggest something," grumbled Mac. "What was that big crash?"

"They knocked over the shelf unit with all the flea meds and ear washes."

"They did *what*?"

"And I think I hung up on Dr. F."

"Oh Pema—"

"I didn't mean to. I was talking to him when they knocked over the shelf unit and I put the phone down without thinking." She paused and then added, "He might have called back."

"Was he mad?"

"I didn't get to the phone in time."

"Okay, well I can't deal with that right now," said Mac as the dogs sent the oxygen machine spinning into her back. She hung up and grabbed the broom by the door to the large animal ward. She slammed the handle on the stainless-steel lift table to get the dogs' attention. They startled, but Perky, the darker of the two pits, used the moment to throw his rear leg over Pinky's belly, who was on his back on the floor, kicking like crazy. Perky grabbed up a mouthful of his prostrate brother's neck and shook vigorously. Pinky kicked at his brother's groin until Perky let go of his neck, repositioned his butt, then snatched a mouthful of the other side of Pinky's neck and shook again. This time Pinky somehow managed to catch hold of his brother's cheek with his teeth and pulled down hard, causing Perky to open his mouth and emit a long, loud howl of pain.

Mac realized that eye contact with the fighters was not going to happen at this point, so she approached them with the broom out in front of her like a shield and stepped on one of the leashes. Something drew her attention to the small animal ward and she glanced up to see Waylon sniggering—*sniggering!*—at the dogfight. She caught his eye, pointed at him, then pointed down at the other leash, and beckoned. Come. Here. Now.

Waylon eased out of the ward and cautiously stepped on the other leash.

"Stop!" Mac yelled at the pit bulls, banging the handle of the broom on the lift table again. They fought on. "Pick that leash up and tie it on the door handle," she informed Waylon.

Waylon leaned down, grabbed the end of the leash, and quickly made a figure eight, pulling the handhold of the leash through the top of the eight and looping it over the handle of the door to the small animal ward. It cinched tight with the muscular grappling of the dog on the other end of it.

Mac let the broom fall to the floor. "Give me that water bottle," she told Waylon.

He bent over and picked up an unopened, sixteen ounce bottle of water that had rolled off the workstation. He passed it across to Mac.

She unscrewed the top and poured the contents down onto the dogs' heads until they sprang to their feet, irritated by the intrusion. She dropped the bottle and grabbed up the leash under her foot, then darted toward X-ray before the dog on the other end knew what was happening. When she turned around, she realized she had Pinky, the one with the pink around his eyes, on his muzzle, and on his underbelly, and brown and white patches elsewhere. She guessed that the owner might be regretting the delicate names she'd given these dogs now that they'd turned into such hoodlums, but she was English, so who knew? Mac dropped the leash back on the floor and stood on it, effectively keeping the dogs just far enough apart that when they lunged again, they found they couldn't make contact with each other. They bit and snapped and growled into the air between them, straining full force on their leashes to get at each other. Perky was fully restrained, but Mac felt her legs start to splay apart as Pinky's determination to get back to his brother dragged her foot along the wet floor with the leash underneath it. She tried to lean over and grab the broom again, thinking to block his path with it, but his urge to fight overrode her lean, and she pitched forward, landing hard on her knees as Pinky threw himself at his lassoed brother. Waylon skittered away to the safety of the autoclave as Perky yelped and fell backward, spilling garbage the length of the hallway.

At exactly that moment, Carly burst through the double doors, yelled, *"What the . . . ?"* and slid on a patch of wet soap to land hard on her butt on the floor. *"Oww!!"* she cried out.

"You okay?" Mac asked as she picked herself up from the floor. The usually humming treatment room was a cacophony of angry barking and snarling and mewling, not just from the pit bulls engaged in the fight but from every other animal in the clinic that wanted to know what was going on.

"I must've been in that room for twenty minutes," Carly exclaimed, pointing back at exam 2 as she stood back up. "Trying to get that cocker spaniel to stop barking and hold still so I could look at his constricted pupil and then explain to his owner that he might have Horner's syndrome. It took a helluva lot longer than it should have with this *ruckus* going on! It's time it *stopped*!"

Mac noticed the young vet's face was almost the same plum color of her scrubs. Probably a mixture of anger and pain, she thought, seeing Carly rubbing her coccyx with her left hand.

"What we need are some Tasers!" the young vet declared.

"I think Pema carries Mace," said Mac.

The two women locked eyes, a frisson of *I'm game if you are* passing between them. Then they both let go of the idea.

"Your dad would never go for it."

"Yeah, no," agreed Carly. "Although if my butt's too sore for me to ride my horse tomorrow," she yelled at the plundering dogs, "I'm coming after you with my Smith & Wesson."

"I'm going in," Mac said, marching toward the dogs, her mind made up.

Carly slapped the patient file she was holding down on the workstation next to her. "I'll take the broom."

Mac kept her feet a good distance away from the snarling, snapping fray, reached her right hand forward, and snatched the skin at the back of Pinky's neck. She gripped it tight in her fist, so he wouldn't be able to turn his head, and dragged him back with just his hind legs touching the floor. His weight was oppressive for one arm, but her grip had a paralytic effect on the dog from his chest up, and he walked backward passively, his front legs stiff and unmoving out in front of him.

Once Perky shook himself upright and figured out his brother had backed off, he flew at him full force, but Carly was ready with the broom. She thrust it in front of his face, and he ran right into it, let out a yelp, and slumped down on his belly, swiping at his muzzle with both front paws. "Don't let my dad know I did that," she said.

"I'm ready for you to suture the incision," came Dr. Murphy's voice from behind Mac.

The vet tech stopped moving and sucked in a breath. So far she liked working with Dr. Murphy, but she was definitely high energy and lacked patience, just like Dr. F. "Erm, I'm kinda busy here," Mac replied.

"Well, as soon as you can," answered Dr. Murphy, adding, way too cheerily for Mac's taste, "Looks like you've got things under control here."

That was true. But Mac knew it would take one wrong move and the two pit bulls would be back at it. "Waylon, come tie this one up."

"Sure thing." Waylon edged past Perky and scooped up the end of Pinky's leash. He made the same figure-eight hitch and looped it on the door to X-ray. "Done," he said, then hustled away to a safe spot behind the wet sink.

Mac turned Pinky to face X-ray, and stepped back toward Carly as she let go of him. Pinky jumped around to face his brother again, and Mac leaned in with some powerful *obey me* body language. *"Down!"* she commanded.

The dog lowered his head and sank to the floor, subdued. There was a bloody tear on one side of his face and blood dripping out of his mouth, although Mac didn't know if that was his blood or his brother's. She stared hard at the dog. He closed his massive mouth, put his chin meekly on his front paws, and flicked his eyes away, then back, spent.

The door to treatment eased open. "Um, Vera says she's found her Taser now and you can borrow it if you want," came Pema's voice.

Mac looked at Carly; Carly looked at Mac.

"Fu-ck!" they said.

*****

It was almost three thirty by the time Leo got out of his lawyer's office. John had been right about the boilerplate questionnaire; if Leo had taken it home, he would have blown off filling it out. Not only were the questions invasive, half of them he didn't know the answer to because he never cared that much about the finances of the clinic. As long as he was paying his bills and the staff was happy, he was content to leave that aspect of his business with Mary Jo, his part-time bookkeeper. She kept him updated on the overall financial health of his practice but spared him the minutiae. The trouble was, it was the minutiae that John needed.

Leo spent a tortuous hour and a half intermittently poring over the questions, muttering angry commentaries about how it was nobody's goddamn business as he penciled in answers, staring out the windows trying to remember how much he charged for certain procedures so he could calculate his revenue, and then disturbing Mary Jo at home to get real figures.

It was just as well he'd gotten it over with, he thought as he hustled down the steep staircase from John's office, Lono beside him, and burst through the double doors to the sunlit cobblestone square outside. Blue skies had drifted in from the Puget Sound, and Leo could see the rainwater on the surface of the cobblestones steaming under the sun's warmth. There was still plenty of time to go home and uproot the tomato plants, he thought to himself as he rounded the corner, heading for his Jeep. Although just because it was blue skies down here in Mount Vernon didn't mean it wasn't still pouring with rain farther up valley, at his house. The undulating hills and vales running both sides of the Skagit encouraged an abundance of microclimates, and he knew he could drive in and out of rain and sun, sometimes even snow, before he got home. He turned and looked at the sky east of where he was standing, pulling open the driver's-side door for Lono to hop in. Yep, it still looked pretty overcast up there.

Plus, he thought as he climbed in next to Lono, he probably ought to stop by the clinic. It was closed now and most of the staff, he imagined, had gone home already, but Mac would probably still be there and could catch him up on what had happened today. "Maybe if it was something terrible, I won't want to fight to keep it," he joked to Lono. "Then I can spend my time gardening and riding my horse."

Lono stretched his head forward to rest his chin on Leo's thigh.

"Oh okay," the vet conceded. "And play with my dog." He stroked Lono's baby-soft fur, feeling glad he'd had a chance to dry out in John's office, then put on his seat belt and drove across town to the clinic. He was glad to see Mac's car parked around the side when he pulled in, but he was surprised to see Carly's rig there, too. This was one of her days off, so why . . . ?

He pulled past the general parking for clients and wound around to the back of the clinic. That was when he saw JJ's *and* Pema's vehicles. What on earth was going on?

*****

"Well, that was no fun," said Carly. She was standing by the wet sink, untying her surgical cap at the back of her head when Mac and JJ came out of the ward where they'd put Snickers with her six puppies. They stopped in front of her and Mac got the sense that they were shell shocked, like the room around them. It had been a difficult C-section on top of an exhausting and incident-filled half day that had turned into a three-quarter day at the clinic. The walls of Snickers's uterus were so thin they'd started to rip when Carly tried to lift it back into her belly after delivering the puppies.

"She needs a hysterectomy," she said to Mac.

Dana Erdahl was standing outside the door to surgery, banished from coming in and watching the procedure because she couldn't keep her hands off Mac's surgical instruments, which made Mac feel like she had to either keep her out of surgery or stab her hand with a scalpel. But she wasn't standing so far outside that she didn't hear Carly's pronouncement.

"Noooo!" she screamed, pushing the door open so they could be sure to hear her. "No hysterectomy!"

"The uterus is coming apart in my hands," explained Carly, her voice soft, as if she empathized with Dana but these were the facts.

"Stitch it up," insisted Dana. "That's what I would do."

Carly stared at Dana for a long moment, and Mac knew what was going through her mind. She knew she was walking that uncomfortable line between doing what was right and doing what the client wanted. And she was assessing how much time it might take to convince this hardheaded client of the dangers of *not* doing what was right while the uterus sat exposed to possible infection and the dog remained under anesthetic. It was a no-win situation for Carly and Mac really wished she could hold a hand out to support her in walking this line. But all she could do was send her positive vibes across the operating table.

"You realize we might lose her if we do that," Carly explained to Dana, her tone somber.

"I have to get one more litter from this dog before I stop breeding her. So you *have* to save the uterus."

Carly nodded and then carried out the client's wishes. But Mac felt the mood drop in surgery. Poor Snickers.

"I'm just worried Snickers isn't going to make it through the night," said Carly, stuffing her surgical cap in the pocket of her scrubs.

"I'll come by after my show tonight and check on her," said Mac. "I was planning to go over to the theater early, but I think I'll stay with her as long as I can." She looked around her at the chaos the pit bulls had made of treatment and added, "And clean up this mess."

"I'll help with that."

"You don't have to, Carly."

"No, I want to," countered the young vet. She shrugged. "I'm not ready to leave Snickers just yet anyway."

"You want me to set up an ICU out here in treatment for her?" JJ asked.

Carly thought a beat, then nodded. "After we clean up that might be a good idea. I suggested Dana take her to the emergency clinic but of course she didn't want to spend the money on that. I thought dad was going to fire her as a client?"

"Me too," said Mac.

They looked at each other for a second, the walls around them seeming to echo the devastation of the day, then they all moved in unison.

"I'll get the mop," said JJ.

"I'll pick up everything that came out of the sharps bin," said Mac grabbing another pair of latex gloves out of the box.

Carly crossed to the sink and turned on the faucet. "And I'll help Pema," she said. "I saw her trying to sort out the flea meds when I was talking to Erdahl out in reception."

"What did Dana say when you told her to wait at least one heat cycle before she breeds Snickers again?" Mac asked Carly.

"Nothing. She heard me, I know, but I'm not sure she'll do it." Carly looked weighed down by sadness, but she lifted her head and smiled gently at Mac. "How's your chin?" she asked.

"Sore." Mac had the mask she'd been wearing in surgery down over her chin with a small ice pack taped on behind it. "I'm going to look at it right now before I start cleaning up this mess. If that's okay with you."

"Do it," said Carly. Her eyes drifted away and Mac glimpsed her lost in that bleak inner darkness where a little light would be so welcome. "Maybe I'll try calling my dad," muttered Carly before leaning forward to let the water run over her hands.

*****

Leo walked in the side door with Lono and tsked at the sight of all the garbage strewn through the hallway. "Someone needs to pick up this garbage," he called out as Lono trotted across it and stopped by the overturned bin to sniff the base of the wall by the small animal ward. Leo navigated his way around the mess, with a quick glance at what was catching Lono's attention. That's when he saw the blood.

He got to treatment and his jaw dropped at the obvious ransacking; aside from even more garbage on the floor, there were pools of brown foamy liquid under the workstations, machinery was toppled, the sharps bin was upside down and backward, and it looked like someone had Jackson Pollocked blood across the floor and up the walls.

JJ rounded the corner from the large animal ward holding a mop and a bucket of soapy water. Her mouth dropped open as if she'd been caught doing something she shouldn't. "Dr. F," she gasped.

"Is that my dad?" Carly called out. She rushed into treatment from Leo's office and saw him across the room. "Thank God!" she exclaimed. "D'you have time to talk?"

"What happened here?" he said, not yet able to take his eyes off the floor.

"This?" asked Carly, waving her hand over the carnage. "This was just a dogfight."

"A dogfight?"

Mac blew into the room, her mask gone, her chin bloody and

swollen. She stopped as soon as she saw Leo.

"Did you get *bitten*?" he asked, even more incredulous at the sight of that than at the mess on the floor.

"Dammit!" she cried.

"What?"

"You can see it?"

"Yes, I can see it," he told her. "Of course I can see it. Your chin looks about three times its normal size."

"Dammit!" she cried again, reaching into the pocket of her scrubs and pulling out a square of gauze. She held it up in front of the bite to hide it. "I thought I put enough makeup on it."

"Your chin looks like it belongs on a zombie," Carly informed her, her face wrinkled with skepticism. "You ain't covering that with makeup."

"I know. I know," conceded Mac. "But I had to try. We have a public dress rehearsal tonight, and I'm supposed to vamp it up as the queen of Egypt, not look like some stupid vet tech that let her guard down."

Leo felt a surge of empathy for his number-one assistant. She did a lot to make his work seamless, and the only thing she asked in return was support for what she did onstage. He scanned his memory for the few lines of Shakespeare he'd learned in high school and said, "I thought the vilest things became themselves in Cleopatra."

"Oh, very funny!" Mac shot back, although he could tell by the softening of her posture that she liked the reference. "I doubt Shakespeare was thinking of a fresh dog bite when he wrote that line."

"You quoting Shakespeare now, too?" Carly asked her dad.

"That's what twenty years of working with someone will do," he replied.

"Nineteen," said Mac.

"Okay, nineteen. Did I at least get the line right?"

"'She makes hungry / Where most she satisfies, for vilest things

/ Become themselves in her,'" Mac said, her posture softening even more as she quoted the Bard.

"So I was pretty close."

"What's it mean?" asked JJ.

"That Cleopatra drives men nuts with her beauty," explained Carly.

"Yeah, I'm not looking forward to trying to convince the audience of that tonight with my chin like this," Mac said, her eyes on the floor.

Lono moved on from the blood on the wall. He sniffed in a narrow zigzag past JJ and her mopping toward his dog bed, stepping gingerly over the puddles and paper cups and plastics littered about the floor, with frequent stops to ascertain the details of the scents he was catching.

"It's not your fault your chin got in the way of a dogfight," Leo told his vet tech, pulling his eyes away from his dog.

"Oh this?" said Carly, pointing at Mac's oozing chin. "This wasn't Vera's pit bulls."

"Pinky and Perky? That's who made this mess?" he queried, pointing down at the floor. "Didn't I neuter them a couple of weeks ago?"

"Yeah, but apparently not all their aggression was in their balls," Carly informed him.

"But then who . . . ?" Leo started to ask when the room suddenly filled with a long, single-tone, plaintive cry, like something wild was in distress.

All heads whipped around to look at Lono.

"Did you just *yodel*?" Leo asked his dog as soon as he quieted again, amazed that such an intense noise could come out of his mouth.

Lono tipped his head back and repeated his cry.

Pema burst in through the double doors. "Is everything okay?" she cried, obviously panicked. Then she spotted Leo. Her mouth dropped open. "Dr. F," she exclaimed, "I'm so sorry I hung up on you."

Leo blew off her apology with a sideways smile and a flap of his hand. "You had other things to deal with," he said, waving at the mess on the floor.

Lono cried again, long, high, piercing, like it could break a wineglass.

"Has he ever done that before?" Carly asked her dad in the pulsing silence after the screech.

Leo shook his head no. "I've heard him bark twice, both times at the cat, so I thought there wasn't that much basenji in him."

"Yeah, they don't bark, do they?"

"No. This is what they do," said Leo, pointing at his dog. Then he shrugged. "At least, as far as I know. I'm not that familiar with basenjis, to be honest. It's not a dog I would have chosen for myself, and I don't think we've even had any at the clinic. Have we?" he asked, glancing across at Mac.

"We had that one client that bred them. Didn't we?"

"That's right," he agreed. "Briefly."

"Right. I think she got put off when her bitch got accidentally knocked up by the Aussie shepherd next door."

JJ chuckled.

Carly clicked in the side of her mouth. "Gotta pay attention when the bitch is in heat."

Leo looked at Mac again. "Didn't we deliver that litter?" he asked, but before she could answer, Lono yodeled high and loud again. They all winced and waited him out.

Pema stared down at Lono, apparently fascinated. "Do they make that sound when they're happy or mad?" she asked.

Leo raised his shoulders and shook his head, smiling. "I have no clue," he answered. "Could something be bothering him?"

Lono was standing about two feet from his dog bed, craning forward to sniff it. His nostrils flared once, twice, three times, and then he pulled back, tipped up his head, and yodeled again.

JJ ducked, covering her ears with her hands. But as soon as Lono stopped yodeling her eyes bugged like she'd had an ah-ha moment. "I bet I know what it is," she said. She dropped her mop in the bucket, resting the length of it against the back counter, and raced to snatch Lono's dog bed up off the floor. "Sorry, sorry," she cried, clasping it to her chest. "I was going to wash this with all the blankets that got bloodied by the pits but forgot. I'll do it now."

"Why? What happened to it?" Leo asked before JJ could disappear into the large animal ward.

"Dr. Murphy's dog, Kent, slept in it."

Leo gasped dramatically and looked down at his dog. "Was someone sleeping in *your* bed?" he teased.

Lono craned forward and sniffed hard at the floor close to his bed, then tipped his head back and yodeled again.

Leo half winced and half laughed at his dog's persistence. "Enough!" he cried out when Lono stopped. "I get that you didn't like some other dog near your bed."

"He's probably smelling all the mucus Kent sneezed on the floor."

"I'll scrub it with disinfectant, I promise," JJ reassured Lono, who walked a big circle around the offending smells and stopped next to her. He bowed his head and pushed his forehead against her leg as if he was saying thank-you.

"Awwwwwwwww!" erupted all the women in the room.

And Leo just rolled his eyes, smiling.

*****

Lono's antics had definitely lightened the mood in the room, which had felt like a pall of bewildered exhaustion to Leo when he got there. The calm after the storm, only it didn't feel like calm so much as resignation. Sadness, even. Especially in his daughter and Mac.

Leo knew the ups and downs of veterinary medicine could weigh on the soul, and he wondered what else had happened in his absence. He pulled on a pair of latex gloves to help clean up the mess and placed himself alongside Carly, picking up stray wads of cotton and used bandages that had fallen out of the trash. "What was it you wanted to talk to me about?" he asked.

Carly slowly opened up about the C-section she'd had to perform on Snickers and the interaction she'd had with Dana Erdahl that had left her feeling so inadequate as a vet. Leo listened, keeping his eyes on the random trash he was picking up, so she couldn't see how angry this was making him.

"I sent her a letter telling her not to come back," he assured his daughter when she finished retelling the whole incident. They were both standing now, pulling off their gloves to drop in the bin with all the trash they'd picked up.

"You know, I wondered," said Mac from below them. She crab walked forward and put the righted sharps bin back under the wet sink. "She claimed she wanted to see you but she wasn't nearly as pushy about it as she normally is, and I wondered if she knew today was your day off and risked coming in with Snickers because she wouldn't have to run into you."

Leo was watching Carly, whose eyes were still down on the floor, as if she was ashamed of the choice she'd had to make. "Snickers is still here, I'm guessing," he said to her.

"Yeah," said Carly, meeting his eye now and shaking her head sideways. "There was no way I was letting her go home."

"Good," Leo declared with a reassuring nod. He stepped forward and wrapped his arms around his daughter. "You made the right choice."

"JJ's going to set her up in an ICU out here in treatment once she's cleaned the floor."

"Great idea," attested Leo. "So who did bite you?" he asked Mac, seeing her dabbing at her chin now that she was upright again, her eyes watering in pain.

"Harry Rea's Shih Tzu."

"I thought it was gonna be Earl Grey that got you," JJ joined in from across the room.

"The cat with the splint removal?" laughed Carly. "Oh. My. God. He was a holy terror, wasn't he?"

"Oh, but I'm glad he didn't," said Mac, her spirit sounding revived, too, with the rambunctious way they were telling the story. "A cat bite would've been worse!"

"Yeah, you would've been the one getting the shot instead of the Shih Tzu," teased Carly.

"That's why the Shih Tzu bit you?" said Leo, surprised. "Over a vaccination?"

"Yep. And I had tight hold of him, too."

"So did Earl Grey's owner," said Carly. "But man, he got mad, didn't he, when I tried to touch his leg to check it?"

"You should've seen it," Mac told Leo. She crossed her arms in front of her and grabbed her shoulders tight, as if she was cold. "His owner had him cinched down tight against her chest—"

"But he twisted this way and that," Carly went on, "so *maniacally* that he forced her arms apart—"

"—and shot out into the room like a chicken from a cannon."

"MRRAUWWWWWW!!!" Carly and Mac imitated together.

"I heard that noise out in reception!" gasped Pema. "And did he hit against the door when he sprang out of his mom's arms?"

"Big time!" declared Carly, her lips making a popping sound with the way she emphasized the *b* in big. "I think his mom nearly had a heart attack she was so shocked."

"It's been that kind of day," said Pema.

"Did any of you get any lunch?" asked Leo.

"I didn't," Carly answered as she started to stack the charts in tidy piles.

"Nope," said Pema and JJ.

"No time," put in Mac.

"How about I order you all some pizza?" Leo suggested. He looked at Mac. "That way you'll get to eat now and have more time at the theater for makeup."

"Sure," she agreed.

"You want me to stitch that?" Carly asked, looking more closely at the bite on Mac's chin as the vet tech handed her the last of the papers that had fallen to the floor.

"Nah. I think I'll just put some glue on it."

"I have some gold glue you could use," offered JJ. "Then you could paint the rest of your face gold to go with it. That'd work for Cleopatra, right?"

"No, no, put a slug over the bite and say it's one of her asps," joked Carly.

"Eww! I am not putting a slug on my face."

"You could borrow a snake from someone and have it coil around your neck," said Pema, "then rest its head on your chin to cover the bite."

Leo let himself bask in their banter for a moment, enjoying the resilience it showed after such a trying day. This, he thought as he put the phone to his ear to call the pizza parlor, this was definitely worth fighting for.

Spike

His head was too quiet. It felt like someone had erased the home page of all the conversations that he was used to tuning into, and now he couldn't find any of them. He didn't like it. It was very disorienting.

He wasn't sure he could live without the constant discourse. He was so used to his head being full of chatter that the quiet was decidedly eerie. Like he was standing on top of the world in a place where the only sound was the wind whooshing across a barren landscape. Plus how would he do what he was supposed to do if he couldn't hear the unspoken conversations?

He sighed and closed his eyes. Maybe it would all come back to him when he wasn't so tired.

Chapter 7

The following Monday Leo sat on the steps of the front porch at his house trying to figure out what he did and didn't want. He'd felt so sure when he'd told John on Thursday that he wanted to keep the clinic but ever since he'd been second-guessing himself. Not that he thought it was the wrong decision necessarily; more that he didn't know why it was the right one. Had he made it just to thwart Sheena or because he so loved his work that he didn't want to give it up? He did love his work, but there were times—

Harley thumped down onto his side a few inches from Leo's shoulder. They had been sitting together, Leo on the third step down, Harley above him on the deck, waiting for the sunrise, but Harley must have become bored. Leo swung around and saw the old dog had his front paw lifted, exposing his belly. "You want me to pet you?" he asked. He put his coffee cup one step down, under his legs, and rubbed the palm of his hand up and down Harley's belly.

He kept coming back to the look in Carly's eyes when she'd told him about having to save Snickers's tattered uterus. He knew that look; it was anguish over not being able to do what was best for the animal. And he knew how much that anguish would tarnish Carly's enthusiasm for being a vet. Fortunately Snickers had survived the C-section but if she died farther down the line, somehow related to the procedure, that tarnish would harden into a patina over part of Carly's heart. He knew because he'd felt it happen to him. And what he couldn't help wondering yesterday, when he was rattling around alone in his house, was whether Sheena had bumped up against that hardened part of his heart and that's why she'd left him. In which case, why would he want to keep doing something that drove the people he loved away from him?

He felt a little chin slip onto his knee and turned around to see Lono sitting between his feet, two steps down. "You'd know what to do, wouldn't you?" he said, stroking the soft, tufty fur on top of the dog's head. Lono pulled his lips back into his cheeks and sneezed hard. "Are you catching a cold?" Leo asked, perturbed. He ran his thumb over Lono's forehead; he did feel a little warm. But that could have been from chasing round with Venus. *Who was where?* Leo wondered, peering out across the pasture in the still dark of the early morning. That was the problem with his life right now; he didn't know where things were or where he stood in them. He felt like he was sitting in a boat in the middle of a lake with a tangled knot of fishing line in his hands. Part of him wanted to just cut off the knot but it was the only line he had and he couldn't fish without it so he felt compelled to try and untangle it. The weird thing was the harder he tried, the more he felt his boat drifting away from where the fish were, and he couldn't figure out what was making it drift.

Lono nudged his hand with his nose. "Okay, okay," conceded Leo, stroking his head again. "I'll stop thinking so much."

Venus ran around the corner of the house just as the first wisps of peach appeared in the sky. She bounded up the front steps and clambered onto Leo's chest with her front paws, licking him effusively on his face, her tail banging in time with her excitement against the railing behind her. He smiled and eased her down into his lap with both hands, watching the horizon above the mountain ridges opposite billow to a full canvas of burnt orange and fire red with a seam in the center of bright near-white yellow. Enter the sun, he thought, as the ridges in front of the rising orb turned purple behind a veil of smoky white, adding to the illusion that the sky was on fire. And then, just as quickly, like shaking an Etch A Sketch to start a new image, the sky cleared and it was daylight.

"And on that glorious note," Leo announced to his dogs as he picked up his coffee and slowly rose to a stand, "let's go face the day."

*****

"Uh-oh. Looks like you're going to be busy," said Chad as he turned the Honda Element into the parking lot. "Have you got a bunch of surgeries scheduled for today?"

Mac reluctantly opened her eyes. She counted four cars already parked alongside the clinic as Chad drove past them and the clock on the dash indicated it was still only six-fifty. She yawned. "I don't think so, no. They're probably just the 'need-to-get-our-pet-to-the-vet-first-thing-Monday' crowd."

Chad pulled in next to Dr. F's Jeep and parked but left the engine running. "Is Carly in today?"

"Yep."

"Well that'll help."

Mac leaned across the seat and kissed him on the lips. "See you later."

"Hey, don't forget your Cruella de Vil outfit," he told her as she stepped out of the vehicle. She looked back inside and saw that he was pointing at the *101 Dalmatians* scrubs on the floor in front of the passenger seat. She reached back in and picked up the shirt with all the spotted puppies on it. "How's my chin?" she asked, tipping it up toward him.

"Not too bad. Did you bring any of that cover up you used for yesterday's matinee?"

"Yeah. I'll put it on when I do my hair."

She blew him another kiss, closed the door to the Honda and walked around the back of the clinic. When she got to the side door she was aware of Pema pulling up, but she slipped inside without acknowledging her so as to avoid any of the clients thinking that might be their cue to get out of their cars and follow her.

Once inside the hallway Lono trotted toward her. Mac paused to bend over and tickle his ear. "How are you doing today?" she asked.

"Not so good," Dr. F answered, stepping out of the shadows in treatment. He was looking down at a thermometer.

"What's going on?" Mac asked. She straightened back up and moved past Dr. F to put her purse in the break room.

"He's been sneezing off and on," she heard him say as she slipped out of her jacket and pulled on her scrub shirt.

"It's chilly out there," she said as she came back through X-ray into treatment.

"Yeah, I noticed that too. Feels like fall."

"Did you check on the Doberman?" she asked, pointing at the large animal ward.

"I did. She can go home today."

"I'm not sure I want her to," said Mac with a small pout of regret. "She's so mellow." She was standing facing Dr. F and he nodded as if agreeing with what she said but he was still staring down at the thermometer, his brow furrowed. "Whose temperature did you take?" she asked, then crossed to the back counter and booted up the first computer.

The side door beeped three times. Mac glanced to her right as she moved down the counter to the second computer and saw Pema coming in. Lono started down the hallway toward her and Mac found herself tilting her head in surprise. *Did he just*—? But whatever it was she thought she'd seen was gone before she could complete the question.

"Lono's," answered Dr. F.

At the sound of his name the dog turned around and trotted back to the vet.

Mac opened the door to the oxygen closet and someone mewed in the small animal ward.

"Hi," said Pema on her way by to the break room.

"Hi," they both replied.

"It's a little elevated," Dr. F told Mac. The dip in his brow deepened.

Mac looked down at Lono. He was holding his head a little lower than usual but other than that he looked fine. "You think he caught Kent's sinus infection?"

"Kent?'

"Dr. Murphy's dog."

"Oh that's right. That's a possibility, I guess." He wiped the end of the thermometer with alcohol gauze and walked over to the sink, crossing paths with Pema. She turned on the rest of the lights in treatment and continued on out through the double doors. Lono padded over to his bed under the viewing station and tucked himself in a curl.

The phone rang and the side door beeped again. "You want me to do a chest X-ray?" asked Mac as she went to boot up the scheduling computer over by the doors. She heard Waylon and JJ talking together and the phone rang again. She looked up at the clock; it was two minutes before seven.

Dr. F walked back toward Lono, tossing the paper towels he'd used to dry his hands into the small trash can at the end of the wet sink. "I think I'll do a swab first," he said.

Pema pushed open the door. "Mrs. Biagi's here with her Rottweiler."

"That's our amputation," said Mac, reading it off the computer.

"I'll go," she heard Waylon say and then smiled a greeting at him as he went past her out the door. The phone rang a third time. Mac started to follow Waylon, to go fix her hair and make-up before the day took off completely, when she felt Dr. F's anxiety from across the room like a chill in her bones. She turned around, walked between the workstations and crouched down beside him in front of Lono. She felt like they were on an island in the center of a busy market with the sounds of the clinic clattering into action around them. Lono looked at them with a small furrow in his own brow, as if worried about the trouble he was causing them. Either that or he was picking up on Dr. F's apprehension, Mac thought. Now that she was this close to the pup she could see how ragged his breathing was.

"You want me to start him on cephalexin?" she asked the doc.

"Let me check the swab first," he replied.

"Okay." Mac waited to see if he'd give her more direction but his eyes were glazed over, his face somber, and she could almost see all the worst-case scenarios running through his mind.

"I just need him to be okay," he muttered finally.

"I know," she said.

"Dr. F," came Pema's voice from the doorway. "Your lawyer's on the phone."

"Already?" he groaned. He sprang upright like someone had stuck a pin in his butt and looked at Pema across the room.

"He said he tried your cell but it was too important to leave a message."

"Okay, I'll take it in my office. Can someone put this on a slide?" he asked Mac, handing her the swab.

"Sure."

And then he took off. Mac shifted out of the way of the incoming Rottweiler, passed the swab to JJ and headed for the bathroom before anything else could stop her.

*****

Two and a half hours later Leo was standing in front of the staff schedule pinned to the wall by the entrance to his office, trying to persuade his daughter to work an extra shift.

"No," Carly told him like he hadn't understood. She touched the calendar with her index finger. "I'm not down to come in again 'till Thursday of this week."

Leo drew in a big breath. His stomach was already beginning to feel like a car battery submerged in acid. He reached into the pocket of the sweatshirt he had hanging next to the staff schedule and pulled out a small bottle of antacids. He had a patient in exam 3 that needed to be brought back and he knew Carly had started her day on the run when her shift began at nine so he'd really been hoping this wouldn't take too long. "I know that," he clarified. He popped two antacids into his mouth and chewed them quickly. "I know you don't usually come in Tuesdays and Wednesdays. What I'm saying is can you make an exception and come in tomorrow morning?"

"I can't. I promised mom I'd cover for her at the kitchen tomorrow."

"Where's she going?"

He watched his daughter vacillate, swinging her head side to side, her eyes rolled up, like she didn't really want to say. He wondered why. "She's going hiking up in the North Cascades before the weather changes," Carly answered finally.

"Your mother??" Leo spluttered.

"I know," said Carly in a conciliatory tone. "She's got some new boyfriend."

Leo glanced across at Mac who was doing a dental procedure on a poodle at the wet sink. He saw her eyes drop as soon as he looked her way and knew she'd been watching for his reaction. She was aware, from the times he'd mentioned it over the years, how much he'd wanted Sheena to go hiking with him but she never would. And now here she was, taking his assistant vet from him so she could go with some other guy? Lono came around the workstation and sat tucked in against Leo's foot. He leaned into Leo's leg and tipped his head up to look at him. Leo stroked the underside of Lono's muzzle feeling his anger subside. "You should be in bed," he whispered down to the dog.

"Why? What's wrong with him?" asked Carly.

"He's got a sinus infection."

"Oh. Well you don't look like you're suffering," she baby-talked down to the dog, tickling him on top of his head.

Leo looked up at the staff schedule again.

"Why do you need me in tomorrow anyway?" Carly asked. "Aren't you going to be here?"

"In the morning yes." He cupped Lono's head gently in his hands and whispered, "You go lie down." Lono obeyed.

"But look," said Leo, stepping forward to the scheduling computer and motioning with his fingers for Carly to follow him. He touched the keyboard and the screen lit up. "My morning is full of appointments and there's a medial patella luxation that *has* to be done—"

"I can't do an MPL," argued Carly. "I'm not that comfortable with surgery yet."

"Yes, I know," Leo agreed. "I was hoping you could take some of my appointments in the morning so *I* can do the MPL."

Carly shook her head no. "Sorry. I just can't. Why don't you schedule Dr. Murphy to come in?"

"I did already," said Leo. "But she can only come for the afternoon, which doesn't help me—"

"Dr. F," interrupted Pema, leaning in through the double doors. Leo looked at her, inviting her to continue. "Louisa Miller's on the phone, and she wants to know Pred or Pred combo for her cat?"

Waylon pushed the door fully open behind Pema and came in around her, holding a chart up in the air for Leo to see. "Where do you want your ten forty-five?" he asked, dropping the chart in the stand by the door.

"Who is it?"

"Cedric Rogers. His Chihuahua isn't walking right."

"What's open?"

"I have people in exams 1 and 2," Carly put in.

"Okay, then. Exam room 3," Leo told Waylon.

"You've got an impacted bunny in exam 3," Mac reminded him.

"That's right," said Leo, irritated with himself for forgetting. "Exam 4, then," he told Waylon. "And I have to look at Calvin's chart—that's the name of her cat, right?" he replied to Pema. She nodded yes. "Okay, so I have to look at his chart before I can say. Find out if I can call her back?"

"Okay," Pema agreed and let the door to treatment close as she followed Waylon back out to reception.

Leo stood for a second, recalibrating. He crossed to the chart stand and picked up the patient file Waylon had left there. "Let me think on it," he said over his shoulder to Carly.

"There's not much to think on since I can't do it," Carly informed him, then pushed the door open for him to walk out ahead of her.

*****

Mac was scraping tartar off the poodle's teeth and found the piercing whirr of the dental drill good white noise for her contemplation of Dr. F's dilemma. She could reschedule the MPL for Wednesday, but she knew he didn't want to make Maisie wait because the poor dog had a Grade 4 luxation and her kneecap was about an inch out of place. It was obvious she was in great pain.

Dr. F should have just told her he had a lawyer's appointment after his Rotary lunch, Mac thought. But she also understood his need for privacy. Her divorce had been pretty brutal, and the only way she'd been able to stop it from trashing every other part of her life was by keeping it to herself. Plus, he probably didn't want to say anything in front of Carly.

The poodle jumped a little, and Mac stopped the drill and looked at the oxygen machine. She pressed the button on the side, and the ticker tape of her heart rate printed out for her to read. It looked stable. Must have been a reflex. She heard Lono hum contentedly in the back of his throat and looked across at him. He straightened his back in his sleep and pushed all four paws out, stretching. He arched his neck back, his legs quivering in satisfaction, then he suddenly let out a small cry and pulled his legs back in. He curled on top of them and threw Mac a sheepish glance as if embarrassed that she might have seen. She thought about the cry, wondering if he had something else going on besides the sinus infection. She'd checked his temperature before she started work on the poodle and it was lower than when Dr. F had taken it so she assumed the cephalexin was kicking in. Maybe he was just achy, she thought, the way she got when she had the flu.

She lifted the drill and went back to scraping. She really liked how quickly Lono had fit in at the clinic. Not only did everyone love him, but he never got in the way, unlike other dogs the staff would bring in. That surprised her because he was almost always at Dr. F's heels, trotting along beside him from station to station. She kept expecting him to trip someone or get trodden on, but it was as if he could see one move ahead of the rest of the staff and dance out of the way before that happened. Mac chuckled; had she just made Lono an honorary staff member?

The poodle's body jumped again. Mac moved on to the next tooth wondering why Dr. F hadn't asked her to schedule a relief vet for tomorrow? She might have been able to find him someone other than Dr. Murphy, someone who could work the morning with him so he could take care of the MPL. But then often, if it was a vet who'd never worked at the clinic before and Dr. F was around, they'd pester him with questions about protocol and Mac knew that made him edgy. "I bring them in to save me time, not to cost me time," he'd complain. She imagined he'd called Dr. Murphy after he'd hung up with his lawyer, thinking she already knew the protocol of the clinic, and when she'd said she couldn't work the morning he'd told her to come in anyway for the afternoon and then tried to talk Carly into covering the morning with him. Mac sighed; it was going to be a long few weeks at the clinic with Dr. F juggling his divorce on top of everything else. And if the set of his jaw was any anything to go by when Carly said no, they were going to be weeks when it might be hard for him to stay positive.

She peered at the poodle's teeth; they looked clean. She switched off the drill and wiped them with some dry gauze. She wished there were something she could do to help Dr. F, she thought as she stood up, untying the bandage holding the endo tube in the poodle's mouth.

The doors to treatment pushed open and Carly trudged in groaning, her head slumped forward, her shoulders down, like a kid being made to do homework.

Mac laughed. "Whaddaya need?" she teased. "A martini? An Irish cabana boy? A nap?"

The young vet shook her head. "I need to do an endoscope. Can you help me with that?"

"I can. Yes."

Mac hung the endo tube back on the oxygen machine and waited for the poodle to wake up.

"It's for the Yorkie in exam 1," said Carly pulling a tie out from the pocket of her scrubs and capturing her long locks in a ponytail.

"I'll get Waylon to bring him back." Mac nudged the poodle. "What'll you be doing in your mom's kitchen?"

"Making salsa." Carly started down the hallway to her dad's office. "While drinking wine, I hope."

"Nice," said Mac and felt the poodle stir under her hand.

$$*****$$

When Leo walked into exam 4 Cedric was sitting in the corner by the examination table with Poppy on his lap. "Hi there," he said, dropping the Chihuahua's chart on the table. "We've got some kind of hitch in our giddalong, is that what's going on?"

"What's that?" said Cedric. He was in his midseventies, Leo knew, and retired now from his work as a chemist at the local refinery. He was tall and lean, with narrow, gentle features, and Leo really enjoyed him as a client even though there was something distant and strangely forlorn about Cedric. The old fellow's right hand caressed Poppy constantly, almost reflexively, his long fingers kneading her skin like a baker with his dough. The little dog stood for this, absorbing the massage like it was a private pleasure while nervously eyeing Leo.

"Poppy's having trouble walking?" Leo asked.

"Not since the last time," said Cedric.

Leo hesitated, wondering if he meant that as an answer or not. "Which was when?"

"What's that?"

"When?" Leo repeated.

But Cedric's eyes drifted to a spot above the floor, his mind elsewhere, his hand palpating Poppy.

Leo flipped open the Chihuahua's chart; maybe he'd find something helpful in there. He felt fruitlessly for his cheater glasses in the top pocket of his teal scrubs; then he reached up and found them in his hair. He propped them on his nose and read his notes in the blissfully quiet room. It felt good to have a moment when he wasn't being peppered with questions or demands, when he couldn't hear the phone ringing or the animals complaining about being left out in the wards. He found the information that he needed; Poppy had been in before for IVDD. He slapped his hand down on the chart and pushed it across the table, drawing Cedric's eyes back to him, then he asked loudly, "Did this come on all of a sudden, Cedric?"

"Yes. She looked at the stairs yesterday and didn't want to come up them."

"And did you see anything happen that would have made her leery of the stairs?"

"What's that?"

"Did she fall? Or jump off the couch?"

"She always comes up the stairs," said Cedric, his hand still fondling the skin on Poppy's back.

Usually Leo got nine tenths of his diagnosis from listening to what the client said about the patient but he'd forgotten how bad Cedric's hearing was. Or maybe it wasn't this bad the last time he came in. He glanced at Poppy's chart; that was six months ago. Cedric's hearing could well have deteriorated in the past six months. He decided to try a different tack. He smacked twice on top of the hollow-sounding surgical steel. "Okay, why don't you put her on the table," he said.

"You want her up there?"

"I do, yes." said Leo with a strong nod.

Cedric unfolded his long legs, leaned forward, and gently placed Poppy on the table. Then he sat back, folded his legs the other way now, curling the entire front of his foot around behind his shin, and went back to gazing off at nothing. The room hushed again, perfect for Leo to listen to Poppy's heart rate. It was not elevated. He pulled off his stethoscope and gently moved Poppy's head from side to side, looking for the stiffness that might indicate her intervertebral disk disease had returned, but it moved easily, without any noticeable distress to the dog. He felt her abdomen, waiting to see if she shook; she didn't. He switched his focus to her rear legs, flexing them both and listening for that ominous clicking sound, which would indicate she'd torn her ACL. "Did you notice if she was favoring one of her legs?" he asked Cedric, when he didn't hear anything.

"Her legs, yes."

"All of them?"

"That may be why she didn't want to come up the steps," said Cedric.

Leo moved on to Poppy's hips and Cedric's eyes wandered away again. Leo stared off at the wall as he rolled each hipbone gently in its socket, trying to find something out of place. He kept hearing John's voice, telling him that he'd arrived at work to a message from Sheena's lawyer rejecting their counter proposal. He hadn't sounded too bothered by that but then his voice had become heavy. "There is something else," he'd said. He wouldn't say what exactly. Just said that they should meet again as soon as possible. Or maybe he had said, because Leo remembered the words motion and finances and support but the weight in John's voice when he'd said, "There is something else," had so soured the inside of Leo's stomach that he couldn't focus.

Leo heard a soft "humph" and glanced at Cedric. He was still staring off into space, having an unspoken conversation with someone, trusting Leo to take care of Poppy. Leo felt sad watching him. How could he be sure that Cedric would trust Sheena the same way if she became the vet here? And if he didn't, what would happen to Poppy? Suddenly the silence felt treacherously uncomfortable, like it might encourage all his private fears out of hiding.

"Can you put her on the floor for me?" he said, not having found anything amiss in Poppy's hips or legs. "Let me see her walk?" He held his palm open down toward the floor

"You want me to put her down?"

"Yes, please."

Cedric leaned forward, picked up his dog and set her on the floor.

Leo waited for her to move, but Poppy just stared indignantly at him. He stepped out from behind the table, crouched, making encouraging kissing sounds for her to come to him. Poppy trembled. Cedric bent forward and pushed her butt with his hand. "G'won," he said. Poppy propelled forward a few steps, and Leo could see that her gait was stiff, a sign that her IVDD might be recurring.

"Okay, you can pick her up now," he said, bouncing back up and returning to the chart on the table.

Cedric reached down and scooped up Poppy.

"It says here that last time she had this we gave you a bottle of carprofen," said Leo pointing at his notes. "But you brought it back. Do you remember why?"

"Is it the same as last time?"

"I think so yes," said Leo. He looked at Cedric, pulled off his glasses and dropped them on top of the chart. "And I'd like to put her on carprofen but did she have a reaction to the medication last time? Is that why you brought the bottle back?"

"You put her on meds last time," Cedric told him, massaging Poppy's back again.

"That's right. Carprofen," said Leo.

"I don't remember what they were called," murmured Cedric to himself, his eyes drifting away again.

Leo opened his mouth to tell him then decided an example might be quicker. "I'll be right back," he said and scooted out to find one.

*****

Mac and Carly were following the lens of the endoscope on the screen when Dr. F burst through the doors to treatment like a bird through an open window, looking for a way out now that he was in. Mac could see him out of the corner of her eye and she turned slightly away so he'd know she was busy right now. As she shifted she noticed Lono sit up in his bed across the room and tilt his head looking at Dr. F as if wondering what was bothering him.

"There's some definite inflammation in the stomach," Carly murmured, pointing at the screen.

"Do you want a photo of that?" Mac asked.

"Please."

Mac pressed the button on the control panel. There was a small electronic hum and the photo slid out. She tore it off and turned around to look at Dr. F.

"Can you get me some carprofen?" he said.

"Sure. Just let me finish here," she answered, pointing at the endoscope.

Apparently that wasn't the answer he wanted. "Where's JJ?" he went on.

"Outside, trying to get the Doberman to poop before she goes home."

She watched him process that information then he asked, "What about Waylon?"

"Can you get that, too?" interrupted Carly, pointing at the screen again.

Mac turned and looked at what she was indicating then pushed the button for another image. "I had to send him out to the hardware store because we needed light bulbs for surgery," she told Dr. F.

"You sent *both* vet assistants out at the same time?" he grumbled.

Mac stayed calm. "JJ's not *out*," she explained. "She's just outside with the Doberman."

"But that doesn't do me any good."

Carly flicked a look at Mac. "Go help him," she said, nodding.

Mac strode past Dr. F and took a bottle of carprofen out of the cabinet above the controlled substances' log in her alcove. When she strode back towards him she saw Lono trotting across treatment to get to him too. Once again she thought she saw the dog falter in his back end, as if he might be limping. But then it was gone just as quickly as she'd seen it.

"Why couldn't Waylon have gone for the light bulbs during his lunch break?" Dr. F niggled as she handed him the bottle of tablets. "I won't be in surgery till after lunch."

"Well for one thing," said Mac, feeling her easygoing nature being more than a little tested. "Because Waylon's lunch break is for his lunch. And for two, because I thought you said you wanted to do the amputation before lunch."

She watched his mouth drop open and she knew she'd got him. Then it closed again and tightened, as if he was laying for her.

Pema slipped inside the door. "Dr. F," she said but before she could go any further, he lifted his hand into the air as if to silence her.

"I know. Louisa Miller," he rapped out without turning around. "I'm getting there."

"Erm," said Pema, her face pinking up. She grimaced her embarrassment at Mac and Mac responded with a reassuring nod for her to continue. "Mr. Wong is here with his Lab," said Pema.

"*Now?*" barked Dr. F. He spun around and looked up at the clock above the doors behind Pema. "It's almost ten already."

"*Dad!*" Carly complained from her spot by the endoscope.

"No, but clients need to be told to bring their pets in by nine," Dr. F justified to his daughter as Pema's face went from pink to red. Mac saw him open his mouth to continue when Lono stepped forward and kissed the fingertips of his right hand. The vet looked down at his dog and closed his mouth. There was a long pause then he turned back to Mac. "Can we still fit the Lab in?" he inquired, sounding much calmer.

"What's he here for?" she asked Pema.

"Neuter."

"Then I don't see why not," said Mac going back to the endoscope.

"Good," said Dr. F.

Mac heard the door swing open and closed and figured he'd fled before he could get in any more trouble.

*****

"Okay," said Carly as soon as he was gone. "What's making my dad act like a turd?"

Mac shrugged as if she had no idea.

"Well I'm going to talk to him about running marathons again. This time with me," Carly said, pulling off her mask and giving Mac a devilish smile. "I'm done here by the way."

Mac watched her walk off in the direction of Dr. F's office and noticed that Pema was still standing by the door looking uncomfortable. "Find out if the Lab has eaten anything today," Mac told her as she pulled the endo tube out of the Yorkie. "And if the answer's no, buzz me and I'll come talk to Mr. Wong."

Pema's face relaxed. "Thanks," she said.

The side door beeped and JJ called out, "Okay, the Doberman can go home now."

"I'll call her owner," Pema offered on her way out the door.

Mac picked up the Yorkie who was already awake but still a little groggy. "I'm going to start prepping the Rottweiler for his amputation," she told JJ, who was heading back to the large animal ward with the Doberman.

"Okay, I'll help once I've got this one back in her kennel."

"Where's Lono?" asked Mac, seeing his empty bed as she crossed the room. But nobody answered. She looked around. Everybody had left. She glanced under the workstations but didn't see the little basenji anywhere. She rolled her eyes and opened the door to the small animal ward; like she didn't have enough to do chasing around after Dr. F!

*****

Leo pushed the door to exam 3 ajar then remembered that wasn't the right room. At least he didn't think it was. He took a half a dozen steps and put his eye to the peephole in the door to exam 4. There was Cedric, still staring calmly off into space with Poppy on his lap. Leo envied him the calmness. He was usually much better at compartmentalizing the different strands of his life so his personal crap wouldn't spill over into his professional life. He stepped back, almost knocking into Pema, who was skating behind him, on her way back to reception. He looked down and saw Lono standing beside him. "I'm not getting that right today, am I?"

Lono's eyes were gleaming up at Leo, caring and non-judgmental. "I know, I know," Leo went on in a tight whisper, not wanting to be overheard by anyone out in reception. "I was too harsh with Pema. But I need her to keep the clients in line right now."

The dog leaned forward and kissed the tips of Leo's fingers again. Leo started to decompress. He slipped the carprofen in the pocket of his scrubs, crouched down and ran both hands over the gloriously soft, coppery fur on Lono's back. The dog's tail swished through the air. "The thing is," he confided to the dog. "It feels like my schedule is crammed to overfull right now so I don't need anyone adding to that by trying to squeeze in clients that can't make it in on time." Now that he said it out loud he could hear how ludicrous it sounded. Mr. Wong's Lab had already been on the schedule for today and it wasn't Pema's fault that the client didn't make it in on time. What hadn't been on the schedule, Leo realized, was the early morning call from his lawyer.

He slumped to a sit, his back against the wall opposite exam 4, his left shoulder up against the shelf unit holding all the flea meds and ear washes so he was partly hidden from reception. He thought for a second in the quiet, his head tipped back, his eyes running over the ceiling. "What I need," he concluded with a big sigh, "is for someone to pack my schedule so the clinic won't fall apart when surgeries get tossed around by my lawyer. But I'm pretty sure there isn't a way to do that."

Lono crept forward and nuzzled Leo's neck, tickling him. Leo laughed, his spirit on the upswing. "You just made me feel two hundred percent better, d'you know that?" he told the dog. "I'll have to find some way to repay you."

At that moment a bunny hopped out of exam 3. Lono looked at it, then at Leo. "Yeah, not that way," said the vet, springing to his feet and shooing the bunny back inside the exam room. He glanced around for the owner then remembered she'd gone off to work. He saw where the bunny had eaten a hole through the mesh window on front of his cloth carrier to get out. "No wonder you're constipated," Leo whispered to the bunny before he closed the door to the exam room.

Lono was still sitting outside exam 4. "I'm glad you're feeling better," said Leo as he walked around him. He pointed at the door to the exam room. "But that still doesn't mean you can come in here, you know that, right?"

Lono looked past Leo's knees, straight out at reception.

Leo paused; he knew what the dog wanted him to do. "Okay, okay," he conceded finally. He turned and walked forward, his eyes on the smiling Mr. Wong. "Did your pup have anything to eat or drink today?" he asked, glancing down at the black Lab on the end of the leash.

"No, no," Mr. Wong assured him. "And I'm sorry that I ended up being late—"

Leo cut him off with a friendly wave of his hand. "It's not a problem," he said. "We'll be able to fit him in." He looked across at Pema. "Could you buzz someone to come bring him back?"

"I did already," she replied, back to her usual perky self.

"See," said Leo to Mr. Wong. "I have the best staff." He leaned across the counter and whispered to Pema, "And is someone coming for the bunny in exam 3?"

"Oh. I thought Waylon got him." She picked up the phone.

"Is that who's coming for the Lab?"

"No. Mac is."

"Great." Leo looked back at Mr. Wong as he started toward exam 4. "My vet tech will tell you everything you need to know."

*****

But Mac wasn't on her way out to reception. She had been but before she could turn the corner in the hallway she was stopped by the sound of Dr. F's voice. He was saying something about being too harsh with Pema and that he needed someone to keep something in line. His voice was low, like he was whispering, and even though Mac couldn't hear all the words, she could tell that they were heartfelt. She heard him mention his schedule and then something about not squeezing clients in. She didn't necessarily want to listen in to his conversation but, then again, she was curious about what had made him lose it with Pema. Even his worst days didn't usually include snapping at the staff. Mac wondered who he was talking to? She leaned slightly right, trying to see around the corner without being seen, and glimpsed Lono's tail swishing through the air and Dr. F's hands stroking the fur on his back. Of course he was talking to Lono. "How far that little candle throws its beam," she quoted in her mind.

"What I need," she heard Dr. F say more clearly, with a big sigh, "is for someone to pack my schedule so the clinic won't fall apart when surgeries get tossed around by my lawyer. But I'm pretty sure there isn't a way to do that."

Oh, there's a way, Mac thought to herself delightedly. She swung around and headed back into treatment to call Maisie's owner. If there was one thing she was good at, as resident queen of the football standard surgical tray, it was packing things so they wouldn't fall apart when tossed around.

Chapter 8

By six-thirty the next morning, Dr. F was holding the small orthopedic handsaw over Maisie's trochlear groove ready to cut down through the cartilage and into the underlying bone. "Will you look at that," he'd complained when he'd opened up the dog's knee and revealed the patella stuck off to one side of the groove where it was supposed to rest. Mac could see that the trochlear groove was not grooved at all but smooth and flat like a river rock. She could also see that Maisie's medial trochlear ridge was sloped down so when Maisie's patella had shifted inward, it had slid down that slope and stayed there. Ouch, thought Mac. She knew why Dr. F had complained; inbreeding had created the abnormal bone structure somewhere back in Maisie's ancestry but humans had decided they liked the look of the inbred dog and purpose bred more, creating generations of dogs with kneecaps that did not luxate the way nature intended.

Dr. F moved the orthopedic handsaw back and forth, incising down into one side of the trochlear groove with the care and precision of a master craftsman sawing the f holes in a violin. Mac mopped up the beads of blood with gauze after the doc withdrew the blade. She looked at Maisie's breathing; it was steady. The heart monitor beeped rhythmically, unintrusively, and Dr. F positioned the blade on the other side of the groove to repeat the process.

Once he got both sides, he laid the orthopedic saw down on the surgical tray and said, "If I haven't said this already I am very grateful that you set this surgery up to happen before clinic hours."

"You have. And you're welcome," said Mac, handing him the bone chisel. She grasped the femur and tibia so the leg wouldn't move while Dr. F hammered into the cartilage between the incisions. "And honestly, it wasn't that big a deal. The client even said it helped her out, because she could get to work on time if she dropped Maisie at six instead of seven."

Dr. F kept tapping the bone chisel until a small length of cartilage lifted like a tiny wedge of pumpkin from a Halloween carving. "It helped me out, too," he admitted, moving the chisel to the exposed bone underneath the cartilage. "I was worried I wouldn't be able to get to it."

"I know," said Mac. "You should've just said that's what you needed."

"I didn't know I'd need it before John called yesterday," he explained. He bent over and tapped the end of the chisel again, gently chipping away at the surface of the bone. "And then after he called I couldn't think straight to see this as a possible solution."

"Will this be the only time we need to come in early this week?" asked Mac.

"What d'you mean?"

What she wanted to ask was why his lawyer had called yesterday but she knew if she was that direct she might never find out what she really wanted to find out; which was what impact was the divorce going to have on the clinic? After all, Washington was a community property state, which meant that Sheena was entitled to at least half the clinic. Was the doc going to have to sell it to give Sheena her share? Mac knew she might have to brush up her résumé if that was the case. Unless he planned to open another clinic. He'd already done that once before, fifteen years ago, and had taken Mac with him when he'd made the move. She'd move again if that was what he needed.

"I guess I mean are you seeing your lawyer again this week?" she asked. "After today?"

"Not that I'm aware of," he muttered. He paused, looking down at the bone as if assessing whether he'd removed enough of it, and then added, "But I'm sure I'll find out more this afternoon."

Mac waited even though she wanted to probe more. She knew that if he was going to tell her, the impetus would have to come from him, not from her asking him.

He must have decided the bone looked sufficiently lowered because he laid down the instruments, picked up the small wedge of cartilage and slipped it back in place. It now fit so the trochlear groove had a solid dip throughout the center. "Okay, flex it for me, please," he said.

Mac made Maisie's leg bend and flex, bend and flex, as if she were operating a hand pump. The patella moved up and down the groove the way nature had intended. Dr. F nodded his satisfaction.

He picked up the bone chisel again. "Sheena rejected my proposal for the separation of our assets apparently."

Uh-oh, thought Mac.

"That's why John called. She has something else in mind."

"Like what?"

He bent forward and started chiseling the insertion point on the tibia to remove a bone chip, which he would then pin back to the tibia in a different location to prevent the patella tendon from wanting to twist inwards again. Mac knew she should get him the pin he needed but she was waiting for his answer. She felt like they were on stage and he'd dropped his line. She wanted to prompt him only she didn't know what the line was. She stared at the blue and green Seahawks surgery cap covering his hair and pierced through into his brain with her eyes. *Tell me!* she insisted wordlessly.

He glanced up, as if he'd heard her, and said. "Sheena wants the clinic." Then added, "Kirschner pin, please."

Mac heard him but she couldn't move. What did he mean, Sheena wanted the clinic? All of it? So he'd be out of work?

He finished chiseling and shot her a questioning look. "The pin?" he said.

She swung around to get what he needed out of the drawer but her mind was still reeling. It was one thing to have wondered what she would do if she had to find another job but it was another to hear her fears confirmed. She couldn't just leave his statement hanging. She couldn't. "Are you going to have to sell the clinic? Is that what Sheena wants?"

"Nope. She wants to run it."

Mac froze, her hand over the packaged medical equipment. "As the office manager?" she said finally, pulling out the pin he needed.

"Nope. She's going to become a vet."

"*Sheena is?*" exclaimed Mac. She ripped open the blue plastic packaging and dropped the sterile pin onto the green drape.

"That's the threat," he said. "And I'm supposed to keep the clinic warm for her while she gets her degree."

"Are you going to?" Mac balked, thinking this was a very bad idea.

"I don't want to," he admitted. "The notion of me doing what I do here for the next five years—or however long it takes her to get her veterinary degree—just so I can hand it all over like some spoils of war makes me want to close up shop and run." He deftly pushed the pin down through the bone chip into the tibia creating a ridge that would keep the tendon aligned over the center of the trochlear groove.

Mac was racing through possible solutions in her mind, trying to find one that would allow the clinic to stay open without Dr. F feeling like he was being emasculated. She handed him the cutters for the excess pin. "Why does Sheena want to become a vet?" she said.

"I have no idea," he replied.

She hadn't really expected an answer. If there was one thing Mac knew from all her years of being around Sheena, it was that she was a hard woman to figure out.

Dr. F snipped off the end of the pin, handed her back the cutters and said, "Can you move it again for me, please?"

Mac lifted and lowered Maisie's leg. The patella luxated smoothly up and down the trochlear groove but she was hardly noticing. All she could think about was how everything that had defined her for the past twenty years would suddenly be over if Dr. F had to walk away from the clinic. "That looks good," she heard him say somewhere off in the distance. Her mind was stuck on the idea of Sheena expecting him to play nice with the clients so she could have them when she was ready for them.

"I'm sorry to drop that on you," interjected Dr. F, pulling her back to him. She stopped flexing Maisie's leg and looked into his eyes across the table. They were filled with kindness and understanding.

She sighed: now for the other thing she didn't really want to have to talk to him about. "Talking of dropping things," she said, and saw his eyes cloud with concern. "Did you spill a bottle of tramadol by chance?"

"No. Why?"

"I can't make my log tally with the number in the bottle. But I'm only a few off so I thought maybe one of us had dropped the bottle and then not picked them all up."

"Have you looked?"

"As much as I can," she said. "But I also need to ask Dr.

Murphy. She may have forgotten to enter what she prescribed in the controlled-substance log."

Dr. F rolled his eyes the way she knew he would and shook his head in exasperation. "Relief vets," he groused. "Like I don't have enough to worry me."

"'When sorrows come, they come not single spies / But in battalions,'" Mac quoted.

"So my lawyer would have me believe. Okay, let's get this sutured," Dr. F announced, glancing at the clock on the wall above the counter. "I brought Venus down with me today and I'd like to take her out for some quick play time before my first appointment."

*****

JJ walked into surgery while Mac was suturing Maisie's skin back together. "Did you do surgery already?" she asked.

"Yep."

"Why so early?"

Mac kept her eyes down on Maisie's incision. "He's got a lawyer's appointment this afternoon."

"Oh. You okay?"

There was a long pause while Mac tied off the suture and snipped the end of it. Her emotions had mushroomed from shock to anger but she didn't want to dump that on her friend. She took a deep breath and made eye contact with JJ. "Sheena wants the clinic in the divorce."

"So she can sell it?"

Mac gave a small shake of her head no. "She's going to become a vet."

"A *vet?*" JJ paused and the word hung in the air like a bad smell. "What in the world . . .? I thought she didn't even like *him* being a vet—"

"Me too."

"So why . . .?" JJ trailed off, her face scrunched up in confusion.

Mac empathized. She'd been equally confused. She'd had a little more time to process the information, however, and had come up with a possible motivation. "The only thing I can think," she said, her shoulders relaxing into the repetition of her hand movements, "is that Sheena wants to get inside Dr. F's head somehow." She stopped and looked over at JJ again. "You know how he can be unreachable when his head's full of the next thing; maybe she needs to live that to get it out of her system. Like they say some people have to do what was done to them to purge themselves of the memory?"

JJ contemplated this for a second, then said, "Nah. I think she wants to get inside his head by showing she can do this better than him."

Mac couldn't argue with that. She'd noticed how competitive Sheena had become with age. She went back to her rhythmic suturing rather than let herself get angry again.

JJ hustled toward her and started throwing the surgical instruments that Dr. F had used into a stainless steel tray. "Have you got any idea what this might mean for us?"

Mac shrugged. "I don't, no. I think—from what he said—that she wants him to keep the clinic till she's qualified to take it over and then, well," —she flapped her hand in the air away from herself— "take his leave."

"What's he say to that?"

"He'd rather take his leave right now."

"I don't blame him. I'd run the clinic right into the ground if I had to hand it over to Sheena 'cause that's all she's gonna do with it."

"You think?"

"I do. I can't see her caring about the clients and the patients the way he does. She's more about the money."

"So you're thinking she'll raise the fees—?"

"—and drive away the clients. Yep. Especially if she can't make nice with them the way Dr. F and Carly do." She picked up the small trashcan and started to toss squares of bloody gauze into it. "Hey, here's an idea," she went on. "Maybe Dr. F could turn the clinic over to Carly. She probably wouldn't mind working for her mom. Or even *with* her mom. And I'm sure Sheena would love working with Carly."

"Well her dad certainly does," murmured Mac. She stopped suturing as the significance of the words she'd just uttered hit her. "Maybe *that's* behind her bid for the clinic," she said. "Sheena's jealous because Dr. F's working with Carly!"

JJ looked skeptical. "That's a lot of schooling for a little jealousy," she suggested.

"I had rather be a toad / And live upon the vapor of a dungeon / Than keep a corner in the thing I love / for others' uses," quoted Mac.

"Ooo. Nicely put, Mr. Shakespeare." JJ put the trashcan back on the floor and began to gather the soiled gowns and drapes. "So what are we gonna do about all this?"

"I'm thinking I'll get out my cauldron," said Mac.

"Whip up some eye of toad for Sheena?"

"Something like that." Mac tied off the last of the sutures, cut the ends and then dropped the rat-tooth forceps and needle drivers in the stainless steel bowl. "I'm just hoping that Dr. F keeps us in the loop so we can make our exit before the curtain comes down."

"Hmm," grunted JJ. She started for the door with a bundle of green cloths in her arms. "I might not wait for the curtain. I've got kids to feed. I might get me a new outfit from the thrift shop and see if that spay and neuter clinic across the river needs any vet assistants." She turned back and looked at Mac again. "I'm going to start a load in the washing machine. Does Dr. F have any other surgeries this morning?"

"Nothing scheduled, no. But we have an Irish wolfhound coming in that's got a problem with his penis. That might be surgical."

"The Horovitzs' dog?"

"Clement, yes. How'd you know?"

"They were in the parking lot when I came in the side door."

"Oh. Will you see if the Emergency Clinic sent over his X-ray?"

"Sure."

"And JJ," Mac said as her petite assistant started backing out the door with the laundry. "Let me know if the spay and neuter clinic needs a vet tech."

*****

Leo walked out of surgery and over to the sink to wash up. He hadn't really wanted to tell Mac that he might lose the clinic in the divorce but he also didn't want to foist any unplanned surprises on her. But now that she knew, he was worried she'd look for work elsewhere. And he couldn't do what he did without her. Why did Sheena have to put him in this bind, he grumbled to himself.

He heard a whine and knew it was Venus standing on her back legs, her front paws balanced on the top of the baby gate over the entrance into his office, her tail rocking behind her. It was almost seven and all the lights were on in treatment and out in the hallway so he guessed Pema had arrived. He pulled some paper towels down from the roll above the sink and ambled toward his puppy. "You want to go out for a walk?" he asked, drying his arms in a spiral motion.

Venus ruffed once, her tail rocking harder behind her. Leo looked between the workstations at Lono. The basenji was still curled up in his bed, watching Leo but not moving to join him on a walk. And he definitely knew the meaning of *that* word.

Leo tossed the paper towels in the trash and walked over to Lono. "Are you still not feeling great?" he asked the pup, crouching to pet him. "I noticed you were moving more slowly." He stroked the dog's head.

"Hi, Dr. F," said JJ passing beside him to go into the large animal ward.

"Hi, JJ," Leo replied, distracted.

"Is he doing okay?" he heard Mac ask him.

Leo stood up and turned to face her. She had Maisie lying across her arms to go back into a kennel. "I'm not sure. His temperature was back up to 103.5 this morning."

Mac frowned and he knew she was wondering why. "I'll ask Dr. Murphy later if she noticed the same thing with Kent," she said.

"I'd appreciate that."

"Of course. And just so you know, Eugene and Frieda Horovitz are out in the parking lot. Frieda called my cell this morning and said she thinks Clement broke his penis."

"His *penis?*" said Leo, surprised. This would be a new one for him.

"I brought his X-rays up on the viewing station," JJ called out from the large animal ward.

Leo touched the keyboard in front of him and an image popped up showing the small tip of Clement's penile bone had broken off. He pulled down his medical bible from the shelf above the computer and let it land with a thud on the counter above Lono. He flipped to the index at the back.

"Apparently they took him overnight to the emergency clinic but she wanted to bring him to you for treatment."

Leo nodded his agreement. He'd been caring for Clement since he was a puppy and really enjoyed Frieda and Eugene. Plus he'd never done a broken penis before.

Venus whined louder and Leo stopped looking at the index, spun around, walked back between the workstations, around the charts' table and slipped through the baby gate. Venus skittered along beside him as he strode down the narrow corridor, past his bathroom and around the corner into his office. He snatched his deep-red sweatshirt, supporting his alma mater, off the back of his chair. He pushed his arms into the sleeves and zipped up the front, feeling in his pocket for her tennis ball. It was there. He reached out to pick up his phone off his desk but changed his mind before he touched it. Did he really want to find out that his lawyer had called him already today? Nope.

He swung around and unhooked Venus's leash from where it was hanging between medals from marathons he'd run more than a decade ago. "You know what we're going to have to do," he said, bending forward and rubbing the warm puppy fur on her torso in opposite directions. She wriggled ecstatically under his hands. "We're going to have to start running together so you can help me train to run marathons with Carly. She's got one in mind at Disneyworld. Doesn't that sound fun?"

He clipped her leash, hearing the side door beep in the distance, and walked her back down the narrow hallway and out through the baby gate. When he swung around, to head for the side door, he saw Frieda and Eugene Horovitz standing at the entrance to treatment, smiling across at him. Clement, their gangly Irish wolfhound, was standing between them.

"We hope you don't mind that we brought him in this way," Frieda whispered across to Leo. She was short and rotund with thick, curly, dark hair. Very different from her husband, who was a tall, stick insect of a fellow with just a few strands of gray hair stretched across his scalp. But for all their physical differences they both had gentle dispositions and both took the health of their dogs very seriously.

"We didn't want him to be embarrassed in front of the other patients out in reception," Eugene explained. He was carrying an IV bag of fluid that was attached to Clement.

"How's he doing?" Leo asked as he put Venus back behind the baby gate and unclipped her leash. She whined miserably but he bent forward, kissed her and whispered, "We'll come back to this. I promise." He pulled the tennis ball out of his pocket and bounced it down the hallway. Venus took off after it.

Leo hung her leash on the wall hook beside the staff schedule on his way over to Clement. He crouched in front of the gentle giant and made long, downward strokes on either side of the dog's neck. Clement's mouth was open, his head tipped up, as if he might catch more air for his lungs that way. He was definitely struggling.

"Well he's still bleeding, as you can see," said Frieda.

Leo glanced under Clement and saw some spots of blood on the floor. He tracked them to the side door. He stood up and looked directly at Eugene, then Frieda.

"So what happened?" he asked.

Frieda began the narrative. "Well, Eugene has this cot out in his man cave—"

"Only because someone gave it to me," her husband interjected, as if he didn't want Leo to think it was something he would ever buy. "I never use it."

"No but Clement does," explained Frieda.

"When I'm doing my carpentry work."

"I think he likes the music Eugene plays."

Eugene grinned. "I'm a big fan of the Beach Boys."

"Anyway, he was out there on the cot yesterday—"

"In the afternoon. I was finishing up this shelf unit I've been building for Frieda's yarn and stuff."

"And I went in to get him—"

"Clement that is," clarified Eugene.

"Yes, Clement, so he could go for his pre-dinner walk with Judy. Our poodle." She pointed back to the side door. "We left her out in the car."

"And as soon as he saw her with his leash, he started to climb down from his cot," said Eugene.

"Only it has a metal frame on it—"

"A metal frame with springs holding the canvas," explained

Eugene. "I put memory foam on top of the canvas inside a nice cover Frieda knitted for Clement."

"Only Clement doesn't move so easily anymore and when he got down his front legs must have gone out from under him and he caught his . . ." Frieda swallowed hard, her dark eyes shifting left and right as if worried she might be overheard. *"Potty part,"* she muttered.

"In the tight gap between the metal and the canvas," Eugene finished for her.

"That's what we *think* anyway."

"We didn't know what he'd done at first," Eugene went on. "Because he let out this huge screech and we couldn't see anything wrong but, of course, we didn't think to look at his—" He glanced at Frieda.

"Potty part," she interjected. "But then, when we took him out for the walk," she continued, "we noticed that he didn't . . ." She stopped, and looked at Eugene, as if not sure how to say it.

"He didn't go number one," Eugene told Leo.

Leo nodded.

"But we thought it was because he didn't need to."

"Did he look like he wanted to?" asked Leo.

"What do you mean?"

Leo searched his mind, wondering how to be discreet about asking if the dog cocked his leg. "Did he walk up to a tree?"

"Oh yes. More than one," Frieda assured him.

"But nothing happened?" asked Leo.

"Nope," said Eugene.

"Not a drop," said Frieda.

"I thought it was because he's getting old," Eugene went on.

"He's how old again?" asked Leo.

"Ten," said Frieda.

Eugene leaned forward and whispered to Leo. "And you know how it gets for us guys as we get older."

"Eugene!" chided Frieda.

Her husband chuckled. "Well it does."

"Anyway then later last night, I saw drops of blood on the carpet in our bedroom. I said, 'Eugene, Did you cut yourself?'"

"And I said, 'No. Not that I'm aware.' But I checked," he told Leo. "Just in case."

"His hands and his feet," Frieda added quickly. "Not his . . . you know."

"Well, no, not that!" Eugene said looking at his wife. "I mean I would know if *that* was bleeding."

"So we followed the blood trail—"

"And found where it went to on . . . you know,"—he waved his free hand over the front of his pants—"Clement," he finished. Then he grimaced. "That had to hurt."

Leo nodded; he could imagine. "So he spent last night at the Emergency Clinic?" he asked.

"Yes because you weren't open that late," Frieda answered. "And with it bleeding we didn't know what to do."

"Well you did exactly the right thing," Leo assured them. "Did you see the X-ray at the Emergency Clinic?"

"No they didn't show us anything. They just said they thought it was broken."

"The small tip broke off," explained Leo, walking them over to the computer. He touched the keyboard and brought up the image. "But I think I can put a suture around it to hold it in place while it heals."

"But you'll give him an anesthetic before you do that, right?" asked Eugene, clearly worried. "Because if not,"—he rocked his eyes left and right—"*Ouch-ie.*"

"Yes, we'll *definitely* give him some gas," Leo reassured him. "Because by definition this is a surgical procedure. And we'll keep him overnight. What I need you both to do when he comes home is make sure he doesn't chew on it."

Frieda's face flushed red.

"The suture I mean," amended Leo.

"Can't you put some tape over it?" she asked.

Leo hesitated. "Erm . . . not in that location, I wouldn't think so, no."

"That would be ouchie times two," Eugene explained to her and this time his face flushed a little red.

"We'll take good care of him," Leo assured them. He took the IV bag from Eugene and the leash out of Frieda's hand and passed both to JJ. "Would you take Clement into the ward, please," he said.

Then he stretched his left hand out and guided Frieda and Eugene toward reception.

*****

By the end of the morning Mac could feel the tension in her lower back. She watched Dr. F take off for his Rotary lunch and decided to get herself a cup of coffee from reception after she got Clement back in the ward. She'd prefer a massage, she thought as she and JJ hefted Clement down onto a blanket on the floor in surgery, but she'd settle for a cup of coffee. A cup of coffee and some lunch would be ideal. Chad had packed her pork dumplings in a thermos and she was really looking forward to eating them. "You ready?" she asked JJ.

"Yep."

They each grabbed two corners of the blanket, lifted Clement a few inches up off the floor, and started shuffling toward the door.

"You want me to clean up in here?" JJ asked, the strain of hefting Clement apparent in her voice.

"No. I'll do it," said Mac. She took another breath and added, "I'm getting some coffee first though."

She backed out through the door to surgery and held it open with her foot. JJ scuttled through it.

"Can you get me a latte?"

"I'm not going out," Mac grunted. "Just to reception."

"Okay," gasped JJ.

They carried the dog into the ward and set him down on the blanket inside his kennel. They both paused, to catch their breath again, then JJ crouched and rubbed Clement's forehead, encouraging him awake.

Venus whined and scrabbled against the door in a kennel two doors down. Mac stopped in front of her on her way back out. "You could have stayed in his office," she told the golden retriever, "if you'd have left Mary Jo alone to do her work." She tickled the pup's nose through the openings of the wire-mesh door, then walked back out into treatment. Venus yipped her dismay.

It was almost noon by the clock above the door. Dr. Murphy was late again but Mac didn't care. Her body was beginning to warm to the fact that it was no longer hunched over in concentration. She'd done two sets of dental work after Maisie's MPL as well as pinned down a dog who needed an ear examination but didn't want his ears touched, changed bandages, prepped vaccinations, and then assisted Dr. F when he sutured Clement's penile bone. She still had to go over her controlled-substance log again, but for now, all she wanted to do was hold her head upright and not think of anything.

She started to hum the tune to "Be Our Guest" from *Beauty and the Beast* as she pushed through the door to treatment and breezed around the corner, headed for reception. It looked empty except for Pema, who was sitting in her office chair behind the counter, scribbling something in the appointments book.

"You know you have a voice like melted chocolate, right?" she said as Mac came up alongside her.

"I do?"

"All warm and rich and yummy."

"Stop. You're making me hungrier than I already am," Mac said, although the compliment had fed her a great deal.

Pema lifted her chin and nudged her eyes over Mac's shoulder as if indicating someone was behind her. Mac swung around and glimpsed the top of a baldhead on the other side of the turtle tank. She leaned right and saw an elderly man sitting in one of the chairs against the sidewall, his head tipped back, his eyes closed, his mouth slightly open as he snored softly. She wondered that she hadn't woken him, talking to Pema, but then she glimpsed the hearing aids curled around his ears. Maybe he had them turned off. There was a little girl on the chair next to him. She was maybe seven or eight years old and had her arms wrapped tight around a cage on her lap. Her eyes were puffy and red, like she'd been crying, and she glared at Mac when she caught her looking at the cage.

Mac turned back around and whispered to Pema, "What's going on with them?"

"No, I put it on the shelf over here," said Pema, jumping up out of her seat and leading Mac away from the counter.

Mac followed without question, knowing this was code to get them to a place where they could talk more privately. Pema trotted a few steps down the hallway and tucked herself in beside the shelf unit of flea meds and ear washes. "The little girl's pet rat is in that cage," she whispered. "with a big tumor on its leg that's stopping it from walking. That's what the grandpa said. He's the one out there with the girl."

"So he wants us to remove the tumor?" whispered Mac.

"No, that's the thing. The grandfather doesn't want to spend any money helping the rat 'cause it's old." She gave a little, nervous laugh. "He wants it put down."

Mac thought about the girl's puffy eyes and the way she'd glared at her. She guessed the little girl didn't agree with her grandpa. "How old's the rat?" she asked Pema.

"Three and a half."

Mac giggled.

"What?" said Pema.

"Just the way you said 'and a half.' So earnest." She chuckled again.

"That's how the little girl said it," explained Pema and then apparently got the humor too, because she also chuckled.

"Okay," said Mac, returning to business. "When Dr. Murphy gets here, I'll have her look at the tumor."

"The grandfather doesn't want to wait. He said his granddaughter's on a very strict eating schedule so he needs to get her home for lunch." She leaned in closer to Mac. "I think he's the one that's on the eating schedule though."

"All right," sighed Mac. "Let me go see if Dr. Murphy's arrived yet. If not, I guess I'll text Dr. F for permission to do the deed."

*****

The short blonde with the infectious laugh wasn't at the Rotary lunch that Leo could see, and he was disappointed. Not only had he been looking forward to lunching with her again but he'd been toying with the idea of asking her out. After all, if Sheena was hiking with some other guy then he figured that gave him permission to avail himself of a little company.

He picked up one of the white china plates at the end of the table holding the buffet and smiled at the young man serving the food.

"Roast beef or chicken?" the server asked, the plastic hair net over his beard crinkling as he spoke.

"Beef, please," replied Leo.

"Do you know how this works?" came a woman's voice over his right shoulder.

Leo twisted to see if the voice was talking to him while the server speared some slices of roast beef onto his plate. He saw a slender, fair-haired lady who looked to be in her late forties. Although she could have been younger. Or older, he supposed. He smiled at her. "I've been here before, if that's what you mean," he answered.

"Potato salad?" asked the server.

"Yes, please," said Leo with a nod. He smiled at the woman again and saw her shoulders relax, as if he'd made her feel more comfortable by talking to her. He noticed her gently weathered olive complexion and the dark brown of her eyes and eyebrows, and guessed she wasn't a true blonde. "What do you need to know?" he asked, looking down at the chicken and salad on her plate. She obviously didn't need help with the buffet.

She pointed out at the numerous round tables spaced across the floor in the main room of the Historic Museum, where the Rotary Club always held its luncheons. "Do I just sit anywhere, or do we have assigned seating?" she asked.

"I think you're supposed to sit next to me," said Leo.

The woman's eyebrows popped up; then her smile widened. It was a warm smile of a soul at peace, and Leo found himself feeling vicariously more peaceful too. Like he was standing in a sunbeam. "As long as you don't mind taking this newbie under your wing," she said, bringing him back to the present with the movement of her lips.

"Not in the least," declared Leo. "Just let me finish getting my lunch." The server put some green beans and a roll on his plate; then he walked to the end of the buffet, lifted a knife and fork out of the utensil tray and a napkin off the pile. "Come on," he said, motioning with his head for her to follow him.

"I'm Leo, by the way," he said as he led her to an empty round table.

"I'm Joan," said the woman. "Joan Doherty."

They set their food and drinks down next to each other and sat, immediately making themselves comfortable. Leo picked up his fork and dug it into the potato salad. "I take it this is your first time at a Rotary lunch?" he said to Joan.

"Here, yes," she replied, buttering her soft roll. "But I did go to a couple of Rotary lunches in Seattle a few years ago. They were set up more formally than this, with people wearing name tags and such, so when I walked in here today, I thought—*Uh oh! Now what do I do?*" She chuckled as she swung toward Leo and added, "So thanks for helping me out."

Leo had been looking at her hair. It was blonde, but it had a luminescence to it, as if she'd added glitter to a hair dye. He dropped his eyes to meet Joan's when she swung toward him, but she must have caught where he was looking, because she said, "It's an interesting color, isn't it?"

"It is, yes. And I'm sorry if that's rude. I didn't mean to stare."

"No, no, I don't mind. I appreciate that you're honest with me. Some people that I catch looking at it try to lie their way out of it, and I think, *why?* It's just a wig."

"Is it?" said Leo, overtly staring at it now.

"Uh-huh. See?" Joan flicked the scalp side closest to Leo up, and he could see her baldness underneath it. "Cancer," she said, in answer to his unasked question. "I figured if I had to lose all my hair, I may as well get a wig with a bit of sparkle to it." She lifted her buttered roll and took a small bite out of it, the edges of her mouth curled up in a smile.

Leo watched her, thinking how she already had a bit of sparkle to her. He was curious to know more. "Is your cancer in remission?" he asked.

"It is. And so am I," she said with a definitive nod. "I have a new leg and a new head of hair, so I decided to get myself a new life to go with them."

"A new leg?" Leo remarked.

"Uh-huh. I had a sarcoma and had to have my leg amputated, so my son—who's only nineteen—says to me that he's been reading about prosthetics made on 3-D printers, and if he can find a way to get me one, can he design the cover for it?"

"And did he?"

"What?"

"Get you one?"

Joan grinned. "He did. And he drew a comic strip about a dragon on it."

"So I can read your leg," said Leo, impressed.

"Only if you buy me lunch."

Leo laughed.

"Would you like to see it?" asked Joan.

"If you don't mind."

"Not at all. I love showing it off." She pulled up her right pant leg and showed Leo a hard plastic prosthetic that reproduced the shape of a lower leg with black-and-white drawings of a dragon on it. Where the dragon was supposed to be talking, the artist had added the only color on the drawings: orange to suggest flames around the speech bubbles.

"That's *cool*," exclaimed Leo, fascinated. "I've read about 3-D printer prosthetics, but I've never seen one. Can I touch it?"

"Oh, you'd have to buy me dinner for that," teased Joan.

And Leo roared with laughter.

*****

When Mac walked back into treatment she was immediately hit by the aroma of food. It smelled good—warm and spicy. She followed her nose to the break room. She heard a loud beep as she went through X-ray and found Waylon opening the door to the microwave. "Have you seen Dr. Murphy?" Mac asked.

"Uh-uh, not yet." Waylon pulled a plate out of the microwave that held a hefty mound of something smothered in tomato sauce and cheese. "Leftover Mexican," he said lasciviously.

"Mmm," murmured Mac. She bustled out of X-ray and peeked through the door to surgery, looking for Dr. Murphy. She wasn't there, but Mac was reminded, looking at the operating table, that she still had to clean up from Clement's procedure.

She pinched a pair of latex gloves out of the box and pushed through the door, tugging them on. She picked up a small, square garbage can labeled "NO POOP PLEASE" and glided around the operating table, tossing used gauze pads into it as she contemplated the upcoming auditions for *Mary Poppins*. She'd had a busy couple of months it seemed, between performances of *Antony and Cleopatra* and rehearsals of her lead role in a new play that was going to open soon at the community college. Did she want to keep up this pace by auditioning for the winter musical? That was the question.

She put the garbage can back on the floor and began making neat loops in the heart monitor cords, quietly humming "A Spoonful of Sugar." She'd never minded the grunt work of being a vet tech. In fact, she thrived on it. Especially when she could be alone in this room, with its cool acoustics, and see the Disney version of her chores playing out in her mind.

She pushed the mobile oxygen machine back from the table and started dropping all the instruments onto one tray, her shoulders canting from side to side as she sang the words to the song in her head. Her humming seeped into every corner of the room, like the smell of good soup in a kitchen, and before she knew it the surgical instruments were flying through the air into sealed sterile bags, then dropping into place in the drawer. Mac spied some small drops of blood on the floor under the operating table and pushed a towel into them with the tip of her toes. Then she bent down, scooped the towel up, and spun once, twice, in tight chorus-line circles to drop it theatrically in the pile by the door.

"'That a spoonful of sugar . . .'" she sang to herself as she toe stepped back across the room and lifted the instruments tray off the operating table. "'. . . The medicine go down,'" she sang out loud.

"Mac," Pema said from behind her.

Startled, Mac dropped the tray she'd just picked up, and all the harmony in the room disappeared in a deafening clatter.

"Oh, I'm sorry," said Pema, rushing toward Mac. "Was that my fault?"

"No," said Mac, looking down, mystified, at the surgical instruments on the floor.

"What's the matter?" asked Pema.

Mac looked from the instruments to the drawer, then back. "I'm just wondering how they all got in the tray?"

"Didn't you put them there?"

"Did I?" Mac looked at the concern on Pema's face. "I thought I snapped my fingers and they all magically tidied themselves away . . ."

Pema's lips wrinkled into a smile now. "You're such a good actress."

"But not such a great witch, I see," Mac replied. She bent down and began picking up the instruments. "Has Dr. Murphy arrived yet?"

"No. And the guy out front woke up and says he doesn't want to wait any longer."

"Okay," sighed Mac, standing back up and pulling off her gloves. "I'll go text Dr. F."

*****

Joan pulled her pant leg up even farther and showed Leo the mechanics of her leg as he ran his fingers over the hard plastic, feeling the connectors for what would be the knee on this prosthetic. He could visualize many different uses for this kind of 3-D prosthetic in animal care.

"Your son's very talented," he said as he sat back up in his seat and let Joan drop her pant leg down again. "Is he considering making a career out of his artwork?"

"His artwork *and* 3-D prosthetics," Joan answered. She tore another piece off her buttered roll before she continued. "And that's where my new life comes into it." Leo raised his eyebrows in interest and Joan went on. "I worked in PR down in Seattle, in a firm that had a lot of contracts with some of the Pacific Northwest megabusinesses, and my life was all about climbing the ladder of success. Then I got diagnosed with this sarcoma, and none of that career stuff seemed important anymore. Especially when I started to get that sixth sense that the firm might let me go as soon as my chemo was over. My son, Justin, who was eighteen when I was diagnosed, in his final year of high school, put his social life on hold so he could research these 3-D prosthetics, and I saw that and thought about the things that mattered to him. Things that I'd denied him because . . . well, because of my own emotional pique, I guess is the truth of it."

She pushed some salad onto her fork, looking down at her plate, and Leo felt poignancy in her aura. He waited for her to go on. Joan ate a mouthful of greens and then continued.

"He'd always wanted to live closer to the mountains, closer to his dad, and I'd never made that a priority. So we started coming up here between my treatments, just to get a feel for the area, and found a lovely little property with a small home on it and a large workshop, just outside Mount Vernon. By that time Justin had passed on his opportunity to go to the Art Institute to study graphic design and was talking in earnest about making a career out of designing 3-D prosthetics, and I said, why not? I got a *huge* price for our home in Seattle, plus a golden handshake from my PR firm—who *did* want to let me go—and I thought, *Why not invest it in a business for Justin?* So that's what I did. I bought a state-of-the-art 3-D printer and some fancy computer system that I don't really understand, and Justin loaded it with CAD software, and he's making and drawing on prosthetics in the workshop on our property. And I'm using my PR skills to try to market them." She speared some grapes from her salad onto her fork and smiled at Leo. "That's why I'm here, of course. Trying to make those business connections."

Leo nodded as he chewed some roast beef. His mind was turning the possibilities of 3-D printer prosthetics in the surgeries he did on small animals. He'd read about them being used for animals, but he'd never actually seen or met anyone in the industry. He wondered how much a printer-generated prosthetic for a dog, say, would cost. Whether it would be a viable option for his clients. He'd have to learn how to attach it to the bone, of course.

His cell phone buzzed in his pocket. He pulled it out and glanced at the text on the screen: *Can I euthanize a 3 yr old rat w/ tumor that's dragging? Belongs to a client's granddaughter.*

"Would you excuse me for a minute?" he said to Joan, holding up his phone.

"No, go right ahead," she replied, forking some more salad into her mouth.

Leo texted back—*yes*. Then he slipped the phone back in his pocket and turned to Joan again. "Sorry," he said. "That was work."

"Oh. What is it that you do?"

"I'm a veterinarian. Small animals."

"As opposed to . . . ?"

"Large animals." Leo could tell by her expression that she didn't get the distinction. "Horses and cows and such," he said. "I deal mostly with cats and dogs."

"Vets don't do all animals?" asked Joan, as if this was something she hadn't considered.

"No," replied Leo. "That's a common misconception, though. Perpetuated by the movies, if the ones I've seen are anything to go by." He drank some water from his glass before going on. "Vets tend to specialize anymore. Some like to go out to the farms and help with the livestock, and others, like me, see people's pets."

"And what made you want to help cats and dogs?"

"A horse."

"O-kay," said Joan, seeming amused. She lifted a chicken wing and started to nibble on it.

"I know, it sounds strange," Leo admitted. "But that's exactly what happened. I was nineteen—maybe twenty? I forget—but I *do* remember that I was trying to impress a girl. She liked horses, and even though I had no idea what I was doing, I agreed to ride with her—and the horse threw me. And there I was, lying on the hard ground under the blazing-hot summer sun over in Eastern Washington, wondering if I could get up as sore as I felt . . . and the horse came back to check on me. And I remember looking up at him and thinking—*yeah, this is all right.*" Leo's head nodded at the memory of the epiphany that changed his life. "That's when I decided I wanted to be a vet," he told Joan. He pronged two beans with his fork and pushed them into his mouth.

"Sounds like a calling," said Joan.

"I suppose. Yes."

"And does it?"

"What?"

"Call to you? I mean, do you miss it when you're away from it?"

"Does it call to me?" Leo repeated, thinking about the question as he watched Joan drop the clean chicken bone onto her plate and wipe her fingers on her napkin. "Well," he ventured, "I like it, of course. I like the work very much. But I also like to think of myself as more than just a vet." He shrugged. "I guess I don't want my work to be the only thing that defines me." He narrowed his eyes, wondering if what he'd just stated was true. "On the other hand," he went on, "animal care is pretty much what I think about most of the time. So would that make it my calling? I don't know. When I'm away from it, like on vacation, I do find myself getting a little antsy to get back."

"Why's that?"

Leo considered this as he ate another mouthful of potato salad. What *did* create that feeling in him? "It's the animals," he declared.

He'd been staring out the window opposite him at Mount Baker, her broad, snow-covered shoulders and flat top sitting high above the agricultural fields, but now he turned back to face Joan, to watch her reaction to his explanation. "There's a connection I make with them the minute I put my hands on them. I find relationships with animals so uncomplicated. Much less transactional than relationships with humans. They have their needs." He held out his hand and ticked them off with his fingers. "Food, water, shelter, exercise—but even if we don't meet those needs, they're still willing to give us every ounce of their love to help us feel right with the world. Because that's their mission: to take care of us, not the other way around. And usually I step in when they're not being able to meet this mission because they're not well." Leo put both hands out now and cupped them as if he were holding a Chihuahua. "I touch them to find out why they're not well, and it's like they infuse me with a little of their ability to feel right with the world. As a thank-you. Which sounds transactional, I know, but it doesn't feel that way. It feels natural, unbidden. Like walking through a field of wildflowers and getting pollen on my pant legs." He put his hands back in his lap. "That's what connects us," he finished up. "So tight that I believe all the animals I care for belong to me, and I'm just letting their owners borrow them. So of course I worry about them when I'm not around them."

"That must make it so hard for you when you have to put an animal down," said Joan, her dark eyes brimming with compassion.

Leo felt a catch in his breath. "It does, yes." He immediately changed the subject. "How about you? Do you have any pets?"

"Not anymore," Joan answered. She had just finished her salad and set her fork down, then wiped her mouth with her paper napkin. "It was hard to have pets, living in the city. We tried a dog at one point because Justin really wanted one, but we couldn't keep him."

"Maybe now that you're living in the country you can try again."

Joan crumpled her napkin between her fingers. "Maybe," she said.

Leo pushed his plate away and slipped his elbows onto the table. He scanned Joan's face, seeing the lines of her past, her pains and her joys, worn so easily there.

"I'm just not sure I'm ready to go through that again," she confessed, making eye contact with him. "You know, loving an animal, then losing it. How do you cope with that, caring for animals the way you do?"

Leo looked out the window at Mount Baker again. If there was one question he didn't have an answer for, it was that one.

Chapter 9

Mac hovered by the door to treatment, waiting for Waylon to hang up the phone. She could tell from his end of the conversation that he was talking to a doc; she just didn't know which one. She was hoping whoever it was would save her from having to make that little girl out in reception look unhappier than she already looked.

"Was that Dr. Murphy, perchance?" she asked, bouncing the knuckles on her thumbs together like steel balls in Newton's cradle.

"Uh-uh, no," said Waylon as he put down the receiver. "It was Carly. She's coming in, apparently."

"How soon?" said Mac, jumping at the possibility of an out for herself.

"I don't know. She didn't say. But I got the impression it wouldn't be till later. Why? What are you trying to avoid?"

"Putting down a rat."

"Oh."

Mac's stomach growled loudly.

"Was that you?" asked Waylon.

"Uh-huh. I need my lunch."

"And your stomach's *gnawing* at you?" teased Waylon. "Get it? Get it?"

"Yes, very funny," said Mac, giving him a testy look even though she did find it amusing. She changed direction, deciding to get this over with. "Will you bring the rat back for me?" she said, heading for the safe to get the blue stuff.

"Sure."

"Where's Lono?" asked Mac, suddenly noticing his absence. He would have helped her through this.

"I moved him in with the cats."

"Be-cause . . . ?"

"Dr. Murphy might bring her dog in again."

"Oh right. And you don't want Lono reinfecting Kent."

"Well, I was kinda thinking of Lono getting reinfected, but yeah, sure, we can go with Kent."

Mac chuckled. "Don't you like Dr. Murphy's dog?"

"No, I like him. It's Dr. Murphy I'm not sure about."

"I thought you said she was great!" countered Mac, surprised.

"When she first got here, yeah," said Waylon. "But then she started closing the door on me when she was with clients, like she didn't want me in the room . . ." He dropped his head, embarrassed, and he suddenly looked very young to Mac. "I don't know," he muttered. "There's just something about her."

"Ah," sighed Mac. "'Love is not love / Which alters when it alteration finds.'"

"Whatever," scoffed Waylon. He picked up the two prescriptions he'd just labeled and put them in the basket by the chart stand. With his hand on the door, he asked, "So where is our death-row rat?"

"Ouch," said Mac, not liking that image at all. "In reception."

She walked around and unlocked the controlled-substances safe, pulled a twenty-one-gauge needle out of the drawer, and half filled it with the blue stuff. The rat wouldn't weigh very much, but it was better to be sure. She relocked the safe and was just about to cross to the wet sink when Waylon pushed open the door for the old guy and his granddaughter.

"There she is," announced the grandfather, pointing across at Mac. "That's the lady who says Lily has to be put down."

Mac couldn't move. She felt like a deer in headlights, standing there holding the needle loaded with Fatal-Plus. And the rat's name was *Lily*! she thought miserably. Her stomach hurt.

"Why?" asked the little girl, her eyes filling with big watery tears.

"Because Lily's got that bad lump on her," said the grandfather.

"Why can't she do an operation to take the lump away?" asked the child, one of the tears escaping and running down her cheek.

"It's too expensive."

"I have my allowance. I can pay for it," argued the little girl.

Mac hated this part. It wasn't so much the suffering animals that made euthanasia so hard; it was seeing the grief in their owners. She still couldn't make herself move.

"Honey, the lady said Lily *has* to be put down," the old guy explained, lifting the cage out of his granddaughter's hands. He opened it and took out the rat.

Mac could see that Lily's perfect white fur and little pink feet were marred by an ulcerated tumor ballooning from her belly up her left front leg. It was possible one of the vets could remove it, but at Lily's advanced age, it was risky. Maybe the grandfather would let his granddaughter hold Lily while Mac put the gas mask over the rat's nose, so she could see how the rat would get very relaxed and not even notice what Mac was going to do after that.

She tried to make her mouth move to suggest that, but the old fellow already had the rat down in front of his granddaughter. "Say goodbye to Lily now," he said.

The child's chin wobbled as she fought to hold in her emotions. She tickled the top of the docile Lily's head and then let everything explode out of her. "I *hate* you!" she sobbed at Mac and tore out of treatment without looking back.

The grandfather gave Lily to Waylon and started after his granddaughter. "Thanks," he said back to Mac, with a wink and a thumbs-up.

Mac wanted to let her emotions explode, too, but she caught Waylon watching her pityingly, so she swallowed them instead.

"Dr. Murphy just pulled in," he told her. "She could do it if you want to get your lunch."

"Yeah," said Mac, feeling sorrow like heartburn in the center of her chest. "I'm not hungry anymore."

*****

The sun disappeared behind a barrage of dark, thunderous clouds. Leo watched them step across the sky, slowly crowding out the light until the afternoon mirrored the darkness inside him. He wondered if there was a direct correlation between the weather and his mood inside his lawyer's office because last time he was here it was as stormy outside as it was inside his head. Today was no different. He was listening to John describe the monthly allowance Sheena wanted put before a judge even before they got into mediation, an allowance for "living expenses" she claimed when Leo knew damn well that it was for her payroll. It was making him wish very bad, very dark things on her.

He'd asked Mac once how she was able to play characters with murder in their minds when she wasn't that kind of person. "We all have that potential," she'd explained. "We just have to get pushed in the right way. So when I'm playing the character, I try to imagine what in my life would push me to that point."

Leo hadn't really gotten it at the time, but he did now. Not that he wanted to murder Sheena. But he wouldn't mind if somebody else did. He snapped away from the pillows of black in the sky and forced himself to focus on John again.

"If we could offer her a monthly sum now," his lawyer was saying, "before anyone twists your arm, I think it would look very good at the mediation."

"I'm already paying her $3,000 a month," said Leo.

John jumped his hands up off the conference-room table and did a double take at Leo. "You are? Why didn't you tell me that?"

"Because it's none of your business!" snapped Leo. He immediately pulled back. "I'm sorry. I'm sorry. I didn't mean it to come out that way."

"It's okay—"

"No, it's really not. And it's not who I am at all—"

"I understand."

"—but I don't feel like I should have to expose my every move when I'm *trying* to do the right thing."

"I get it," agreed John. "But the court needs to *know* you're trying to do the right thing."

"Should I bring them in a stool sample, too?" griped Leo.

John burst out laughing, and the sound bounced off the walls in the quiet room, thawing the hard spot that had begun to set up in Leo's chest. He heard himself chuckle.

"Okay," said John, coming down from the humorous interlude, "I'll respond to this document with a letter saying that you're already providing for Sheena, although it would be very helpful," he specified, giving Leo a meaningful look, "if you could give me some proof that you've been making these payments. Hopefully you wrote her checks . . ."

"I did," said Leo. "I can get my bookkeeper to pull up images of the checks from my bank statement if you like."

"Perfect. And if you have proof that they were cashed, that would be awesome."

Leo pulled his phone out of his pocket to text Mary Jo and something fell on the floor. He bent forward. It was Joan Doherty's card. He slipped his fingers underneath it and read her name as he pulled himself back up to a sit. Then he stopped, caught off guard by a sudden thought. He slipped the card and his phone back into his pocket and levitated out of his seat.

"I'm sorry," he told John, "but I have to go check on my dog."

"Is he out in the car again?"

"No, he's at the clinic, but he was running a fever this morning, and it's just occurred to me that it might be connected to his leg."

"His leg?" queried John. "What's going on with — ?"

But Leo was already halfway out the door.

"Don't forget to e-mail me those check images—" was the last thing he heard before he slammed the door closed behind him.

✶✶✶✶✶

Mac walked out of treatment with a handful of gauze pads and some chlorhexidine. She crossed the hallway to exam 2 and hesitated outside the slightly ajar door. She could hear Dr. Murphy's voice, low and soft. Muted almost, as if she didn't want to be overheard. She was probably cooing to the Lab, Mac thought, to calm him down.

She eased the door open and saw Dr. Murphy explaining something to the tall, bearded, heavyset guy who owned the Lab. Her back was to the door, her arms spread out, her dark, wavy hair bobbing along with her animated speech pattern, and Mac could tell by the way the guy was looking at her that she had his full attention. *"She's beautiful, and therefore to be woo'd; / She's a woman, and therefore to be won,"* Mac quoted in her mind.

". . . no, but that's what I'm saying," Mac heard as she slid in behind her. "When I get my own—"

The Lab's owner's eyes flicked toward Mac, and Dr. Murphy spun around to see what had caught his attention. Her mouth stopped moving and she looked awkward, guilty almost. Like she'd been caught doing something she shouldn't. Mac suddenly felt uncomfortable, excluded. Was this what Waylon had meant when he'd accused Dr. Murphy of closing him out?

If that was the case, she thought as she put the antibiotic flush and the gauze swabs on the examining table, then what kind of conversations could Dr. Murphy be having with clients that would make her want to exclude the rest of the staff?

*****

Leo parked right in front of the side door to the clinic and hopped out of his Jeep, moving with rapid determination. "Where's Lono?" he called out, when he saw the dog wasn't sitting in the hallway to greet him. He did a double take; he wasn't in his bed either. His anxiety ramped up a notch.

"Oh hi, Dad," said his daughter.

Leo looked at her blankly. "What are you doing here?"

"Nice to see you, too," Carly shot back, her eyes big like his when he was making a point.

"I just want to know where my dog is," he informed her.

"Well, you don't have to bite my head off to find out."

Leo didn't know what to say to that. He just wanted her to answer his question. She must have picked up on his internal apprehension because her demeanor toward him changed. Her look softened, and when she spoke, she enunciated clearly, the way she did when she was trying to reassure a client.

"I only got here about fifteen minutes ago, but there haven't been any emergencies that I know of. And I don't know where Lono is, but I'm betting"—she turned around and pointed at Waylon as he walked into treatment—"Waylon does."

"Waylon does what?" the vet assistant asked.

"Know where Lono is?"

"Oh sure. He's in with the small animal ward."

Leo spun around and peered through the window in the door to the small animal ward as he grabbed the handle to go in. He could see Lono sitting on the other side of the door looking up at him. How dogs could foresee their owner's arrival was still a mystery to Leo, but every time he was privy to it happening, it impressed the heck out of him.

He pulled the door open and Lono stood to greet him, his head tipped up, his breathing steady and his tail swishing excitedly through the air. "You don't look nearly as bad as I feared," declared Leo. He crouched down and tickled the fur on Lono's head. He still felt warm but not nearly as warm as earlier. Plus the ward was stuffy, Leo noticed, with all the kennels full of patients. He fumbled to find a thermometer in the pocket of his scrubs, then realized he wasn't wearing his scrubs. He reached forward to examine Lono's left rear leg but an arm slid across his back and he turned to see Carly crouching down beside him. She tipped her head down to rest against his shoulder and kept her arm around him, holding him in a loving embrace. It was the first affection Leo had received from another human in a while, and it felt good. He reached across with his left hand and gently cupped her face, tipping his head down to rest on the top of hers.

"Is he okay?" she asked.

"Seems it."

"So panic abated?"

"I should take his temperature, but I think so, yes."

"Good." She stood back up and Leo followed suit. "You know, we would have noticed if something was really wrong with him."

"You're right." He looked at her. It suddenly occurred to him why her presence at the clinic had confused him. "I thought you weren't coming in today."

"I wasn't. But then Mom and her friend couldn't get to the trailhead because of trees across the road, so they came back early. They're going to hike someplace in BC next week, apparently. So I came in for the rest of *today* because Mom wants me to cover for her then."

"It's not going to be next Tuesday, I hope, because you'll be at the conference in Florida with me then."

"I know," she said, a little testy as if he should know that she knew. "Stop fretting, Dad. I'm on top of it. Thursday is the day next week Mom wants me to cover for her, and since I'm usually off Thursdays, I said yes."

"Hmm," grunted Leo. He glanced down at Lono again, who was sniffing at the pocket of his sweatshirt with intense focus and alacrity. Leo reached for the tennis ball in his pocket then remembered he'd thrown it over the baby gate for Venus earlier. "Why is he in here anyway?" he asked Waylon, who was standing behind them in the open doorway.

"Oh. Because Dr. Murphy was coming and I thought she might bring her dog, Kent, again."

"And she didn't?"

"No, I did," said a cheery voice behind Waylon.

The vet assistant backed up, and Leo saw an attractive woman wearing dark-blue scrubs.

"But I left him outside in my car." She reached forward toward Leo with her right hand. "I'm Kelly Murphy," she said.

"Oh hi!" said Leo, stepping out of the ward and shaking. Her hand felt tiny in his, her grip confident. "A fellow Irishwoman," he said, smiling back.

"That's an interesting juxtaposition of genders," laughed Dr. Murphy.

"Hey, I'm trying to be PC here."

"Actually I'm not Irish. Murphy is my ex's last name. I kept it after the divorce because we have twin daughters together and I didn't want my name to be different than theirs."

"How old are your daughters?"

"Seventeen."

"That's a good age. At least it was for my daughters."

"Maybe for you," joked Carly. "I don't remember it being that good."

Leo laughed. "This is one of my daughters," he told Dr. Murphy.

"Yes, I got that," she said. "And thanks for coming in today and helping out again," she told Carly. She looked at Leo, squirming a little like a naughty child. "I'm sorry that I've ended up being late both times I've worked for you. You must think that I make a habit of it, but in my defense I couldn't find the clinic the first time, and then today I thought I was expected at one thirty, not eleven thirty, 'cause that's what Mac told me on the phone."

Leo glanced at Mac, surprised that she would make such a mistake. She was labeling a prescription, but he caught her eyes lift and treat Dr. Murphy to a scathing look. Fortunately Dr. Murphy was bending toward Lono, who had dodged out of the ward with Carly and taken his place next to Leo.

"And who is this little guy?" she crooned.

"This is Lono."

"Lono, as in the owner of the dog bed that was under the counter last time I came in?"

"That's the one," said Mac from her alcove.

"Well, it's good to meet you, Lono," said Dr. Murphy, reaching out and fondling the top of the basenji's head. He sprang away from her, tipped his head back, and yodeled. The high-pitched sound filled treatment and started the dogs in the large animal ward baying.

"Oh my," laughed Dr. Murphy again. "Does he greet everyone like that?"

"No, I think he must reserve it for you," chuckled Leo. "The only other time I've heard him do that was the last time you were at the clinic."

"But I didn't meet him then."

"But he smelled that Kent had been in his bed," Mac informed her as she stepped away from her alcove and dropped the paper from the back of the label in the recycle bin. "And maybe because he caught Kent's sinus infection," she added before continuing on out the door.

Leo saw Carly lower her eyes to the chart in her hand.

"Oh no! Did he?" exclaimed Dr. Murphy, looking mortified.

"We don't know that for sure," Leo responded. He knew Mac felt justified in pointing the finger at Dr. Murphy for Lono's infection, but he couldn't—and wouldn't—go there. "Lono got drenched by the rain last week, so that could be what's behind the infection. Plus he seems to be on the mend." He looked at his daughter. "Makes me embarrassed that I came charging back here. I wonder what signal I thought I was picking up on?"

"Maybe he needs to pee," said Carly.

"Has anyone taken him out today?"

"I don't think so," she replied.

"I haven't," added Waylon.

"You want me to do it?" asked Dr. Murphy. "Try to get back in his good graces?"

"Dr. Murphy," Pema said from the doorway. She was holding up a chart. "Can you see a Dalmatian that's having trouble standing up? I put him in three." She shifted right to let Mac come back into treatment and spotted Leo. "Oh hi, Dr. F. Do you want to do the Dalmatian?"

"No, no, I'll do it," said Dr. Murphy, touching his hand with her fingertips. "You go walk your dog."

Leo followed her partway across the room and watched her take the file from Pema. He was suddenly conscious of Mac's eyes on him and wondered why he'd walked this far. Then he remembered. "Is Venus in my office?" he asked, taking her leash down from the hook next to the staff schedule. He heard a yip from the large animal ward and smiled. "I guess not."

"I'll get her if you like," offered Mac, already on her way to the ward.

"And then could you bring up the X-rays for the Jack Russell with congestive heart failure in exam 2?" Carly requested.

"Sure," said Mac.

"Thanks." Carly scooted around her dad saying, "I thought if I left the client alone for a moment, she'd say her goodbyes and we'd be good to go, but she's changed her mind."

"It's really hard for some owners to make that decision."

"Oh, I get that," agreed Carly, moving toward Pema. "Totally. So I'm going to show her his X-ray. Maybe that will help."

"Do I have anything else pending?" Leo asked Pema before she followed Carly out of treatment.

"The spay you did Saturday is back in."

"The dachshund?"

"Yes," said Mac coming back into treatment with Venus.

"What's up with her?"

"She was in heat when you spayed her, remember?"

Leo nodded. Venus bounded up to him and stepped on his toes. He bent down, petted her, and clipped the leash on her collar.

"Well a dog tied with her once she got home and now she's bleeding from the vagina." Mac explained. "You want this, too?" she asked, showing him a tennis ball.

"Thanks," said Leo, sighing. He pocketed the ball mentally berating the clients who couldn't seem to contain their pets after surgery. "Okay," he said, starting for the side door, Lono sniffing his pocket again and Venus sniffing Lono. "Remind me to take Lono's temperature when I come back in if you would." Then he pulled the hood up on his sweatshirt before bracing the rain with the dogs.

*****

Mac found the X-ray Carly wanted on the computer and double-clicked it open. She heard Carly's voice behind her and turned to see the young vet coming in through the doors to treatment, leading two women wearing hijabs. The younger of the two women was cradling a Jack Russell wrapped in a cream-colored blanket, and drawing in rapid, staccato breaths through her nose, as if she'd just been sobbing.

"I can give him three more of Lasix, yes," Carly was murmuring to the young woman as she led her to the viewing station. "But that won't be enough for him to make it through the night. If you look at his X-ray," Carly went on, pointing at the screen, "his lungs are full of fluid. So you'll end up having to take him to the Emergency Clinic for his final moment because we won't be here after six."

Mac saw the client start to cry again. She grabbed a couple of tissues from the box on the counter and handed them to her, then went and pulled a thermometer out of the drawer for Dr. F. "But won't that give me a chance to watch one more movie with him cuddled on my lap?" she heard the client ask.

Mac glanced back and saw Carly lean forward and stroke the Jack Russell under his chin with the same kind of compassionate tenderness her father exhibited in this situation. She felt her own eyes well up with tears and hastened away, putting the thermometer next to Dr. F's pile of charts before pushing through the door.

"You might get that," she heard Carly concede. "But he's really struggling to breathe—"

The door swished shut behind Mac. She knew from the film on the fourteen-year-old Jack Russell that he wasn't going to make it through the night, and she really didn't want to have to put him down. Puck, her own Jack Russell, was almost thirteen now, and Mac didn't want to be reminded that it might not be long before his "little life" would be "rounded with sleep." She decided to go get herself the cup of coffee she'd been wanting earlier.

She rounded the corner in the hallway and heard Dr. Murphy in exam 3, consoling the client with the Dalmatian. Mac had picked up on the chemistry between her and Dr. F; they may have thought they were hiding it, but Mac was good at reading body language. And theirs said they liked each other.

She doubted Dr. F would act on the attraction, but on the other hand, he was pretty vulnerable right now. And human. She was glad that his mood had lightened, though. This morning he'd been wearing worry lines like he'd slept in them, and now it was like he'd had a shower and a shave and a complete change of heart. If anything, Mac felt a little jealous. She wouldn't mind a little mood lightener herself right now. Maybe she'd call Chad, she thought. *After* she'd gotten some coffee in her.

She walked past Pema, who was entering something into the computer, and out to the coffeepot. Her shoulders sagged when she saw that it was empty. Then she realized that reception was empty, too. A nice, big empty space in which she could do anything she wanted.

"Sun roll!" she announced.

"Really? Here? In the middle of reception?" said Pema as she danced around the counter to stand next to Mac.

"You bet. I need to loosen up my back and give myself a bit of a wake up."

"Okay," laughed Pema.

The two women bent forward in the center of reception and touched their hands to their toes, then quickly unraveled, thrusting their ankles, knees, hips, torsos, and finally arms up toward the sun. Even though there was no sun right now because of the rain.

"That felt good," said Pema.

Mac smiled. It still impressed her that of all the staff members she'd shared her theatrical warm-ups with, Pema—the shyest— enjoyed doing them the most. "Want to go again?"

Pema glanced out at the road leading into the parking lot, then over her shoulder toward the exam rooms. "Sure," she giggled.

They repeated their sun roll with Mac letting out a loud

vocalization as she threw her arms up into the air. "Oh, that's much better," she said, tugging her scrub top back down from where it had gathered above her boobs and straightening it over her narrow waist. "I came out to get some coffee, but I think the sun rolls did the trick." She pointed across at the coffeepot. "Plus you're out anyway."

"Oh, but I'll make more," Pema reassured her, walking over to pick up the coffeepot. "I'll bring you a cup when it's ready if you like."

"Thanks."

Mac walked back toward treatment wondering if she had time to eat before Dr. F would be back inside, wanting her to prep the Dachshund for a redo of her spay? The door to exam 3 opened as she walked past it this time, and Dr. Murphy came out and fell in step beside her. The relief vet made a face like she regretted what she was about to say. "They have a beautiful Dalmatian in there that can't pull her hips up to a stand anymore. She's a lover of a dog and she's only three, but the owner knows she has to be euthanized."

Mac's stomach dropped. She felt like she'd avoided one trap only to walk into another. Her face must have shown it, because Dr. Murphy jumped right back in with, "I'll do it. I just didn't know whether I should do it in the exam room or in treatment. Plus which euthanasia med do you use here?"

"Fatal-Plus," said Mac quickly, before Dr. Murphy could change her mind. "It's in the safe—where I showed you the tramadol—but please remember to log what you take out."

Dr. Murphy winced. "I think I may have forgotten to do that with the tramadol."

Mac wasn't good at playing the heavy so she just lifted her eyebrows, to acknowledge the mistake, then pushed open the door to treatment. It was empty.

"Do you have the key to the safe?" asked Dr. Murphy.

"No, it's in the drawer right underneath," said Mac, pointing toward her alcove. "Make sure you put it back when you're done."

"Will do."

"And you can euthanize the dog here in treatment. With the client present if they want. Or not. Their choice."

"Okay, good to know," said Dr. Murphy.

Carly leaned into the room behind them. "Mac, are you available to euthanize this Jack Russell?" She was talking low, as if she didn't want to be overheard.

Mac's shoulders slumped. "I was thinking of getting some lunch," she said.

"I can do it," offered Dr. Murphy. "Since I'm already doing the Dalmatian."

"If you wouldn't mind," agreed Carly. "Only I have a feline bacterial infection in exam 1 that I need to get back to, and I don't want the owner of the Jack Russell to agonize any longer if she doesn't have to."

"Sure," said Dr. Murphy. "I'm happy to help."

She smiled and Mac thought she caught a little relief in the smile. Compassion washed through her for how hard it must be for anyone to be accepted into the tight-knit group that consisted of her, Dr. F, and now Carly. And to add to that, she'd been thinking negatively about Dr. Murphy ever since Waylon had said what he'd said, and she didn't honestly know why. Maybe she ought to forget Waylon's change of heart and go a little easier on Dr. Murphy.

She smiled back, and went in search of some pork dumplings.

*****

It was raining but not enough to dissuade Leo from walking the dogs around the back of the clinic and onto the adjoining, empty quarter-acre lot that he also owned. He'd bought it thinking he might extend the parking for his clinic out here but ended up preferring it as a place for the staff to walk dogs. The land was covered in tufted quack grass and a smattering of scraggly trees around the perimeter, but it also had a long stretch of river frontage and was far enough away from the main city road to feel peaceful. Maybe he could build a second clinic here, he thought, if Sheena got the existing one. Then he could compete from up close. But did he even want to compete, he wondered as Lono charged at the brush on the river side of the lot, heading for the water. "Lono, no," he called out. The dog stopped and tipped his head to one side, looking at Leo.

"I don't want you going down there," said Leo. "Just do your business up here." He motioned with his hand to the flat, grassy sprawl in front of them.

Lono stared at him, as if waiting for Leo to change his mind.

"No, we're not going down there," Leo insisted.

Lono looked down toward the river, then at Leo, then toward the river again.

"Come," commanded Leo.

Lono came, his head and tail down to show his reluctance. Leo unclipped Venus from her leash, and she leapt up and down in front of him expectantly.

"We're not playing right now either," Leo told her. "You're just out to do your business. Go," he said, throwing both hands up in the air. The dogs turned away from him and trotted toward the trees on the other side of the lot, Venus stopping and squatting partway across.

Leo felt himself smile as he thought back to the zing he'd gotten when Dr. Murphy had touched his hand. And the way she'd looked at him with those velvety blue eyes, making him feel special. Wanted. He wouldn't mind, he thought. But then again, at fifty-eight he knew these things were never as simple as the heat that fueled them. Sex was like glue, sticking people together who really had no business being together. And then, when they tried to pull apart, they tore at each other, leaving a bloody mess that was raw and ugly. And painful.

He glanced at the dogs; they were sniffing along the tree line. He turned back to the river, watching the raindrops make fleeting dimples on the cool-green surface. He remembered how intoxicated he'd been with Sheena when he first met her. How much she'd occupied his thoughts and made him hungry. Not just for her but for life. Like he'd wanted to conquer it so he could take back the spoils and see her smile. And she had smiled, often and beautifully. Had he stopped noticing her smile, was that what led to them ripping apart? Or was it that his spoils had become not enough, and she'd decided to show him how she could do better? In which case, why did she have to take his practice to do it? Why couldn't she start from scratch the way he had? Why—?

Venus burst into his thoughts, leaping up and down and bumping the pocket of his sweatshirt with her nose. Without thinking, Leo reached in and pulled out the tennis ball. The golden retriever's eyes became glassy, her focus entirely on the ball, and in one synchronized move, Leo hurled the ball across the lot and Venus took off after it. He saw Lono watch her from the other side of the lot. He could have undoubtedly beaten her to the ball but Leo noticed that he tended to cede the retrieving to Venus, enjoying just the chase when he had a mind to chase.

Leo turned away, leaving the dogs to their game, and walked toward the river. He really loved where he'd chosen to situate his clinic and couldn't imagine he'd find a better place if he had to go through this whole process again. He felt his stomach begin to act up again. Why did Sheena have to destroy him in the process of leaving him? She wanted her freedom; then fine, she could take it. But she didn't have to take everything he'd worked for. Or denude him of his ability to trust the way he felt about other women. If Dr. Murphy was interested in him, why couldn't he just yield to the pull and get himself a little company?

That was the problem, he thought; he was lonely. And he didn't want to start something just because he was lonely. Even if the woman did have Egyptian-blue eyes. He felt the ball bounce on his foot and snatched it up, hurling it again into the trees on the other side of the lot. A flash of gold sped after it as Leo allowed himself to think back to the feel of Dr. Murphy's fingers on his hand. He got another zing. Did he dare? he asked himself.

Before he could answer, there was a loud cry, and suddenly everything changed.

Part Three

Spike

It was coming back. At least, somewhere he got a passing scent of something that reminded him of her. He still wasn't hearing her thoughts, but he felt pretty sure those would come. He'd been so busy since he got here, helping the people around him with the things that *they* wanted, that he hadn't had time to just sit and pay attention to the ether. Watch all the molecules bumping and rolling against each other, some of them round, some of them flat, some of them pinpricks, some of them large and gelatinous, all of them moving in that never-ending mass of fluidity to get to their destinations with the messages they were carrying.

Eventually he'd get back to that, but for now he had to take care of his new boss. There was no point trying to bring back the past when the present needed so much work, he told himself. Fortunately he was in a good place now, and he liked the people around him. But he had a lot to do to take care of his boss's needs, and he wanted to do it well. He was *very* grateful for this chance he'd been given.

He'd get his moment to sit and zone out. But for now he would just have to be glad that a passing scent had rekindled her memory in his mind.

Chapter 10

The following Saturday Leo decided to play hooky from work. It had been one heck of a week, and he just couldn't bring himself to go in for the half day. He needed to go watch the training of future world champion performance horses at Rhodes River Ranch. He texted Mac that he wasn't coming in, took a long ride on Dreamer, showered, shaved, and then walked Venus down to her kennel. "I won't be late," he whispered to her as she whimpered at him walking away. He didn't want to leave her home, but this had to be Leo time.

It was the first day of October, and a balmy Indian-summer sun warmed the front of the Jeep as he drove it down the steep, curved driveway leading away from his house. It was just after ten o'clock in the morning, and even though his journey down the hill to the highway was uninterrupted by other traffic, he found a steady stream of vehicles heading upriver once he got to the highway. Leo didn't mind. He took the pause to mess with his phone and find the audiobook that Pema had downloaded for him yesterday. He hit "Play" just as a spot opened up for him to pull out onto the highway.

He didn't usually listen to things when he was driving,

preferring the company of his own thoughts, but with everything that had happened over the past few days, he needed to stop his brain from festering on the negative. A Robert Crais mystery would be a great way to do that. As he listened, his eyes feasted on the honeyed hues of the autumnal alders and maples scattered among the conifers on the mountain ridges on either side of the highway. Fall could often pass without a show in the Skagit because the rain would quickly tumble the dying leaves to the ground; but this fall was being more dry than rainy, and since the spring had been wet and the summer hot, conditions were perfect for eye-catching bursts of caramelized amber.

Most of the color was a distance away from his vehicle as he settled into a fifty-five-mile-per-hour groove alongside the river, but when he got to Rockport and followed the highway between the old-growth trees of the state park, he was treated to a sentinel trellis of translucent yellow, as if the leaves were holding the sunrise for him to pass beneath. It filled his spirit with warmth and made him glad he wasn't closed inside the clinic today. For all that he loved communing with the animals, sometimes nature could bring him back to center in a way that no creature could. What was it Wendell Berry said in his poem "The Peace of Wild Things?" Leo turned down the story he was listening to and ran the words through his head as he crossed the narrow green bridge over the Skagit River in Rockport: "For a time / I rest in the grace of the world, and am free." Today the world around him was certainly graceful.

He started down the more heavily shaded Highway 530, with the sapphire blue of the Sauk River meandering in and out of sight through the trees on his right, and glimpsed a field of blueberry bushes set back from the road on his left, their fall leaves and stems a striking copper red in the sunlight. Immediately he thought of Lono and how his coat would catch the sunlight in exactly the same way. It made him wish Lono were sitting on the seat beside him, looking out the window the way he preferred.

Leo turned the stereo in his Jeep back up and let Robert Crais transport him away from his thoughts again.

*****

Fifteen minutes later he slowed the Jeep and pulled in between the wrought-iron gates with the three Rs logo of Rhodes River Ranch. He continued on down the wide, curvy gravel driveway and turned to park in front of a large, barnlike building with a gambrel roof, tan siding, and red trim that had a sign above one of the doors for the restaurant. He eased his Jeep in between two Ford pickup trucks, noticing that there were quite a few other vehicles parked in front of the barn and even more parked over in front of the paddock; the restaurant had to be pretty full if the parking lot was this full at eleven already, Leo thought. Or was it eleven? He glanced at the clock on the dash of the Jeep; it was eleven forty. It must have taken him longer to drive here than usual. Mind you, he couldn't be sure what time he left, since he wasn't paying attention to the time, not wanting to be on the clock on his day away from work.

He turned the engine off and tried rolling the window up on his side yet again. It wouldn't budge. It didn't really matter, given how warm it was today, but if he didn't get it fixed before the fall really set in, then he was going to have to find a way to cover that eight-inch opening; otherwise he'd be a very wet driver. What bugged him was that he knew the window *could* move, because sometimes he came out and found it open wider than eight inches. He just couldn't figure out how. Or why. He sighed. He just had to take the moment to go to a scrapyard and find another scissor-type window regulator for his old Jeep because his had obviously become sloppy with use.

He climbed out and locked the vehicle, looking across at the passenger's seat, expecting to see Lono. He whirled around and strode over to the main entrance. He pulled open the glass door and took the few steps across the hallway to the elevator. The red door trundled open immediately, and he stepped inside and pushed the button for the second floor. He waited, feeling a little anticipatory excitement. It had been too long since he'd been here. The elevator bumped noisily upward and then stopped. The door opened again. Leo stepped out and immediately looked down at the indoor arena where the riders trained the horses. It looked like a skating rink with a sandy floor and a waist high wall on Leo's left, which opened out to a row of stables and a wide barn door. Where Leo was standing, behind three short rows of stadium seats with an open and uninterrupted view down to the arena, he could smell the unmistakable aroma of clean hay, a smell that he loved. To his right was the restaurant, which stretched the length of the arena and had large, sloping windows so diners could watch the horses without smelling anything other than the aroma of good food. The arena was empty at the moment but Leo knew it wouldn't be long before one of the trainers came out with a horse and he'd get to watch them work together.

"Is that my favorite vet?" a voice called out from his right.

Leo turned and saw a buxom woman with a wide smile, tight jeans, and cowboy boots coming toward him. She planted a wet kiss on his cheek and threw her arms around him in greeting.

"Hi, Angie," he said, returning her hug. He could smell her perfume, strong and citrusy, like her personality, and felt immediately at home.

"Are you here for lunch?"

"I was hoping," said Leo with a nod. His eyes scanned right, past the hallway, at the number of tables against the window already filled with people eating. "If you have a table."

"We will," she assured him. "Do you mind sitting here while you wait?" Her hand was out, palm up, indicating the risers directly in front of Leo. He didn't mind the idea of waiting there, but he was pretty sure Angie would be needed inside the restaurant proper, and he wanted to be where he could talk to her *and* watch the horses.

"Can I sit at the bar?" he asked.

"We can put you a stool to one side of the bar, sure," replied Angie. "You want a beer while you're waiting?"

"That would be great."

She slipped her arm through his and led him down a narrow hallway into the much wider restaurant. To their right was a small bar area with a doorway off to the kitchen, and in front of them were numerous dining tables, set up like angled parking against the sloping windows, so everyone seated had a view down to the horses. Angie's boots clunked on the high-polished wood floor as she walked Leo over to a stool next to the bar and left him to go deal with a staff question. He sat facing out, with his back to the bar, so he could watch the horses when they came out into the arena. Country music piped into the space through overhead speakers. Leo wasn't a fan of country music—it could set his teeth on edge as quick as a fingernail scraping down a chalkboard—but this music was on low enough not to bother him.

Angie returned almost immediately, carrying a frothy amber ale in a pint glass for him. She knew what he liked. She came around the counter and set it in his hands. "This one's on me," she said, easing her buttocks up onto the stool next to him. She propped her elbows on the bar behind her and looked out at the arena like Leo. "That way I feel justified making you talk to me while they find you a table. Although I'd feel justified even without the beer, because it's been too long since I've seen you," she chided.

"Yeah, I know. I'm sorry. I've been working a lot," said Leo. He took a swig of his beer. It tasted good.

"You need to find another vet to come lessen your load."

"I have," he told her. "My daughter."

"Carly's working there now?"

"Uh-huh."

"Well, that's good news," she said. She gave him a playful slap on his arm. "And it's still taken you all this time to come by for a visit?"

Leo took another swig of beer before meeting her eye. "I've spent a lot more time with my lawyer of late than I'd care to."

"This about your divorce?"

"Uh-huh."

"Oh gee." She nodded, and Leo knew this was familiar territory for her. "I was hoping y'all would have that signed and sealed by now. What's the holdup?"

He rumbled, low and deep in his throat. "Sheena wants the clinic."

"Well, why would she . . . ?" Angie scrunched up her face. "Hasn't someone explained to her that she can't get alimony out of someone who doesn't have a place to work?"

A waiter with shoulder-length black hair and a nose piercing breezed in front of them, carrying two pints. He turned slightly sideways to make it past them without touching and grinned at them both as he did so. Leo and Angie both scooted upright on their stools, so their knees wouldn't be intruding into the passageway so much.

"Apparently I'm to find work elsewhere to pay her alimony," Leo informed Angie.

"Oh boy." There was a long pause, and then Angie slapped her hands down on her knees. She shook her blonde hair off her shoulder and turned her big brown eyes on him. "Well, I'm gonna tell you the same thing I told my oldest son—she can take it all away from you, but she can't stop you from building it up again. You did it once," she declared, holding her index finger up in the air. She touched him on the knee with the same finger. "You can do it again."

"I'm not sure I want to do it again," he told her honestly.

"Why ever not? You're such a great vet."

"Maybe—thank you—but I'm not twenty anymore."

"Which means you're not as dumb as you were then."

Leo laughed. "I guess there is that. So how's it going with the

Lost Dogs of Snohomish County?" he asked, changing the subject. The waiter breezed past them again, on his way back to the kitchen this time, and a rider came into the arena with a beautiful, honey brown stallion.

"So good!" crowed Angie. "Who would ever have thought? We're up to twenty thousand members now."

"I saw that."

"And we're not even trying. People just find us. Talking of which, were you able to help that stray I sent your way?"

Leo pushed up his lips, trying to remember. "Which stray?"

"Earlier this summer. He didn't have a name tag, and he looked like he'd been roaming the streets?"

The various rescue societies around the area were always sending Leo stray dogs, but he couldn't remember one coming from the Lost Dogs of Snohomish County.

"Unconscious? Hit by a car?" Angie prompted. "Pretty badly banged up?"

"That was *you*?" he exclaimed, realizing she meant Lono.

"Not me directly, no. One of the sponsors of the Lost Dogs. He was in Mount Vernon for some function at the college and drove past a dog lying in the road. Nearly drove over it, I guess. But he said the dog was still breathing when he lifted him out of the road and wrapped him in some T-shirt he found kicking around."

"A black T-shirt with yellow bands on it?"

Angie shrugged. "I don't know. He didn't tell me that much. Just said he'd found something on the sidewalk to wrap the dog with because he thought one of his legs might be broken. I think that's what he said. To be honest, he called me around one in the morning when I was with a bunch of girlfriends, drinking margaritas . . ."

Leo chuckled, getting the picture.

"He said the dog needed medical care, and the only person I could think of close by was you. He didn't tell you that when he dropped the dog off?"

"I never got to meet him," Leo explained. "He just left the dog on the ground outside the clinic."

Angie's brown eyes got bigger. "I didn't mean for him to do *that*."

"Oh, don't worry. People are always dumping critters outside the clinic, so we're used to it. That's how we got the turtle. Someone left three of them outside the front door one night in a box, but we only managed to save one."

"I thought he'd keep the dog till the morning, then bring him to you. Mind you, I did get the impression he was on a hot date . . ."

"Fortunately we were called in to the clinic early that morning for an emergency; otherwise I don't think we could have saved him. Mac thought the T-shirt was just a rag somebody had left there, and when she went to throw it away, she found Lono wrapped up inside it."

"Lono?"

"That's what I called the dog. After the Hawaiian god of peace and prosperity." He scooted his knees left for the waiter to go by with two plates of steaming hot food. "I was hoping he might bring me a little of both to counterbalance all the crap I have going on in my life right now."

"So you saved him?"

Leo watched the young female rider start to do lazy figure eights in the sandy arena with the stallion as he answered. "I did, yes. With Mac's help. And then I kept him because I discovered he was a pretty special dog."

"You should have brought him along," said Angie, cuffing Leo's forearm with the back of her hand. "I would've liked to have met the little guy."

"Yeah," muttered Leo, his heart heavy again. He threw Angie a sheepish look. "He had a little setback in his recovery."

Angie swiveled around on her bar stool, so she was facing Leo. She was a hale and hearty rodeo-riding cowgirl first, but having raised four sons, she also had something a little earth mother about her. Her brow wrinkled, and she lifted Leo's left hand and held it in both of hers. "Tell me," she said.

*****

Mac had the pork dumpling between the chopsticks and up to her mouth when she heard the cry: the howl of an animal in distress. For a split second she worried that it was the Dalmatian Dr. Murphy was putting down, but then she caught the three-beep tone of the side door to the clinic being opened, and the howling intensified. The pitch crept higher and higher as the sound got louder, like a child screaming for attention. Only that was no child, Mac realized; that was Lono.

She bit off the end of the dumpling and dropped the rest back in the thermos. It wasn't very warm anymore and it was likely to be cold by the time she actually got to eat, but it sure tasted good. She set the thermos and the chopsticks on the counter next to the sink in the break room, licked her lips, swallowed her mouthful, and rushed out toward the sound. As soon as she turned into X-ray, she could see Dr. F scrambling down the hallway, Lono balanced across his arms, Venus running at his side, bobbing up and down trying to get to Lono. The basenji's head was stretched out, his mouth a perfect O, as he cried his pain out to the world.

Waylon and Dr. Murphy both hurried across treatment to help, but Dr. F made a beeline for Mac in X-ray.

"What is it?" she asked.

"It's his left leg. Can you do an immediate X-ray?"

"Yes, yes. Bring him in," said Mac, turning sideways and motioning toward the X-ray table. Her mind jumped back to the couple of times she thought she'd seen Lono limp. Why hadn't she said something to Dr. F? She should have trusted her instinct and maybe prevented this.

"Somebody put Venus back in my office, please," Dr. F called out. "And bring me a thermometer and a stethoscope."

Waylon bent forward and trotted after Venus, managing to grab her just as Dr. F went through the open door to X-ray.

Mac backed up to give Dr. F room. Lono was lying on his right side over Dr. F's arms, but his head was on the vet's left arm, putting him facing the wrong way if Dr. F just slipped him onto the table. He needed to turn him around, so the dog's legs would be toward Mac for the X-ray. Mac waited till Dr. F had Lono's head and shoulders on the table, and then she stepped in and helped him ease the dog into the right position. Lono quieted, his lips relaxing from their tight O into open-mouthed panting, his eyes fixed on Mac. She saw fear in them, because of the pain no doubt, but something else, too. A pleading kind of shame, as if he was embarrassed to be putting them to this kind of trouble again. She stroked Lono's head. "It's okay, baby. We've got you."

"I can't believe I let him go outside," said Dr. F, snapping his tongue against the roof of his mouth, his eyes on Lono. "Let alone chase a ball!"

"Is that what happened?"

"I don't know. I don't know," said the vet, throwing his hands up in irritation. Waylon slipped into the room and handed him the thermometer and the stethoscope. He took both without acknowledgment.

Mac knew he was irritated at himself, not at her. She took her lead apron down off the hook to give him some privacy while he wrangled with his thoughts.

Dr. F put the stethoscope to Lono's chest and listened for a moment. Then he wrapped the stethoscope around his neck and lifted the dog's tail. Mac saw Lono's left leg flinch. There was definitely something going on there. The vet slipped in the thermometer and cautiously lifted the leg that he'd pinned and wired. Lono licked his lips in pain. Mac saw Dr. F's jaw flex in anger; she knew how he felt.

He glanced up at her. "I was in my head, you know, not paying attention, and I threw the ball for Venus . . ." He blinked away and stared down at Lono again.

Mac slipped her protective apron over her head.

"I think his implant's infected," he admitted finally. "And I *knew* . . . well, I had a sense of it, but I didn't trust myself and I let him . . ." He trailed off. The thermometer beeped. He pulled it out and barely glanced at the reading before giving Mac a pained look. "Did you see him limping?"

Mac reached up to lower the X-ray arm, wishing she didn't have to answer this but wanting to at the same time, because she felt responsible and that weighed on her. Lono's eyes moved from her to Dr. F and then back to her again. "I thought I might have," she admitted, with the same uncertainty she'd felt when she spotted the hesitation in his back leg. "But then, you know, when I looked again, I didn't see it."

"How could I have let this happen?" protested Dr. F. "I get mad at clients for being careless about their pets' recovery, and here I go and do something just as bad. If not worse."

"Don't torture yourself," Mac reassured him. "You've got a lot on your mind right now."

"Yeah, that's no excuse," he said, more to himself again than to her.

She gave a sideways nod of her head: *Yeah.* But that didn't mean it wasn't valid.

A trundling sound interrupted them; it was Dr. Murphy pushing the oxygen machine into X-ray. She stopped and dropped a shaver and a needle with some liquid in it down onto the X-ray table. "I thought you might need these," she said.

Dr. F kept his eyes on Lono.

"Thanks," said Mac. She nodded at the needle. "Is that morphine?"

"Uh-huh. And cefazolin in the bag on the oxygen machine. For the IV. Do you need anything else?"

"I don't think so. Not right now."

Waylon leaned in, one hand resting on the doorjamb, the other holding a chart. "Dr. Murphy, there's a Jack Russell that needs debarking in exam 1 . . ."

"What's your policy on debarking?" she asked, looking at Mac and taking the chart from Waylon.

"We'll do it if they give us a good reason," Mac replied.

"Such as?"

Mac looked at Dr. F, but he was still staring down at Lono.

"A sheriff's order to euthanize the dog if the owner can't keep him quiet."

Dr. Murphy nodded, then followed Waylon out of sight.

X-ray fell silent again. Mac stared at Dr. F staring at Lono. His face was filled with anguish. "What was his temperature?" she asked him.

"104."

Her stomach fell. He was septic. "Okay, well, I'll hook him up to the IV as soon as I've taken the X-ray. Do you want to remove the pin and the wire today?"

"If we can get his infection under control. Do I have anything else on the board?"

"Just the dachshund."

Dr. F gave her a blank look.

"Vaginal bleeding post spay," she reminded him.

Dr. F tipped his head back, eyes closed. "Oh, that's right." He looked down at Lono again. "We can't fit this in before we close."

"I can stay late."

"But you started early."

"I know." She looked at him, waiting.

"What?" he said.

"You need to step outside. So I can take the X-ray."

"Oh." She watched him trudge to the door, hesitant to leave. "He'll be all right, you know," she assured him.

"I know." He looked back at her. "It's me I'm worried about."

*****

"Did he make it?" Angie asked, her eyes filled with concern.

"Who, Lono?"

She nodded.

"Oh sure," said Leo. "We did the surgery to take the pin out on Wednesday morning, and he was back up and shadowing me around the clinic Thursday first thing. The only reason he's not with me today is I'm leaving for Florida tomorrow, to go to a dermatology conference with Carly, and since I decided he was safer sleeping at the clinic the first few nights after the surgery, so he wouldn't be jumping in and out of my Jeep when my back was turned, I figured I'd leave him there till I got back from Florida next Wednesday."

Angie was looking at him as if she didn't understand. "Don't you have to break the bone again to get the pin back out?"

"Uh-uh, no," said Leo. He gulped another mouthful of beer, and then put the pint glass back down on the bar and made fists with his hands out in front of him. He pushed them together so his thumbs and forefingers were touching. "If these are the two parts of the bone," he explained, "I put the pin through them both but leave the end sticking out of one side. That way I can come in and pull the pin out later if I need to." He found a pen in his shirt pocket and did a demonstration.

"Well I'm glad everything turned out okay," said Angie, "but I'm still bummed you didn't bring him with you today." She leaned back and studied his face discerningly. "I'd like to see what he's got that captured your heart."

Leo chuckled. "You could always come and visit me, you know."

"Yeah, but that usually involves a bill, and this way *you* pay the bill," she teased, her cheeks dimpling into a big smile. She nodded at someone in the distance. "Looks like your table's ready," she said, tapping Leo on the thigh and pointing across the restaurant at an empty table. She stopped herself and looked down at the thigh she'd just tapped. "Hey, have you been working out?"

"I have," said Leo, pleased that she'd noticed. He stood up and started to follow her to his table, carrying his beer with him. "I've been running again. Training for a marathon Carly wants me to do with her."

She looked back at him with some noticeable skepticism. "In the spare time that you don't have?"

"In the moments in between the spare time I don't have, so I won't have to think about how I don't have any spare time."

"That's what running does for you?"

"Marathon running, you bet."

She stopped beside a table with one place setting, her hand open to show it was his. "I prefer to ride my horse," she said.

Leo set his beer down on the table. "Well, me, too. I ride for bliss and I run long distances to scramble my brain."

She shook her head. "You need to take more time off, my friend."

"What d'you think I'm doing here right now?" he told her. He put one finger to his lips. "Shush," he said, "I'm s'posed to be at work."

"Oh, well, now I wish I'd ordered you more than just a burger," said Angie, surprised. "To show how glad I am you skipped work to come be here."

"Did you order my burger with bacon?"

Angie grinned. "You know I did. You gonna relax while you eat it? Or are you gonna worry that the clinic's falling apart without you?"

"Are you kidding? I bet they're having a blast without me."

*****

And they were. At almost exactly the same moment that Dr. F made this statement to Angie, Pema and JJ burst through the doors to treatment, rocking with laughter. Lono skittered in behind them.

Mac put her clipboard down and grinned at them. "Tell me," she said.

"It was hilarious," Pema squealed.

"Who'd you get?"

"Barb Peterson," said JJ.

"Oh, she's a good sport."

"Yeah, she laughed *so* hard," said Pema. "Except for the moment when she first saw him."

JJ giggled. "Yeah, then she screamed."

"I heard that—"

Waylon bounced in through the double doors and interrupted Mac. "I'm guessing it worked?" he said.

"Are you kidding?" said Pema. "You *totally* freaked her out."

"Where'd you hide it?" asked Mac.

"In the toilet-paper closet in the bathroom," said Waylon, "with the door open so it looked like he was peeking out."

"Ni-ice!"

Carly bumped in behind Waylon. "What's going on?" she asked, her face eager, as if she thought she was missing out.

Mac told her. "Waylon hid that stuffed schnauzer I found at the thrift store in the TP closet in the bathroom, and Barb Peterson went in to take a pee—"

"And when she sat down she saw him looking at her and screamed," Pema finished.

"But the best part was Lono sat outside the door to the bathroom, so when she stepped out he was staring at her, and she about jumped out of her skin. Then she fell about laughing."

Carly looked down at Lono, who was sitting in the middle of them all, watching. "Yeah? You like playing jokes with us?"

Lono stood up as if ready to go again.

"You know what I want to do with the schnauzer?" said Carly. She leaned in closer and dropped her voice even though there was no one else around to hear them. "I want to drop him down in the turtle tank on his back, so his feet are up in the air, like he croaked gorging on the turtle."

"That would be hilarious," agreed Pema. "Except getting him wet might change the quality of his fur. I like how real he looks."

"We could set him on the counter above the tank with his butt up in the air and his chin perched on the edge, like he's waiting to grab the turtle in his mouth," suggested Waylon.

"Yeah, that's another great idea," agreed Mac. "But I want to get Dr. Murphy first. Pay her back for always being late."

They put their heads closer together.

"How?" said JJ.

"I don't know. I've been thinking about it, and all I've come up with is putting the schnauzer in Dr. F's bathroom 'cause she always goes in there first thing," said Mac.

"Why don't we give him a name?" said Carly.

"Who, the schnauzer?" asked Pema.

"Yeah, I was thinking that, too," agreed Mac. "How about Titus? Or Mercutio?"

"No, we're always using names from Shakespeare," complained Waylon.

"'Oh, teach me how I should forget to think,'" Mac admonished tartly.

"Yeah, I know. You like Shakespeare," insisted Waylon. "But we've got an Ophelia and a Hamlet—"

"Which one's Ophelia?" Pema whispered to Carly.

"The turtle."

"Oh."

"No, the cat's Ophelia and the turtle's Hamlet," JJ corrected.

"No-o," Mac corrected again. "The turtle's Bottom, the cat's Ophelia, and the *cockatoo's* Hamlet."

"We have a cockatoo?" said Carly, surprised.

"Used to," said JJ. "At the old clinic. Before Dr. F built this one."

"So no, then."

"See, we can't even keep the names straight when they're all from Shakespeare," Waylon complained again.

"Okay, then you suggest a name," said Mac.

"Can it be after a musician?"

"Sure."

"I've always called the cat Fifi," whispered Pema. "I had no idea she was Hamlet."

"She's not Hamlet," Carly whispered back. "That's the cockatoo?"

"We have a cockatoo?" Pema looked confused.

"No. Not anymore."

Pema looked more confused.

"How about Beethoven?" said Mac.

"I thought *I* was suggesting," griped Waylon.

"Then *suggest*," said Mac. "She'll get here if we're not careful."

"Fifi's an abbreviation for Ophelia, I think," Carly told Pema. "So you had the right name for the cat, you just didn't know it."

"Barry," said Waylon. "After Barry White."

Carly, Pema, and JJ all started making circles in the air with their two hands locked, singing, "Duh-duh-duh, duhduhduhduhduh, duh-duh-DUH—"

Everyone laughed.

"Okay, so what are we going to do with Barry to scare Dr. Murphy?" Mac asked.

"We could put him in her car," suggested Waylon.

"How?"

"Well, she always does the same thing when she gets here."

"She drops her bag by the surgery board—" acknowledged Mac.

"—and her keys on the counter—"

"—and then she runs into Dr. F's bathroom," finished JJ.

"And *then* she asks if she can bring in Kent," said Waylon. "Which, can she today?"

Mac looked down at Lono. "I don't see why not. His fever's gone and he hasn't sneezed in a couple of days."

Lono dropped his front shoulders down, legs extended, and lifted his hips and tail, ready to play.

"So one of us grabs her keys," explained Waylon, "while somebody else goes and gets Barry and sneaks him out the front door. Then we meet at her car and slip Barry in before she goes out to get Kent. We should be able to get her that way."

"You're good at this," Carly told Waylon.

"Okay, but what'll we do if she doesn't bring him today?" JJ speculated.

"Who?" said Pema, sounding lost.

"Dr. Murphy," JJ clarified.

"No, I meant—"

"Yes, hello, I'm here," Dr Murphy called out over the three beeps from the side door. She jogged into treatment and dumped her tote bag on the floor by the surgery board and her keys on top of the counter, just as predicted.

Waylon slipped out of the room, making a quick gesture to Mac with his left arm curled in front of him and his right hand stroking. She took the gesture to mean that he was going to get Barry, and she gave him a surreptitious thumbs-up.

"I need to get back to reception," said Pema, taking off after Waylon. "Good to see you, Dr. Murphy."

"Yeah, you, too. I'm sorry I'm a bit later than I said I'd be. I had to wait for my ex to show up to take the kids to their game," said Dr. Murphy, approaching their little huddle, flattening her hair on one side between her thumb and fingers. "I'm just going to pop into the bathroom," she added, "and then I'm ready. What's first up for me?"

"We have a cat with uterine pyometra."

"Needs an ovariohysterectomy?"

"Spaying, yes," agreed Mac.

"Okay, I'm on it."

She walked into Dr. F's bathroom, and Mac whispered to JJ, "You watch out from here."

"Okay, sure."

"Can you prop the side door open, please, JJ?" Carly said very loudly. "I think one of the cats in the ward had a problem, and it's stinking up that hallway?"

Mac used the cover to snatch up Dr. Murphy's keys and hustle outside to the parking lot. Waylon was already there with Barry.

"Shall we put him on the floor in the back, peering up between the front seats, so when she opens the door to let Kent out, she sees this face staring up at her?" he asked, peering into the Prius.

Kent was watching them from the front passenger's seat.

"She's probably going to come out and unlock the passenger's-side door to let Kent out," said Mac, "and unless she leans in, she might not see Barry. Let's set him on the driver's seat."

"Okay."

Mac unlocked the driver's side, and Lono, who had slipped out alongside Mac without her noticing, jumped into the Prius and continued on past the seat to the floor in the back.

"You can't be in there," Waylon told him. "Come on back out."

Lono set his chin on the console between front seats.

"Oh, that's even funnier," said Waylon, laughing out loud.

"Okay, quick, put Barry on the driver's seat," said Mac. "Lono, you'd better not screw up in here."

Lono looked at her, nonplussed.

Mac relocked the door and fled back into treatment, Waylon heading in via reception. JJ had propped the side door open with a rubber wedge, so she didn't give away her reentry. She dropped the keys back on the counter just as Dr. Murphy opened the bathroom door. Mac slid around into her alcove and had her controlled-substance log in her hand before Dr. Murphy was at her side.

"Do you mind if I bring Kent in today?" she asked.

"No, that's fine."

"I thought I saw Lono around," said Dr. Murphy, glancing around the floor.

"Yeah, he's somewhere," said Mac. "But he's doing much better now, so I don't see the harm in bringing Kent in."

"Thanks."

Dr. Murphy grabbed up her keys from the counter and trotted out the side door. Carly, JJ, Waylon, and Pema all appeared at Mac's side. They huddled at the end of the hallway coming in from the side door and waited, listening. And they weren't disappointed. Dr. Murphy squealed loudly. Then there was a pause, and she squealed again.

And they all fell about laughing.

*****

The waiter with the black hair and nose ring set the fat, sizzling bacon burger down on the table by Leo's beer, smiled, and walked away without a word. The meaty, straight-off-the-grill aroma hit the back of Leo's palate and kicked his salivary glands into action.

"That gonna suit you?" asked Angie.

He beamed at her. "It's perfect. Thank you!"

She made a short drumbeat with her hands on the shiny surface of the table, her rings, with their big turquoise stones, rapping against the wood. "You're welcome. I'm gonna come back and let you tell me more about this wonderful dog I set you up with, but I need to organize a large group we have coming in for lunch." She pointed back toward the door. "Enjoy your lunch." She took three steps away and added, "And the horses."

The rider on the stallion had gone, but as Leo picked up his burger, he watched another young woman ride a three-toned brown mare out from the stalls and onto the sandy arena. She walked the little mare around the arena two or three times before chivying her into a trot. The older man who had pushed open the red wooden gate for them to enter the arena, watched for a few seconds and then went back to hanging reins from hooks closest to the big barn door to the outside.

Leo could hear the people behind him at the next table talking about the rider and how she was moving the horse into a canter now. Leo easily tuned them out, letting the sounds of the restaurant become background as he relished the return of his appetite. He'd had acid stomach for days, it seemed like, but the pleasing, easy atmosphere of the restaurant encouraged him to let go of his worries and relax. He savored the contrasting textures of the burger: the smoky crispness of the outside; the moist, juicy inside overlaid with the salty bite of the bacon. He felt his stomach filling as he focused on what the rider was doing with the horse. The young woman pulled the reins to the right, obliging the mare to change direction, and she did, without bucking or complaint.

Leo noticed that at some point during her training session with the mare, someone had thrown the big barn door open. Sunlight illuminated the wide entrance, drawing Leo's eye to the trees hanging like wisteria on both sides of the opening and the crisp emerald green of the paddock in the distance. He watched the older man let the young rider out and then come into the arena himself with a bigger, shiny black Thoroughbred. The horse was saddled, but the man was working him from the ground, holding the reins. Leo chewed a sliver of tomato that had fallen out of his brioche burger bun as he watched the man grab a hold of one side of the saddle and push against the horse. The horse resisted without backing up, turning his head toward his saddle as if he wanted to bite the man's hands. But he didn't. Leo wondered if that was what the man was training the horse to do: to take a shock without fighting.

He swallowed the last of his burger and dropped his napkin onto his plate just as he heard, "You know, you could probably get a job as an in-house vet for all the horses they board here."

Leo smiled at Angie as she dragged the seat opposite him around the table and sat with her knees almost touching the side of his leg. She put her right elbow on the table and rested her face on her hand.

"I'd have to go back to my studies to be able to make horses my specialty at this point," he told her.

"Why? You know about horses' health, don't you? I mean, you still have a horse, right?"

"Yes, but that doesn't mean I'm current on all the latest meds and procedures for horses."

"Ah. Got you."

"And I'm not sure I'd want to stay with veterinary practice anyway."

"No? What would you do?"

"That's the part I'm trying to figure out."

She sat upright and tipped her head to one side, as if she didn't get it. "Are you talking, like, complete career change here?"

"I'm not talking anything, Angie. I just find that my mind has started asking questions. Questions that it didn't used to ask because it was set with what I was doing. All I had to do was ask what was next. I get up at a certain time, I go to the clinic, see clients, do surgeries when needed, see more clients. And then something came along that made me see things differently."

"A divorce will do that to you."

Leo shook his head no. That wasn't it. "The divorce kind of just makes me want to dig my heels in harder and stick with what I think belongs to me. I think it's Lono that's making me see things differently."

"How so?"

"Well, you know, he had a life somewhere, right, before he got hit by a car and ended up almost dead in the road. And then someone brought him to me, and I helped save him, and he found himself in a completely different life, and he adjusted. And I see that in his eyes when I'm wanting things to stay the way they've always been. It's like he's in my head saying, yeah, you could fight this but you could also step sideways and let it not be an issue anymore. Like a force of nature. You think you can build a house strong enough to avoid it, or you can build a house somewhere else and actually avoid it."

"Ahhh," mused Angie. "So the universe brought you this dog to cope with change. I mean, that's what you're struggling with, right? The divorce brought it front and center, but maybe you were already chafing at the bit to re-prove yourself. Or learn something new. Wanting that rush we get when we figure something out and the sense of value from bringing it out to show others. It's funny that we all get so much out of that struggle, yet we shy away from it, preferring to stick with the known, the predictable."

"The comfortable," Leo put in.

"Right. So Lono comes along and reteaches you that it's not that hard, especially if you open your hand and trust the universe to show you the way."

"Ye-ah," acknowledged Leo, thinking about it as he said it. "Maybe I got that from Lono. Or maybe from this woman I met at the Rotary lunch . . ."

"Ah, now we're getting to it," teased Angie, shifting in her seat like she was ready to hear some gossip. "Is she cute?"

Leo looked at her, surprised. "Who?"

"This woman."

"Joan? That's her name; Joan Doherty. No. I mean, I don't know. I wasn't thinking about her like that." He trailed off, thinking back on how comfortable he'd felt chatting to Joan. "Anyway," he went on, "she's started a business for 3-D printer prosthetics, and

I've found myself thinking about that quite a bit since. What that might mean for dogs that have to lose a leg to bone cancer. It's been intriguing me ever since I met her."

Angie tilted her head, looking into his eyes. "It's okay if you *are* attracted to her, you know that, right?"

His brow crinkled, wondering what she meant by that.

"I mean, you're allowed to date again."

"I know," he said, laughing. He thought about Kelly Murphy's dark-blue eyes and felt a rush in his belly.

Angie's head tilted even farther, watching the expression on his face. "I guess you do," she remarked, smiling.

"What's that mean?"

"Well, someone's tweaking your fancy."

He was a long way from his usual haunts, talking to a woman he almost never saw, so he decided to just say it. "Uh-huh. But she's a relief vet at the clinic, so I don't know that I can."

"Oh yeah, that's a hard one," agreed Angie. Her face lifted as she caught the eye of a waiter two tables down. "Do you want coffee?" she asked Leo.

"Please," he said.

She mouthed the word "coffee" at the waiter, pointing at Leo's place setting, then held her forefinger up in the air for him to hold on for a second. She looked at Leo. "We've got some fabulous apple pie right now if you want a slice?"

He shook his head no. "Carly and I are running a 10K on Monday in Florida as part of her 'get-Dad-back-in-shape-for-a-marathon' plan,"—he laughed—"and there's no way in hell I'll run 10K on Monday if I eat pie today."

*****

It was almost one thirty when Mac got to her controlled-substance log. The clinic was very quiet now that all the appointments had been taken care of and Pema had dimmed the lights in all the rooms except treatment. Waylon was still futzing around in the large animal ward, but Pema, JJ, and Dr. Murphy had all gone home. Carly was somewhere; Mac just didn't know where. Wherever she was, she didn't need Mac, which was just as well because Mac felt like she *had* to figure out where she'd gone awry with the tramadol count.

The computer said they should have 544 tablets and the handwritten log came up with the same, but she'd counted and recounted the tablets in the safe and there were only 530. She had been interrupted every time she'd tried to count them, so maybe, she thought, therein lay the rub. She picked up the container of tablets one more time.

Lono, who'd been sitting beside her, pawed her knee.

"What?" she said down to him. "You want to lend me your paws to count?"

He rested his chin on her knee, looking up at her with his big brown eyes. Mac smiled and caressed the fur on his head. Then she went back to the tablets.

But instead of counting her mind got sidetracking re-running the day's activity at the safe. She'd seen Carly there, but she didn't see an entry for her having logged out any tramadol. Mac turned to the page for the morphine doses; yep, Carly had logged out four ccs for Mocha. She flipped back to the tramadol. She had a vague recollection of Dr. Murphy at the safe, too, but she didn't see her handwriting on any of the pages for today. She racked her brain, trying to remember when she thought she'd seen her there.

Carly suddenly appeared beside her. Mac stopped fixating on the tramadol and looked at her. She'd changed out of her scrubs and into jeans and a silky black blouse. She'd also brushed her long hair out and put on a little makeup.

"You got a hot date with your hubby?" Mac asked.

"I wish," said Carly. "But he's working at the gym till eight tonight." She flipped her hair off her shoulders. "I just wanted to freshen up is all."

"How'd it go with Steve Rengen?"

Carly's shoulders slumped. "Not my favorite part of the day. Mocha has bone cancer—"

"I saw that."

"I think Steve's leaning toward amputation 'cause Mocha's only two and she's so important to Noah, but of course I had to tell him that there's no guarantee the cancer won't pop up elsewhere even if we take off the leg with the tumor in it. Fortunately they kept one of Mocha's puppies, so, you know, Noah won't be without a connection to her if they opt to put her down."

"You gave them some tramadol to take home for her?"

Carly shook her head no. "Carprofen," she said. "And a shot of morphine for today because it was obvious she was in a lot of pain. They made another appointment for next Thursday, I think. To see Dad." Her eyes clouded. "Noah was trying so hard not to cry when I said bone cancer, but when I said maybe six months to live, he lost it. Made me hate myself to have to tell him that."

Mac put down her clipboard and wrapped her arms around Carly. "I think it's the cancer you've gotta hate," she whispered. She broke away and picked up her clipboard again wishing she didn't have to do this part. "You logged everything you took out of the safe today, right?"

"Are you fucking kidding me?" protested Carly, back to her usual salty self. "After the dressing down you gave us all on Wednesday?"

"I did not give you a dressing down."

"You did, too." Carly sniffed, playacting wounded. "I felt thoroughly thrashed."

Mac laughed.

Carly left the alcove and walked over to the board. "So it looks like Dr. Murphy covered all the surgeries?"

"Uh-huh. She did the feline pyometra first and then neutered some of Greek pantheon."

"I see that. Apollo, Zeus, and Poseidon," Carly read, pointing at the board. "Those were the five-month-old Rotts?"

"Yeah." Mac laughed, remembering something. "And in between Apollo and Zeus—I think it was those two—she put Barry on his back on the wet sink and covered most of him with a sterile drape. And I came in and thought, *Where's this dog's testicles?*"— she laughed through the rest, Carly laughing with her—"before I realized it was the stuffed schnauzer."

"I'm glad she has a sense of humor." Carly swung around to face Lono, who'd followed her to the board. "And she's trying to fall in line with policy. She asked me how we'd handle the English bulldog with the kidney disease."

"Chuckie? Yeah, he's already gone through a change of diet."

"That's what Dr. Murphy said." Carly shrugged, then bent forward and sliced her hands through the air, one over the other over the other, in front of Lono. He jumped and nosed toward the moving targets, loving the game. "I told her if the disease is back and the clients are not ready to say goodbye, we'd recommend either sub-Q fluids or dialysis. But probably the sub-Q fluids." She stopped moving her hands and knelt on the floor. Lono climbed up onto her knees and let her hug him. "That'll buy them some more time with their baby," she murmured into the dog's neck. Then she looked at Mac again. "But I told her it's really up to the client."

Mac looked askance at her. "You realize you're going to get dog hair all over your shirt."

"Oh, I don't care," said Carly, letting go of Lono and brushing the red and cream hairs down off her shirt. Then she cupped Lono's muzzle in her hands and pulled it right up to her face. "You're such a *sweet dog*."

Mac heard a noise and looked across treatment. Waylon came out of the large animal ward carrying the mop and a bucket of soapy water. She picked up the container of tramadol, spilled the contents into a tablet counter, and started her addition again.

"Okay, I'm out of here," Carly announced behind her.

Mac stopped counting and looked up in time to see Carly disappear down the hallway to the side door. "Have fun in Florida," she called after her.

"I will," Carly called back.

Lono dropped to the floor, sphinxlike, stretching his chin out onto his front paws, his eyes on the side door.

"I told you Dr. F's not coming in today," Mac said to the dog.

"Is Lono sleeping here again tonight?" Waylon asked from across the room.

"What's that?" said Mac. She looked up and saw that he was mopping under the lift table. His question finally registered and she answered it. "Oh. No. I'm taking him home with me tonight so he's not . . . *lone*-ly," she crooned down to the dog.

"I thought you were in tech rehearsals?"

"Not today. Hell week starts on Monday." She smiled at him, wanting to ask but not wanting to pressure him.

"I'm coming, if that's what you're wondering."

Mac's smile widened. "You are?"

"Yep. Opening night. Got my tickets already."

"So you're bringing your girlfriend?"

Waylon nodded. "And my mom. She's excited to see this new play. And to see you in a lead role." He started to mop again.

"Awww, thank you," said Mac. She looked down at the tablet counter again and was suddenly very tired of rechecking. "Hey, did Dr. Murphy prescribe any tramadol today?"

Waylon shook his head. "Not that I'm aware of, no."

Mac searched her memory yet again, hearing the rhythmic sound of the mop swishing across the floor. Where had she gotten the impression that she'd seen Dr. Murphy at the safe today? Was she misremembering and thinking about last Tuesday instead?

She heard a splash and looked up to see Waylon holding the

bucket with the mop sticking up out of it.

"When I've poured this out," he said, "can I be done for the day?"

"What time is it?" said Mac and swung around to see the clock above the door. She almost jumped out of her skin. Barry was on the counter by the chart stand. She fell about laughing.

"Gotcha," said Waylon, grinning.

"Okay, yes, you can go," said Mac once she got a hold of herself again and noticed it was already one fifty.

"Thanks." He disappeared back into the ward with the bucket, and Mac heard him empty it into the big sink.

Lono got up suddenly and trotted over to his bed under the viewing station. He sniffed it cautiously, then climbed in, turned a full circle, and laid down in a tight ball. Waylon came out of the ward and breezed past the dog without seeing him.

"Enjoy your weekend," he told Mac.

"You, too," she replied.

She heard the three beeps of the side door, and then there was peace. She looked down at the tablet counter and began adding the whole numbers again. But she knew it wasn't going to come out any different than the first ten times she'd counted them. She sighed. The real problem was she'd found a discrepancy in the morphine on Tuesday when she'd gone over the log. But she'd worked a really long day Tuesday so had talked herself into believing that the error was more about brain fatigue than missing morphine. But now, with the tramadol, she wasn't so sure.

She poured the tablets back into the container and walked it over to the safe. She thought hard. The only variable on Tuesday and today was Dr. Murphy. *Had* she seen Dr. Murphy go to the safe today? She ran flashbacks of the morning through her mind. Yes, she had. After she finished the feline pyometra.

She crossed back to her clipboard and began flipping through the pages. She didn't see Dr. Murphy's writing anywhere on today's log. She flicked back to Tuesday's log; she *did* see Dr. Murphy's writing there. So either Dr. Murphy was still forgetting to log all of the controlled substances she took out of the safe, Mac thought, seeing Lono watching her from his bed.

Or they had a bigger problem. A much bigger problem.

Spike

This was what he loved most: sitting on the porch, watching the world do its communicating. He'd always thought that it was a gift he'd been given, to be able to see the connections between everyone in the ether. He just had to close his eyes partway and then let them get fuzzy—blur them, just a little—and bingo, he could see that honeycomb of tiny circles fusing along all around him. He could sit for long stretches like this, just watching the world do its communicating. He liked the fast-moving messages the most. Zip. Like shooting stars. Blink and he'd miss them. He still hadn't figured out what happened when some of the circles just disappeared. Did they get swallowed up by other circles and make mixed messages? Or did they just explode out of existence like those bubbles kids blew with soapy water, so the message had no chance of being received?

The thing was, with a gift like this did he have a responsibility to deliver some of the messages? He never knew the answer to that. He tried, when it was stuff he thought could help the people that he loved, but sometimes they came so thick and fast he couldn't keep up. Still, that shouldn't stop him from trying, he thought.

Chapter 11

The plane was still taxiing into the gate when Leo reluctantly pulled his cell phone out of his pocket and turned it back on. He almost didn't want to look. It had been very liberating not to receive any calls or messages from his lawyer for the last three days—at his request, since Leo had told John that whatever news there was could wait until he was back in the state and could take care of it—but now that he was back in Seattle, all bets were off. Sure enough, as his screen rebooted there were several messages, the last one being from John. *Please call me when you get a chance.*

Leo looked out the window at the big, puffy white clouds surrounding the terminal. So different than the blazing sun of Florida. And so welcome. It was funny; he'd thought seeing a message from John would just set his teeth on edge and start his stomach acids foaming, but actually he didn't feel too bad. It was just a reality right now, the divorce stuff, something that a year from now he'd wonder why it had gotten him so upset.

"You going to stop by the clinic on the way home?" Carly asked him as the plane lurched to a stop and he heard the sounds of a hundred-plus people unbuckling their seat belts.

"I've got a couple of things I want to do on the way, but yes. I want to pick up Lono."

"You going to call Steve Rengen?"

Carly had told Leo about the bone cancer and he hadn't dwelt on it, but he had been thinking about it since they got on the plane to come home. He'd been trying to envision how he would attach a prosthetic leg to Mocha if they amputated. There was no reason he couldn't screw it into the bone marrow, like he would a surgical pin, and then the tissue would grow around it. He'd have to do more research and he'd have to find out if Steve was willing, but he was warming more and more to the idea. First, though, he'd have to stop at Joan Doherty's and see if her son, Justin, could design a leg for Mocha. He could go elsewhere, to designers already working with animal prosthetics, but he wouldn't mind throwing Joan and Justin the work. Especially since they were local, and—he didn't know— but if he got into this kind of work, maybe they could collaborate on more animals than just Mocha.

"No," he said in answer to her question. "Steve made an appointment to see me tomorrow. I'll talk to him then." He pulled himself up in the narrow space and kept his head hunched forward so it wouldn't hit the overhead luggage bin. "Right now I just want to get home and take Dreamer for a ride."

"Where's Venus?"

"One of the neighbor's daughters wanted to keep her for a 4-H project, so she's at their house. I'll swing by on my way home and pick her up. What about you? Are you headed home?"

Carly moved into the aisle and Leo edged forward to her seat so he could straighten up. He watched her flip her hair back off her shoulder, and capture it in a ponytail. "Yep," she said. "Todd sent me a list of groceries that we need, so I'll stop and shop, then head home. I wouldn't mind a moment to ride my horse, too, especially since Mom wants me at the kitchen by seven a.m. tomorrow." She rolled her eyes. "She's worse than you."

Leo threaded his way out to stand behind her in the aisle without commenting on her remark. He reached up and pulled his carry-on out of the overhead luggage, letting it fall down onto the seat where Carly had been sitting; then he pulled her bag down. He set it on the floor between them and went one more time into the overhead to pull out his laptop bag. He tucked the ribbon holding his medal from the 10K farther down into the side pocket and realized how good it made him feel to have earned that medal. "I had a good time," he told Carly. "You know, doing the race."

"Yeah, that was definitely the highlight."

"The dermatology conference, not so much."

She turned and looked into his eyes. "So you think you want to do the Walt Disney World Marathon in January with me?"

"The World Marathon yes. But the Dopey Challenge—"

"—the forty eight miles in four days?"

"Yes. That one not till *next* January."

"You got it," agreed Carly. And then they started edging forward.

*****

Dr. Murphy came up beside Mac, dropped a chart onto the counter, and leaned her hands on top of it, lifting one leg up in the air behind her, as if her feet were tired. "Did you do the specific gravity on the golden's pee yet?"

Mac was counting amoxicillin tables into a pill bottle. She stopped, knowing Dr. Murphy wouldn't wait for an answer, lowered her hands, and turned toward the vet. As she did so, Dr. Murphy backed away, her nostrils flaring and her lip curling in a way that Mac had seen others do around her today. And she knew why— because there was a bad smell coming from somewhere; she just didn't know where. But since she'd bathed and put on her clean

Casper the Friendly Ghost scrubs today, she didn't think it could be coming from her.

"Yes. It was 1.005," she told Dr. Murphy.

"Oh, not good. More water than urine. Do we have room to keep him overnight?"

Mac ran all the patients in the large animal ward quickly through her mind. "I'm pretty sure, yes. But you won't be here tomorrow."

"No. Not unless Dr. F needs me to come in I won't. Will he take over on the golden?"

"Him or Carly, yes."

"Carly's not in tomorrow," said Waylon. He was standing by the fridge, holding the golden retriever he'd just brought back for Dr. Murphy.

"She's not?" said Mac, alarmed. "'Cause we have a lot of appointments tomorrow." She put down the antibiotics and hurried past Waylon to verify what he'd said on the staff schedule. He was right; Carly wasn't coming in. She saw him step back when she lingered beside him. Dang, maybe that smell *was* coming from her.

"Let me text Dr. F," she told Dr. Murphy, "and see if he wants you to come in tomorrow."

"Sure. I'm happy to take appointments off his hands."

"At least the ones that aren't coming in to see him specifically," Mac corrected.

"Well maybe those too," joked Dr. Murphy.

Mac glanced at Waylon; he was looking at her in a way that suggested he didn't think the relief vet was joking.

"That poodle you held for me while I took an ear swab," said Dr. Murphy, moving right on to the next thing. "Did you put the swab on a slide?"

Mac walked over and checked that it was still in the microscope. "Yes, it's here," she said. She saw Dr. Murphy's nose crinkle in distaste again. She shifted away.

"Yes," muttered Dr. Murphy, peering down through the microscope. "That looks like it needs a good dose of amoxicillin." She bounced back from the counter and turned to Waylon. "Why don't you put the golden in a kennel while 1 explain to the client what's going on with her, and then bring me three ccs of amoxicillin to exam 2 for the poodle." She ruffled the fur on the golden as she walked by. "We don't need Dr. F here to keep things running smoothly, do we?"

Waylon threw Mac another knowing look before heading off to the ward, and this time she found herself agreeing with him. It did sound like Dr. Murphy had some kind of agenda that didn't involve the rest of the staff at the clinic. Not even Dr. F himself.

She looked down to see Lono at her side, sniffing her pocket.

"What is with you today?" she admonished. "I already told you I don't have any treats in there." She frowned thinking maybe she did. She reached into her pocket and felt something dry and crumbly. What was that? she wondered. She lifted a small piece out. "Oh, crap," she muttered.

"What?" said Waylon coming back out from the ward.

"That poodle pooped in my pocket!"

*****

The sun had reemerged by the time Leo stepped out of John's office, and the puddles of rainwater on the ground were steaming into the air. It made him wish he were at home, feeling the moisture from the trees against his cheeks as he rode Dreamer through the woods. He'd felt so calm when he'd arrived back in Seattle, and had been sure he could handle whatever news John had to give him without letting go of that calm. But Sheena's request that he give her $5,000 a month in exchange for her not taking a percentage of his revenue during the first year of her studies had blown his calm.

"You don't have to agree now," John had told him, "but

because we're in mediation on Friday, you need to come to some kind of decision."

Which had blown Leo's calm even more because he'd totally put Friday's mediation out of his mind, and being reminded of it just seemed to heap onto everything else he needed to do after three days away. He glanced at his watch as he unlocked the Jeep. It was almost four p.m. already. Maybe he should pass on going out to see Joan Doherty's 3-D printer business and just head straight for the clinic. Maybe even do a little work once he got there.

He climbed into the Jeep and slammed the door. He thought about how he'd been looking forward to taking Lono for a walk once he got home. Lono and Venus and Harley. He pictured Lono looking at him when he got to the clinic, with those eyes that seemed to understand everything. He'd surely wait while Leo did whatever he needed to do, but the thought of making him wait suddenly didn't feel right to Leo.

He slipped the keys into the ignition, then sat back in his seat, his eyes staring out the windshield but not really seeing what was out there in front of him. That was the problem with this divorce stuff. It put everything out of focus that Leo wanted in focus. He looked at the steam drifting out of the puddles again. It was dense where the heat met the moisture, but then it dissipated into nothingness higher in the air. It made him think that he'd taken what John had told him and let it stir him up; but he could just as easily let it go.

He felt his insides decompress. He'd run over six miles, in Florida heat, after all these years. He felt himself nodding; he had this. He'd get done whatever he needed to get done tomorrow.

He reached into his pocket and pulled out his wallet. He opened it and found the business card that Joan had given him. He was beginning to get the sense that this was the whole purpose of Sheena's demands; to rattle his cage and force him to stumble. So what was the best way to deal with that? Stay focused.

He pulled out his phone and dialed Joan's number.

*****

Mac had changed her scrubs and was trying to tighten the green drape around the large surgical tray to her specifications, but she was also trying to watch Dr. Murphy. Chuckie was back after three days with sub-Q fluids at home, and Mac knew that Dr. Murphy had just given the client the news that he wasn't going to be able to stay with them much longer. So either she was at the safe to get some Fatal-Plus, or for some morphine to make him comfortable at home until they could let him go. Mac wasn't interested in which medication she chose; she just wanted to be sure the log got updated after Dr. Murphy was done. She lifted the tray by the tuck in the top; *dammit!* It wasn't tight enough. She pulled it apart and started again.

"Mac, there's a client out front that wants to talk to you," said Pema. She corrected herself with an embarrassed smile. "Actually she wants to talk to Dr. F—"

"I can talk to her," Dr. Murphy yelled from around by the safe.

Pema looked at Mac and pulled one side of her mouth down like she didn't know what to say.

"It's okay, I'll go," said Mac.

"Okay," said Dr. Murphy, pulling a liquid out of the safe and lowering it to the counter. Mac couldn't see from where she was standing which liquid it was. "Just trying to be helpful," added Dr. Murphy.

"Do you know who it is?" Mac asked Pema.

"I think her name's Fuqua. She's got a cocker spaniel that she's pretty sure has eaten something that's upset her tummy."

"Is it Charlie?"

"Charlie Fuqua?"

"No, the dog."

"Charlie and Chuckie," mused Dr. Murphy. Max watched her lock the safe and drop the key back in the drawer.

"Charlotte, that's what she called the cocker spaniel," said Pema.

"Yeah, that's Charlie," said Mac. She glimpsed Dr. Murphy pick up the needle she'd loaded with medicine and turn around, her left hand still on the counter.

"What are you looking at?" the relief vet asked.

Mac stood on tiptoe and peered across the charts table to see Lono sitting at the end of the workstation. "He's probably waiting for Dr. F to come through that side door," she said.

"No, I get the impression it's me he's waiting on. For something. I don't know what. But he's been eyeballing me all morning."

"Is Kent in his bed again?" asked Pema, peeking around the post between the wet sink and the lift table to see.

"Uh-uh, no," said Mac.

"I left him at home with the girls," said Dr. Murphy, breezing out of the alcove, one hand holding the needle, the other in her scrubs pocket. "They've got colds, and I told them to stay home from school today. I think I may be coming down with it, too." She pulled a tissue out of her pocket and wiped her nose.

"I'll be out to see Charlie in a minute," Mac told Pema, not wanting to put Dr. Murphy on the spot in front of her.

Pema took the hint and backed up out of the door. "I'll tell her," she said.

Dr. Murphy went to follow, but Mac stopped her. "Did you log what you just took out of the safe?" she asked.

Dr. Murphy swung around midstep and headed back to the alcove. "You know," she confessed, "I'm going to get this right. I promise I am. I just have to stop getting sucked into other people's conversations."

Mac watched her from across the room as she wrote, feeling the drape on the surgical tray cinch really tight this time.

"There you go," said Dr. Murphy, dropping the pen back down

on the clipboard. She marched over to the door, and Mac watched her leave. She heard the door to exam 2 open and close. She picked up her surgical tray by the fold on the top: tight as a tick. She walked it around from the wet sink with two others to put in the autoclave but stopped next to the controlled-substance log first. Dr. Murphy had recorded three ccs of morphine. Mac would check that after she put the trays in the autoclave. She freed her right hand, pulling the trays in up against her body with her left, and thumbed through the clipped pages to see the logs for tablet medications. There were no new recordings since ten thirty-five this morning. She lifted her head and pushed up her chin, thinking. She could have sworn she'd heard the rattle of tablets in a plastic bottle when she saw Dr. Murphy's hands go back into the safe before locking it.

She looked down at Lono, who was still sitting tucked in against the post at the closest workstation. "You and me, bud," she said softly. She put two fingers to her eyes, then out toward Lono's eyes and finished by pointing them in the direction Dr. Murphy had just gone. "You and me."

*****

Leo drove the back way out of Mount Vernon, past the community college and on down a long, rambling hill with spacious, high-end homes at the top and wide stretches of verdant pasture cradling the bottom. This was floodplain for the Skagit River, green and lush right now but sometimes so far under water that the road could not be driven. Leo glanced at the hurried directions scribbled onto the back of a receipt he'd had in his wallet when he called Joan.

"Yes, Leo, of course I remember you," she'd said, sounding delighted. "And yes, now is a great time to come out. We've pretty much finished our workload for the day, so we'd love to show you around our office-in-a-barn. Let me tell you the best way to get here."

He found the school-bus turnout at the end of the road where she lived and made his right-hand turn onto it. He drove the tight S curve that she'd described and then, sure enough, saw the mailbox being held in place by a red-and-black 3-D prosthetic hand. He could imagine how someone from Seattle would enjoy all of the proximity to town while feeling like they lived in the country in this location.

The driveway bumped up a short incline, at the top of which was a small house with cedar shingle siding, a light-blue metal roof, and sage-green wood trim on the windows and door. Colorful pottery planters adorned the front steps, most of them brimming with untamed late-season flowers, and Leo could see wind chimes and dream catchers and single glass beads hanging from the long beam over the narrow front porch. There was nothing austere about the welcome to this home.

Joan had indicated that Leo should follow the driveway past the house, down to the barn at the edge of the neighbor's pasture. He let the Jeep creep forward as he took in a small plot of tilled soil with some bright-orange pumpkins on browning vines in one corner. That must be their garden, he thought. He braked as a scarecrow came into view behind the pumpkin patch. It was life-size, made of interconnecting, bold spectrum-colored plastic, with cornhusks stuffed here and there into the torso and a battered felt hat on its head. Leo smiled. Somebody had found a way to practice his 3-D printer skills.

He took his foot off the brake and let the Jeep drift down a wide tongue of gravel surrounded by grass to a building that looked more like a tractor shed than a barn. It was maybe sixteen feet wide, with a pale-blue, sheet metal roof, which matched the one on the house, and silvering cedar board-and-batten siding. Someone had hung a metal rendition of a sun face surrounded by long, wavy rays on the front of the building and, underneath, two plastic 3-D arms, one yellow, one orange. The yellow one, on Leo's left as he looked at them, was bent at the elbow, and the orange one fully extended, both with their pointer fingers out, indicating the way in. Leo laughed as he parked under the sun. He liked this kid's creativity.

He walked around the back of the Jeep and past a long window into the space, then stopped in front of the door. The top half of the door was a window, too, and Leo could see Joan talking to a young man with shoulder-length dark hair who was sitting on a stool in front of a drafting table. Her son, he imagined. Two west-facing windows to the right of the door were unabashedly pouring afternoon sunlight into the space, which was littered, front to back, with tables and desks, computers and printers.

The sound of a banjo, or maybe a ukulele, strummed enthusiastically through the walls accompanied by some rhythmic tambourines and cymbals. The music was loud but inviting, an upbeat and festive celebration that set Leo's shoulders rocking, and as he turned the handle and opened the door, he heard a beautiful female voice come in to harmonize with the music. The door was tight in its frame, so Leo had to push it hard to get it closed again. The slamming sound caused Joan to turn her head toward him, and her face broke instantly into a smile as wide and crinkly as the one on the metal sun.

"Hi, Leo," she called out, then looked down at her son.

The young man picked up a cell phone from his drafting table, touched the screen, and the music lowered to background level.

"Hi," Leo replied, smiling, too. He walked toward them. "You didn't have to turn the music down for my benefit," he assured them.

"You like Kuinka?" asked the young man, standing up and stretching his right hand out. "I'm Justin, by the way." He was tall, over six feet Leo guessed, and youthfully skinny, with warm brown eyes like his mother, and the start of a dark beard on his chin.

"Hi, Justin. Good to meet you," Leo replied, shaking the proffered hand. "I don't know who Kuinka is, but if that's who was playing, then yes, I like them."

"They're a local band, from Mount Vernon," Justin told him,

nodding his head in time with the music. One side of his hair slipped down over an eye as he rocked, and he pushed it back. "I really like them."

"I'll have to look them up," said Leo. He turned to Joan and smiled again. "Good to see you again, too. Thanks for letting me come and check your work out."

"Are you kidding? We're thrilled that you want to see around. Where do you want to start?"

Leo looked at Justin again. "How about you show me how you figure out the joints on a limb?"

*****

JJ backed into treatment and turned around to reveal a beautiful Abyssinian cat in her arms. "Look who I've got," she said with obvious delight.

"Amber," Mac cried out with glee. She loved this mischievous feline. "What's she doing here?"

The slender, shorthaired gloriously ginger cat with the bib of white on her neck and chest sniffed JJ's chin and then rubbed the top of her head against it.

JJ laughed. "She's not peeing enough. You got time to help me siphon off some urine?" She craned her head around and looked up. "'Cause I know you want to get out of here early today for tech rehearsal."

"I do, but I want to clean this one's teeth before I leave." She glanced down at the miniature pinscher on the wet sink in front of her and gently shook his belly. His eyes popped open above the mask she was holding over his mouth. He still wasn't quite asleep. Mac leaned forward and whispered to JJ, "Plus I want to talk to Dr. F about"—she nodded her head toward the safe—"you know."

"Ah," muttered JJ, her face implying she got it. Her eyes dropped to the wet sink. "That's the min pin with the caution on his chart?"

Mac stood upright again. "Yep. I'm being careful."

The Abyssinian climbed up one of JJ's arms and rubbed against her temple. JJ giggled and stroked the length of the cat down to her tail. "You could be Lono's sister, you know that, as coppery as you are?"

"Yeah. If it weren't for the fact that she's a cat," agreed Mac. She smirked at JJ.

"Where is Lono? Maybe I'll see if they bond."

"He's fixated right now," said Mac, nodding toward the hallway by the side door. "Watching for Dr. F to come through that door."

"He's here?" asked Dr. Murphy, buzzing into treatment behind JJ. She stopped on the other side of the wet sink from Mac, holding her hands out in front of her like she was ready to receive something.

"Not that I'm aware of," Mac replied. "But according to Lono, he's close. He moved to that spot about a minute and a half ago, so I'm guessing"—she glanced up at the clock above JJ's head—"that in another three minutes—"

"Dr. F will walk through that door?" finished Dr. Murphy.

"Uh-huh. Why? D'you need something? Because he's really only popping in to get Lono. He said he'd look at Charlie's X-ray but that's it."

"*Charlie's* X-ray?" questioned Dr. Murphy, walking over to the sink in the corner. She turned on the faucet and pumped chlorhexidine liberally on the palms of both her hands.

"The cocker who ate her blankie."

"She ate her blankie?"

"That's what it looks like on the X-ray." Mac shook the min pin again. His eyes remained closed. She swiveled right to look at Dr. Murphy. "I thought you were leaving at four?"

"Oh no, that's okay. I figured I'd help you clear the waiting room before I left. And I wanted to ask Dr. F about this Shar-Pei in exam 3. He has *really* oily skin. I mean, excessively oily." She shook her hands over the sink and snatched out three paper towels to dry them. She scratched at them with the towels in a way that suggested they still weren't free of oil. "I was hoping he'd learned something at his dermatology conference that might give me a clue how to help this poor pup."

"I'm sure if he did, he'll share," said Mac, removing the mask on the min pin. She peeked up from under her brow at JJ, wondering if she was thinking the same thing as her. They'd been gossiping yesterday about the chemistry Mac had felt between Dr. Murphy and Dr. F and now Mac was thinking that Dr. Murphy's resistance to leaving was because she wanted to bump into Dr. F again. JJ shot her back a look. Yep, she was thinking it too, Mac decided. She shifted the min pin farther up the table, so they could drain some urine out of Amber, but the dog wasn't as far asleep as Mac had perceived, and he grabbed a hold of her left thumb and bit down hard. *"Ahhh,"* she screamed.

"What?" said Dr. Murphy. She dropped the paper towels in the sink as JJ deposited Amber on the counter beside it, and both of them rushed to help Mac.

"Get him off me! Get him *off* meeeeee," squealed Mac, smacking the min pin's nose with her free hand in an attempt to make him let go. The min pin glared at her. Mac spun her body right, toward the counter behind her, trying to escape the pain. Dr. Murphy and JJ slipped into the opening, JJ bobbing under Mac's outstretched arm to be on the other side, so they both had room to work. Dr. Murphy clutched the dog's head in her hands and pulled back as JJ gripped both parts of his muzzle with her thumbs and forefingers, trying to pry them apart. The min pin just bit down harder.

"AHHH," screamed Mac, her head rocking side to side in the air.

Pema burst through the double doors. "What d'you need?" she cried out, reactionary.

"Grab a needle," ordered Dr. Murphy, "and I'll jab him with it."

But Lono was already there, his front paws on the side of the wet sink. He reached his muzzle forward and bit down on the end of the min pin's tail. The min pin's mouth popped open with a yelp. Mac fell forward, clutching her left hand with her right between her knees. JJ slapped the mask back over the min pin's mouth, and Dr. Murphy dropped down to reward Lono for his quick thinking with a hug. But he wouldn't let her. He backed up before she could touch him and trotted the long way around the other workstation back to his post.

"Boy, he is definitely a one-man dog," Mac heard Dr. Murphy complain. She wanted to snipe that this "one-man dog" had just saved her thumb, but she was focused on breathing through the throbbing agony that was her left hand and arm.

"Let me look at it," JJ whispered. She was crouched close to the floor, her head tilted to one side to look up into Mac's face.

"I'll get the first aid kit," she heard Pema say behind her.

She knew they all wanted to help, but she couldn't make any words come out. Not just yet.

Beep, beep, beep went the side door, and then Mac heard Dr. F greet Lono with, "*There* you are. You ready to go home?"

She forced herself to roll back to a stand, not wanting the doc to see her succumbing to the pain. She pushed her left hand forward for JJ to examine. It was shaking. It wasn't so much that the min pin had pierced the skin, although the area between Mac's thumb and forefinger was soaked in blood; it was the way he'd crushed the proximal phalanx bone that was killing her. Dog bites were like that, crushing rather than piercing, and Mac knew already that she'd be bruised on that thumb for a long time to come.

"What is it?" she heard Dr. F baby-talk in the distance. "You've got something to show me?"

Mac glimpsed Dr. Murphy move away from the wet sink to stand facing Dr. F's entrance; then she closed her eyes, not caring about anything except the pain.

"Hi, there," she heard Dr. Murphy call out.

"Oh, you're still here," came Dr. F's voice. "I thought you'd be long gone by now."

"Lot of late appointments today."

"I appreciate you covering for me."

"Of course. You're welcome. Are you headed right back out, or do you have a minute?"

"I'm not sure quite what my agenda is yet," she heard the doc say, his voice closer. "All I know for sure is Lono wants to show me something . . ."

Mac heard the soft bounce of his footfall, she felt JJ shift slightly, and she opened her eyes to see Dr. F standing in front of her, looking down at her hand, Lono on the floor between them.

He looked at her thumb, his jaw clenching and unclenching the way it did when he was trying to figure out the best way to help an animal in distress. He looked up into her eyes, his own filled with caring. "I guess first up is I'm taking you to the hospital."

And Mac felt her eyes fill with tears.

Spike

The best part about watching the world do its communicating was the light show. He could only see that at dusk, when the shadows were stretching across the sky, flattening the daylight; and even then, only when it was clear. Today was the right kind of day. He snuck out to the front porch before dinner was called, feeling the October nip in the air, and settled down to wait for that moment when his eyes would tune into the clear, iridescent messages fusing with just enough color to create an aurora borealis of grays and blues and yellows and greens. Of course, the color came from the messages that weren't so good but he always marveled at the fact that the universe found a way to incorporate them into something so beautiful.

The bitter, malicious messages were probably the darkest: real cankers that looked grayish-brown and corroded, like a battery left out in the rain. He had to believe those thoughts couldn't be good inside a person's brain. Their darkness softened when it came up against the pale green of the messages filled with sadness. He could always recognize sadness because those molecules didn't shimmer the way the ones holding happy thoughts did. As if sadness dulled the thing that was carrying it. And then there was anger, flashing across the universe like lightening. Except dark yellow. Almost the same yellow as love. In fact the two were so close in color it didn't surprise him that people slipped from one to the other so easily. He always thought it was a no-brainer to stick with love, since that was the more satisfying of the emotions, but the light show made him understand just how tricky anger could be.

The toughest one for him to see was pain. It was gray and lifeless and sifted onto the scene like smoke from a wildfire. He wished he could blow on it, vaporize it into a silvery aura that backlit the fusion of warmer colors. But it didn't work like that. And he knew it.

He knew he had to take the good with the bad because otherwise there wouldn't be a light show. He might come at life from a place of love but he knew that others had to be shown the way. After all, love wasn't as obvious as people made it out to be. Sometimes it was downright scary.

Maybe that's why the universe worked so hard to set it in the right light.

Chapter 12

It was still dark when the alarm went off, and Mac felt the nip in the air as she pulled her arm from under the covers to silence it. Fall had definitely arrived. Chad rolled over and wrapped himself around her. "You don't have to go in today, you know," he muttered, his voice early-morning husky.

"I know. But I want to."

"It's gonna be hell for busy."

"I know that, too." Puck scooted up the bed till his nose was resting by her face. She freed her fingers from under the covers and stroked his head. "It'll be more streamlined if I'm there."

There was quiet for a moment, then, "How's your thumb?"

"Okay right now. But I took two more Ibuprofen at four this morning, when it woke me up."

"I'm gonna stop at the pet store on my lunch hour. Get Lono a treat."

Mac smiled. "Make it a big treat."

The room fell quiet again, both of them enjoying the last seconds of comfort before having to face the day. Then Chad threw the quilt off on his side.

"Okay," he said, "let me get the space heater going in the bathroom before you get up."

*****

Leo woke well before his alarm and lay in the shadowy room, staring at the space above his bed. He wasn't really looking at anything; his mind was just too busy to let him sleep anymore. He kept hearing John's words, that he had to come to "some kind of decision," but he had no idea what kind of decision he was supposed to come to. Was it a decision to give Sheena more money? To give her the clinic? To keep the house? To give her the house and the clinic? All of these decisions seemed predicated on what *she* wanted, not what he wanted. Because if *he* was to make a decision, it would be that his life be left alone. He'd get to keep his clinic and his home and keep doing what he was doing. But apparently that wasn't an option, which felt, to him, like he didn't have a decision to make. So may as well leave it up to the judge or the mediator, and then he, Leo, would live with it.

Lono was over by the window. Probably watching the deer eating the drops under the apple tree by the light of the moon, Leo thought. The dog must have felt Leo's eyes on him because he turned around, trotted over and sprang up onto the bed. He stepped over Venus, flopped down and slid his chin onto Leo's belly.

Leo moved his right arm from where it was folded on the pillow and stroked the soft hair on the dog's head. He let himself relax and began to imagine how his life would play out if Sheena were awarded the clinic in the divorce. He'd still get to work there for the next four or five years but maybe he wouldn't feel so tied to it. He could slowly let Carly take over, helping her when she needed it but giving himself the time to drift in another direction. Toward that whisper on the wind that he kept sensing rather than hearing. Like a change in the seasons. Was that what it was? The autumn of his years calling to him? He frowned, a realization hitting him; would he really have time to answer that call if he had to come up with another $5,000 a month in overhead?

Lono knocked against his hand—*Pet me more*—and Leo looked down the bed at him. In the soft light from the almost-full moon Leo could see that the dog had his eyes open, intent on him. He smiled. He had a lot sweeter things to think about than this divorce ugliness. Like the dinner date he had last night. The way they'd talked had felt so easy, so comfortable. And then when she'd leaned forward and kissed him on the cheek. He could still feel the explosion of fireworks he'd felt in every part of him at that kiss. He'd caught her hand as she leaned away, and kissed her on the back of it. She'd blushed and looked down, making him want to scoop her up in his arms.

Leo glanced over at Venus, who was snoring soundly against the folds in the quilt on the far side of the bed. He felt Lono nudge his hand again and stroked the length of the pup's back down to his left leg. Lono didn't resist. He stretched out under Leo's gentle touch and let him palpate the site of the injury to make sure it had returned to normal. It was a hand movement so familiar to Leo, so much a part of his everyday life that it felt like a reflex. A habit. And he couldn't imagine a life where he'd choose to give up that habit.

He rested his hand on Lono's belly and watched the dog's eyes close, his breathing become steady, his posture relax completely. Leo felt his own eyes start to close and was surprised, two hours later, when he woke having missed the alarm.

*****

It was seven fifteen in the morning. Mac was standing in front of the board trying to figure out what she might do to streamline things for when Dr. F finally arrived. The trouble was, the words were there in front of her, but they weren't actually registering in her mind. Because Dr. F was never late.

The door to treatment swung open behind her and she turned, hoping it was him. It was Pema. "Mrs. Fuqua's here, wondering about Charlotte."

Mac nodded. She looked at Waylon, who was standing next to her, waiting for instructions, and said, "Go see if Charlie's pooped in her kennel, would you?"

"Sure thing." Waylon ambled away.

"And if she hasn't"—Waylon stopped—"take her outside and see if you can get her to poop."

"You got it."

The side door beeped. Mac turned to see if it was Dr. F. It was JJ. "What?" said JJ.

"Did you see Dr. F out there?"

"No. Why? Isn't he here?"

"Not yet."

"Oh shit. There are a lot of cars out there already."

"I know. I know," said Mac, agonizing.

"Did he call?"

"Don't know. My cell's in the break room."

"Maybe you should check."

"Good idea."

Mac swung around to act on the suggestion, but JJ stopped her with a question. "What about Dr. Murphy?"

"What about her?"

"Yep, she pooped," said Waylon from the door to the ward.

"What?"

"Charlie pooped."

Mac felt like a juggler trying to keep two balls in the air while navigating the impasse of what to do if Dr. F didn't appear soon. Or at all. Because he was never late.

JJ set her coffee down on the catchall table. "Isn't she due in?"

"Who?"

"Dr. Murphy."

"Oh," said Mac. "Yes. She is. But she's late again." Mac turned back to Waylon. "Was her blankie in it?"

"What? In the poop?"

Mac nodded.

"I don't know. I didn't check." His eyes tipped up like he was wondering about what he'd just said. He must have come to some conclusion because he suddenly added, "But it was blue, if that helps."

"Yes, it does. I'll go tell Mrs. Fuqua." She looked at JJ. "Would you bring back Midnight? He's the black Lab out in reception."

JJ looked at the surgery board. "The torn cruciate ligament?"

"Uh-huh. And put him in the Lost Boys because he's loud."

JJ nodded and made for the door.

Mac paused for a second, trying to remember what she was doing next. Mrs. Fuqua, she reminded herself. She headed for the door asking Waylon, "Is she eating?"

"Who?"

"Charlie."

"Oh yeah. She ate all her breakfast."

"Good. Then you can clean up the poop if you wouldn't mind." She pushed through the doors and bustled after JJ to reception. Mrs. Fuqua was standing by the side window, worrying the purple-and-yellow scarf hanging around her neck. Mac walked over to her. "It looks like the laxative did its job," she said with a reassuring smile.

The petite, gray-haired lady lifted her hands excitedly. "Oh good," she said. "So does that mean she won't need surgery?"

"Well, I can't answer that till Dr. Friel gets here," said Mac, her eye catching the arrival of the doc's Jeep through the window behind Mrs. Fuqua. She also saw Dr. Murphy's Prius pull in directly behind him. They parked side by side and Dr. Murphy jumped out, all smiles, and hustled around the front of the Prius to stand next to Dr.

F as he got out of his Jeep. "But it's looking pretty hopeful. Do you know how much of the blankie she ate?"

"I brought it with me," said Mrs. Fuqua, turning toward a bag that she had set on the seat under the window. Mac took the moment to watch the interaction between the two vets out in the parking lot. Dr. Murphy had dumped her tote bag on the hood of her Prius, the strap hanging down toward the wheel well. She had one hand on the roof of her car and the other on the door to Dr. F's Jeep, effectively blocking his path. Dr. F didn't seem bothered by this, which bothered Mac because he *had* to know he was late. But he was busy messing with something on the inside of the door. Then he moved his hands to the top of the open window in the door and tugged upward, as if trying to make it move. Dr. Murphy moved in closer to him and took over tugging while he reached around her, presumably to roll the window up. It all looked very friendly. And intimate.

Pain shot up Mac's arm, and she realized her fists were clenched, stressing her bad thumb. She relaxed her hands, surprised to think that she might be angry over what she was watching. After all, Dr. F was an adult, and a free one at that; he could do whatever he wanted. Her eyes narrowed, seeing the flirtatious maneuverings of the woman in front of him. *But maybe not with Dr. Murphy,* Mac thought slowly.

Lono barked a couple of times, as if trying to tell his boss it was time to go, but when nobody paid attention to him, he suddenly tugged Dr. Murphy's bag down off her Prius by the strap and ran off with it, heading toward the side door. Dr. Murphy immediately gave chase, leaving Dr. F to slam his Jeep door and hustle after them. Mac was so surprised she heard herself snort a laugh and slap her hands together, an involuntary applause for Lono's ingenuity. Then she winced as her thumb throbbed its displeasure.

"That looks painful," said a voice in front of her.

Mac realized Mrs. Fuqua was now facing her again, holding up a clear plastic bag with some folded blue flannel in it. She looked down at her thumb and the nasty bruise mushrooming around the bandage. "It's not as bad as it looks," she reassured the sweet older lady.

"Maybe not," said Mrs. Fuqua. Then she leaned in closer and added, "But I'd be careful trying to work with it."

And by the way she glanced out the window toward the vehicles in the parking lot, Mac wondered if she meant her thumb or the vet stealing Dr. F's attention.

*****

Leo breezed down the hallway to treatment, Lono leading the way, and found Waylon and JJ standing by the surgery board. "Don't you have things to do this morning?" he said to them before they could reprimand him for being late. "To at least make yourselves *look* busy," he continued. JJ hurried away with the black Lab she was holding on a leash. "Who's that?" Leo called after her.

"This is Midnight. Your TPLO."

"And what about you?" he said to Waylon, who still hadn't moved.

"There's a Doberman with a botched ear crop in reception."

"Did I do the ear crop?" questioned Leo.

"No. They're not clients of ours."

Leo started moving toward his office again. "Okay well talk to Pema and see if we can fit a new patient in this morning. If not, the owners will have to take the dog to the Emergency Clinic."

"Don't you hate it when you have to remind them to work?" commented Dr. Murphy, who was close on his heels, following him into his office.

"Oh no, they're fine, really," said Leo, suddenly defensive. He dropped his personal items on his desk and swung around to head right back out and nearly ran headlong into Dr. Murphy.

He stepped left to go around her just as she stepped right to get out of his way. They nearly collided again. And then they repeated it in the other direction, laughing at the obvious silliness of the situation.

Leo finally stopped moving, folded himself to the right, and waved her through, all the while wondering why she was in his office in the first place.

Much to his surprise, she dropped her bag in his office chair.

She pointed at it, apparently picking up on his surprise. "You don't mind if I leave it here, do you? Only that's where Mac told me to leave it."

"No, that's fine," he said, wondering why Mac had chosen his office rather than the break room for Dr. Murphy to leave her personal items. But he didn't argue the point. Instead he hustled along to the bathroom next to his office. He closed the door, pulled off his sweatshirt, and lifted a clean, neatly folded gray scrub shirt off the pile on top of the cabinet. JJ was really good at keeping him in clean scrubs. He should remember to thank her for that. He glanced in the mirror before he pulled it on and saw that he had bed head. Probably from piling out the door and into his Jeep without showering this morning once he realized he'd overslept. He put the scrub shirt back down, pulled off his T-shirt, and bent over the sink for a dousing. When he stood back up, his face and hair were wet and cold water trickled down his neck and onto his chest. *I'm awake now*, he thought. He toweled off, and then pushed his fingers through his wet hair to tidy his coif. He slipped back into his T-shirt, pulled on the clean scrub shirt, and swung the door open.

Dr. Murphy was hovering in the hallway just outside the door. She smiled at him, and he was struck again by the beauty of her eyes. "Sorry," she said, "I need to . . ." She pointed into his bathroom.

He waved her in graciously with his hands and managed to get out of her way without doing the step-in-the-same-direction shuffle this time. He bounced into treatment, ready to attack the day, and then heard a strange scuffling noise. He turned and saw Lono running out of his office, dragging Dr. Murphy's purse along the floor behind him.

"What is *with* you this morning?" he objected, embarrassed by his dog's antics.

Lono kept running until he was under the counter by the surgery board, and then he let go of the bag and trotted over to his bed.

JJ was writing a feline neuter on the board and answered the vet without looking down at the tote bag. "He's just putting stuff where it belongs."

"What do you mean?"

"That's where Dr. Murphy usually leaves her bag."

"Oh," said Leo. He looked back at his office; *then how come—?* he asked himself, then let it go as a loud, monotone, evenly spaced bark started up in the ward.

*****

When Mac walked back into treatment, she found JJ over by the wet sink, lining up surgical instruments to be sterilized, and Drs. F and Murphy shoulder to shoulder, poring over the charts at the chart stand. She looked hard at them, trying to see if she could detect whether they'd been up to anything together.

Dr. F glanced up at her. "What?" he said.

"Did you get a flat?"

He chuckled. That was the excuse Mac always used when she was late. "No," he replied, shaking his head. Then he changed the subject. "Do you remember what the story is on Romeo?"

"The golden with the loose stool?"

"I prescribed metronidazole," said Dr. F, looking down at his notes on the chart.

"To take care of the infection causing the loose stool," said Mac, reading upside down. "But his stool sample showed roundworm—"

"Right."

"And you called the client to say that metronidazole doesn't work on roundworm and they need to bring Romeo back in. But they didn't." She pointed at the handwritten sticky note on the chart, which showed he'd called the client.

"How's your thumb?" he asked.

"Colorful."

"Did they have to stitch it?"

Dr. F had driven Mac to the hospital, but then Chad had taken over from there, so the vet could go home and spend some time with his animals. At least that was what he'd told her he wanted to do. "Uh-uh, no. They just glued the tooth marks and gave me some antibiotics."

"Hopefully some good narcotics, too," said Dr. Murphy, staring at Mac's bruised and swollen hand.

"I'm fine with Ibuprofen."

"What's in the bag?" asked Dr. F, looking at Mac's other hand.

"Charlie's blankie."

"Ah." His eyes narrowed. "Does that mean you're looking to make a comparison?"

"Yep. She pooped out something blue—"

"And very slimy," added Waylon, who was coming out of the large animal ward. The single, repetitive bark intensified with the door to the ward open and Mac could tell it was Midnight letting them know he wasn't happy.

"Have you already cleaned up the poop?" she asked Waylon.

"Ummm . . ."

Mac paused, waiting for him to confess one way or the other. An insistent yapping savagely overlaid the single bark. So savagely that Lono leapt out of his bed and came over to sit up against Dr. F.

"Close the door to the ward, would you," she told Waylon, "as you go in to clean up the poop."

"Is that Kaiser?" asked Dr. F, looking surprised.

"The min pin? Yep. I put him in with the cats."

Waylon closed the door to the large animal ward, and the volume on Midnight's bark lowered again. Kaiser stopped yapping.

"I thought you were doing his dental work yesterday?"

"That was the plan. Until he bit me."

"Ah."

"He's going in the boo box today—"

"The *boo* box?" exclaimed Dr. Murphy. Apparently this was the first time she'd heard the term.

"That's our hypocoristic," JJ said from behind them.

"Say *what*?" said Dr. Murphy.

JJ grinned. "Our pet name—"

"—for the anesthesia chamber," clarified Mac. "Usually reserved for cats that won't stand for an injectable. But today,"—she gave a smug smile—"I'll let Waylon put Kaiser in it."

"Yeah I know what it is," said Dr. Murphy. "But why 'boo' box?"

"Because 'boo-hoo, sucks to be you' I think," said Mac. She smiled at Dr. F. "Do you remember why we started calling it that?"

He shrugged. "I thought it was because the cats cried when we put them in it."

"And what did you call it?" Dr. Murphy asked JJ.

"A hypocoristic." She grinned at them all again, looking very pleased with herself. "You can use it as an adjective or a noun. It means a term of endearment or pet name. It was one of my words from last week."

"Your words?" questioned Dr. Murphy.

"Word of the day calendar," explained Mac.

"Ahh," acknowledged Dr. Murphy. "Okay, one more terminology question if you don't mind, before we start the day." She had her index finger up in the air.

"Go ahead," said Mac.

"Why is the ward in the back called the 'Lost Boys' ward?"

"Because it's for the dogs that won't ever shut up, which sounded like the boys that won't ever *grow* up, also known as,"— Mac flipped her hands out at her sides for a *TaDa* effect—"the Lost Boys. From *Peter Pan*. I was doing that show when we named it." She turned her attention to Dr. F again. "Anyway, I'm putting Kaiser in the boo box this time, to make sure he's asleep before I intubate him. Do you want an X-ray to confirm that there's no more blockage in Charlie?"

"Please." He pointed at something in the chart he was holding. "So now Romeo's back with diarrhea *and* a cough?"

"That's what they're saying."

Dr. F flashed his blue eyes at Dr. Murphy. "D'you want to take this one?"

"Sure." She held out her right hand and said, "'Give me my Romeo.'"

Mac chuckled.

"Exam 1?" asked Dr. Murphy on her way to the door.

"Yep." Mac watched her as she walked away. When she turned back around, she saw that Dr. F was also watching Dr. Murphy walk away. She raised her eyebrows at him.

"What?" he repeated.

"I need to talk to you about something."

"Oh, I'm sure," he replied, rolling his eyes. "But not before I've seen the snoring French bulldog." He let one of the charts drop back down into the stand. "Why is Mocha not in here?" he asked.

"I don't know. Did you look up their appointment time on the schedule?"

"I thought that's what I had you for."

"Watch it," she warned him, lifting her bandaged thumb. "I could take your eye out with this."

He laughed, then motioned her away with his fingers. "Go— examine some poop."

*****

Sometimes the staff could slay a busy day at the clinic like a bunch of tennis pros lobbing balls back across the net to land with precision inside the court, and sometimes it seemed like they spent their time ducking to avoid getting hit by the balls. Leo felt like they were on track for it to be a good day, despite his late arrival, because every interaction he'd had so far in the rooms had gone well. He and Dr. Murphy kept crossing and recrossing paths out in the hallway *without* repeating their side-step shuffle, and she seemed to intuit the cases that she could take off his hands without him having to go into it. Which left Mac enough time to get Kaiser fully knocked out, so she could pull the rotten tooth that was infecting his gum.

"Look," she said, holding the tooth up for Leo to see. "I think that's part of my thumb."

Leo peered at it, pretending to play along. "No, I think that's part of yesterday's breakfast."

Mac swung around on her seat and placed the tooth on a piece of gauze on the counter behind her. "He didn't have any breakfast yesterday," she said, throwing the forceps into a sterilizing tray. "He was on nil by mouth from midnight because I knew I'd have to give him an anesthetic for the dental work."

"And you made him wait all day to take care of him?" teased Leo. "No wonder he bit you."

"Yeah, Mac, he was hungry," Waylon piped in.

"Oh ha ha," drawled Mac. She pulled the tube out from the min pin's esophagus. "For that, *you* can take him back to his kennel."

"No, no!" Waylon mock wailed. "Don't sic Kaiser on me."

But he came around the wet sink and lifted the still-inert miniature pinscher.

"Did you take the X-ray of Cobweb's colon?" asked Leo.

"The cat in exam 2? Yeah."

"I couldn't find it."

Mac stood up and peeled her gloves off. "Look under Glendenning. That's the owner's name."

"Thanks. And then if you wouldn't mind prepping my TPLO."

"Midnight?"

Leo was looking down at the chart in his hand. What was he looking for on Cobweb again? *That's right, constipation.* He scanned the top of the page for the name—Glendenning—then looked up at Mac. "Yes, Midnight." He bounced over to the viewing station and quickly found the X-ray he needed.

"So what's happening with the French bulldog?" asked Mac.

"She needs a soft palate surgery."

"Not a spay?"

He heard the door swing open behind him. "A spay, too. But I told the client we couldn't do both under the same anesthetic, so she chose the soft palate surgery for today."

He faced Mac, having seen what he needed to see on the X-ray. Dr. Murphy was now in the room, over by the chart stand, and he caught her and Mac exchanging a look. It meant something, he could tell; he just didn't know what. "Could you do the soft palate surgery on the French bulldog?" he asked Dr. Murphy, walking toward her.

"Sure. Is that the one that was snoring?"

"Yep. Every time she breathes." He lowered his voice. "The client took the dog to a vet in Seattle, and he wanted five grand to do both surgeries. Which, he said, had to be done at the same time."

Dr. Murphy sucked in a whistle of air, and Leo noticed the perfect circle she made with her lips as she did it. "That would be dangerous to keep her under long enough to do both."

"That's what I said. I also said I'd do the soft palate surgery for $500 and the spay for $125."

"Oh well, I'll only do the soft palate for $2,000," Dr. Murphy informed him.

Leo's eyebrows popped up.

"Only kidding," she said with a laugh and a quick squeeze of his upper arm.

Leo smiled. "Where's Lono?" he asked Mac, crossing to the door. "He's been my shadow all morning."

"No idea," she replied.

He breezed through the door, then stopped on the other side: Exam 1 or 2? He put his eye to the peephole in the door to exam 2. That was the one. But instead of walking straight in, he decided to wander out to reception to get an idea of who was there. It helped him prepare mentally, to know who was waiting for appointments, and he was ahead of schedule enough that he could take a little moment to greet them.

He walked the few steps to the corner, smiling at the way Dr. Murphy had teased him, then swung around it to find Lono prostrate in the middle of the short corridor, an aggressive schnauzer biting down on his throat.

"Hey!" yelled Leo. He dropped down onto his knees, sliding along the linoleum floor like a baseball player stealing first, and smacked at the schnauzer with the chart in his hand. The dog fell backward with a clunk, his legs stuck out stiff and straight. Lono leapt to a stand, his head up, looking at Leo, eyes bright, mouth open, tail curling in the air behind him. He looked very pleased with himself.

"You guys," exclaimed Leo, then giggled like a schoolgirl at the joke.

Pema and Waylon were standing at one end of the hallway, giggling with him, and Mac and Dr. Murphy were at the other.

"Who set this up?" he asked.

"Lono, of course," said Mac.

Lono stretched forward on his front paws and play bowed. He skittered over to Leo, who was still kneeling on the floor, and sprang into his arms.

"Well, you certainly got me," Leo said, rubbing the dog's belly with both hands. He was still laughing when he let go of Lono and stood back up. "But I'm gonna find out who put you up to it," he announced, lifting the schnauzer, a look of diabolical pleasure on his face, "and get. Them. *Back.*"

*****

Mac loitered in the hallway after the comic relief rather than rushing back into treatment. She wanted to talk to Dr. F before he shot into exam 2 ,and she wanted to do it where they couldn't necessarily be overheard. She waited while he scanned reception, and then she fell in step beside him as he started back toward the exam rooms.

"Did you see who was out there?" she said, sotto voce.

"The Wallaces, for one." He looked at her, as if to confirm that was who she meant. She nodded. "Why? What's going on?" he asked.

"I'm pretty sure they're here to put Chuckie down. He's got kidney disease."

"And they've tried diet and sub-Q fluids?"

"Yes. And when they were here yesterday, Dr. Murphy sent them home with some morphine to keep Chuckie comfortable overnight."

He looked at her like he didn't get what might be the problem. "Okay. It sounds like Dr. Murphy's on top of it. I assume she'll take care of them today."

He took a hold of the door handle to exam 2, implying the conversation was over from his perspective, but Mac couldn't let it end there. She'd been trying to find a way to approach this subject, and this situation seemed to have the right degree of clouding to allow her to present her concerns without having to be direct. She stepped around to face him, implying the conversation was *not* over from her perspective.

"I was hoping you would take care of them."

"Why? If Dr. Murphy's been treating Chuckie—"

"Well, for one thing, you've been his vet since the day he was born. You even delivered him—"

"By C-section." He looked her in the eye. "I remember."

Now was the part that Mac had been dreading. "And for two, I'd rather Dr. Murphy not have to go to the safe today."

He scrunched up his face like this made no sense to him. "She'll have to go to the safe if they opt for euthanasia, because she'll need the blue stuff."

"That's why I'd prefer *you* to see the Wallaces."

"You don't need me to get the blue stuff out," he argued, pushing down on the handle to the door. "Just—tell her where it is and make sure she fills out the log."

Mac opened her mouth to explain why that wouldn't work, but he jumped in again with, "And can you bring some Laxatone in for Cobweb?" and immediately went into Exam 2.

She closed her eyes for a second, willing herself to stay calm. When she opened them again, she saw Lono staring up at her. "I hope you have better luck communicating with him," she muttered, then slapped open the door to treatment.

Lono skittered in ahead of her, stopped, and sat at the end of her alcove facing away from her. Mac glanced over; there was no one in the alcove. In fact, there was no one in treatment at all that she could see. Then her eye caught what Lono was looking at; Dr. Murphy was crouched close to the floor, fumbling through her tote bag for something. She found whatever she'd been looking for almost as soon as Mac saw her, and straightened herself to a stand. "Do you know who moved my bag?" she asked.

"Moved it?" questioned Mac. "I thought you always left it there."

Dr. Murphy turned and looked at her bag like the question surprised her. "I guess I do," she agreed. She popped something into her mouth and held her hand out toward Mac.

"You want some gum?"

Mac looked at the sheaf of bubble-packed white squares. "No, thanks," she said.

"So I was going to do the soft palate surgery next, but then I think I spied the English bulldog with end-stage kidney disease out in reception when we were playing the prank on Dr. F. Am I right?"

"Chuckie. Yes, he's back."

"Okay, but here's the thing. I think it would be great if Dr. F could see them, because it was obvious from my interaction with them that part of the reason they were holding on for so long was because they wanted Chuckie to have the chance to say goodbye to Dr. F."

Mac nodded. "I know. I just talked to him about that."

"And?"

"He thinks you should take care of it because you've been seeing them."

"Do you mind if I talk to him about it? Maybe I can persuade him just to see them, even if I do the euthanasia."

Mac startled a little at the kindness of the gesture. "That would be great," she said when she found her voice again.

"In the meantime, I think I'll get Chuckie and his owners into a room. Do you have his chart?"

Waylon walked in at that exact moment, holding a chart up for them to see. "I put Chuckie in exam 1," he said and slid the manila folder into the chart stand. "And we have a cat that's just in for shots." He slipped right back out the door.

"Okay, I'll go see Chuckie and make sure it's the end," said Dr. Murphy, heading to the chart stand.

"And I need to get some Laxatone," said Mac, walking into her alcove. She reached up to the cupboard above the microscope and heard the door swing open, then closed. She craned her neck around the fridge to double check that Dr. Murphy had stepped out, and then slid open the drawer holding the key to the controlled-substances safe. She had placed the key very specifically on one side of the drawer this morning, just in case. It was still there.

But it was definitely turned around from the position she had left it in.

Spike

Sometimes, at night, he would wake up missing her and he would crawl out of bed to go sit by the window and watch the sky. That's when he could see the unresolved messages. They were the ones that bothered him the most. Because eventually everyone died.

People believed that ended their unresolved business with the dead person, but he knew they were wrong. Because the messages kept coming. Yes, the communications were from farther out in the stratosphere, because of everything that needed to be said—or thought—between the people still alive on earth; but farther out didn't mean gone. If anything, it meant brighter and louder when they did get sent, like the stars up in the sky. And that brightness could reach down into someone's soul and create an ache like none other.

He couldn't let that happen to the people he loved. So he had to try extra hard to make sure he helped them resolve things before it was too late.

Chapter 13

"**O**kay, so we *are* constipated," announced Leo as he walked into exam 2. Cobweb, the silver-and-white eight-year-old cat, was looking out at him from her carrier on top of the examination table while her owner, a woman about Leo's age, and her owner's mother hovered close by.

"Oh, we are?" said the mother. She pushed a pair of almost nonexistent eyebrows together, creating a set of new wrinkles in her paper-thin skin. "Are we eating enough fruit?"

"The cat, Mother," said her daughter. "The *cat* is constipated, not Dr. Friel."

"O-oh," said the mother, looking from Leo to her daughter and back again with the same kind of visual concern she had expressed when she thought that *Leo* was constipated. "I thought you . . . well, I suppose it . . . I mean, people *do* get constipated."

"Yes, they do," agreed Leo. "Fortunately *I'm* not, but Cobweb *is*," he added, bringing them back to the matter at hand. "So I'm going to have my vet tech bring you in a laxative for tonight, and then she'll talk to you about increasing the fiber in Cobweb's diet."

"Do you have high-fiber foods available here at the clinic?" the daughter asked.

"I believe so, yes. But maybe ask Pema out in reception. She'll know." He smiled and started for the door.

"And what about the mange?" asked the mother.

Leo hesitated. This was the kind of moment that could start a day going sideways for him: the unexpected addition to the original reason for the patient's visit. "The mange?" he asked.

"Yes. You know, where the hair falls out."

"Yes, I know what mange is, but I didn't see anything about that on the chart."

"You didn't see the patches of bare skin on her left side?"

"I told you it's nothing, Mother."

"I only had a note to check for constipation," said Leo, making a point of looking at the chart again, even though he wasn't reading it because he knew it didn't say anything about checking for mange. Instead his mind replayed Mac's words about not wanting Dr. Murphy to go to the safe, and it suddenly clicked that she may have been signaling something with that remark. But what?

"She's been pulling out her fur, which she does when she gets stressed," he heard the daughter say to her mother.

Leo looked up, thinking this explanation resolved the matter.

"It looked like mange to me," persisted the mother.

"That's very unusual in cats," Leo told her. "But are you current with her flea medication? Because if she was itchy from fleas, she might overgroom and that can cause constipation."

"Fleas can?"

"No, not the fleas, Mother; the fact that she keeps worrying her fur. She gets hairballs, and they plug up her digestive system."

"Exactly right," said Leo, grateful that the daughter understood and was able to explain it to her mother, providing him with an out. If he jumped on it, he might still be able to keep his day on track. Except now he was worried about that thing Mac had said.

His hesitation cost him, because the mother turned to him and said, "So she has fleas?"

"I . . ." He shook his head gently, looking down at the chart. "I couldn't say. I didn't check her for fleas. I only—"

The door opened and Mac walked in. He could tell by the set of her jaw that she wasn't happy with him, and since he couldn't do anything more for Cobweb right now, he took this as his cue to leave.

"Here's Mac with the laxative," he announced, way too brightly for the room and the subject matter. "She can talk to you about choices in flea medication."

He slipped out the door and pulled it closed behind him. Lono was waiting for him in the hallway. His tail immediately swished across the floor, left, right, left, right. Leo loved the fact that he never had to guess what his dogs were thinking about him. He'd been slightly rattled by the change of direction in the room, but now he felt his focus come back to center.

The door to exam 1 opened and closed behind him, and Dr. Murphy came out.

"Is that the Wallaces?" Leo asked, nodding at the exam room.

"Uh-huh," she whispered. "They've made the decision."

Leo lowered his voice, too. "Do I need to go in? Because Mac was saying—"

The door behind him opened and Mac stepped out. Lono's tail swished across the floor again.

"I was just asking Dr. Murphy if I should go in to see the Wallaces—"

Waylon spun around the corner. "Oh, Dr. F?" he said, seeing him there. He held up a chart. "Steve and Noah Rengen are here with Mocha. Do you want me to put them in a room or bring them back to treatment?"

"A room, please."

"Okay, it'll be exam 4," said Waylon, spinning back the way

he'd come and pointing toward the exam room.

"Go ahead," Dr. Murphy told Leo, flapping her hand to indicate he should follow Waylon. "I thought the Wallaces might be waiting for you to help them make the decision but I think they were just dragging their heels. Trying to get in a last few moments with Chuckie." She gave one sharp nod of her head. "They seem ready now."

Mac was staring at her and Leo caught the disgruntlement in her stare. "What is it?" he asked. "D'you not want to have to do the euthanasia?"

Dr. Murphy jumped back in. "It's okay. I'll do that," she reassured Mac.

Mac didn't say anything.

Leo tried again, hoping to resolve whatever was going on here before it could balloon into something bigger. "Except there's an issue with you getting the Fatal-Plus out of the safe," he told Dr. Murphy. He kept his eyes on Mac, hoping she'd give him some indication that he'd addressed the problem. She didn't, so he pressed the point. "Is that right?"

"I know I've been really bad about writing things down in the log," confessed Dr. Murphy, shaking her head and hands in a self-deprecating manner. "I'm just used to the computer keeping records."

"Yes, but—" Mac started.

"But I get it," Dr. Murphy continued. "And I'm sorry if I've screwed up the tally. I'll come get you when I need Fatal-Plus from now on, okay?"

Mac looked at Leo. He shrugged. It was her decision, but it sounded good to him. He started toward exam 4, but Lono blocked his way. He looked down at the dog.

"What?" he said. But he knew.

He knew he should go in and help the Wallaces say goodbye to Chuckie no matter how ready Dr. Murphy thought they were. They had been clients for a long time and Chuckie had been a patient of Leo's his entire life. It was just hard, having been the one who brought Chuckie into the world, to have to be the one who sanctioned taking him out of it, too. Lono's brown eyes stared up at him, patiently waiting for him to make the right decision.

"Okay," Leo decided, swinging back around to face Dr. Murphy. "Give me a moment with the Wallaces, would you? And Lono," he said, looking down at his dog, "you come in, too."

*****

When Leo walked into exam 1, the two stout Wallaces were sitting in the chairs up against the far wall, their dying English bulldog spread at their feet. They looked up at the vet, their jaws tight, as if they were sure a different outcome could be found and they were daring him to defy them in this certainty. He knew how tenderhearted they both were and believed their angry looks were because they were mad at the situation, not him. The air in the room was too dense for the space, and Leo wanted to push the walls out with some kind of superhero strength he didn't possess so they could all breathe. Before he could say anything, Lono trotted across the room, sniffed delicately at the shallow-breathing Chuckie, then sat at Mrs. Wallace's feet and slipped his chin on her knee. And apparently that was all they needed. Tears trickled down each of their cheeks, and they looked up and nodded at Leo: *It's time.* He didn't know if it was seeing a healthy dog alongside Chuckie's suffering that did the trick, or if Lono just offered them the solace they needed to be strong. All he knew for sure was that he had been right in taking Lono into the room with him.

He strode forward, mentally awarding his dog the superhero status he wished he had himself, and hugged each of the Wallaces. Then he crouched and ran the back of his fingers gently over Chuckie's bulging belly, remembering how he'd fit in the palm of his hand when he'd first arrived in the world.

"I'll get Dr. Murphy to come back in," he told them as he stood back up.

"Can this one stay with us while it happens?" asked Mrs. Wallace, stroking the top of Lono's head.

"Of course," replied Leo.

Maybe that was what the clinic needed when clients were really struggling with letting go of their pets, he thought; a comfort dog.

He left the Wallaces and made his way to exam 4 where Steve half rose, welcoming Leo with his usual self-effacing smile. Noah was busy playing tug-of-war with a tubby ball of chocolate-brown fur on the floor. Mocha was standing to one side, watching them, her head down, eyes bright, tail wagging, as if she was hoping to get a chance at the short length of knotted rope, too. Leo felt his face break out into a wide smile.

"Who's this little rascal?" he asked. The pup had one knot on the rope between his sharp little teeth and was systematically jerking his head back, trying to get the rest of the rope away from Noah.

"This is Woody," laughed Noah, obviously enjoying the game. He let go of the rope and the puppy fell backward, then righted himself, eyed Leo, and skittered over to sit leaning against Noah.

"It's okay," Leo assured the pup. "I'm not going to give you any shots today."

"But he does need his follow-up shots," said Steve. "That's why we brought him along."

"To keep Mocha company," Noah put in, "*and* to get his shots."

"Yes, but *I'm* not going to give them to him," said Leo. "I know better than to give shots to a little puppy because that's how he'd always think of me." He knelt down close to Noah, scooped up the wriggling puppy, and pulled him in against his chest, his hands moving in their easy, practiced way, gathering and releasing the pup's warm, soft fur. Woody became still in his arms, as if listening to the language they'd spoken together many times.

"How'd you make him do that?" Noah marveled in his six-year-old way.

"Practice," said Leo. He smiled at Noah's obvious pleasure in the puppy. "I'm going to take this little bundle of joy out to my vet tech, Mackenzie, and she'll give him the shots he needs while we talk about Mocha. Is that okay?"

Noah nodded. Mocha followed Leo to the door, watching Woody the whole way. "Mocha, you have to stay here," said Noah. She trotted back toward him and sat.

"See, you've got it," Leo reassured the young dog owner. He opened the door behind him and saw Waylon coming down the hallway. He held the door open with his foot and lifted Woody into the air. "Would you give this one to Mac for shots, please?"

"Sure. Does she have his chart?"

"Don't know. This is Woody, and the client's name is Steve Rengen."

"Got it."

Leo turned back and braced himself for the rest of the visit. The door clicked closed behind him. He walked over to the examination table and popped open Mocha's chart. "You both know what's going on with Mocha, right?" he said, looking from Steve down to Noah on the floor.

"She has bone cancer," answered Noah, nodding soberly. He stroked Mocha's head. She pushed up into his gentle touch.

"Yes," confirmed Leo. "In her right rear leg." He pushed away from the table and crouched down next to Mocha. He felt the swelling at the lower end of her femur. It was warm to the touch. He jumped back up and looked at Steve. "Did you decide how you want to proceed?"

Steve looked down at his son and then back up at Leo. "We want to know if she really only has about six months to live if we do nothing?"

"Yes," said Leo. "Maybe even less." He hated to sound so

matter-of-fact, but he didn't want to mislead them. They were both staring at him with incredulity. "I'm sorry," he said, softening his voice. "But bone cancer can go fast."

Steve spoke again. "And if we have you amputate her leg, she might have a year or more?"

"That depends on whether the cancer has spread, but yes, that's what we hope." He double-checked something in Mocha's chart. "I see my daughter, Carly—Dr. Tremper," he corrected, looking up at them again, "the vet you saw last week—had our vet tech take an X-ray of Mocha's lungs, and there's no cancer in them, which is a good sign. Usually that's where it metastasizes to after it's in the bone."

Noah threw his arms around Mocha's neck and hugged her fiercely.

"We talked about it," said Steve, rubbing his hand over his son's head. "And we decided that if she were a human, we'd help her as much as we could—"

"Because she's our *friend*," Noah put in.

"The only reservation I have is the cost, and even that is a small reservation because for all she's done for us, she's worth whatever it costs."

Leo looked from one to the other of them again. "I understand. And I'm very willing to amputate her leg, but I have a special request for you. I'd like to have someone I know design her a prosthetic leg." He looked at Noah. "Do you know what that is?"

The little boy shook his head no.

"It's a replacement leg."

"Won't that be expensive?" asked Steve.

"Not this one. Because Justin—the designer—would make it on a 3-D printer. I've never tried this before, so you'd be my guinea pigs—well, Mocha would be—and because of that I'd be willing to give you a family discount for the amputation, and I wouldn't charge you for the prosthetic."

"No, I'm not trying to suggest—" started Steve, shaking his

hand in the air at Leo.

But Leo interrupted him. "I know you're not. And I'm not trying to sell you on the idea by not charging you. This is just something I want to try, but because it's not going to affect how long Mocha might live, I don't want you to have to pay for it."

"So it won't give her more time."

"No, not necessarily. But it could make the time she has more bearable. Because she'd still have four legs to run on."

Steve looked at Noah. "I don't see why not."

"Would it be brown, like her leg now?" asked Noah.

"Well, that's something that we could talk about," Leo replied. "Because Justin is an artist, and I've seen a leg he designed that had drawings of a dragon on it."

"She could get a *drawing*?" said Noah, sounding impressed.

"If that's what you want, yes. A drawing, or some bright colors . . ."

"How long would the design take?" asked Steve.

"I'm not sure. But I'd do the amputation as soon as possible, if that's what you're worried about. I just need the implant to screw the prosthetic onto before I do the surgery, so I can attach it before we sew everything back together. But I think my vet tech can lay her hands on one pretty fast. We might even have one here already that will work, I don't know, I haven't asked Mac. But if you want, you could leave Mocha with us. Did she eat this morning?"

"No, because the other vet said not to feed her when we brought her in next time," said Noah.

"That's good," said Leo. "But I still can't promise I'll get to the surgery today. But either way you'd have to leave her overnight, so if I don't do it today I'll do it tomorrow morning first thing."

"Okay," agreed Steve with his effusive smile and head nod. "Do you have any way we can look at Justin's work on previous prosthetics? Just because I'm curious."

"As a matter of fact, I do."

*****

Mac had the black Lab pressed up against her chest, her arms wrapped under his belly and up over his shoulders and hips, his head lolling over her right elbow since he was fully asleep from the preanesthetic she'd just administered, when Waylon walked into treatment, looking very troubled. "What's the matter?" she asked.

"Do you know anything about Dr. F leaving us?"

Mac stopped, even though Midnight weighed a pressing ninety-eight pounds. "I know there's some talk in his divorce about him losing the clinic, but that's not supposed to happen for a while. Why?"

Waylon's brow dipped, and he opened his mouth and paused, as if confused about whether he should continue or not. "It's just," he said, apparently deciding he should, "I helped the Wallaces carry Chuckie out to their van, and they said how sad they were that Dr. Friel was leaving because he'd always been such a good vet."

"Where did they get that from?"

"I don't know. But then they said thanks for having given them the chance to meet Dr. Murphy because they'd feel more comfortable going to her new practice, when it opened, having worked with her already."

"What new practice?"

Waylon pointed at Mac like he'd been vindicated. "See, that was *my* question."

"Did you ask them?"

"Well, no . . ."

Mac thought for a second, the weight of Midnight beginning to pull down on her shoulders oppressively. On the one hand, this would explain Dr. Murphy's secrecy when talking to the clients; on the other, there was no way she could know the pending details of Dr. F's divorce. Unless—

Midnight slumped even farther in her arms. "They probably just misunderstood," she threw out, then bumped her butt against the door to surgery to go put Midnight on the table.

*****

The day started to get away from Leo when he walked into treatment and asked if someone was available to go bring Mocha back. Waylon was assisting Dr. Murphy prep the soft palate surgery, and Mac was wheeling the second oxygen machine out of X-ray.

"I don't know that we have anyone right now," she told him in a tone that suggested she had other things to do and couldn't this wait?

"Where's JJ?" he asked.

"In surgery," she informed him. "Helping me prep your TPLO."

"Can you send her out when you get back in there?"

"Can you wait till I've intubated Midnight?"

Leo paused, wondering who else they had. "I'll ask Pema," he said, thinking it was dealt with now.

But apparently Mac had another agenda, because she stopped pushing the oxygen machine and gave him the look: the stubborn, sometimes-you-ask-too-much-of-me look. He'd like to say he was sensitive to this look, because he did ask a lot of her and he knew she did always give 200 percent; but a part of him was pumped to move forward with this case. So he challenged the look and immediately felt his day start to go sideways.

"What?" he said.

"Are you expecting to do the amputation today?" she retorted. "Because the board is full—"

"I can see that," Leo interrupted, looking at the surgery board in front of him. "If you can find me the implant, then yes, I'd like to do it today."

"Implant?"

"Yes—you know—the one we'll need to screw the prosthetic onto when it's ready."

He avoided any further conversation on the subject by picking up the phone on the desk to his right and buzzing reception. "Pema, could you bring Mocha back from exam 4, please?" he said into the receiver and then hung up when she agreed.

Behind him he heard the wheels on the mobile oxygen machine start to rattle again and assumed that meant Mac had accepted that they were on for the amputation, so he hurried through into his office to call Justin so he could move forward with Mocha's 3-D printer generated prosthetic. That was when the day went even further sideways. Because as soon as he picked up his cell phone, he saw the missed call from his lawyer. He tried to ignore the fact that he'd left a voice mail, but it was Thursday already, and tomorrow they were all going to find themselves sitting with mediators, trying to hash this divorce out without having to go to court. So could he avoid hearing what was up? He didn't think so.

As he listened to the words of the message, he heard, and felt, a strong pulsing in his ears, which he suspected was his blood pressure spiking. *What?* Now Sheena wanted him to sell the house they owned so she could use her share to pay for veterinary degree? He thought she was going to let him live there till she *finished* her degree. Was she going to leave him with *anything*? He hung up, flexing his jaw in anger, his stomach already aching with acidity.

He couldn't make himself call Justin—or even Joan—the way he was feeling, so he just texted to say that the amputation was a go and to start work on the prosthetic as soon as possible. While he was texting, Dr. Murphy came in.

"I hate to bother you," she said, "but I need someone to go to the safe for me, and Mac is busy prepping your TPLO."

Leo flexed his jaw again. Why Mac had to choose today of all days to become so touchy about the controlled-substances safe, he didn't know. He hit "Send" and was about to turn around and go get

Dr. Murphy whatever it was she needed, when JJ ran into the room.

"We need someone," she cried out. "The French bulldog's heart's stopped."

They all charged out of the office, and Leo assisted while Dr. Murphy ably and very calmly gave compressions to the dog's chest to get her heart pumping again. It was a momentary aberration, but coming on the heels of the phone call and the look, it all started to pile on in Leo's mind.

And kept on piling on. Midnight had a torn meniscus, complicating the tibial plateau leveling osteotomy Leo performed on him, another dog hemorrhaged, an emergency that sent the whole clinic into panic mode, and a smashed-leg-bone, feline versus automobile, arrived needing to be squeezed into the day's workload if the cat were to have a chance of walking again. Reception never seemed to empty.

So when Mac brought up what was undoubtedly a legitimate concern about the controlled-substances, Leo should have been able to hear it, but he couldn't. Or wouldn't. They were both poring over the jigsaw puzzle the vehicle had made of the cat's femur, trying to figure out which piece of bone went back where, when Dr. Murphy popped her head in the door to surgery.

"Can I trouble one of you to get me some tramadol out of the safe?" she asked from behind her mask.

Leo didn't even look up. "It's for a prescription?" he said, thinking he'd gotten one of the shards in the right place and then realizing it was nowhere near right. His shoulders slumped in frustration, and the quick burn across his neck made him realize how tightly he'd been holding them.

"Uh-huh."

"Then you can get it," he proclaimed.

"Okay, thanks," she said and popped back out.

Mac had stopped piecing and was glaring at him above her mask.

"You going to make me feel bad about that?" he challenged her.

"Bad about what?" she responded coolly. But he could hear the sarcasm in her tone suggesting she was, indeed, going to make him feel bad.

His pique at the situation rose. "About the fact that I overrode your proprietary lock on the safe."

"Oh, I'm sorry," she shot back, not sounding sorry at all. "I didn't mean to appear proprietary. In fact, how about I let *you* update the controlled-substance log, and while you're at it, *you* can answer to the state over why it doesn't tally with what's gone from the safe."

"Oh please!" he countered. "You've had a mis-tally before and always found the error."

"Because before it was always just about someone forgetting to log out what they took." She leaned forward across the table, as if she were jabbing him with her words. "This time there are drugs missing."

"That can't happen with the tablets because the computer keeps a tally when she enters the script."

"It keeps a tally of what she enters, yes."

His mind processed what she'd just said. He slid a look at JJ, who was standing next to the heart monitor at the end of the surgery table. She looked away. "Are you accusing Dr. Murphy—?"

"All of the meds went missing on the days she was working."

"Then you should talk to her about it."

"Maybe *you* should talk to her. She's your friend."

Which blew Leo's fuse. He looked back down at the femur puzzle, his mouth clamped shut. The conversation was over.

*****

And then Carly walked in. A beacon of hope in the midst of the storm. Leo heard her voice out in treatment while he and Mac were still trying to piece together the jigsaw and was immediately grateful for her unexpected arrival. His mind started to play out the things he could do now that he had a third set of veterinary hands, but when she pushed open the door to surgery, he could see her ashen complexion around the mask she was holding over her mouth. And then he met her eyes and saw the pain.

"What is it?" he asked.

Mac even swung around to see, picking up on the concern in his voice.

"Dad, it's Mom."

Leo's hands stopped moving, a tiny piece of bone balanced on the tip of each forefinger. "What?" he asked.

"She fell when they were hiking today. They think she broke her brain stem."

Everything that Leo knew to be true at that moment suddenly stopped, like someone had thrown a switch on a large engine and all the parts quit moving at the same time. His autopilot kicked on. He laid the two pieces of femur down on the sterile gauze, snatched at his gown, untying it one-handed in the back, and moved toward his daughter. "Someone get me another sterile gown, please. I'll be right back after I've washed up again." He made eye contact with Mac on his way by. "Can you keep working the problem?"

She nodded.

He tossed his gown and gloves on the way to the door, stepped outside, ripped off his mask, and pulled his daughter into his arms. She sobbed. He let her get past the worst of it, then he asked, "Where is she?"

"They airlifted her to the trauma hospital in Seattle, but Dad . . ."

She stepped back and he waited, watching her swipe the tears away from her face. She finally settled enough to continue. "They have her on life support." Her face collapsed in anguish. "She's not breathing."

Leo pulled her back into his arms and let her emote. When her cries settled again, he stepped back, nearly knocking into Lono, who had come to stand with him. "I have to get back," he said to his daughter, nodding at surgery. "You know that—"

She wiped her face with her sleeve, and Lono pawed her leg. Leo watched as Carly reflexively bent forward and scooped the dog up into her arms. He crawled upward on her chest and buried his head under her hair, up against her neck. "I do know that," she said, her voice thick from crying.

"But what can I do to help?"

"Clarissa's on a flight in from Hawaii already. I think she's s'posed to arrive at Sea-Tac around eight tonight. Can you go get her and bring her to the hospital?"

"I can."

Seconds went by that felt like hours. It was eerily quiet, as if even the animals in the wards had sensed the seriousness of the situation. Leo waited, not having any words that could make this better, watching his daughter struggle internally with this bomb that had been dropped on her life. Finally she flicked her eyes back at him. "What am I going to *do*?" she cried.

He put a hand on each of her shoulders and dipped his forehead, holding her eyes with his. "You're going to drive down to the hospital and talk to the doctors. You're a doctor, too, so you're going to ask to look at the X-rays. I assume she has a head injury . . ."

Carly nodded, the tears starting back up again. Lono tucked even closer. She pushed her lips together before speaking, as if biting back a sob. "Yeah. A skull fracture."

"Okay. Go look at the film and make an assessment from there. Don't take anyone's word for it. Go make your own judgment."

She nodded, as if coming to the conclusion in her own mind that this was the way to proceed.

"Do you need someone to drive you?" he asked as an afterthought.

She shook her head, one hand stroking the length of Lono's

back, her breathing settling with each stroke. "No. I'm fine," she said, and he could hear the decisiveness in her voice. "Thanks, Dad."

She turned, still holding Lono, and strode away from him, acting on her courage before it slipped away again.

Leo headed for the sink. "I'll finish up here and go get your sister at the airport," he said, turning on the faucet and letting the water run over his hands and arms. "Then we'll come directly to the hospital, and you can fill me in." He twisted his torso to make eye contact just in time to see her bury her face in the soft fur around Lono's neck before setting him back down and taking off. Now she had what she needed to face the worst.

Chapter 14

Death, or the proximity of death, brought everything into focus; that was what Leo decided as he pushed along on Dreamer by the light of the full moon. He'd woken in the wee hours again, and today not even Lono could ease him back to sleep. He had too much to think about. He wanted to linger in bed, hoping that he would reclaim sleep, since he knew the day would be full, starting with an early surgery to take care of Mocha before he got on the road again to the hospital. He'd made a quick run out to Joan's place before heading down to the airport last night to give Justin the dimensions of the implant Mac had tracked down. He could have just texted the details to Justin but something had made him want to make the journey, and he was glad he did, because standing in their workspace had been a welcome respite from everything that had happened in his day. And even now, riding on Dreamer across his pasture, he could feel the calm it had brought to him. He could get used to that calm. It was a feeling that had been talking to him ever since, making him wonder again about continuing to work at the clinic. Even though the danger of losing the clinic was now over. He wanted to say it was on hold, but he knew that wasn't the case. The news from Carly had not been good.

He'd driven Clarissa from the airport to the hospital, trying to involve her in a conversation to contain the huge airbag of fear that he could detect ballooning around her, but she wouldn't be drawn away from her thoughts. It was as if she was sitting very still, either hoping that the onslaught would miss her or bracing herself for when it hit. Clarissa was petite and athletic, like her older sister, but there was a wispiness to her personality, as if she might blow away in a strong wind. She wasn't *that* fragile, he knew, but she was definitely a tropical flower that preferred full sun to shade. And Carly was a bold and bright and hardy flower that flourished no matter what the weather. But despite their differences, when Carly had finished recounting that Sheena had, indeed, injured her brain stem and was in a vegetative state, both daughters had looked at him like they were standing in the middle of a disaster zone and needed saving.

But Leo couldn't save them. Not from the decision they had to make about whether to turn off Sheena's life support. He couldn't even advise them about what *he* would do, even though that was what they wanted. Desperately.

"Why not?" pleaded Clarissa.

"Because your mother and I weren't together anymore. It wouldn't be right."

"You're still her husband," stated Carly. "Technically."

He just looked at her. He wasn't going to argue. But he also wasn't going to make this decision. He tried a different tactic, stepping away to hunt them down some warm, sweet tea while they talked together. But when he came back ten minutes later, he found them holding hands, staring out the door that he had walked through earlier, waiting for him to return. Like they were little girls again, standing outside the grade school for him to come and pick them up. It broke his heart.

He put the two paper cups of tea down on the mobile tray next to the bed Sheena was in, trying not to look at her all tubed up and immobile, and pulled both his daughters toward him. He knew that this was a mirror image of all the times he'd had to help clients make an end-of-life decision about their pets, except that this time, the mirror was clouded with conflict of interest. He couldn't even present the medical ramifications of leaving Sheena on life support. He had to stay completely neutral while infusing his daughters with as much supportive love as he could. He had to be Lono.

Cantering across the pasture on Dreamer he could see the basenji, running out ahead of him with Venus, their coats intermingling to look like rose gold under the gentle glow of the full moon. The sight of it shored him up for the task ahead of him. The big task, the one that he knew he had to do first, before everything else on his agenda for today. The fence he had to mend.

*****

The moon radiated a calm, flat light over the parking lot of Riverside Animal Clinic and made the surface of the Skagit River an inviting, milky teal just beyond. Leo was surprised to see Mac's car already in the lot, since it was only just five twenty in the morning and they'd agreed last night, when he was waiting for Clarissa's flight to land and Mac was backstage at her dress rehearsal, that they'd start Mocha's surgery at six. At least, he thought that was what they'd agreed. The truth was, he'd jumped to respond to her text saying she and JJ were a go to help him again, because he was so relieved that she'd gotten past the way they'd left things during the feline femur reconstruction. He had been even more relieved that he'd gotten his head out of his own problems long enough to ask how her dress rehearsal had gone. This play was a big one for Mac, and he didn't want to be the guy who didn't care.

He pulled in alongside her Honda Element and switched off the engine. It was blissfully quiet in the front of his Jeep, and he could see the day ahead of him laid out like a cross-country marathon course. He wouldn't mind the early stretch, where he got to stay in the known landscape of his surgery, but beyond that the terrain looked loaded with peril. He knew his daughters would still be anxious for him to make the decision about their mother, because that was what happened at the clinic: people not wanting to have to be the one to say that a loved one's life was over. It was the part of euthanasia that weighed the most on him, because he completely understood. But he also understood what the flip side of not helping an animal let go looked like. And he didn't want that for Sheena. Despite all their differences, he didn't want her to lie in a vegetative state indeterminately. But could he tell his daughters that switching off the life-support machine didn't mean they were switching off her life? Could he tell them that what it really meant was they were giving her a chance to see if she could *live* a life? And if she couldn't, well, then the machinery had just been giving them false hope.

He chewed on that for a moment, wondering if such a statement would put him over the line? The line between what was practical and what was medical. As a vet he had to walk that line almost daily, working hard not to lose sight of it. But it was a fine line, and sometimes, like the white line at the edge of a road in heavy fog, it could momentarily disappear, and then he'd be left wondering if he'd missed it. He couldn't risk that with Sheena. Not when he had his two girls to face after whatever happened. He already felt guilty enough about thinking bad thoughts about her, wondering if that was what had caused this to happen. After all, if someone could pray or think good thoughts for *improvements* in another's health, then what would be the result of thinking bad thoughts?

He was suddenly aware of Lono up against his face. He had stepped his front paws across from the passenger's seat and was sniffing Leo's sideburn. As soon as Leo became aware of his presence, he felt Lono lick him delicately on the cheek. A reassuring lick that tickled and took Leo out of himself. He smiled, turning his face toward the pup. "You're going to have to stay at the clinic today, you know that, right?" he said.

The tip of Lono's tongue shot out and licked Leo on the nose.

Leo laughed. "Yeah, don't try talking me out of it."

He swung the door open and climbed out of the Jeep, Lono jumping down after him. He closed the door and hesitated, that last moment of quiet before his day would begin. Then he turned and headed for the side door.

*****

Mac heard the door beep open and sighed. She'd hoped to have more time, before Dr. F arrived, to go over her controlled-substance log again, but apparently he hadn't been able to sleep either. Lono trotted around the corner and greeted her. She leaned down, the pen still in her hand, and tickled the top of his head. When she straightened back up again, Dr. F was next to her.

"Good morning," she said. "How's—"

But he stopped her with a palm up in the air. "I'm sorry," he said simply. Then added, "For being such a butthead yesterday."

Mac hadn't been expecting this. She stared at him for a second. "A poopyhead," she corrected.

"There's a difference?"

"Probably not in your case."

He chuckled. He lifted his chin toward her log. "Is there more missing?"

"Yep," she conceded, brushing her hand across the page. "Some fentanyl patches this time."

She watched him shake his head very slowly, his jaw flexing. She wondered if now was the time to tell him the rest. She saw Lono sit, like he was ready, and pushed on. "I think she's also been poaching your client list."

He looked confused. *"Poaching?"*

"There have been rumors of her opening a practice—"

"Not if I turn her in to the veterinary board, she won't," Dr. F declared.

"Is that how you're going to handle this?"

He paused, pushing his lips up as he cogitated. "Do we have any proof?"

"Apart from the fact that the meds have gone missing on the days she's been working for us?" He nodded. "No. I've been trying to keep my eye on her, but—you know—that's hard to do. I'll have JJ and Waylon help me today."

"Are you going to let her come in today?"

"I don't think I have a choice. With you and Carly both out and a full day of appointments . . ." She put her clipboard down on the counter and stretched back, feeling her shoulders and neck start to warm with the increased blood flow. "Plus, by the time we get finished with Mocha I think it'll be too late for me to get another relief vet." She could see she'd added to his anxiety for the day and tried to relieve it with a smile. "I'll let her know first thing that I have my suspicions."

He shook his head no. "Don't. She already knows you're suspicious, because of the talk about her not going to the safe yesterday. I'll be back this afternoon, and *I'll* talk to her." He flexed his jaw. "With or without proof."

"What's going on with Sheena?"

"She's brain dead," he stated. "It's just a matter of switching off the oxygen."

"Is that what you're going down to do?"

"No-o, not me," he said, shaking a hand definitively in the air. "I'm not any part of that. I'm just going down to support Carly and Clarissa."

Mac grimaced. She wouldn't want to be either of them. "Where's the boyfriend? The one she went hiking with?"

"No idea. Carly said he skipped out as soon as he could. Too much reality for too soon in the relationship would be my guess."

There was a pause then Mac changed the subject since there wasn't anything edifying she could say about Sheena's condition, and she knew he didn't need it anyway. Not now, at least. Maybe that would come later. "JJ's coming in early to assist with Mocha's surgery," she said.

Dr. F just nodded, a far away look in his eyes, and she wondered if he'd heard her.

"She'll watch the monitors so I'll be free to hand you whatever you need." He still didn't say anything. "The implant's in the sterile closet with everything else."

He raised his head, inhaling a deep breath. "Great. When do you want to start?"

"As soon as JJ gets here." Mac replied.

The side door beeped.

"I'll go get changed then scrub up," said Dr. F.

Mac dropped the pen she'd been holding down on to the clipboard. "And we'll start prepping Mocha," she said.

*****

Leo sliced confidently through the skin on Mocha's leg and peeled it back like a banana. It was coarse and rubbery, like cutting through linoleum, and he wanted to leave enough to be able to sew it back over the opening once the leg was gone. The heart monitor beeped repetitively in the quiet room, and JJ took thorough notes on Mocha's stats while Mac watched him from across the table. He sliced down through the subcutaneous skin and into the soft tissue, being careful not to cut too deeply too quickly. Tumors had a tendency to push things out of position, so he had to watch carefully for the unexpected and clamp it off before he cut it off. He was grateful for the extra supply of hemostats that Mac had ready on the mobile surgical tray to help him with this.

"Did you get a good audience last night?" he asked. Mac grasped the bandage she'd put on the paw and used it to hold the leg firmly in the air while he made his incisions.

"Actually we did," she said. "I think it was the biggest audience I've ever seen for a dress rehearsal of a new play."

"That's good," Leo heard himself reply. He was wondering how much soft tissue to leave. He needed a certain amount but not enough to give the tumor a place to grow back. That was a definite risk with an amputation, not going deep enough.

"I'm excited," said JJ.

"When are you coming?" Mac asked her.

"Tonight."

"For the opening?" asked Leo.

"Yep," said JJ.

"I can't make the opening," he said, exposing the femur bone above the tumor. "But I've got tickets for the matinee next weekend."

"You do?" said Mac, a hint of surprise in her voice.

"I do," he confirmed. He switched instruments so he could saw through the femur and complete the amputation. He looked at Mac and teased, "And since it's the last performance, I'm hoping you'll have gotten it right by then."

Her eyes narrowed above her mask, and she shook her head, a shake of sarcasm. But he could tell he'd made her happy. He didn't usually go to the plays she was in.

"Do we have the implant ready?" he asked.

"Uh-huh." Mac pointing at the surgical steel strip with the nut on the end of it that was lying on the sterile drape. "I'll get the pins out when you're ready for them. Or will it need screws?"

"Threadless screws," he told her. "So essentially pins." Then he bent forward again and started sawing.

*****

Surgeries passed without anyone really knowing how long they took. Mac had a rough idea from all the times they'd done the same surgery, or at least she could tell when something took longer than usual because there'd been a problem, but she never really paid attention to the exact time. Today the amputation had gone smoothly, and pinning the implant for the future prosthetic went much quicker than she'd feared. JJ must have been worried about that, too, because she asked, "Why do you even need to put that in? Can't we just strap the prosthetic onto Mocha after she's recovered from surgery?"—and she almost never asked questions.

"We could," said Dr. F. "But I watched a bunch of videos of animals using prosthetics, and when they were strapped on, the animals tended to move awkwardly, like they wanted to shake the thing off. This way," he went on, "the prosthetic just becomes the new normal. At least that's the way it looked to me. The thing to be is bold," he said as he sewed the sub-Q skin back together around the implant. "If it doesn't work, we can always take it out."

"It looks weird, doesn't it?" JJ said to her after Dr. F had gone and Mac was finishing up the suturing.

She tied off the last suture and looked at her handiwork. It still looked tidy, the way she liked, but there was something strange about the piece of surgical steel sticking out of the sutured skin. "Maybe it'll look better once there's a leg attached to it."

She dropped the suture kit into the surgical tray next to her, and she and JJ started cleaning up and unhooking Mocha from the gas and heart monitors. They worked with their practised ease and efficiency until the mess had returned to order and they were on the same side of the operating table, lifting Mocha down onto her blanket on the floor.

"I'll put some coffee on if you'll stay with Mocha till she wakes up," said Mac, backing up toward the door.

"Yeah, that's fine," agreed JJ.

They walked Mocha into her kennel and laid her on the floor. Mac kept moving. She wanted to get surgery cleaned up and another two surgical trays made and in the autoclave before the clinic opened. She glanced at the clock above the door on her way through treatment and was surprised to see it was six thirty-five. Plenty of time.

Lono trotted over to her from his watch outside Dr. F's bathroom and sniffed her hand, his wet nose making little kiss sensations on the tips of her fingers. "You going down to the hospital?" she asked him, scratching him behind the ear.

"No, he's staying here," said Dr. F as he burst out of the bathroom, looking like he'd put his head under the faucet. His face was pink from being freshly scrubbed, and his hair was wet and slicked back across his scalp. But he couldn't wash away how tired he looked.

"I'm about to put some coffee on," said Mac. "D'you want to wait for a cup to take with you?"

"No, that's all right. I'll get one from the stand down the road before I hit the freeway."

"Okay," she said, pushing open the door. "Good luck today."

"Thanks."

*****

The hallway from treatment to reception was still in shadow because no one had turned the lights on out here yet. Mac liked it. It had the feel of waiting in the wings backstage before the curtain went up, filled with the wonder of how it might go. She breezed past Pema's counter and on across the clean, empty space and picked up the coffeepot. She turned around to go fill it with water in the bathroom and jumped at the sight of Barry balanced on his hind legs, his front ones propped against the bottom of the counter, like he was trying to see who was up there. Who'd put him in that position? she wondered. Waylon, probably, to scare Pema when she came in this morning.

She filled the coffeepot in the bathroom, walked it back across reception, and poured the water into the machine. She took a clean paper filter out of the box and put it in the plastic one above the pot, heaped two tablespoons of coffee into it, closed the lid, and clicked the switch to "On."

She gazed out the front windows, marveling at the moon's ability to light the landscape while still being soft enough for people to sleep by. She thought about Sheena and how she'd never be able to gaze upon the moon again. It made her sad to think of her life coming to such a harsh and sudden conclusion.

She turned away from the front windows, hearing the gurgle of the coffee machine, and saw Dr. F marching out to his Jeep. This was going to be easier on him now, she thought. No more having to hand over his clinic or his home—or anything, for that matter—to Sheena. She watched him walk between her car and his and reach into his pants pocket for his keys. He switched hands and reached into the other pocket. Maybe he couldn't think about the upside to Sheena's death yet. That would probably make him feel guilty. Maybe. She watched him try the door handle, and when it didn't open, he cupped his hand around his eye and peered in through the driver's-side window. Then he turned and headed back to the side door.

Honestly, she had no clue how a guy would think in this situation. Dr. F might be privately sounding the battle cry of triumph that Sheena had gotten her just desserts. And she wouldn't blame him, given how acquisitive Sheena had been of late. The smell of coffee brewing crept across the room, and Mac inhaled deeply, then let out a little gasp when she saw Lono skittering toward the vehicles. Did Dr. F know he was out? Before she could finish that thought, she watched him bound up onto the hood of her Honda and nimbly leap in through the open window of the Jeep. Only it wasn't open far enough for him to get through. Her mouth dropped open in astonishment as she saw him rock his torso left and right, forcing the window down a couple of inches, so he could get his hips, tail, and back legs in. Then he disappeared out of sight.

She couldn't help but laugh. That little minx. Apparently he was going to the hospital after all.

*****

The first available space in the hospital parking lot that Leo came to had a perfect view out to Mount Rainier. It wasn't always possible to see the towering giant, but today she shimmered bold and beautiful on the horizon, backlit as she was by the morning sun. He switched the Jeep off and stared, trying to imagine how many tons of snow were on that rocky mass. As he stared he felt something against his right ear, something soft and wet. He whirled around, startled, to find Lono's big eyes staring at him.

"What are you doing here?" he snapped.

Lono ducked, acknowledging his wrong doing in a submissive pose.

Leo turned back around and looked at his window. How did that—? He shook his head; it was what it was. He felt the tip of Lono's chin on his shoulder and slipped his left hand over to stroke the dog's nose. His glanced right to look directly at Lono. "You know you're going to have to stay in the car, right?"

Lono edged his chin farther forward till it was nestled in the crook of Leo's neck. It reminded Leo of something and gave him an idea. "Okay, wait here," he told his dog, pulling the keys out of the ignition and opening the door of the Jeep. He climbed out and went to lock the door, then looked at the position of the open window again. He tugged it up a couple of inches, using both hands, and then watched it shudder downward again. He really had to get that fixed.

Lono had moved onto the front passenger's seat and was watching him. Leo held up his index finger. The dog looked away.

"You stay," Leo warned him. "And don't give me that I'm-not-looking-at-you-so-I-can't-hear-you nonsense." Lono flicked his eyes back to Leo. *"Stay,"* he commanded, and the pup curled up on the front seat.

Leo hustled into the hospital and made his way directly to the ICU. When he stopped at reception, he could see his daughters down the hallway, sitting outside Sheena's room, staring at the wall in front of them. He smiled at the nurse on the other side of the desk, behind the computer. She was a young Asian American with a tight ponytail of dark hair and a dimpled smile. Her name tag said Kate B. "Hi, I'm Dr. Friel," he said. He pointed down the hallway. "My estranged wife, Sheena, is in room 4b. On life support. I was wondering if you have a policy about support dogs in the hospital?" He waited but the nurse didn't say anything, so he went on. "I'd like to bring my dog in to help my daughters. They have to decide what to do about their mom."

Kate B pushed back from the desk, using the rollers on her office chair, and said to someone behind a makeshift screen, "Dr. Haney? Could you come talk to Dr. Friel?" She lowered her voice and added, "About Sheena Friel. Room 4b."

A man about the same age as Leo came out from behind the screen. He was slim with sparse gray hair, a goatee, and round glasses. He exuded friendliness. "Oh, I'm glad to meet you," he said, extending his right hand toward Leo as he came around from behind the desk. "I'm Dr. Haney. I talked to your daughters a little bit ago about turning off their mother's life support and told them I'd be willing to do it for them, but they're still hesitant. Are you here to help them with the decision?"

"Kind of. I was hoping you'd let me bring in my dog. He's the one I think can help them."

"He's a therapy dog?"

"Not exactly. But he's helped clients at my veterinary practice make the decision to euthanize their pets—"

"You're a doctor of veterinary medicine?"

"Yes."

"Well then, sure, let's bring in your dog."

*****

Leo could see Lono sitting in the driver's seat, watching for him through the window, and shook his head in amazement. How did he know that Leo was going to come back for him? Or maybe he didn't. Maybe he had just made a show of curling up to go to sleep, but really he spent his time peering through the window, wishing Leo would come back. Either way, Lono stood as soon as he perceived Leo walking across the parking lot toward the Jeep and jumped out when he opened the door, his tail wagging happily.

"You ready?" said Leo as he clipped a leash to his collar. He was glad to be trying this with Lono and very grateful that Dr. Haney had acquiesced so readily. Lono seemed glad, too, if the way he was trotting along beside Leo, his tail lifted high in the air, was anything to go by.

Leo speed-walked him into the hospital partly because he was keen to get to Carly and Clarissa and partly because he didn't want anyone to have a chance to stop him and say he couldn't bring the dog in. But the only acknowledgments they got as he walked Lono down the long corridors to the ICU were adoring smiles down at the dog.

Dr. Haney saw them approaching and fell into step beside them. He walked quickly, like Leo, and chatted easily. "What a handsome dog," he said with obvious pleasure. "He's got great coloring. To be honest, I'm curious to see how this goes, because end-of-life stuff is so hard. I'd love to provide a way that makes it less wrenching for some of the relatives."

When they got to Sheena's room, the door was open and Carly and Clarissa were inside, sitting in two chairs that they'd pulled up close to the side of their mother's bed. Leo unclipped Lono from his leash and watched him trot around behind their chairs and then slide in between them, the tip of his tail just barely flickering. In Leo's mind he remarked on how sedate Lono's entry had been compared to his usual enthusiastic bounding and was sure that the dog sensed the seriousness of the moment.

"Ohhh," sighed Clarissa, immediately immersing her slender fingers in the fur on his head and neck. "You must be Lono."

Carly wrapped her right arm around Lono, and her hand began rhythmically caressing the side of his body. "Isn't he lovely?" she whispered to her sister.

"Gorgeous," said Clarissa.

Dr. Haney closed the door behind Leo and then stood with his back up against it. It made him a presence in the room but an unobtrusive one, leaving the family in a position where they could all see each other. Leo waited, watching his dog comfort his daughters, expecting—well, he didn't really know what he was expecting. He waited some more.

Carly turned to him after a few moments. "We know we have to turn off the life support," she said in her clear, well-thought-out way. "It's what's right. And it's what Mom would have wanted."

"Yes," agreed Clarissa.

"But . . ." said Carly.

There was a long pause. They both looked at their mother in the bed.

"We're scared for her," whispered Clarissa.

Carly looked at Leo again, her eyes wet with tears. "It doesn't make any sense, I know . . ."

Leo thought about this, wondering how he could help. He looked at Lono, who was watching him while Carly and Clarissa petted him easily, unconsciously. The dog moved his eyes to Sheena in the bed, and Leo's eyes followed. It was the first time he'd allowed himself to really look at Sheena. And what he saw was a woman trapped and helpless, overtaken by the tubes and monitors. As he took that in, he saw Lono step forward from between the chairs, just far enough to place his chin on the edge of the bed. Leo automatically came forward to join him. This he could do for his daughters, he thought.

He lifted Sheena's left hand and held it, limp and lifeless, in his own. He tried not to see the woman who lay inert in the bed but the one he'd loved. His eyes blurred as she came back to him, young and beautiful, vibrant with dreams for their future and full of laughter. He remembered her smile when she'd sat in a hospital bed just like this one, holding baby Carly. How happy she had been. And how tenderly she'd shown Clarissa to her big sister in another hospital bed. The way she'd looked across at him, so proud of their little family, her eyes soft with love. In the background he was aware of Carly and Clarissa leaning forward and placing their hands on Lono. He heard Dr. Haney's gentle yet confident tread as he walked behind their chairs to the breathing machine and switched it off. Then the sound of the flat line, and it was over.

He laid Sheena's hand back down and knelt in front of his weeping daughters, putting one arm loosely over their laps as Lono crept forward and sat against his knees. He wrapped his free arm around the dog. "If it helps," he told them softly, "I've held a lot of animals in that final moment, and I've come to know when the end is just a continuation of what's already come to pass." He paused, looking from one to the other, and added, "Your Mom was gone long before the machine was switched off."

*****

They agreed that they would all meet up at the clinic later, after Carly and Clarissa had called the funeral home and started the process of bringing their mother back to the Skagit. Leo would finish whatever work he needed to do before he could leave, and then they'd all drive up to the house on the hill above the Skagit River and spend the night up there as a family. Carly's husband would come and join them, and they'd share memories of Sheena, possibly, but not the business of death. Not yet.

Leo walked back to his Jeep, feeling pretty peaceful, and he didn't think it was because the decision had been made or even because Sheena had now gone, leaving him free of the worry that had been eating at him recently. He opened the door, and Lono jumped in and bounded across to the passenger's seat, then turned back to face him and sat. "You're pretty good at what you do, you know that?" said Leo as he climbed in beside him. Lono's neck straightened, his nose tipping up, as if proud. Leo stroked both sides of his neck, feeling the baby-soft fur smooth out, then spring back under his ministrations. He nudged Lono's head back down, and pushed his own forehead up against the dog's. "Thank you," he whispered.

He let go and faced front, feeling rejuvenated. He slipped the keys in the ignition. "Now for the part of my day I've really been dreading," he said. "I doubt you can help me with this."

Lono threw his head back and yodeled a single tone, loud and piercing.

"Okay, *okay*," yelled Leo over the noise, laughing as he held his hands over his ears.

Lono stopped.

"You wanna give it a whirl?" he asked his dog as he started the engine. Lono stayed quiet. "Okay then, let's go do it."

Chapter 15

Mac tried to hold her tongue until Dr. F got back; she really did. However not only did it make her anxious every time she knew Dr. Murphy had gone to the safe when no one else was in treatment, but she'd just called the French bulldog's owner to follow up on the soft palate healing and make an appointment for the spaying, only to be told that the client was thinking of waiting until Dr. Murphy had her own practice, since Dr. F would be out of business soon. That way she'd have continuity of veterinary care.

She hung up the phone and whirled around to face Dr. Murphy. "I know you had your client list stolen from you, but that doesn't give you the right to come here and try to do the same thing to Dr. Friel."

"What are you talking about?" said Dr. Murphy in a derisive tone. "I'm not trying to steal his client list."

"Then why are you telling people that he'll be out of business soon and they should come to you?"

"I'm *not*."

"Yes, you are," Waylon joined in from across the room. He

stuck a label on a box of blister pack medication and tossed it angrily into the prescriptions basket. "I've talked with at least three clients who've said they'll be sad not to see me anymore—"

"And Mrs. Horovitz gave me a big hug the other day, when she came for Clement's follow-up, and said how much she'd miss me," Mac snapped out, emphasizing how much this made her mad by jabbing the air with her forefinger.

She was having her showdown with the relief vet in front of the surgery board, effectively blocking JJ, who'd come out of the small animal ward, holding an armload of stinky bedding.

"I thought that was because they were moving or something," JJ added to the conversation.

"Look, I don't know what you *think* you've heard," argued Dr. Murphy. "But I am *not* trying to steal anyone's client list. If people want to tell me what a great job they think I did and ask about working with me again in the future, then I think I have every right to let them know I might be opening a practice. That's not stealing; that's just being honest." She had her right hand out, palm down, her shoulders rocking from side to side as she spoke. Even angry, her big dark-blue eyes had the power to captivate the onlooker, and Mac hoped Dr. F hadn't succumbed to this dissembling harlot.

Dr. Murphy powered on, having obviously found her groove. "And by the way," she sniped, "you guys have no say in this anyway. They're not *your* clients, they're Dr. Friel's, so it's not important what you think I *may* or may *not* be doing with them—"

JJ had propped the side door open to clear the stench from the small animal ward, and Dr. Friel had walked in, unseen by Dr. Murphy.

"Yes, it is," he interrupted coolly. "It's very important what they think." He came up alongside her, Lono at his heels, and shrugged. "To me, at least."

Dr. Murphy smiled a small, nervous smile. "I don't think you understand—" she started to say.

"Let's go into my office and talk," interrupted Dr. F, waving her forward with his right hand.

But Dr. Murphy stepped away from him, marching around the catchall table to put herself in the middle of the room. She slapped the chart she was holding down onto the charts table. "No," she countered. "There's nothing to talk about. I can't help it if you surround yourself with sycophants that don't understand the nature of building relationships with clients—"

Dr. F moved forward to stand on the opposite side of the charts table from her. "It's what's missing from the safe that I want to talk about," he said with quiet compulsion. He held his hand out again to indicate passage into his office.

Mac crossed discreetly into her alcove, or as discreetly as she could, given the circumstances. She picked up the clipboard holding her controlled-substance log, to be ready, and turned around in time to glimpse the shock on Dr. Murphy's face.

"How *dare* you," she spat. "I'm not going to stand in your office while you accuse me of some fantasy scenario cooked up by your vet tech."

With that she sprang across the room to grab her tote bag and keys, planning—what looked like to Mac at least—a self-righteous and stormy exit.

But Lono sprang quicker. The dog grabbed the bottom of Dr. Murphy's bag in his sharp little teeth before she could get to it and ran headlong toward Dr. F, spilling the contents of the bag out on the floor behind him.

And there, among the personal items, were some fentanyl patches and a little plastic baggie of what Mac assumed was tramadol.

*****

Leo came out of his office twenty minutes later, after Dr. Murphy had taken her leave, and went in search of Mac. It was almost one forty-five and he wanted to know what was next, because he was hoping to get a moment to do a little shopping for his evening guests. And get some lunch, if at all possible. And maybe call Joan.

Treatment was empty except for Lono, who was curled up in his special bed under the computer. Leo peered through the window into the small animal ward; Mac wasn't there. He scurried past Lono and poked his head into the large animal ward; she wasn't there either. There was a sweet-looking Bernese mountain puppy standing in a kennel to the left of the door, watching him quietly, and then Mocha, stretched out on her blanket two kennels down. Leo stepped into the ward and walked down to Mocha's kennel. He opened the door and went in, his eye on her breathing, which was steady. He looked at the neat stitching job Mac had done; it made it easy to forget it had been a bloody, gaping hole just a few hours ago.

He knelt down and gently laid his hand on the site of the surgery, feeling to see if it was warm. It was not. Mocha lifted her head and looked down where he was touching. A wondering, nonargumentative look, suggesting it didn't hurt either. Leo took both as good signs. He edged forward and stroked her head. "You're a good girl," he muttered. She let him pet her until her head relaxed back down to the floor.

He hurried out of the ward and continued on into surgery. That was where he found Mac stacking sterile surgical trays in the cupboard above the counter next to the operating table. He let the door close behind him.

She glanced over her shoulder at the sound and asked, "How'd it go?"

"What?" he replied.

"Your talk with Dr. Murphy."

"Oh." His mind had already moved on from that, but he brought it back to center. "It was fine. I told her she had to bring the drugs back or I was going to report her to the veterinary board. All of the drugs."

"What if she doesn't have all of them?"

"Then I'll report her to the veterinary board." He walked farther into the room and leaned against the mobile surgical tray, which was up against the wall. "I might report her anyway. I don't know yet." He stretched his legs out at an angle, one foot propped over the other. He watched Mac put the last tray in the cupboard and close the door, then tidy away the little footstool she'd been standing on into the cupboard beneath the sink. "But if we have to talk to the state," he went on, "then she's doing the talking. I made that clear. And I also made it clear that I was going to talk to my lawyer about drawing up something for her to sign saying she wouldn't work in Skagit County again."

Mac opened the drawer where all the vacuum-sealed surgical instruments lived and sifted through them. "And will you?" she asked.

"Will I what?"

"Talk to your lawyer?"

"I already did."

Mac looked over at him and he could tell she hadn't been expecting that answer. "I'm sorry if it bummed you out," she said.

"What?"

"Having to talk to Dr. Murphy like that?"

Leo was confused. "Why would it? I don't want her stealing our controlled-substances, or any other clinic's for that matter."

"Did she tell you why she took them?"

"Something to do with an old soccer injury but honestly, I wasn't listening. I don't care what's behind her drug habit. Just that she not impose it on me. Not in my place of work at least."

Mac didn't reply. She looked like she was trying to detect something in his face, but he couldn't imagine what. He pushed himself back to a stand, eager to keep moving.

"What's with the Bernese mountain dog?" he asked.

"He bit a chunk out of his paw, and his owner tried to glue it back but it didn't work."

"So we're stitching it?"

"Uh-huh."

"Anything else?"

"Dr. Murphy was partway through a border collie mix in exam 2. Her owner says she's got something wrong with her ears, but Dr. Murphy looked and couldn't see anything. So she had me take a blood test but was on her way back in when we cornered her. Or I cornered her, I guess."

"And that client's still waiting?" exclaimed Leo. "I mean, that was what?"—he glanced up at the clock—"twenty some minutes ago."

Mac closed the drawer. "Yeah, but the client's Jim Savage and I went in and talked to him—told him there might be a bit of a holdup—and he didn't seem to care." She frowned, her hand resting on the counter. "He doesn't look that good . . ."

Leo nodded, remembering. "He had leukemia a couple of years ago."

"Uh-huh. And my guess is it's back. His skin's real gray. I got a pretty strong sense that it's not the dog that's sick . . ."

"Okay, I'll go see him first," said Leo, heading for the door. Mac followed him. "Do you know where the chart is?"

"No, but I'll find it for you. And you have a nonspecific dermatitis waiting in reception who's scooting all the time."

Leo pushed through the door and smiled blithely back at Mac. "So business as usual," he quipped. But for once he was comforted by that reality.

Part Four

Chapter 16

The following Thursday Leo was toward the end of an OCD surgery on Tinker, a mastiff with torn cartilage in his shoulder joint that would flap open and cause lameness until it flapped closed again. "It's called osteochondritis dissecans," Leo had explained to Tinker's owners. "And he can live with it for a while, maybe taking a painkiller like carprofen or Rimadyl, but eventually that cartilage is liable to break off and roll around in his shoulder. And that's really painful. It would be like walking with a chunk of gravel in your shoe." Tinker was already lame more often than he wasn't, so his owners had opted for the surgery.

Leo had already incised the loose flap of cartilage and was just finishing curetting the rest away from the bone when the door opened and Pema put her head in.

"Dr. F, Steve and Noah Rengen are here with Mocha. Do you want me to put them in a room or bring them back into treatment?"

"A room would be fine," he answered, scrutinizing the bone to make sure he'd gotten all the cartilage off. "What do you think?" he asked Mac, but she wasn't looking down at the mastiff's shoulder.

"What?" he asked.

"Will we get to see the prosthetic?"

Leo turned back to Pema. "Okay, bring them back to treatment," he amended. "Are Joan and Justin here yet with the prosthetic?"

"No."

"Then maybe ask Steve to wait in reception until they get here. Unless—are there a lot of animals out in reception?"

"Nope. Just Mocha. And we don't have any more appointments till after lunch."

"What time is it now?" Leo asked.

"It's eleven forty," answered Pema. "The Rengens' appointment isn't until eleven fifty. They're early."

"We might even get a lunch break," Leo told Mac and then checked his handiwork on the mastiff one last time.

*****

He washed up quickly in his bathroom and smacked a little cologne on his cheeks. He pulled on a clean white T-shirt and then picked a dark-blue scrub top off the pile and pulled that on, too. He was feeling a buzz of excitement. He had some mouthwash in here somewhere, he thought, eyeing the metal shelf unit to the left of his sink. He found it next to a supply of disposable razors, unscrewed the top, and took a slug in his mouth. He sloshed it around as he screwed the lid back on the bottle, sucking it in and out of his teeth, and finally gargled for a few seconds before spitting it out in the sink. He heard the door to treatment swish open and closed, and voices sound greetings. He thought it was Steve and Noah because he could hear the clicking sound of a dog's claws on the tile floor. That could be Lono but—

He threw the bathroom door open and stepped out. Sure enough, Steve and Noah were over by the lift table with Mac, and all three of them were looking down at Mocha. As Leo came around the catchall table, he saw Lono was with them, too, sniffing Mocha. He wasn't sniffing at the site of her surgery, though, which Leo took as a good sign.

"How's she doing?" he asked as he got closer to the group.

"She's doing great," announced Steve with a huge smile. He threw his left hand out like he was showing her off, and Leo accepted the offering by kneeling down next to her and looking at the place where her back leg used to be. Mac was already down looking at it, Lono sitting next to her, watching.

"She might not even *need* another leg," whooped Noah. "She can even run almost as fast as Woody."

"But aren't you excited to see how fast she can run with a bionic leg?" asked Leo.

"Oh yes," stated Noah.

The doors swung open, and Leo rose to see Pema leading in Joan and Justin. Joan was looking around treatment, her face filled with the kind of wonderment that someone gets when they're discovering something new. Something new that they like the look of. Leo felt a little proud.

"He-llo," she called out when she caught sight of him. "What a great place to work—"

Lono yipped, a happy, over-the-moon yip that electrified the entire room. He darted around Leo and ran between the workstations to stop opposite Joan and Justin, his tail wagging like crazy, his mouth open expectantly. Leo laughed that his dog was giving the newcomers such an enthusiastic greeting, but then he looked up at Joan's face. She was staring down at Lono as if she didn't believe it.

"Spike," she exclaimed, her voice spilling over with excitement. "Is that *you*?"

And Lono bounded forward.

*****

"Do you know this dog?" asked Leo, pointing at Lono, who was allowing himself to be petted vigorously and unashamedly by both Joan and Justin. The others had all come around from the lift table to watch the lovefest happening in front of the doors. "I mean, obviously you know this dog," he corrected with a laugh, "so do you know where he came from?"

"This is our dog," said Joan, a catch in her voice like she might cry. "The one that we lost—"

"Lost? I thought you said you couldn't keep him?"

Joan nodded, her hands still moving over Lono's fur. The dog tipped his head back and rubbed his nose over her chin. "What I meant was we couldn't keep him in our yard down in Seattle, even though it was fenced. He'd always manage to find a way out."

Leo looked down at the basenji and thought about all the times he'd found him in his Jeep and couldn't figure out how he'd got there.

"But he'd always come back," Joan continued. "Until one day last winter—about eight months ago, right, Justin—?"

Justin was sitting cross-legged on the floor, both arms wrapped around Lono, the side of his face pressed up tight against the dog's spine. He nodded his head yes without lifting it off Lono as his mother kept caressing the dog's ears and muzzle.

"—he just disappeared altogether," Joan continued. "And we thought he'd gotten himself lost . . ."

"I guess he had," said Leo. "Because how did he make it from Seattle to Mount Vernon?"

"I *told* you," Justin whispered to his mother.

Joan looked at Leo. "Justin thought he might have seen Spike climb into the back of the carpet cleaner's van, and they were a company out of Conway—"

"Just south of here," said Mac. "That's definitely a lot closer."

"And if he'd followed the river," Leo suggested, his mind running the journey the basenji would have made to get to where he was found on the road not far from the clinic.

Joan looked at her son again. "But I did call that company and they said they checked all the vans and didn't find any stowaways. And we did our own search," she went on, looking back at Leo. "We looked everywhere. We put up fliers and contacted the local humane society, but nobody had seen him. Eventually we gave up."

"Maybe next time, if you get another dog, put a chip in," said Leo. "They're easier to track that way."

"He was chipped," said Joan.

"Not that we found, he wasn't," said Mac.

"But the people we got him from said he was chipped."

"No, they said we should *get* him chipped," Justin corrected, lifting his head off the dog for the first time and looking at his mother.

"Did they?" Her face crumpled and she covered her mouth with her hand, as if acknowledging that she'd missed this and it made her feel badly. "I had so much going on at that time," she said, looking at Leo as she rose to a stand. "I was already tired all the time and didn't know why. Of course then I found out about the sarcoma—"

She was wearing a flowing, knee-length black skirt, exposing her prosthetic. Noah had stepped forward and was staring at the prosthetic.

"Where's your leg?" he asked with the unselfconscious frankness of a six-year-old.

"Noah," said his dad, stepping forward and putting a hand on his son's shoulder.

"No, that's okay," said Joan, and Leo saw the warmth in her eyes again. She had a beautiful way of making people feel comfortable. "I don't mind," she reassured Steve. "In fact, that's why I wore a skirt," she said, looking down at Noah again. "So you could see my prosthetic. I'm like Mocha; I had to have my leg amputated and my son, Justin"—she pointed back at the young man still playing with Lono—"designed me this new leg. Would you like to touch it?"

"Oh yes," said Noah.

"Is that okay?" Joan asked Steve.

He nodded and smiled. Noah crouched down and put his hand on Joan's prosthetic. Leo started to watch, but then his eyes traveled back to Lono and took in how completely he was enjoying being petted by Justin. He felt a stab in his chest; he'd come to love the little dog so much. But he was also marveling at the magic of the scene, all the threads that had come together to make this reunion possible without seeming to be part of the same fabric at the outset. What was it that Angie had said? He had to open his hand and trust the universe to show him the way.

The minute he thought the words, he felt a little hand slip into his own and looked down to see Noah standing beside him.

"Are you sad now?" he asked, looking up into Leo's face.

"Sad?" he questioned. "Why?"

"Because Lono has to go back to his other family?"

"Is that what you called him?" said Justin. "Lono?"

"Uh-huh. We didn't have any identifiers on him when he came in—"

"The tag wasn't on his collar?" asked Joan, as if it should have been.

"He didn't have much of a collar by the time he got to us," said Mac.

"Oh." Joan looked down at Lono again. "So when did he get to you?"

"It was July wasn't it?" Leo asked Mac.

"The same day Mocha had Woody," Noah piped in.

"That's right!" said Leo, impressed. "How did you—?"

"He saw me carrying Lono into the ward just after you did the splenectomy," Mac explained.

"Splenectomy?" asked Joan.

"Yes. He'd been hit by a car when we got him—"

"How did you get him?" interrupted Justin.

"Somebody picked him up off the road and left him outside our clinic."

"So you fixed him up for *free*?" Joan said, the idea obviously troubling her. "Then I must pay you—"

"No, no," Leo started to say.

But Noah walked forward, still holding Leo's hand, and said to Joan, "Maybe you can let him visit with Lono."

"Oh, of course," she exclaimed.

Leo crouched down to be at Noah's eye level, and Lono crept over and sat inside the V-shaped opening between his knees. Leo stroked him as he spoke. Mocha bumped Noah's free hand with her nose, and he started to stroke her, too. "But you know," Leo explained, "this is what I do in my job as a vet. I love animals enough to take care of them until they're better, and then I give them back to their families."

"But doesn't it make your heart hurt to see Lono go away?"

"Yes, it makes my heart hurt," Leo admitted. "Especially since he's such a great dog." He kissed Lono loudly on top of his head.

"And what about when he dies?" Noah's voice was filled with such solemnity that the whole room became still, as if everyone was holding their breath, waiting to hear how Leo would answer.

"Then my heart would hurt worse. For a while, at least. But you know what I read in a book once?" Noah shook his head no. "I read that a new dog never replaces an old dog, it just makes your heart get bigger. So if you love many dogs, your heart will grow very big."

"I still hope Mocha will live a long time," said Noah.

Leo stood up and ruffled the little boy's hair with his hand. "Me, too, buddy," he said. "Me, too."

*****

Three days later Mac peeked out from the wings at the audience filling the seats for the matinee. "Is he there?" whispered Chad, coming up behind her and slipping his arms around her waist.

She leaned back into his embrace, enjoying the tickle of his beard on her neck. "He is. Third row back in the center."

"And who's his date?"

Mac flipped the curtain back a little more to show him and watched his reaction from her lean against his shoulder.

"Ohhh," he said, cracking a smile. "Now *that* I wasn't expecting."

"Me neither."

"She's not even what I would have thought of as his type."

"'Love looks not with the eyes, but with the mind—'"

Chad joined in to finish the quote. "'And therefore is winged Cupid painted blind.'"

"I'm kind of nervous," said Mac after a second. "Knowing he's out there, watching the show."

"Are you kidding? You're a beautiful woman and a fantastic actress. He's gonna love you."

"Thank you," she said, cuddling even deeper into his arms. They stood in the shadowy quiet for a moment, just enjoying each other's company and the sight of the house filling.

"Have you heard anything about what's happening with Lono?" Chad asked after a while.

"I think the plan is that Dr. F's going to drop him off at Joan and Justin's on his way to work and pick him up on the way home, so he spends days with them and nights at his house. At least for now. That's what he was telling Carly at work yesterday."

"But what about his name? Did they switch it back to Spike or leave it as Lono?"

"I have no idea. I don't think he said. He'll always be Lono to me."

"Spike suits him more, though. You know, the way his hair sticks up on top of his head."

"Ye-ah."

"And I think Dr. F definitely got the peace part from the name, but I don't think he's going to get more prosperous. Not if he cuts back to three days a week at the clinic."

Mac let herself observe Dr. F canoodling with his date. He looked better than he had in a long time. "I don't know," she ventured with a small smile on her face. "I guess it depends on your definition of prosperity."

*****

Leo turned his head left and right, looking at how quickly the seats were filling. This was great, he thought. He swung back to face front, pulling his arms out of his jacket, and caught the sparkle in her hair again. He folded his jacket under his seat and sat still for a second, staring at it.

She looked up and smiled mischievously at him, obviously enjoying his fascination with her coif.

"What color will it be when it grows back again?" he asked, nodding at her scalp.

"I don't know," said Joan. "It might come in gray because of my age. Then again, I might not let it grow back. I kind of like my wig."

"Me, too," said Leo.

He glanced around again. "It's packed," he said.

"Yes. I'm glad you made the reservations when you did."

She had the program open in her lap, and he reached underneath it to hold her hand. "You sure you're okay?" he asked.

"About what?"

"About keeping Lono for his name?"

"Of course."

She smiled, and he watched the skin around her eyes crinkle, thinking he'd never get tired of looking at her face.

"I think it's a great name," she assured him. "And Justin loves it. Plus we decided that peace and prosperity are not things we should turn down."

"Exactly," said Leo. "And for that reason I think he should definitely live with you." He leaned across the mutual arm of their seats and added, "Because I'm pretty sure I already have both."

She lifted her hands and slipped them around his chin, pulling him gently toward her. She kissed him lightly on the lips, and he felt the same kind of rush that he'd felt the first time she'd kissed him, more than a week ago.

"Is he out in your car?" he asked, his voice husky.

"Y-es," said Joan. "Because he's going to stay the night with you."

"How about you drive him to my place, so you can both stay?"

She smiled and her voice became husky, too. "I was hoping you might suggest that."

Spike

Today was a good day. It was cold. Cold enough that the moisture on the end of his nose tingled as he bumped it into the air to catch the smell of the apples fermenting under the tree. The ones that the deer had bitten into then moved on. He turned his head and smelled the big leaves on the maple tree crisping around the edges like toast. He bumped his nose higher and smelled the early snow from the high country in the water of the creek.

Today was a good day not just because the rising sun promised a warm center after the cold start, but because they were together. Which meant he'd done what he'd set out to do. Of course, he hadn't done it alone. He recognized that. All he'd really done was go in search of the man with the hands—Leo—and then the universe had stepped in to make the rest come together. He'd spent long moments trying to see the magic behind such moves then decided that sometimes it was better just to enjoy the wonder of it all. Like the way the morning mist hovered over the pasture.

He knew that Leo still hadn't figured out that they'd met before, on the day the vet had delivered him into the world with his big, gentle hands. But he didn't care. That wasn't important to the story. What was important was that *he'd* remembered, and followed his nose back to Leo, trusting that it would all work out. *Bodacious*, that's what JJ had called his move. From her word of the day calendar. Whatever that was.

He yawned. Venus was barreling across the pasture, back toward the house. She'd already gone and done her business but he was waiting for the sun to melt the filaments of frost off the grass. He didn't like it when his paws got chilly. Harley was on the top step above him, willing himself to start the descent. He knew that Leo was aware of Harley's struggle to go up and down the steps, but his heart wasn't ready to let go yet. Maybe Joan would help him with that.

Right now he knew that they were both inside, still trying to figure out the best place for him to live. He didn't mind going from place to place, especially since both places had porches, but he did find his time on the porch, watching the unspoken messages, limited by the constant traveling.

What he wanted—what he hoped for with all his heart—was that they'd figure out a way to live in the same house. Maybe if he let them know that he loved them both—a lot—he could make that happen.

Or maybe he could just trust that they'd figure it out themselves.

Made in the USA
Middletown, DE
13 March 2023

26593106R00194